I0783253

Season
of
the
Corpse
Flower

by

Robert
DEMYAN

DISTANT HORIZONS PUBLISHING

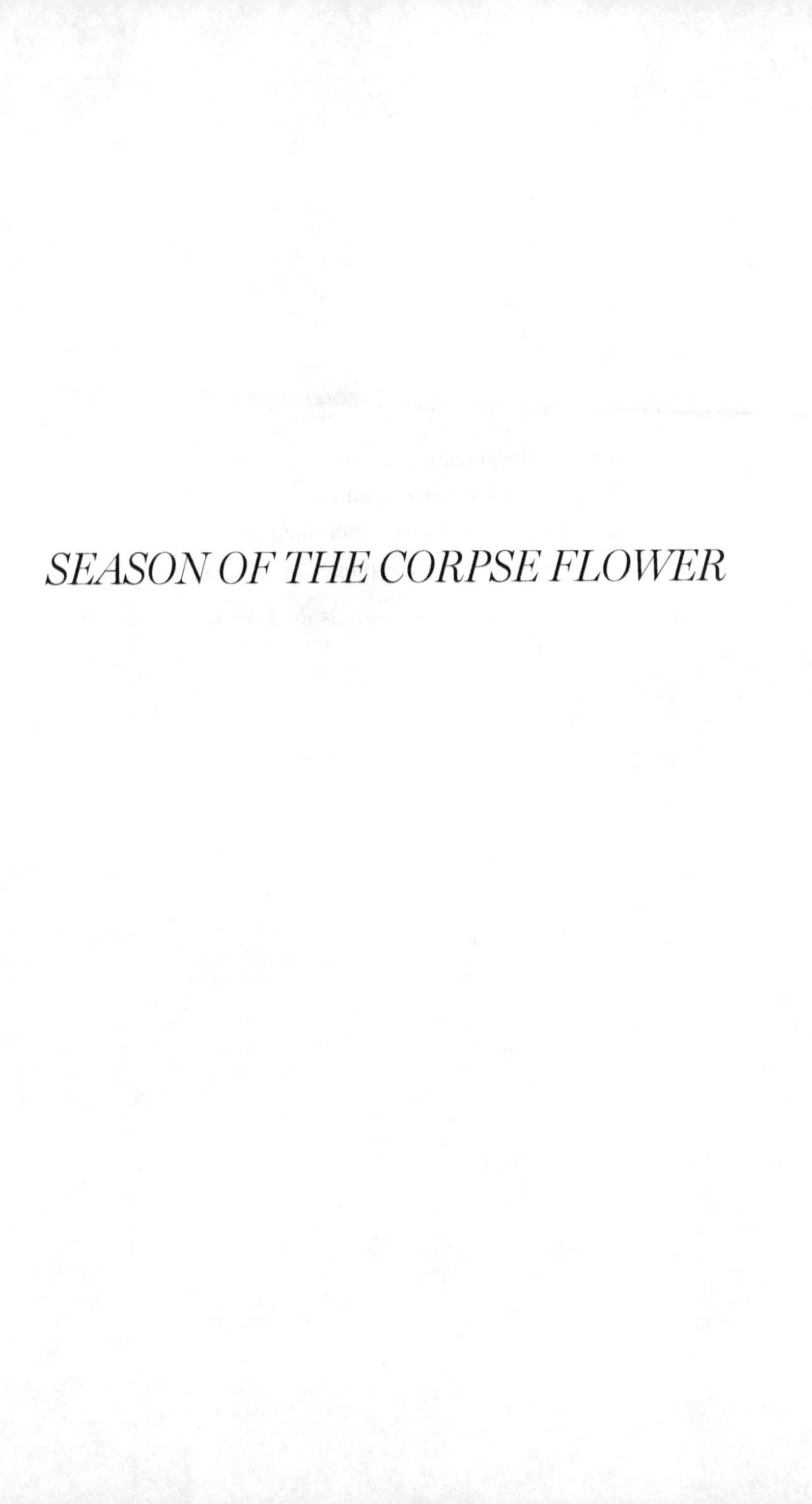

SEASON OF THE CORPSE FLOWER

But whate'er you are
That in this desert inaccessible,
Under the shade of melancholy boughs,
Lose and neglect the creeping hours of time;

---William Shakespeare, As You Like It, Act 2, Scene 7

1.

Los Angeles, 1993

For a city with an unbeatable climate, it was no small irony that people in Los Angeles spent far more time in their cars than they did outside enjoying all that fine weather. A running quip went like this: when it came to the best region in the country for walking from parking spot to shopping center, restaurant, movie theater and the like, Southern California had it *all* over Arizona and Florida. Its year-round balminess had long attracted those looking to flee chillier climes and, over the course of the twentieth century, this sunny southwestern edge of the North American continent swelled with their numbers. They came looking to reinvent themselves or maybe take a shot at show-business; countless others came for aerospace jobs, while many simply washed up on the *West Coast* fleeing debt, ex-spouses, or the law. California — in particular, Los Angeles — was the end of the line, as far west as you could go before ending up in the Pacific.

Such thoughts meandered through Nick Hughes's mind as he kept pace with traffic crawling westbound on the Ventura Freeway, or what most called 'the 134'. Like countless other '*Angelenos*', he had grown up elsewhere, having become acquainted with the Golden State's seductive charms through television shows as a kid in the 1960s and 1970s. On New Year's Day, when the world was frozen and gray outside his window, Nick and his brother would watch the Rose Parade on television, astounded that Pasadena was seventy degrees and green while they were bundled up against January's deep-freeze in Wilkes-Barre, Pennsylvania. Even the parade's setting had a fragrant, vaguely exotic name that rolled off the tongue: *Pasadena.* Many of the television shows they watched were produced in places with equally evocative names like, *Burbank, Studio City,* and of course, *Hollywood.* Back then, California seemed like America's better self, where Januarys were pleasant and the people forward-looking. For ten-year-old Nick Hughes, the Golden State looked to be the nation's future, and quite possibly his.

At the exit for Los Feliz Boulevard, he got off 'the 5' and took surface streets the rest of the way to his rent-controlled apartment near Griffith Park. Figuring out these little routing tricks to save time or avoid congestion had been one of his first adaptations to Los Angeles, where the locals showed a curious pride and somewhat competitive spirit when it came to navigating the city's often-sclerotic traffic. A kind of freeway shorthand had developed that could baffle the uninitiated: '*Take the 110 to the 10 to the 5 then exit at Sepulveda...*'

After parking in his building's shared garage, Nick climbed the stairs that led to the patio landing of his apartment. A rolled-up *LA Times* lay near the front door, which he scooped up with one arm while unlocking the deadbolt with the other. In what looked to be a well-honed routine, he tossed his valise on a chair, found a beer in the refrigerator, unfurled the paper and slid into a plush recliner. At thirty-eight, this little unwinding ritual was an early concession to the approach of middle-age. And yet, he had reached this point with little to show for the journey; two decades into 'adulthood,' and six years after finishing a PhD in English Literature, he had yet to secure a full-time, tenure-track position at a college or university. Deep down, Nick felt foolish for relocating to California without first researching the market for academic jobs. It was a buyer's market and every full-time teaching position advertised ended up wth a mosh pit of qualified candidates holding advanced degrees.

To bide his time, he began taking contract teaching jobs as an *adjunct* instructor at various colleges in and around LA County while he continued to search. Hoping it might only last a year or two, the adjunct gig had since stretched to *six*. Changing this came down to one of two options: look for teaching opportunities *beyond* California or, find another use *here* for his PhD. Option two's stock had risen lately, though Nick had never considered anything other than teaching.

As he flipped a page, a thirty-ish woman with straight, shoulder length sandy hair tucked behind the ears, emerged from the bathroom. She walked over and began picking through sections of the paper he'd set on the table next to him.

"Real estate should be near the back," Nick told her.

Born and raised in the San Fernando Valley, Celeste Draxler subscribed to what Nick viewed as a uniquely Californian gospel, that of prosperity. At its heart lay a peculiar strain of optimism that believed over-priced real estate would only get *more* over-priced. Having arrived at a point of some stability in her career, Celeste now felt confident enough for a plunge into California real estate and wanted to buy before being priced out.

"Santa Monica today?" she asked, settling on the sofa to scan the listings.

"Pasadena City College…" Nick answered. "Santa Monica is *tomorrow*. Another long commute."

From the corner of his eye, Nick glimpsed her carefully scanning the listings, fearing she would use the moment to bring up her ongoing house hunt, a tactic that tended to expose the cracks in the foundation of their relationship. He had come to understand that women generally developed an urge to *nest* at a certain point in life, and, in California, that tended to coincide with a burgeoning interest in *equity*.

By all rights, after five years of co-habitation he should have embraced the house-hunting endeavor with equal enthusiasm, but he hadn't. This ambivalence had begun to chafe at Celeste, a development she had no qualms sharing with him. While eating dinner or having coffee in the morning, Celeste would corner him about purchasing a home together, and Nick would remind her that, without the security of steady, full-time employment, no bank would give him a mortgage. Undaunted, she had floated the idea of potentially securing the loan herself, with down payment help from her family. While *his* role in this arrangement wasn't entirely clear, Nick nonetheless agreed she should pursue it, hoping it might provide some respite from the constant prodding which had fomented deeper concerns he wisely kept to himself — namely, an uncertainty about the long-term viability of their relationship.

"All that driving…" she remarked, with a hint of self-satisfaction.

Nick sighed. She often enjoyed a bit of schadenfreude when it came to the hours he spent on freeways going from one job to another. This sort of passive disapproval was an obvious back-handed attempt at motivating him to change things, as if it were as simple as flipping a switch.

"You hungry?" Celeste asked, after a minute, as she got up and started toward the kitchen.

"Not right now," he answered, flipping a page.

"A couple places over in the Valley look interesting…" she continued from the kitchen, grabbing a plastic tub of yogurt. "I thought we could drive out and take a look this weekend. You know how everything goes so quickly."

Nick muttered an equivocal response, surprised she would consider the sprawling San Fernando Valley to the north and east. Even more than Los Angeles proper, mindless sprawl had overrun the *Valley's* semi-arid Mediterranean landscape with freeways, strip malls, apartment complexes and shopping centers — what he saw as the soulless architecture of a culture on the make.

Sitting back down, Celeste gazed over the top of the Real Estate section. "You have an opinion you'd like to share…? Or maybe you could just grunt and let me know you're awake…"

Wearily, Nick let the broadsheet down. "I'm sorry," he said with a note of sincerity. "That's a good idea. You ought to go look at them."

"Yes, I *ought* to," she countered tartly, "…but I was thinking *we* should look at them, *together*…".

"You know…" he moaned, his tone suggesting familiarity with the terrain, "I had been hoping to spend just one day this weekend *not* sitting in a car."

"I get that," she answered impatiently. "But it's the only time we have together to do this."

At this, he raised the paper again. "You seriously think you could live out there?"

"Why not?" she told him. "It doesn't have to be forever and it's a way to start building equity. We can always sell at some point and buy elsewhere… with some real money in our pocket." Frustrated, she pushed harder.

"Are we about to have the same discussion again? You know, the one where I tell you I don't want to pay rent when I'm retired, that I want to *own* the place I live in with no mortgage hanging over my head."

Nick didn't miss the astringent note in her tone.

"C'mon Celeste," he complained, "That's not fair. I'm just surprised you're considering the Valley. And I don't think we should get cornered into making a decision on something because we're afraid of missing out."

"You make it sound so *coercive*…" she observed, her brow furrowing. "No one's going to *corner* us into anything. I mean, weren't we getting on the same page here…?"

These sorts of exchanges had become a regular feature of their lives. Celeste would lean in and he'd lean back — maybe *too far* back. In her view, they had fallen out of sync when it came to shared priorities; for Nick, he wondered if they ever *were* in sync. Such misfires, he knew, were inevitable in domestic couplings. When the novelty and *heat* wore off, as they inevitably did, couples found themselves at a crossroads where the foundational concerns of lifetime partnering came into sharper relief. Often disappointed, some would dig in for the long haul anyway, convinced in life's essential harshness. Others had a lower tolerance for grinding gears in a relationship and chose to move on.

"All I'm saying is, we should slow down on this a bit..." he told her. "Until I find something full-time..."

"There's that tired old trope again," she countered. "Haven't I said I'll carry the bulk of the mortgage for now...?" Her eyes squinched slightly in the way a parent might telegraph disapproval to a child. "Look, I get it that you don't want to be an adjunct the rest of your life. I don't want that for you, either..."

The thought dribbled off as if she'd grown weary of the topic. She then folded the real estate section under her arm and went to the second bedroom they used as an office. Nick buried himself back in the paper. This *tetchiness* had grown more frequent as of late, adding heft to what felt like already buffeting headwinds.

A minute or so passed in silence, when the phone rang in the office. Celeste picked up and muttered something.

"Sure, just a minute, I'll get him," Nick heard her say as she walked back into the living room with the cordless receiver.

"It's for you..." she said, handing him the phone. "...Says he's your father's lawyer back in Pennsylvania...?"

The words '*father's lawyer*' sent a shiver of dread through Nick as he held the receiver to his ear.

"This is Nick?" he said, off-kilter. "Yes... Hi..."

Celeste unconsciously clutched herself as she listened.

"...I see..." he continued, grimly. "...*When...?*"

2.

Early October storms in the Midwest had delayed their flight, and by the time Nick and Celeste finally landed in Philadelphia, it was almost 8:00 at night and they'd missed the last short hop flight to the Wilkes-Barre/Scranton airport. They went for the only remaining option: a rental car and two-hour drive in the rain.

Nick hadn't been entirely surprised by the lawyer's phone call. After the death of his father's second wife some years back, the old man had gone downhill. Plagued by hypertension and heart trouble, a massive stroke finally hastened the end. Sadly, this marked his first trip east since the second wife's funeral and, as they rolled through the night in the driving rain, he began to wonder if he could have — *should* have — made more effort to look in on his father these last few years, despite the complexity of his own life and the conflicted history they shared.

Celeste dozed off in the passenger seat and, by the time they arrived in Wilkes-Barre, the rain had faded to a drizzle. After several shortcuts through residential neighborhoods and streets filled with standing water from storm drains clogged by leaves, Nick pulled into the driveway of a vintage American 'foursquare', a house built back from the street on a lot rising several feet in elevation from the sidewalk like many in such old Pennsylvania coal towns. Popular in the early part of the century, it sat on a tree-lined street of tidy middle-class homes that took on a forlorn, almost gloomy aspect in the scatter-shot spill of streetlights. The front porch with its boxy rails recalled languid summer afternoons as Nick would stretch out with comic books and watch the world go by.

While punching in the code for the realtor's key box, he recalled the awkward beat of silence on the phone when he told the lawyer he didn't have a set of keys to his father's house. Whatever the lawyer may have inferred from this, he thankfully kept to himself; in places like Wilkes-Barre, notions of filial tethering were stuck in time and the lawyer likely expected Nick would have keys to his parent's home. Pulling the key from the box, he flipped a light switch.

"…*Hey…*" Celeste muttered, stepping ahead of him to gaze at the interior. "…*A real house…*"

Despite their time together, Nick reminded himself she'd never been east with him.

"Look at these details…" Celeste murmured, running her fingers along a chair rail. "…Wainscoting… Crown molding…" She flipped more lights on and noted the kitchen. The furnace had been turned down and the early autumn chill cast the house in a funereal melancholy.

"How about something warm?" she asked, her heels echoing off the linoleum of the kitchen floor. "…Maybe there's some tea here…?" she added, opening cabinet doors.

"…You go ahead, I'm fine," Nick told her while scanning the living room, where the tastes of his father's second wife, Sylvia, ruled. Her fussy, older woman's sensibilities were everywhere: doilies on un-dusted antique end tables, cut glass sugar bowls and vases on built-in shelves, lacy curtains and valances framing windows. There was a shrine-like air about it, as if his father believed changing anything would disrespect Sylvia's memory.

In the kitchen, Celeste rifled through cabinets, opening and closing doors in quick succession as she searched for tea. The sharp sound of the closing doors seemed more distant in the fabric-deadened hush of the living room. Her 'get-to-business' mindset made even simple tasks, like making a cup of tea, feel freighted with consequence.

"…You've got to be kidding…" he heard her say from the kitchen. "… *Instant* coffee? I didn't think people still drank this stuff…"

One of the living room walls displayed framed photos of Nick's father and Sylvia with friends enjoying happy times in various sunny settings. After his father retired and sold the insurance business, he and Sylvia spent much of the year in Florida. They had a good run, thought Nick, recalling his father's devastation at her loss. Sylvia had been the woman he *should have* married — the ebullient, life-loving force that Nick's mother, the volatile, aggrieved first wife, had never been. While Sylvia had been wantonly oblivious to the darker currents in human nature, his mother seemed afflicted by the very notion of their existence, a by-product no doubt, of her working-class childhood in a family where marital difficulties and the comfort of drink featured large.

Running a finger along the edge of a photo, Nick recalled his mother telling him that the apportionment of happiness and sorrow in one's life had already been determined in the 'cosmic lottery of our birth.' Only fools thought otherwise, she'd said.

At that moment, Celeste appeared with two steaming mugs, placing one on the coffee table for him.

"I made one for you anyway," she smiled, sitting down. "Found some tea bags in a cupboard. Probably from your stepmother's time."

"…Actually…" Nick began, as he picked up his cup. "…She *wasn't* my stepmother…"

"*Oh…?*" Celeste perked up, listening.

He walked over to another group of pictures and considered them.

"Did you two get along?" Celeste asked, cautiously.

"*Get along…?*" he replied, as if the question never occurred to him. "Yeah… sure… We got along. She didn't try to be a replacement mother and I appreciated that." He paused a couple beats. "And she made dad happy."

"No kids of her own?" Celeste continued, probing.

Nick shook his head. "Nah… never really interested her. Not everyone has that instinct…that burning desire to be a parent."

"But I thought *all* women wanted to be mothers?" she asked, a bit impishly.

"…I don't know about *all* women…" Nick said, casting a dubious glance her way before turning to another photo. "…but *Sylvia* certainly had no interest in motherhood…"

Celeste glanced around the room. "…You know, I don't see any pictures of you and your brother… *Aaron…?* Was that his name? …" she asked, somewhat tentatively.

"…*Evan…*" he corrected her.

"Evan! Right…that's it… Sorry…" she said, contrite.

"And no, nobody really took pictures when we were kids…"

"No way…?" she remarked, genuinely puzzled. "*Everybody's* got at least *one* picture of themselves as kids. You're going to tell me your folks are the only parents since 19-and-whenever who have *zero* pictures of their kids?"

"No, of course not," he replied. "Probably a few somewhere… Maybe downstairs…"

Celeste noted his discomfort and thought to change the subject.

"Hm…" she muttered, rising to look at one of the photos. "…Now remind me again… About your brother… What happened to him…?"

With a sigh, Nick sat back down on the sofa and sipped at the tea.

"Evan went west…" he explained. "After high school. Said he'd be in touch… A year or so went by with no word and…I don't know… Life just kept going…"

"Really?" Celeste murmured, her expression akin to a bewildered child processing some newly received truth concerning the adult world's unfathomable complexity. "But still…you and your dad must've been worried after a while when you didn't hear from him?"

Nick seemed to hedge on this. "Of course… But we also knew Evan. He could be aloof… Didn't like anyone trying to keep tabs on him…"

"Okay…" she commented, clearly puzzled. "Very different from my family… We're really tight and always in each other's business… Couldn't imagine losing touch with *any* of them for that amount of time."

Staring into the mug of tea, Nick pondered. "Yeah, well, I suppose we'd qualify as your non-typical family…"

Celeste waited for more, unsure what to make of this.

"Listen, I'm beat," he finally declared, running a hand through his hair. "Been a long day…"

3.

Outside the kitchen window, dawn had begun to edge out the night with deep indigo hues as Celeste waited for her cup of instant coffee in the microwave. An edge of the sky had lightened just enough to reveal a low dense band of clouds gathering in shades of gunmetal gray. Her watch said it was just past 7:00 in the morning but you wouldn't have known it by looking outside. A lone streetlight dappled a nearby corner while shadows began to take on a wan, sepulchral gloom. Celeste briefly shuddered at the thought of living day in and day out in such dreariness. Who could muster the enthusiasm for getting out of bed on such dark, cheerless mornings, she wondered?

Thankfully funeral arrangements had been made in advance and paid-for by Nick's father. The will specified a single evening for calling hours and, with the flight delay, he and Carole had missed it. At least they'd be on time for the funeral service, for which a more dismal day couldn't have been scripted.

Nick stepped into the kitchen fussing with his tie, already dressed and ready to go, much to Celeste's surprise.

"Thought you might sleep in a little…?" she commented, noting his attire. "The service and funeral don't start till eleven. That suit's going to be wrinkled by ten."

"I decided to get a last look at him," Nick replied. "I talked to the funeral director before we left. He said I could have a few minutes with him in case we missed calling hours. Before they seal him up." He opened cupboards looking for a coffee mug. "…I know it's not actually him… But it feels better than saying goodbye to a box. Anyhow, I didn't think you'd be up for it."

While Celeste had never met Nick's father, they'd spoken several times by phone. She'd promised to get back there one day, which, of course, never happened. There seemed little point now in having her single memory of him being that of a corpse with overdone makeup.

"No, you're right," she said. "You go ahead. I'll be ready when you get back."

Nick nodded. "Good. See you in an hour or so. I'm sure the coffee maker works so I'll stop and get some decent coffee on the way back." With that, he donned an overcoat and started for the door.

Noon arrived with a cold drizzle and, at the cemetery, a small group gathered under a canopy where Father O'Conglahn from St. Patrick's presided. He stood at the head of the casket, now resting on straps over a freshly dug grave.

Nick and Celeste were to the right of the casket nearest the priest. Stan Dunwiddy, Jason Hughes' longtime employee, stood on the opposite side with his wife, Jackie. Several of Jason's pals from the country club were there, along with Sylvia's sister, Grace, who occasionally daubed an eye with her handkerchief during the eulogy.

Nick stared stonily down at the casket, Celeste wrapping an arm in his. The dearth of mourners felt like a grim testament to time's inevitable diminution of us all, he thought. For most, this is what it came to in the end: few mourners and even fewer words. All the animating passions and vibrancy of an individual life, the exuberance written in blood, bone and spirit, now rendered inert. In another five generations or so, we too would be no more than vapor dissolved in a long-forgotten past, marked only by the weathered headstones in the old pioneer cemetery downtown that no one's visited in generations.

As the service ended, Nick thanked the priest then shook hands with the six or so mourners who'd shown up. Waiting patiently, Stan Dunwiddy and his wife offered their condolences and remarked how much they'd loved Jason and how kind he'd been to them. Nick expressed his gratitude and wished them both well. Finally, Sylvia's sister Grace approached. A tiny woman, maybe 5'2", she exemplified a certain generational sensibility Nick usually found in those who had lived through the second World War. Wrapped in a stylish winter coat that reminded him of Jackie Kennedy at her husband's funeral, and a modest fur-trimmed hat with a thin circular brim, she embraced him, saying he probably didn't remember her.

"Of course, I do…" he replied, "Thanks so much for coming, Grace."

She smiled and glanced at Celeste, whom Nick quickly introduced.

"You know…" Grace said, one hand slightly trembling as she clutched Nick's while clasping his upper arm with the other, "…I always thought the world of your father…" She looked between both of them, sniffling softly.

"He really loved Sylvia and they had some *wonderful* years together..." The emphasis on 'wonderful' had a lilting, unaffected sincerity redolent of a far less cynical age.

"Think how fortunate they were," she continued, coaxing some measure of joy from sorrow. "How many people ever know that kind of happiness in life? Everybody so busy all the time going this way and that, until one day, boom, we end up here..." She sniffed and clutched Nick's arm tighter. Her large brown eyes were glassy from tears and what he took to be some deeper well of sorrow.

"Enjoy each day, I suppose," she said, then looked up at Nick. "Sylvia thought the world of you, you know," she added, as if setting some long neglected account right.

"I know," Nick agreed, "She was a sweetie and made dad very happy. She had a playful spirit."

Grace looked carefully at him, perhaps to gauge his sincerity, then, patted his wrist with a smile. They shared a tacit recognition of the lateness of the hour, a doleful awareness of this goodbye as the last between them, that they would not meet again in this life. She bid them goodbye and soon disappeared in the misty drizzle.

Nick and Celeste remained alone under the canvas canopy as runnels of rainwater dripped from its sagging edges. Hesitating, Nick stepped closer to the casket and gently placed his fingers on it. He silently bid his father goodbye, glancing down into the freshly dug grave and the dark eternity that waited. Fighting back a tear, he gently tapped the casket a couple times then exhaled deeply as Celeste again locked her arm in his and led him away.

4.

After a brief lunch where Nick picked at a club sandwich, he and Celeste went to the law offices of Frank Ciccarelli to take care of the remaining legal business. Ciccarelli had assured them they could wait a day or two but Nick wanted to get it out of the way as soon as possible so he'd only miss a week's teaching back in LA.

It became a quick introduction to the practical legal business that follows a parent's death. Nick had no experience with wills and estates, and his father's death had always seemed a distant eventuality. What he'd be called upon to do in the event had never crossed his mind. Thankfully, Celeste's far more pragmatic nature shored up his own shortcomings in this area.

The house would have to be sold, of course, which wouldn't happen overnight. Ciccarelli, a decent small-town lawyer and third generation offspring of Sicilian immigrants who helped build the Delaware, Lackawanna & Western railroad, said he would act as legal representative at the closing so Nick wouldn't have to return. The remaining furniture, car and household items would be handled by an agency that specialized in estate sales. Any other assets would be sorted out according to the directions in his father's will.

It was therefore a surprise when Ciccarelli told Nick that his father had decided to finance Stan Dunwiddy's purchase of his insurance business eight years ago. As the lawyer explained it, Stan had been unable to secure a business loan without collateral and, since his father didn't actually own their building, the business had nothing in the way of *tangible* assets to back the loan. If Jason Hughes wanted Stan to have the business, he'd need to finance it himself. So, with a very modest down payment, Jason had agreed to finance the rest. But the real kicker came when the attorney added that, according to the terms spelled out in the will, the loan would be considered 'satisfied' upon his death and the business would become Stan's free and clear.

It took a minute to settle in, and Nick finally nodded, agreeing that it made sense. Celeste, on the other hand, expressed confusion.

"Stan strikes me as a really decent guy and I can see why your dad felt for him and his family," she argued, addressing the lawyer. "But what about Mr. Hughes' *own* family? Isn't that business part of his legacy?"

Ciccarelli replied only that these were his client's wishes, specified in the legally binding will. His manner hinted at some deeper understanding of the stipulation's rationale and his favorable view of it. Nick picked up on this and restated his support. 'After all,' he told them, 'Stan had been there for his father in a way *he* had not.' Puzzled by this, Celeste sensed she should back away and let the matter rest. Ciccarelli tried to smooth things by pointing out the bigger picture: Nick still got the house and all other assets.

"There is one thing, though…" the lawyer added, his tone tentative, guarded. He removed his reading glasses and hesitated as he considered how best to approach the potentially delicate nature of what he was about to say. With a glance at each of them, he set the glasses down and clasped his hands together.

"Your father…" he began, quieter now, "Well… he added a codicil to his will specifying that your *brother* share *equally* in the estate if he so wishes…" It suddenly felt as if a shroud had been dropped over the office.

"...Um..." Ciccarelli continued, searching for the right words, "...Given the unusual circumstances, however... Your father set a finite window of *one year* for your brother to come forward and claim his share."

He then cleared his throat, sat back and shifted in his seat, uncertain how much family history Nick might have shared with Celeste.

After an awkward interval, Nick finally voiced his assent.

"Of course," he said, turning to Celeste who leaned back in her chair.

At that, papers were signed, documents copied, and the lawyer assured them the rest could be handled long distance once they returned to Los Angeles. Nick thanked him, remarking that they'd take another day or so to go through the house. They shook hands and Ciccarelli reminded them to take care driving as sleet was in the forecast tonight.

5.

The spitting rain had in fact become an icy drizzle that beaded and smeared on the windshield with each pass of the wiper blade. The chill in the front seats mirrored the gloom outside as Nick concentrated on the road and Celeste stared impassively at the half-frozen precipitation splatting on the glass.

"What's the difference between *freezing rain* and *sleet...?*" she eventually asked, as the fat slushy drops grew almost hypnotic in the headlight beams.

"Are you setting me up...?" he replied, a touch cagey. "...There isn't any, right...?"

"I don't know, that's why I'm asking..." she answered, "On the chance that the guy who grew up here would know."

"Okay, then there isn't any."

6.

Celeste woke the next morning exhausted. Between the strangeness of her surroundings and the events of the previous day, she hadn't slept well. There were troubling dreams — busy, chaotic *Zoloft* dreams she'd gotten used to since starting the drug. The other side of the bed remained untouched, suggesting Nick had dozed off going through his father's files in the basement where she'd left him.

Donning a fleece pullover against the chill, she started downstairs. The kitchen showed no signs of activity during the night — no dishes in the sink or half-filled coffee cups on the table. She flipped the switch on the coffee maker, having set it up last night, and listened as it began to sigh and heave. At the other end of the kitchen, a short vestibule led to a pantry and an open basement door where light spilled up. Celeste leaned her head in and called out.

"What time is it?" came the reply.

With this, she started down into a basement converted into an office and study by Nick's father. The walls had veneer wood paneling and were lined with calendars and various framed sales awards from Jason's insurance days, along with some scattered plaques of golf witticisms. A large L-shaped desk with neat shelves held a sparse collection of books; against the wall, two short file cabinets stood with drawers open and folders flopped about.

On the floor, leaning against a sofa opposite the desk, Nick sat bleary-eyed with legs stretched out, piles of papers, folders and cardboard filing boxes strewn around him. The sofa connected an area of several upholstered chairs scrounged up more for their comfort than appearance. A small television sat on a working bar well-stocked with upmarket liquors and various other accoutrements suggesting a successful small-town Republican businessman's lair.

Oddly, Celeste found it somehow nostalgic and comforting, a reminder of a time when it was still possible to live in the quiet eddy of an American small town, far from the roiling currents of the larger world.

"I'm making coffee…" she said, glancing about at the mounds of excavated paperwork. "You interested…?"

Nick looked up, smiling weakly. "*Please…*"

"You get any sleep down here?"

He exhaled deeply. "Not sure it qualifies as sleep…" he said, running both hands through disheveled hair, "…But I probably dozed off for a bit…"

With a minor swell of sympathy, Celeste sat down on the sofa behind him and began to rub his shoulders.

"How about you come upstairs and I'll make you a nice breakfast," she said cheerfully, hoping to lighten the mood. "Like some oatmeal with butter and brown sugar, hmm…? It's instant, but I can dress it up…"

Smiling gratefully, he thanked her while she noted the assorted piles spread around him. "What *is* all this?" she asked. "Anything important?"

With a slight twitch of hesitation, Nick reached for a nearby folder and stared at it a moment before passing it over his shoulder to her. Celeste's eyes narrowed as she cautiously opened it. The first document, dated 'October 1987', was on some company letterhead with a vaguely 'official' look.

"…What is *this*…?" she asked, warily.

"Go on…" he urged, "…*Read* it…"

She lifted the page and held it closer.

"…It's about your *brother*…?" she muttered, eyes darting line to line before reading aloud:

Dear Mr. Hughes:

Regarding our most recent inquiries into the whereabouts
and activities of your son, Evan Hughes, we regret that we have
not been able to locate anything that might further illuminate his
current status. After an exhaustive search of public documents
and databases we have little more beyond what we had previously
learned.

Our extensive contacts and leads with various law enforce-
ment agencies have likewise turned up very little new informa-
tion. As stated in our prior correspondence, the documentation
we've obtained confirms his arrival in the Islamic Republic of
Malaysia on the dates mentioned, but there's no documentation
confirming he ever left the country. Further queries with the U.S.
Embassy in Malaysia and with Malaysian authorities have thus
far yielded no additional information.

While we are certainly willing to pursue this effort as long
as you deem appropriate, we are of the opinion that it is unlikely
your son's missing person status can be resolved. And, as sug-
gested in my previous letter, any further inquiry would have to be
undertaken in Malaysia, incurring much greater expense and, in
our experience, would likely produce marginal returns.

It's always our sincere hope that our investigation might resolve such matters satisfactorily, but occasionally, these cases go unresolved. We hope that we may have at least been able to draw you as near as possible to a more informed conclusion concerning your son's movements and activities over the last two decades, and perhaps offer some degree of closure to the issue.

We have enclosed a statement for services to date and are always available if you seek further assistance in this matter.

Respectfully yours,

Jack Swarthout, J.D.

Lomax and Swarthout, LLC

For a moment, Celeste held the letter in silence. "…What the *hell* is this…??"

"There's more…" Nick told her, "…Here…"

Celeste reached for the next folder.

"…You've been through *all* this…?" she asked him.

"Several times," he replied, absently rubbing the back of his neck.

The first document was dated July 1987, several months *prior* to the one she'd just read.

"*That* one…" he suggested, "…is a summary…"

Hesitating, she then began to read:

Dear Mr. Hughes:

Our ongoing investigation into the whereabouts of your son Evan has yielded some additional information.

As stated in previous reports, records of your son's work activities in California are intermittent and incomplete. What we were able to obtain showed part-time work unrelated to his academic pursuits: political science and history.

School records indicate he earned a degree in political science with a minor in sociology. Of the former faculty and administration personnel we were able to contact, none had any particular recollection of your son. Some fellow students we were able to locate mentioned a history professor your son had become friends with outside the classroom. This instructor was popular — his classes were very much in demand in the 1960s and 1970s — and he was known to engage with his students in bars and coffee shops. As a matter of course, we looked into this further and determined there was nothing of a sexual nature between your son and this professor, who has since deceased.

While still a student at UC Berkeley, your son applied for a passport in early 1979. In March of that year, he applied for service with the Peace Corps and was accepted into the program. Records we obtained indicate he was assigned to the Islamic Republic of Malaysia. We've enclosed copies of Immigration documents confirming your son's departure from San Francisco on 6 October 1979 and his arrival in Kuala Lumpur, Malaysia on 8 October 1979. Two years later, his service with the Peace Corps was terminated for reasons that, in accordance with federal law, remain confidential.

So far, we have been unable to obtain any pertinent reliable information regarding your son's activities after that. Since he had been in the country on a specific visa affiliated with the Peace Corps, that visa would have been automatically terminated upon his dismissal. To remain in the country after that, he would have needed a tourist visa, which, we were able to determine, he did not obtain. After an exhaustive search of Malaysian immigration records from 1979 right up to today, we were unable to find any-thing confirming your son departed Malaysia. While it is certainly theoretically possible he may have left the country by 'unofficial' means, in our judgment, it's more likely he remained in Malaysia, albeit illegally.

We contacted the US State Department regarding all this and they launched an inquiry with the embassy in Kuala Lumpur. Embassy officials looked into the matter with the Malaysian authorities who confirmed that Evan Hughes' immigration status shows that his Peace Corps visa was never canceled at any official point of departure. They also checked criminal databases, hospital records, and mortuary records, especially any uniden-tified Caucasian 'John Does' who fit his physical description. Nothing came of those inquiries. While this doesn't offer anything conclusive regarding your son's whereabouts, it does suggest that he may in fact still be alive.

The most likely possibility, in our judgment, is that your son chose to remain in Malaysia for reasons known only to him. In the event, we must conclude that any further investigation would have to take place on the ground there. The logistics and expense of such an investigation would, in my estimation, be prohibitive.

We await further instructions re: your wishes.

Respectfully yours,

James Swarthout, J.D. Lomax and Swarthout, LLC

Celeste placed the letter back in the folder, a bit of color drained from her face.

"…*Jesus,* Nick…" she muttered, setting the file down then wrapping her arms as if beset by a chill. "…Your father never shared *any* of this with you?"

At this, Nick got to his feet and stretched.

"…We no longer spoke about Evan… Hadn't in years…"

She folded her arms awkwardly, a frown wrinkling her brow. Nick stepped over to his father's desk and distractedly ran his fingers along its edge.

"…I'd barely turned sixteen when he left…" he went on. "…Caught up in my own stuff, like getting my learner's permit to drive, and Evan and I didn't really cross paths much anymore… We had different friends, different orbits…"

Nick then turned to the shelves behind the desk, distracting himself with a plaque his father had received for some business milestone. Celeste couldn't fathom such a detached sibling relationship; it would have been unthinkable in *her* family.

"…You're saying," she pressed, "He never mentioned it beforehand…? Your brother? Until one day, he told you he was taking off? No word about where or why…?"

Nick shrugged. "…More or less… Like I said, we inhabited different worlds by then…"

A vague but palpable uneasiness floated in the air and Celeste decided to let it go — for now. The basement's drop-ceilinged hush became almost claustrophobic, making the room feel as if some ancient miasma had been stirred. At that moment, a brief chill juddered her, the kind she and her sisters used to characterize as someone '*walking over your grave.*' With it came the sense that their lives were about to be upended in ways neither could imagine.

7.

Later that afternoon Celeste called to check in with her office back in LA. It had been three days and, thankfully, she and Nick were leaving tomorrow. After finishing the call, she went to the kitchen where Nick had just returned from some business in town and was sorting through a pile of mail on the dining table.

"No more surprises?" she warily asked, eyeing the pile.

"Not yet…" he answered, glancing up briefly. "Think we've had enough for now…" He turned back to sorting. "…By the way, your flight is confirmed and you're all set, thank you, Nick."

"Yes, *thank you, Nick…*" she said, puckishly. "…But what's this about *your* flight?" she added, "…Aren't *we* on this flight together?"

He hesitated. "…Um…actually, no… I'm staying in Philadelphia for a few days."

Celeste's eyes narrowed. *"Come again…?"* she asked.

Anticipating such a reaction, Nick sighed and looked up.

"I want to speak with that investigation firm my father hired…" he told her, "…it's just a couple extra days…"

Celeste could feel her chest tighten.

"…*O-kay*…" she said, drawing out the word. "But…what about your courses? Weren't you worried about falling behind?"

"I'll be fine," he assured her. "Someone can cover for the extra day or two if need be. There's a syllabus to follow and the students won't miss a beat…"

She made no effort to hide her skepticism. "Fine… Just asking…"

At this, he put the mail down.

"Celeste…" he chided, "You're not *asking*. You're thinking, *'what the hell is he doing…?'"*

"Well, yeah sure…" she admitted. "Don't I have the right to be concerned?"

"Of course, you do…" he agreed, "…So, go on, speak your peace…"

She crossed her arms in an effort to contain the irritation.

"It hadn't occurred to you to possibly share this with me before making that decision?" she asked.

"No," Nick calmly insisted. "Because I didn't want to debate it with you. I need to do this without having to explain every decision." He paused and met her gaze. "Look, this has been a lot to take in and I need to clear up some things, that's all. Since I'm already here…"

Softening slightly, Celeste tried to dial back her sense of grievance.

"Listen," she told him, "I get it that you're feeling a little unmoored. All this stuff with your father and now your brother… It's a lot…" She considered a moment. "But I don't understand what else you think you're going to find."

"That makes two of us," he answered, shuffling mail again. "I just need to talk to these people in person… He's my *brother*, Celeste. The kid who took the lower bunk bed so I could sleep up top where I felt safer. The least I can do is ask a few more questions."

She recognized the tone — it was the one he used to convey a resolute belief in the application of academic rigor to the vagaries of life.

"Fine…" she conceded, "Just keep in mind…once you start asking questions…it might only lead to *more* questions…"

He paused, unsure how to take this. Like his mother and various other women he'd known, Celeste could drop such nuggets in a way that intimated superior feminine discernment and an ability to see *around* things. Whatever truth there may have been in her caveat, he knew she'd never understand that, for him, turning away at this point was not an option.

8.

Nick's eyelids felt heavy as he looked out from the back seat of a taxi at traffic crawling on the Schuylkill Expressway. After taking Celeste to the airport with time to spare, he returned the rental car and caught a taxi back to the hotel he'd booked in downtown Philadelphia. Fatigue had ground him down and he wondered how his body found the electrochemical juice to fire neurons across synapses.

The taxi driver, a forty-something black man with strands of graying dreads, looked mildly agitated by a talk radio program. A vitriolic male host was dressing down a caller who dared complain about a recent round of tax cuts for the wealthy, ranting on about high tax rates penalizing initiative and discouraging job creation.

"That's some kind of bullshit, ain't it?" the taxi driver commented to no one in particular. "I don't care *who* you are, y'all wanna be in that rich bracket too, and you don't want no one digging in your pockets neither," he continued. "Easy for me to say when I ain't got it. But that don't matter. They give me a chance, I'm gonna get my pile like anybody else."

Nick looked at the driver's face in the rear view mirror.

"And what would you do with it?" he asked. "If you got it. *Your* pile?"

The driver glanced back, gauging his passenger's intent.

"Shit, I'd do what anybody'd do," he assured Nick. "Stop doing this shit, that's for damn sure!" He paused a beat. "No more driving motherfuckers back and forth from the airport all day in traffic like this."

"Can't argue with that," Nick agreed.

As they exited downtown, the streets were humming with the morning's business and the cab pulled up in front of a shiny glass office tower. The driver got out with Nick and went around to the trunk for his luggage. He noted Nick's baggy eyes and wrinkled clothes with a hint of concern.

"You ain't goin' to a hotel first…? You goin' right to business?" he asked, somewhat dismayed. "I mean, it ain't no business of mine, man, but you don't look like you ready for the morning show."

Nick considered the point and smiled as he handed the man a twenty and a ten for the $25 fare, then picked up his bag. The cabbie started to make change but Nick waved him off.

"Thanks, keep it," he said, and started toward the entrance.

Inside, Nick took the elevator up to the eleventh floor where he scanned the directory for the offices of '*Lomax and Swarthout, LLC.*' The firm occupied a suite of offices in a long corridor, and as he opened the glass double doors, Nick found himself in what looked to be the headquarters of a high-end law firm. Hardwood paneling in dark tones, probably teak or mahogany, lined walls appointed with brass sconces that telegraphed a soothing aristocratic confidence and drew a visitor's eye to the main reception desk where raised brass letters spelled out the company name in a classy serif font on the rear wall. With a quickened pulse, he approached a smartly attired receptionist with a slim, barely visible wireless headset. Upon noticing Nick, she asked if he needed help.

"Uh…yes," he replied, stepping closer. "…My father recently passed and I just learned that he'd hired you folks to track down his other son who'd gone missing some time ago," His own lucidity surprised him.

The woman stared impassively, as if disheveled men standing before her were a regular occurrence.

"My father's name was Jason Hughes..." Nick went on, "And I was hoping to find out a bit more about the work Mr. Swarthout had done for him... There are a few things I'm not clear on..."

The receptionist softened ever so slightly as she considered him.

"I'm sorry, but Mr. Swarthout is out of the country this week," she explained, with what Nick took to be a studied detachment calculated to project the firm's high-caliber confidence. She looked at him expectantly as Nick realized his error: he should have thought to call first!

"Of course... my mistake...it's been that kind of week..." he apologized, with an abashed humility that he hoped might squeeze some sympathy from the receptionist. "...I should have called first...but since I was flying back to LA from Philadelphia anyway, I thought I'd just take a chance and stop by..."

This had the intended effect of loosening the receptionist's back and she mentioned that Mr. Swarthout's partner, Mr. Lomax, would arrive shortly and she'd check his availability.

"You can have a seat over there..." she told him, gesturing toward a waiting area with some upholstered chairs and tables. "I'll see what I can do."

Nick thanked her and settled into a large, overstuffed leather chair right out of some Victorian gentlemen's club. The furnishings, like everything else, seemed designed to convey an impression of competence and discretion. It felt like a glimpse into a very foreign world where eminent people with vast interests and deep pockets were willing to pay handsomely for information that could advance their own interests or maybe impede those of their rivals; in other words, not the sort of firm one would hire to snoop on a cheating spouse. The clientele here were the kind of people who landed on skyscrapers and mega-yachts in their helicopters. So, how had his father come to such a place? (He made a mental note: find out how much they *charged* the old man...) As he sat there, the warm and exotic wood tones of the paneling along with the comfortable chair had a lulling effect and he thought how nice it would be to close his eyes, if only for a minute...

9.

"*...Mr. Hughes...?*" a far-off voice was asking. "*...Excuse me...? Mr. Hughes...?*" Closer now... Someone's asking for his father...? "*...Mr. Hughes...?*"

An arm shook Nick's shoulder and he opened his eyes. A large middled-aged man in a suit stood over him.

"Best chairs ever, right?" the man said. "Some outfit in New England makes 'em. I've got two in my house..." He extended his hand —

"Jack Lomax..." he continued, "...I'm Jim's partner."

Nick rose clumsily. "Ah! Hello..." he said, and introduced himself. "...whoa...sorry... Guess I dozed off..."

"I'm sure it's been an exhausting week, Mr. Hughes," Lomax replied, sympathetically. "I heard about your father's passing. Our condolences, of course."

Nick thanked him.

"Andrea said you had some questions," Lomax continued. "I understand. Why don't you come on into my office where we can talk. I've got an appointment in about half an hour, but until then I'm free."

The office was spacious, outfitted with the same richly paneled walls, one of which had been lined with various plaques and framed pictures enhancing the sheen of eminence: 'grip and grin' snaps of Lomax shaking hands for the camera with politicians, celebrities and business leaders.

Lomax seated himself behind the desk and gestured to a posh leather chair across from him for Nick, who thought the man's impeccably groomed and barbered silver-gray hair and erect carriage suggested retired military or law enforcement.

"Something to drink...?" Lomax asked, as he walked over to a well-stocked mini-bar. "Coke maybe? Diet Coke?"

"Sure, sounds good. Coke maybe," Nick answered.

Lomax popped a can of Coke and poured it in a glass with ice before handing both to Nick. He then sat back down and poured a Diet Coke for himself. He had a wariness in his demeanor that Nick associated with cops in general, an 'us against them' mindset that saw the potential *perp* in everyone.

"I actually worked on your father's case," Lomax began, sipping from his glass. Then, after a couple of beats added, "Which, I'm guessing, is why you're here."

Nick nodded as he emptied his glass and set it down. "That's right... I came across your correspondence while getting the house ready to sell... Quite a surprise, as you can imagine... My father hadn't talked about Evan in years."

"I understand," Lomax said, sympathetically. "Family can be complicated... Your father's attorney, Tony Ciccarelli, put him in touch with us."

"Is that right?" Nick answered, surprised. "Ciccarelli...?" He tried to imagine the unlikely conduit connecting a small-town lawyer like Ciccarelli to an outfit like this.

"We knew each other in law school..." Lomax continued, "Tony and me. After graduation, he went into practice and I joined the FBI. Was a special agent for twenty years. Primarily in international fraud and financial crime, that sort of thing.

"Jim and I started this about ten years ago when I retired..." Lomax continued. "...He's ex-FBI as well."

"Looks like business has been good," Nick commented.

Lomax nodded with a wry smile. "It has...though I'm not sure what that says about the state of the republic..." He poured some more Diet Coke and mused on something. "I'm old enough to remember when the formula for Coca-Cola was the world's most closely guarded corporate secret... Seems like a lifetime ago..."

Lomax allowed himself a brief reverie, then leaned back in the chair and crossed his legs in a signal the time had come for business.

"So, your father never talked to you about the work we did?" he queried.

"No..." Nick answered with a flicker of bemusement. "...This was the first I'd heard of it..." He paused to consider something. "Don't know if he shared this with you but... My brother was the unexpected result of a brief encounter between my parents when they were young...my mother was only seventeen. Resulted in an unhappy marriage that didn't last. Evan internalized this, blamed himself, and our parents never tried to convince him otherwise..."

Lomax nodded thoughtfully. "I understand..." he said. "...Things were different back then..." He leaned forward and clasped his hands together on the desk. "At the time, I don't recall your father sharing much of the backstory with us and, in all honesty, it wasn't particularly germane to the task...

"Usually..." he continued, "We refer such cases to other agencies — missing persons aren't really our *bailiwick*. But, Tony Ciccarelli and I go way back, so I agreed to have a look at it..." Here Lomax paused, choosing his words carefully. "...It didn't take long to see there was more to it than we thought...

"We started with the usual protocol for missing persons — credit reports, previous addresses, work and education history, driving history, police records, all that. I assume you saw in our report that your brother made his way out to California and attended UC Berkeley?"

"I did," Nick confirmed.

"Then you know that he graduated in 1979. BS in political science." Lomax exhaled deeply then leaned back again.

"When I was an undergrad, most students pursuing a degree in '*Poli-Sci*' were pre-law or bound for graduate school," he continued. "That wasn't the case with your brother. We found no applications for law school or for graduate studies *anywhere*. In fact, we found surprisingly very little out there about him. No scrapes with the law, no work history to speak of. Nothing, really. The only hits we got were his application to the Peace Corps and subsequent acceptance into the program. We obtained copies of his passport application and immigration records to confirm the dates."

At this, he paused and scratched his head as if puzzling something out. He rose and put his empty soda can in a bin then glanced out a window at the city.

"At that point, the trail went cold," he went on, hands in pockets. Then, he turned back to Nick. "The only thing we were sure of, was that your brother took the assignment in Malaysia and never returned."

"There's something I don't quite get," Nick remarked. "I mean, I haven't traveled that much internationally but…isn't it possible he could have left the country some *other* way?"

Lomax dismissed this. "Not very likely," he answered. "Anything's possible, sure, but that would require an awful lot of effort in a fairly sophisticated country with significant border control capabilities. It's possible he could've somehow crossed a land border into Singapore or Thailand but there again, you're talking about highly developed nations with borders that are *anything* but porous. The question then would be, why? Why do that when he had an American passport that allowed him to go in and out of most countries with ease? Unless he'd run afoul of the law, which we found no evidence of. That only left a couple possibilities: One, your brother *intentionally* stayed in Malaysia for some reason…" At this, he hesitated. "Or…something *else* may have happened…"

"*Something else…?*" Nick echoed.

"Yes, well…" Lomax began, carefully, "In our experience, more often than not, when people go missing in a foreign country, it's usually because they've been victims of a violent crime. A mugging gone wrong, or kidnappers hoping to ransom off a rich foreigner to the folks back home. With women, it's often a sexual assault that got out of hand…" He paused and returned to his chair as Nick distilled his meaning.

"Sadly, it happens more than you'd think…" he continued. "There's a thousand ways to make a body disappear in the tropics. Toss it in the sea and let the sharks have at it, or leave it in the forest for wild pigs and ants. In a couple days it's gone. The police aren't much help. They're poorly trained and underfunded in countries like Malaysia. Bureaucratic foot-dragging, corruption and apathy are all endemic.

"If the victim has any family, someone will eventually contact their government for help. Then the embassy or consulate gets involved which may or may not motivate the local constabulary. There might be an initial flurry of activity, some leads pursued, but it soon fizzles out when nothing's found. All that's left is a fading photo on a bulletin board."

Lomax paused to consider what he was about to say next.

"On occasion…" he began, "We run into the type who's gone missing *on purpose*. People trying to escape something or someone and looking to reinvent themselves. Those sorts don't *want* to be found. Fugitives, deadbeats, misanthropes… More often, they're white-collar criminals who've cleaned out someone else's accounts back home. Which is NOT your brother's story…"

"No skeletons in his closet then?" Nick asked.

Lomax shrugged and shook his head. "He wasn't a jet-setting tax dodger or fugitive trying to beat extradition… Besides, Malaysia doesn't top the list of places people go to fall off the radar screen. It's a Muslim nation, *secular*, to some degree and ostensibly democratic. But still conservative and a bit on the authoritarian side." With a deep breath, Lomax glanced at his watch.

"That's about all I can add, I'm afraid. The only thing we're sure of is that Malaysia was the last known location of your brother. And it's where I'd start if I still wanted answers…" At this, his tone changed.

"Anyway, my 11:30 conference call starts soon and I need to prepare," he declared while starting toward the door. "You know we're here, if there's anything else we can do. Feel free to call."

Nick rose and they shook hands once more as he exited into the waiting area and the same overstuffed leather chair to make some notes. Once more, his head was spinning, but the caffeine was working. Something about the exchange troubled him. He wondered if there might be more in *their* office files on his brother's case and went to ask the receptionist who was on a call. She raised her index finger in a 'just a moment' gesture while Nick smiled awkwardly. After a half-minute or so, he mouthed the word '*restroom*' while pointing in various directions. She nodded and extended an arm toward a hallway.

As he started down it, Nick became taken by the extent and caliber of the operation. Wooden doors lined each side of the hall, enclosing rooms where he imagined agency staff grinding through reams of documents and records as they researched cases. The dark wood paneling continued the intimations of money, power, taste and class, while also conveying the soothing reassurance that *here* lived competence and discretion.

He'd only taken a few steps when a door flung open on one of the rooms and a woman exited with a stack of file folders. She moved briskly down the hall before disappearing around another corner. Nick paused at the door she'd just exited and furtively looked up and down the corridor before reaching for the knob and, in an inexplicable impulse, stepped in. As the door closed behind him, he readied an apology in case anyone was there; thankfully, it was empty. Unlike the agency's public spaces, this room appeared more utilitarian: mostly archives, file storage and a couple computer stations. Shelves containing what must have been hundreds of files ran the length of both walls leading to an open area with a large wooden table and half a dozen architect's clamp-on lamps cantilevered in various positions.

Nick's heart raced. It wasn't like him to succumb to such impulses, but something about the exchange with Lomax felt *incomplete*. He quickly scanned the shelves of files running from floor to ceiling. A sliding ladder provided access to the upper shelves. Perpendicular tabs jutted out from the volumes, each bearing an uppercase letter arranged alphabetically. He immediately located the section for 'H' which was further divided into sub-sections Ha to Hi, Hj to Ho, and Hp to Hz. He homed in on *Hp* to *Hz* and, with his fingers, raced along the surnames until arriving at *Hughes*. Thankfully, there was only one — *Hughes, E.*

He pulled the file and started flipping through it while anxiously eyeing the door. Several pages in, he came upon a manila envelope stamped '*CONFIDENTIAL*' in bright red caps at the upper left corner. With slightly trembling hands, he quickly stuffed the whole thing in his valise, then paused just long enough to breathe and collect himself. He started for the door, preparing a 'wrong door!' apology if anyone happened to be on the other side. Grabbing the knob with his sweaty palm, Nick gently opened the door and stepped into the hall — all clear. The door fell shut behind him and he hurried toward what looked to be an exit.

10.

Frost was in the forecast. Nick sensed it in the air, noting the clarity it lent to the appearance of things. Traffic signals, streetlights, signage — all took on a sharper edge in the crisp afternoon light. He'd been walking for some time now, his mind abuzz with jumbled thoughts. Certain he had the self-conscious, vaguely furtive mien of a second-rate criminal, he avoided eye contact with people he passed.

The pilfered file had unexpectedly kindled a childish thrill that stirred memories of the times he and his brother would stuff the occasional baseball cap in their pants at the downtown Sears and Roebuck. For him, the rush from these petty transgressions usually drowned out any demons of conscience. Evan, he recalled, had been clinical about it, continually refining his techniques of stealth and diversion.

Back at his hotel, Nick ordered a couple beers and a sandwich from room service. He had little appetite but knew he needed something other than caffeine and alcohol in his stomach. A mix of dread and fascination occupied him as he spread the file's contents on the bed, while the ambient blather of a television talk-show played at low volume.

The envelope stamped 'CONFIDENTIAL' had so far offered nothing new, though it did have some finer detail concerning his brother's academic pursuits. For instance, Nick learned that Evan maintained an impressive 3.8 GPA at UC Berkeley and, by his junior year, had been offered membership in several national honor societies. Despite the invitations, nothing in the files suggested Evan ever accepted any of the offers.

As he continued shuffling through the documents, Nick came upon a copy of his brother's 1976 Peace Corps application. In one of the short essay questions, Evan had written that he'd been '*moved by the array of challenges faced by nations in the developing world*' and expressed an interest in '*municipal organization and planning structures.*' He wrote that American leadership meant '*we must foster positive change in the world*' and '*enlist our prosperity*' to help other nations and peoples 'trapped in the *cycles of poverty*'.

Such lofty platitudes seemed at odds with the brother Nick remembered. This stuff sounded like the high-minded blather of a would-be speechwriter, the sort of person he couldn't imagine his brother becoming. But then, what did he really know of Evan? Their years apart now outnumbered their years together, and, in reality, they were essentially strangers.

Nick found one document in the file strangely cryptic. It was an internal memo from Swarthout to Lomax stamped *'Confidential'* and dated 3 March 1987. The subject line read, *'Hughes Case'* and the body was a single paragraph:

'Per our conversation re: Kate Sheneman contact with SD. In our best interest to comply with request. Disengage from current line of inquiry. Firm's interest in keeping channels open should take priority.'

Patches of light from the television screen flashed about the room accompanied by the low-volume chatter of a news program as Nick read the words again: '...*Disengage from current line of inquiry*...'

11.

The next morning, Nick exited the hotel lobby looking drawn and rumpled, like he'd slept in a chair. He hailed a taxi and climbed in. As the driver negotiated traffic, Nick mulled over how to approach Lomax. It hardly seemed to matter as Lomax would not be happy about having a file filched. Even so, Swarthout's internal memo altered the balance of grievance in *Nick's* favor. It didn't take a legal scholar to catch the whiff of something unsavory about it. That they had honored the request of another party to lay off further inquiry struck him as a detail to be rightly shared with his father. Given that, he'd suggest to Lomax that one lapse canceled the other and his only interest now was the meaning of the memo.

The taxi dropped Nick off and, despite his slightly haggard state, he moved with a sense of purpose. With valise in hand, he took the elevator to the agency's floor and walked into the reception area where a different woman was behind the counter this morning.

"Excuse me..." he said, "I was here yesterday — Nick Hughes. I spoke with Mr. Lomax and was hoping I might get just a couple minutes of his time."

She seemed puzzled by this. "I'm sorry...? I wasn't here yesterday. This is in reference to...?"

Nick opened his valise and produced the file. "To *these*. Files from my brother's case. *Evan Hughes*. I took them yesterday as I left."

The receptionist glanced at the files then warily eyed Nick.

"…You *took* these files from *our* office…?"

"I did. From your files and archives room. Yesterday." He let this sink in a moment. "It's what I'd like to speak with Mr. Lomax about."

With an expression impossible to read, she slowly stood up and watched Nick as if he might be some volatile, ranting street person who'd wandered in.

"I'll take those," she said, reaching for the files.

Nick pulled them closer. "Think I'd rather hang onto them myself until I can speak with Mr. Lomax…"

This further unnerved the receptionist. "Wait here a minute," she said, frostily, before disappearing into the back.

Despite the lack of sleep, Nick had an oddly righteous sense of clarity. After a moment, the receptionist returned and gestured to him while holding the door open. "Come with me," she said, coolly, escorting him back to another office where she opened the door and gestured for him to go in.

Nick stepped in the doorway as Lomax watched from a posh leather chair in front of a well-appointed desk with another man behind it who reclined in his chair to regard Nick.

"Come in, Nick…" Lomax said after a moment, gesturing to a chair next to his. "Have a seat…"

The office had the same air of executive privilege and self-regard as Lomax's office, telegraphing a similar sense of experience and competence.

"Thanks…" Nick guardedly replied, as he sat down.

"This is my partner, Jim Swarthout," Lomax continued, nodding toward the man behind the desk.

"Hello Nick," Swarthout said, extending a hand across the desk. As Nick took it, he briefly considered asking him about the 'trip' that kept him out of the office yesterday.

"Sorry, I missed you yesterday," Swarthout continued. "And, of course, I was saddened to hear about your father. He was a good man…"

"I wanted Jim to meet you," Lomax added. "We have a meeting later this morning, but Janice said you were here with something regarding your father's files?"

Swarthout placed his elbows on the desk and clasped his hands in front of his face. In his late fifties or early sixties, his deeply furrowed forehead, thick neck and narrow blue eyes lent him a visage of executive competence. As with Lomax, Nick found something 'ex-cop' in the man's deportment.

"Uh, yes, that's right…" Nick began, glancing between the two. "…When I was here yesterday, I walked into your archives by accident — I was looking for the restroom and the receptionist was on the phone… She pointed down a hall and, well, I walked into the wrong room…" Slightly disingenuous, Nick knew, but fair enough.

"I'm not sure I understand, Nick," Lomax replied, leaning forward a bit. "You went into the *wrong* room…? Thinking it was a *restroom?* And, you… what, decided to look around?"

Nick exhaled, half-expecting this. "I did…" he confessed. "…I'm not in the habit of snooping around in places I don't belong… But, well…I don't know, something about yesterday felt odd, so…yeah, I looked around a minute… And found my brother's files."

He paused and placed the pilfered folder on Swarthout's desk.

"…Good thing too, because I found something in there you didn't share with my father…" Nick waited a couple beats to let this register. "Specifically, a memo, written by *you* Mr. Swarthout, to *you* Mr. Lomax, suggesting the investigation be shut down because of a call your agency received from someone with the initials '*SD*' who *asked* that you lay off. Which, you did… telling my father you'd hit the wall, that the investigation had turned over every stone and Evan's last known location was Malaysia… Mostly true, only you left out the call from 'SD'."

Swarthout and Lomax gazed icily at Nick.

"I'm guessing this is not the way you guys normally do business" he continued, "Considering you're both former FBI, but… It happened…"

Swarthout glanced over at Lomax then regarded Nick a moment.

"I'm afraid it's not quite that straightforward, Mr. Hughes," he said, clasping his hands together on the desk.

"From a legal standpoint, we state up front in all our contracts that sources and methods are *proprietary*, something I'm sure you can understand. We agree to provide the client with a report, *not* a methodology. Any decisions about proceeding with a case are ours to make and there's no contractual obligation to share what methods we may use to make that determination. It's standard procedure in our business."

He then leaned back and took a breath.

"That said," Swarthout continued, a weary resolve in his tone. "…there's no point in knocking about in the weeds here either… I assume you've made copies?"

"I have," Nick replied, after a moment. "And let me just say, I'm not here to get in a pissing match with you guys over contractual fine print or anything else. I just need to *understand*… I buried my father three days ago, and in the process, learned that he'd hired *you* to help locate his estranged son — my brother…"

He glanced between the two men and tapped a finger on the file.

"Who I now understand has gone missing in some foreign country. Maybe in trouble. Possibly even dead…" He held their gaze. "So, like I said, I'm just trying to understand…"

Swarthout hunched forward, forearms on the desk as he clasped his fingers together. Seconds silently ticked away as he considered.

"…It's not a person…" he stated flatly at last. "…S-D…" he spelled out, "It's not a person…at least not any *particular* person…"

Puzzled, Nick looked over at Lomax, who appeared quite content to let Swarthout explain.

"I'm missing something here…? Nick said, confused. "It's *not* a person??"

Swarthout's mouth tightened noticeably. "No…" he explained. "We often use certain shorthand with internal communications… Like S-*D*…" he added, voicing the letters with space between them. "Short for… *State Department*…"

Nick wasn't sure he'd heard correctly.

"Wait…" he said, haltingly. "…You mean, the *US* State Department…?"

Swarthout looked down at the desk while Lomax leaned back.

"…You're saying that…that someone… *somebody* at the *US Department of State,* warned you off…?"

Lomax shifted in his chair, a signal to Swarthout that he wanted this one.

"Kate Sheneman, who got the call, she used to work for the State Department," he explained. "Jim and I had both worked with her when we were at the bureau. After she retired from State, we asked her to join the firm…

"In this business…" he went on. "Contacts are like gold… And Kate brought a wealth of contacts with her." He glanced at Swarthout, then crossed his legs and continued.

"…Of course, it's a two-way street. Runs on good will and trust. There's no way we could jeopardize that trust… So, when Kate got that call regarding your brother, we had to respect it," he added, with finality.

Nick glanced between the two men as he considered this.

Swarthout then got up and stepped away from his desk to gaze out a window. He lingered there a moment with hands in his pockets, then began to speak.

"Ever have to make a judgment call, Mr. Hughes?" he asked looking out. "You know... The kind where your moral compass swings in a direction you're not comfortable with...?" He moved toward his desk and sat on the edge to face Nick.

"...It's true, we chose not to share that information with your father... In my judgment, that was the only option, then *and* now, and Jack agreed." Swarthout paused. "...Even if we *had* shared it, there was no way we could continue the investigation. I'm sure you can see that."

A brief silence followed as Nick took the meaning of the words. "What if he'd gone to the State Department himself...my father?" he then asked.

Swarthout, shrugged. "I think we all know the answer to that..." he answered. "It would've gone nowhere. They'd deny it. Maybe drag their feet for a couple weeks, but in the end, nothing would be found..." He stood again. "So, *yes*, it was a judgment call," he went on, "One of the only times we ever got push-back on an inquiry."

Nick glanced back and forth between them.

"So, there you have it, Nick," Lomax chimed in. "We honestly don't know what's behind the push-back or who Kate was in contact with. She's no longer here and wouldn't betray that confidence anyway."

As Nick listened, it began to feel as if the office was closing in on him.

"Okay, then..." Lomax continued, sitting up in his chair and facing Nick. "I think we're square here..."

12.

From six miles up, the sprawling flat center of the North American continent stretched out to a far horizon where Earth's curvature became noticeable. A high-pressure system had settled in with conditions aviators liked to call, '*CAVU*', an acronym for '*ceiling and visibility unlimited.*' Nick recalled former president George H.W. Bush, a former Navy pilot in World War Two, using the term in a television interview. And while the acronym aptly described the view from his window, little else seemed very clear at the moment.

It would be another four hours before the flight landed in Los Angeles and Nick's restless mind kept him wide awake. He allowed himself to be distracted by imagining the land below as it looked a thousand years ago, a vast sprawling sea of grass stretching to the horizon, an *American Serengeti*. Generations of settlers and the arrival of industrial agriculture had turned these Great Plains into a global bread basket. Seasoned coast-to-coast air travelers had dubbed this ancient seabed between the Mississippi River and Rocky Mountains the great 'flyover' region.

Staring out the window, it struck him that it had been little more than a century ago that pioneer settlers first set plow to prairie sod. The terrestrial patchwork of green and brown squares below still mostly reflected those original 160-acre parcels of the Homestead Act. Through the decades, with the advent of industrialized agriculture, these parcels became more consolidated. He recalled a recent series in the *Los Angeles Times* describing the plight of prairie towns in the Midwest, many fallen on hard times as mechanization and big agribusiness made it nearly impossible for smaller farmers to keep up. Many sold their land or went bankrupt trying to resist economic entropy, contributing to a decades-long depopulating of the grain belt. Once-vibrant communities had become hollowed-out anachronisms, the winds of time picking at their dessicated bones. Towns that had for generations served as the civic, social and business hub of a community were no longer necessary. Nick had to wonder what those original pioneer homesteaders would make of their descendants, now five or six generations on, selling off what their forefathers struggled to create over a century ago to giant agricultural conglomerates.

Eventually, he closed his eyes and let his head fall toward the window. The drone of the jet engines slowly began to dissolve away into voices…a dispute of some sort… There was something familiar about the hollow glassiness at the edges of the words, like the sharp sound of voices in a room of hard surfaces. A kitchen, yes… A kitchen with linoleum floors, porcelain sinks, Formica counters, dishes and glasses…an enameled table with steel legs against a wall where a man absently stirred his coffee while a woman washed dishes at a sink. This was his father's house and these were his parents. A child of seven or so watched from an archway just off the kitchen—*him?* A slightly taller, skinny boy with bony shoulder blades protruding from the back of a dirty tee-shirt stood behind him, a head of unruly blond hair framing his soft features — Evan at nine or ten.

Something had upset his mother.

"What do you know about it?" she barked, "Tell me! What do you think you know about *anything??*"

Nick's father kept his eyes on the table. "Not now," he moaned, irritated. "Not here Janice, please."

"Not now?? Not here?? That's what you always say!!"

"The *boys,* for Christ's sake—"

"Oh, so you're worried about *them* all of a sudden! You don't think they see what's going on?"

"Enough already!! *Stop!!*"

At this, his mother slammed a glass in the sink, shattering it and sending shards everywhere. Blood trickled from her hand and ran onto the white porcelain as his father silently got up from the table and walked out the back door.

Nick watched his younger self turn to Evan, who briefly held his gaze before turning to walk away. Young Nick watched him leave then swung back around, only now he was outside on a bright morning and a year or so older. A green stingray bicycle rested on its kickstand in a corner of a concrete patio area. The banana-style seat had patches of worn duct tape and the wheels had baseball cards attached to the bracket running from fender to fork with clothespins. When the wheels spun, the cards flapped in the spokes creating a thrumming, motor-like sound. He and his pal Jackie Marks would tear around the neighborhood on their bikes sounding like a couple of wheeled buzz-saws.

He jumped on the stingray and rode into an alleyway that bisected their block, standing on the pedals for extra power and kicking up loose gravel that the city threw down on hot tar by way of maintenance every year.

Exiting the alleyway, he turned down Third Street and onto Davis, slowing into his own backyard where he parked the bike on its kickstand and went inside. Immediately, he knew something was off. A man's jacket had been tossed over a kitchen chair but it wasn't one of his father's. The wall clock said it was 11:30 in the morning, and he knew the old man would never be home at that hour.

After a moment, he heard what sounded like his mother upstairs straining at something. There was someone else…a man…

Through the living room to the stairs, he fixed on the grunting sounds of their exertion. At the top of the stairs, he could hear creaking bedsprings and intermittent moaning and heavy breathing. His parent's bedroom door was open a crack and he slowly approached, snugging closer to the wall until he could just peek around the corner into the open doorway. It was dark and the shades were drawn as he peered around to see two darkened figures on the bed. Ambient light from the hallway was just enough to make out his mother on her hands and knees, naked, as a naked man kneeled behind her and repeatedly thrust his groin into her ass. With each thrust, the headboard banged into the wall in time with the slapping of skin on skin. Nick's heart pounded in his chest, accompanied by an onslaught of confusing, contradictory feelings — revulsion, arousal, fascination, and a fury that almost burned. He began to back away when someone started shaking him. Startled, he quickly turned to see a flight attendant standing over him.

"We're going to be landing in Los Angeles soon, sir," she said. "We need you to put your tray table up and your seat belt on."

13.

Almost a week after his return, Nick still seemed out of sorts to Celeste. After sharing what he'd learned from the investigators in Philadelphia, she'd decided to give him some space. At dinner one night, she asked about his classes as he had not yet returned to teaching. He explained that the remainder of his courses for the current term would be covered by other adjuncts. When he added that he needed some time, she became angry.

"But you won't get another assignment until mid-*January...?*" Celeste reminded him, tamping down her irritation.

"Have you actually thought this through?" she asked.

He gave her an 'over-the-glasses-are-you-kidding' look as if she were one of his students trying to explain away a plagiarized paper. Message received, she backed off and they finished dinner in silence.

Most days Nick spent in the public library. He'd written a dozen or so letters and made twice as many phone calls, only to be run around, put on hold or promised call-backs. One solicitous staffer told him, '*everything that could be done would be done*'.

Exasperated, he filed a request under the Freedom of Information Act, for the Peace Corps' assignment records for 1979, the year his brother went to Malaysia. Grudgingly, they eventually complied, providing records of all assignments that year. At the section for Malaysia, he didn't see his brother's name. Reading it twice just to be sure, Evan Hughes name did not appear among that year's volunteers.

He resisted an impulse to contact Swarthout and Lomax with this new and contradictory information; their coziness with the State Department still troubled him. Instead, he tried to track down other names from the records assigned to Malaysia that year. After several futile phone calls however, he realized the fifteen-year-old contact information was useless.

14.

As the weeks passed, Nick made little progress. The bulk of his days were spent making calls from home or chasing down information at the library. Celeste grew increasingly concerned, worried he was becoming 'obsessive' over this. One side of the dining table held a clutter of documents, yellow legal pads and now, various books on Malaysia. She felt helpless as Nick disengaged more and more from the mutuality of their lives, and she reminded herself to be patient, to give him *time*.

Despite her best efforts, things finally came to a head one night while they were having dinner at a nearby Thai restaurant they frequented back when they first started dating.

"This place hasn't changed at all..." she said, looking about the restaurant. "Even the menu is the same."

Nick smiled while distractedly fussing with the label on his beer.

"If it 'ain't broke', I guess..." he concurred, then glanced around. "...You think the 'more rice' guy still works here...?"

This got a smile out of her.

"*That* guy!" she chuckled. "The *rice pusher* — always reminding us we could have *more* rice!"

"Probably hoping we'd forget the *undersized* portions they served..." Nick suggested.

"Right..." she agreed. "He'd hover nearby with that 'deer in the headlights' look, afraid we'd leave hungry." They shared a laugh like old times, then she folded her menu.

"Okay, I'm going for the old standby: Penang curry with tofu," she declared. "You...?"

"Masaman curry with chicken, I think," he replied, still absently peeling at the label of his beer bottle. "With that killer spicy peanut sauce..."

Celeste gestured to the waiter who came for their order. As he left, she clasped her fingers together in silent thought.

"Does it seem to you," she said reflecting, "Things were more fun back then…?"

"Hmmm…" Nick muttered, mulling it. "Maybe… Of course, everything's more fun when it's new. Relationships. Jobs. Places. Life itself, even… Remember when you were a kid, how new things kept coming at you? New school year, new friends, new experiences, new feelings. Like the world had its door wide open for you… And anything was possible…"

The melancholic drift gave Celeste an opening.

"Nick…" she began, cautiously, "What's going on here…? Ever since you got back, it's like you're in some other world… All this stuff with your brother…it's taken over. I'm a little concerned…"

He briefly glanced up then distractedly turned the bottle and sighed. She wanted an explanation for things *he* barely understood himself. For her, ambiguity was an enemy to be flattened out and vanquished, a posture forged by an unshakable belief that life could be *willed* into the shape we desired. It was a mindset suffused with fuzzy notions of 'get what you want' optimism of the sort touted in countless self-help books and life-coaching programs. An essential tenet maintained that '*visualizing*' success would bring it about, that the only obstacles were those in your mind and we could 'will away' the psychic detritus of the past, as if life's tragedies and heartbreaks could actually be *swept* from our minds like so many dead leaves on a sidewalk.

"Can't we just have a quiet dinner?" Nick finally answered, a hint of weariness in his voice.

"*Quiet?* You're kidding, right?" Celeste protested. "That's *all we've had* are quiet dinners. Ever since you got back from Pennsylvania. It's been like dining with a moody teenager…"

"I know… I'm sorry…" he agreed, as if this might defuse her rumbling agitation. She exhaled loudly and put her napkin on the table.

"Look, I've been trying to understand…" she continued, "And maybe I'm not patient enough, I don't know… I get it that you need some time. That this has been a lot to deal with… I understand that. But *this*… this business with your brother? I'm missing something there… I mean, he hasn't been in your life for twenty years. And now you're suddenly obsessed with trying to get answers about where he might be or what may have happened to him? Where's he been for you all these years? What makes you think you owe him all this?"

Their food arrived, defusing the moment. Nick thanked the waiter and they joylessly began poking at the dishes with chopsticks.

"I don't know how to explain it, Celeste," Nick began, while absently pinching a piece of potato in his chopsticks.

"You know…when Evan left…the way he left, I wasn't surprised because…things between us hadn't been the same since our mother's death… Evan took it especially hard… The two of them had a rough history up to that point. And *that's* the way he'd have to leave it… Forever…" He briefly paused, discomfited by something.

"Anyway… Evan grew more distant, physically and otherwise. So, when he took off after high school…it didn't come as a huge surprise. The old man and me, we both assumed that was the way Evan wanted it… The idea that his silence might *not* have been a choice… That never occurred to either of us…"

He lifted his down-turned eyes to her.

"Now I find out my father had doubts… That he'd begun to think something might've happened to Evan and decided to look into it… I don't know how or when that came about as he never mentioned it to me. We never talked about Evan…"

Celeste listened as he grappled with the enormity of trying to explain what evaded explanation.

"How am I supposed to just walk away from this now?" Especially after that business with the investigators…someone from the State Department telling them to lay off. What the hell is that? And why would anyone take the trouble to cook up those immigration records contradicting the ones Lomax had? That takes some doing. Who wouldn't be a little worked-up by it?"

Celeste sighed. "…I don't know, Nick…" she said, wearily. "…I really don't know…"

The undertone of exasperation in her voice underscored the deeper tensions in their relationship. In truth though, Nick had no idea how to explain the complexity of a family history as conflicted and convoluted as his.

"Look, I know all this is hard to understand…" he told her, "But I can't just walk away. Sure, I probably have every right to… But I *can't*. He's still my brother, Celeste, and the bottom line is, there's no one else who'll do this for him."

"Sure, I get that," she agreed. "But where does it end? How long do you put your life on hold for this?"

He held her gaze a moment then leaned back and reached into his jacket pocket, producing what looked to be a ticket of some sort. He held it a few seconds then placed it on the table between them.

"What's this…?" Celeste asked, a heightened concern in her voice. "A *plane ticket?*" She picked it up and read the itinerary: *LAX* to *Kuala Lumpur, Malaysia.* Her eyes then noted the passenger details and she drew in a clipped breath: '*Hughes, Nicholas.*'

"It's just a short trip," Nick explained, as her eyes lifted from the ticket. "I'm not moving there…"

"Oh!" she blurted, mockingly, "Well…*that's* reassuring!"

Nick set the chopsticks down on his plate. "This is why I didn't bother discussing it with you beforehand," he said, leaning back from the table. "I didn't want an argument."

Celeste put the ticket down and slid it toward Nick.

"An argument?" she asked, dismayed. "Really? I thought this was a joint venture, this *thing* between you and me… A partnership… You know…where couples consult each other on things like this."

"Hold on," he objected. "This isn't about *us.* Yes, I should've told you first, I'm sorry, but it wouldn't have changed anything…"

The unfamiliar stridency in his tone further disturbed Celeste, adding to a growing sense of distance between them.

"I can't believe this!" she declared, throwing up her arms. "…Look, I get it that you're frustrated and want answers, anybody would. And I get how you feel, I do… But I don't understand your thinking here. Traveling halfway around the world to do…*what* exactly?"

"I'm not entirely sure…" he sighed, "But I have to try *something*. People don't just disappear from the face of the earth like that… He *was* there and he may still be there. Somebody on the ground in Malaysia must know something, so, I'm going to root around, talk to people and ask questions until I get some answers. Because I can't leave it like this, Celeste. I can't just walk away and forget about it. I owe him that much at least…"

"*Owe* him?" Celeste repeated, pointedly. "Really? Have you ever thought about what he owes *you?* It goes both ways, right? Shouldn't that figure in?"

He held the ticket in front of him, quietly staring down at it.

"It's not like that," he protested, shaking his head.

"No?" she asked, a bitterness in her tone. "Then what, Nick? What *is* it like?"

Turning away, she emptied her wine glass and set it down. For some time they sat there, food barely touched. In the silence, Nick decided further discussion was pointless. He didn't fault Celeste. How could anyone possibly explain the countless unseen threads that bind a soul beyond all reason, to those of their own blood? Such bonds were woven into the very fabric of our limbic systems and exerted an irresistible tidal force not unlike the ancient mechanism that compels salmon from their ocean home to return to the very waters of their birth hundreds of miles inland, driving them upstream in rivers and creeks against furious currents, up and over impossible waterfalls to the place where, at long last, they would spawn and die.

PART II

15.

Wispy patches of cloud hung here and there over the land below, their edges randomly fringed with the crimson hues of another day's first light. At the edge of an endless sky, the tropical sun had begun to peek through as Nick stared out the window of a commercial airliner. Stiff and dehydrated from the stale re-circulated cabin air, he looked around for one of the dutiful and very charming Singapore Airlines attendants. Occasionally, he caught a glimpse of trees poking through the clouds below — *Malaysia*. He had familiarized himself with the terrain from the numerous atlases and books he'd pored over before departing. Situated between the Tropic of Cancer and the equator, he learned that the Malaysian state occupied the bulbous southern portion of the Malay Peninsula, a slender finger of land extending southward from the Asian continent for nearly a thousand miles. To the east, the Gulf of Thailand; to the west, the Andaman Sea. A thin northern piece of the peninsula belonged to Thailand with a sliver sliced off its western edge for Myanmar, formerly known as Burma. Once covered in tropical rain forest, the peninsula had long since been converted to agricultural production, rubber tree and palm oil plantations mostly, as well as countless rice paddies.

They'd be landing for a short stopover in Singapore, the wealthy, somewhat idiosyncratic city-state at the southern tip of the Malay Peninsula. Racial tensions, stoked by fears of Chinese communism in the early days of independence from British rule, eventually led to Singapore's expulsion from the newly created Federation of Malaya in 1965 (Singapore's ethnic Chinese majority, Nick had learned, outnumbered ethnic Indians and Malays three to one.) The new rump city-state eventually developed a unique hybrid form of government merging capitalism and democracy with an idiosyncratic and relatively benign authoritarianism, turning Singapore into a global economic powerhouse.

At one degree north of the equator, the climate was a steamy swelter with no seasonal change, and Nick had to wonder if this played any part in the peculiar civic anal-retentive fussiness Singapore was known for. Laws were on the books that banned chewing gum and prohibited a smelly tropical fruit called *durian* on the subway.

In spite of this, or perhaps because of it, the compact city-state had become an economic powerhouse and the world's busiest port. Singapore's multi-cultural internationalism and robust consumer culture had delivered a prosperity that set it apart from its more sober Muslim neighbors, Malaysia to the north and Indonesia to the west.

Nick would not be here long while waiting for a connecting flight to Kuala Lumpur. '*KL*', as it was commonly known, was the capital of Malaysia, an Islamic republic divided into two geographic and political regions, *Peninsular Malaysia* and *East Malaysia;* the latter being that sliver of the planet's third largest island, Borneo, which Malaysia inherited from the British after independence. A larger chunk of Borneo, almost two-thirds, had become Indonesian territory inherited from *its* former colonial masters, the Dutch. And, a tiny, oil-rich patch of northern coastal Borneo belonged to *Brunei*, a conservative Islamic Sultanate.

"Sir, would you care for some coffee or tea?" said an impossibly pleasant Singaporean flight attendant. That anybody could look so fresh and lovely after a 16-hour flight boggled Nick's mind. As the attendant poured him a coffee, he realized how lousy *he* must look. A quick scan around the cabin revealed a scene that might've been the aftermath of a teenage party when the parents were away — blankets and little airline pillows littered the aisles while passengers slung and twisted in various states of consciousness amid the napkins, straws, and plastic wrappers strewn about their surroundings.

Sipping a coffee, Nick gazed out the window where some of the wispy plumes had begun to dissipate with the sun's steady rise. He felt his pulse quicken, partly from the caffeine but more from the uncertainty of what lay ahead.

16.

Upon clearing customs and collecting his baggage, Nick took a taxi to the hotel. As he rode through the streets, he was struck by Kuala Lumpur's shiny modernity. The city had recently broken ground on what would be the world's tallest skyscraper, the 1,480-foot-tall, Petronas Towers, built with the oil wealth of the eponymously named national petroleum company, *Petronas.*

Though he had read of the city's vibrance, energy and western-style consumerism, the reality still surprised him. That he had subconsciously anticipated something more austere from a Muslim nation served as a reminder how insular his perspective had become living in his LA bubble. All around were fast food chains, jewelry stores, toy stores, clothing chains — all the consumer abundance of a secular market economy. Malaysia clearly seemed intent on becoming one of Asia's economic 'Tigers'. Like Singapore, it was a forward-looking, multi-ethnic state, only with far more real estate. Unlike Singapore, ethnic *Malays* comprised seventy percent of the population. Referred to collectively as *bumiputra,* these ethnic Malays were overwhelmingly Muslim. While Malaysia was officially secular, its constitution had explicitly made Islam the religion of the federation and the bumiputra were obliged to follow Sharia law when it came to family matters like divorce, child custody and inheritance. The remaining thirty percent of Malaysia's population were largely of Chinese and Indian descent, with the Chinese in particular, wielding far greater political power than their numbers would suggest.

Nick had booked a room at an upscale international hotel chain; after the long flight, a little familiarity and comfort would help ease him into this unfamiliar world. Also, one of his guidebooks noted that the global hotel chains here catered to foreign businessmen, meaning they served alcohol in an Islamic country where it was otherwise difficult to find.

The bulk of his foreign travel experience had been during college and graduate school; obligatory trips for the would-be English professor to England and Ireland. There were also a couple jaunts to Baja California and Nayarit in Mexico with Celeste, but these hardly counted as foreign travel since they never left the resort properties. Malaysia was as far afield as he'd ever been, with Kuala Lumpur being his first taste of a sprawling Asian city.

After a nap at the hotel, Nick went out for a quick stroll to get himself on local time and shake off the jet lag. Out on the street, Malaysians were going about their business and looked to be doing fairly well. Prosperity had created an Asian-flavored urban middle-class with distinctly Muslim features. Women sported colorful head-scarves and modest loose-fitting garments that revealed nothing, though they were apparently allowed a wider latitude when it came to color variety, an apt concession given the tropical climate.

The streets pulsed with buses, cars, taxis, scooters and pedal-powered rickshaws. Willy-nilly food carts served kabobs, roasted corn, and other 'grab and go' foodstuffs. Nick imagined his brother walking these same streets, a fresh-faced Peace Corps volunteer and ambassador of American largesse ready to roll up his sleeves and get busy. An impressive skyline had sprouted around the Petronas Towers, giving form to Malaysia's petroleum wealth. Still, beneath all the gleaming steel and glass, an abiding religious current prevailed. As if on cue, the call of the *muezzin* began to echo across the city, calling the faithful to prayers. Part-song, part-incantation, these calls went out five times a day, a reminder to Muslims that piety remained an ongoing endeavor.

17.

Despite the attempt to beat jet-lag, Nick dozed off after dinner and found himself wide-awake at 4 A.M. The hotel café wouldn't open for another hour, so he busied himself organizing the day ahead. A stack of color copies using an old snapshot of Evan sat on a coffee table, ready to hand out. He held one up and gazed at the youthful face of his brother at seventeen, trying to imagine it today.

After a long breakfast in the hotel café, he took a taxi to the embassy. Before leaving Los Angeles, Nick had exchanged faxes with a sympathetic US Embassy employee here that resulted in a meeting with Ambassador Ellen Hollingshead, a woman whose surname certainly fit the part. The Marines at the front gate gave him a thorough vetting, examining his passport and appointment letter while sizing him up.

Once inside, he was escorted into a large and tastefully appointed waiting room with a moldering tropical aesthetic. An assistant soon appeared and guided him through another doorway requiring the swipe of a security card to gain access. Inside, embassy staffers worked at desks with computer terminals and spoke quietly on phones in the overdone air-conditioning. The assistant brought him to a set of French doors, tapping lightly on the glass before entering. A woman seated behind an impressive desk rose to greet them.

"Good afternoon, I'm Ellen Hollingshead," she said, extending a hand. "And you're Mr. Hughes?"

"Yes ma'am, I am," Nick murmured, with a kind of clumsy deference. He found it strange to hear himself say '*ma'am*' like some ex-military guy or southern schoolboy.

"Please, sit down," the ambassador continued, gesturing to a chair. A striking woman in her early sixties with a dignified air of Brahmin self-assurance, she looked the part of career diplomat. He imagined her starting each day with power laps in the Embassy pool followed by a massage at the Embassy spa.

"How was your flight over?" she asked, as an icebreaker. "You know, another few hours and you'd be in Australia," she added, as if this might be preferable.

"Longest flight I've ever been on…" Nick replied amiably. "Don't think I'd want to do it on a regular basis."

"Yes, well, thankfully, ambassadors spend most of their time *in-country*," she explained, "Though some on our staff *do* fly back and forth more frequently and I certainly don't envy them," she added, settling into her seat.

"Now, Mr. Hughes, what can I do for you?" she asked, getting right to the point.

"Thanks for meeting with me, ambassador," Nick graciously replied, shifting more upright in his seat as he opened his valise and handed her a folder.

"I hope you had a chance to read my letter for background on this," he continued. The ambassador placed some 'half-moon' reading glasses on the bridge of her nose then opened the file and began scanning a page while listening.

"As I mentioned… My father recently passed, and while cleaning out his house, I discovered these files from a private investigation firm he'd hired several years back…to find my brother…" Nick paused to be sure she was with him. "He'd lost touch with us…and, uh, I think we both assumed that was how he wanted it."

The ambassador knitted her brow and flipped through the pages like a doctor reading a patient's chart. Nick went on, adding some vague generalizations about family difficulties before sharing what he'd learned since discovering the documents.

"Given all that…" he added, "…I'm obviously concerned…that my brother may be in some kind of trouble or…" He faltered, leaving the last bit unsaid, before pivoting.

"That's why I decided to come here… According to the paper trail, this is the last place he's known to have been."

The ambassador nodded vaguely as her eyes darted about the documents.

"So, let me see if I have this right…" she said, flipping pages. "The immigration documents the investigators found don't agree with those you received from the State Department?"

"Essentially, yes," Nick replied, "You can see in the immigration records the investigators got from Malaysia, that Evan was stamped *in* to the country but never stamped back *out*. When I sent a copy of this to the State Department, they returned this *other* version showing Evan stamped out of Malaysia shortly after his dismissal. They can't both be right…"

The ambassador's mouth tightened as she murmured '*hmm*' without looking up from the file. Some seconds passed before she closed the folder and set it down. Leaning back in her chair, she then removed the reading glasses, tapping them lightly against her cheek in thought.

"Well," she began, "This is *really* quite extraordinary…" She then brought the reading glasses to her pursed lips.

"…Honestly, I'm not sure what to think…" she went on, leaning forward, elbows on the desk. "In my time as a diplomat, I've never run into anything like this. My instinct says there's an innocent mistake here… a mix-up of some kind. We've had some funding reductions with the last couple administrations, so… it's possible staffing issues are to blame…"

"Could be…" Nick agreed. "Only, the investigators couldn't find any record of my brother being in the US after 1979. No bills, no work history, no address or banking records. Nothing…" He let this sit a moment.

The ambassador nodded as she eyed the folder. "I see…" she muttered, a vague distance in her tone. "And, is it possible your brother left unofficially somehow?"

Nick held her gaze a moment. "With all due respect, ambassador, I can't imagine why or how anyone would do that. And…according to your employer, the US State Department, my brother's passport expired eight years ago and has never been renewed."

The diplomat looked genuinely puzzled. "Well…" she began, "I'm at a loss. But there *has* to be an explanation. People do go missing abroad. That's probably the number two thing we do here — helping US citizens with a family member or friend who's gone missing. Right behind the number one thing our office does, which is helping Americans who've run afoul of Malaysian law." She then asked Nick if she might get a copy of the documents.

"This one is yours, ambassador," he answered, gesturing at the folder on her desk. "I've got another full set along with old photos of my brother that are a bit outdated, but they're all I could dig up. I was planning on showing them to the police here."

"Absolutely," said the ambassador. "That's usually the best place to start and we can help with that as well." At this, she hesitated, "…Whenever an unidentified Caucasian body turns up, which, thankfully, hasn't happened in some time, the relevant embassies are notified."

Her tone then shifted. "Also…" she began, treading cautiously, "…we shouldn't rule out another possibility that's unfortunately all-too-common. Every year, a number of tourists here are swept out to sea… They go swimming and underestimate the power of open water; most get caught in currents and panic when they're too far out. Their bodies are rarely found…"

While he hadn't considered this, Nick thought it still didn't explain all the misinformation and stonewalling he'd gotten regarding his brother.

"In any event," the ambassador continued, her tone and body language indicating the meeting was over, "I'll have my staff make some inquiries." She then rose from her chair and escorted Nick to the door.

"It may take a few days, but hopefully we'll get to the bottom of this. Now, how long are you going to be with us here in Kuala Lumpur, Mr. Hughes?"

"I only planned on a couple weeks, but I can change that if necessary."

"Very good," she continued. "Make sure to leave your local contact information with the receptionist. And rest assured, we'll do everything we can."

18.

Outside the embassy, Nick flagged down a pedal-powered rickshaw and pointed to the central police station on his map. As they wove through traffic, Nick reflected on his meeting with the ambassador. Cagey and somewhat guarded, he reminded himself she was a seasoned diplomat and almost certainly a team player. And of course, her team and his were not necessarily the same.

Inside the central police bureau, large fans languidly spun from high ceilings and it wouldn't have seemed out of place to spot Sidney Greenstreet or Robert Morley in white linen suit and Panama hat holding court. Nick approached a counter where a large bulletproof window shielded the police on the other side and stooped to speak into an opening.

"Excuse me…?" he said, "*Hello…?*" A uniformed officer stepped over to the window.

"Do you speak *English?*" Nick asked, hopefully. "*…English?*" he repeated, but the policeman looked puzzled.

Sweat began to bead on his forehead and he quickly began flipping through his Malay phrasebook when another man appeared at the window and said, "*Yes…?*"

"Ah, hello… You speak English?"

"Yes," the man replied. "What is it you need?"

He scrutinized Nick as the uniformed officer made room. Both men had the wary manner of professional skeptics. *Cops*, Nick told himself. The same everywhere, with that suspicious, vaguely contemptuous way of engaging with the world beyond their own ranks.

"I'm here about my brother," he explained through the opening, holding up one of Evan's photos. "An American named Evan Hughes. He's been missing for some time now and his last known location was here in Malaysia."

The man processed this while still sizing Nick up. After several seconds, he said, '*Wait…*' and with a nod to his colleague, stepped away.

The minutes passed as Nick watched people come and go on both sides of the glass. He noticed that a healthy percentage of the uniformed Malaysian police were decked out military-style with fatigues tucked into boots, Kevlar vest and automatic weapon hanging from a shoulder. This militarization of law enforcement had become a growing trend everywhere, it seemed, as if the police were preparing for war with civilians.

Once again he tried to imagine his brother operating in this world. Evan had always been the more fearless of them: riding in the first car of the roller coaster, *diving* off the high-board at Center Street pool, mouthing-off to schoolyard bullies. He alone among their peers would walk long stretches of the foot-wide, thirty-foot tall concrete flood wall built by the Army Corps of Engineers to contain the river as it passed through downtown. Like some punk tightrope walker with arms outstretched for balance, Evan remained oblivious to the river thirty feet below on one side and the scruffy alley behind the buildings thirty feet down on the other.

"Yes, can I help you?" said a voice from behind as Nick turned abruptly to see another policeman in a uniform suggesting a higher rank.

"Captain Patong," he said. "You are looking for a brother?"

"Ah, yes, Captain, I am…" answered Nick.

"I see," the captain replied. "And you are *Australian?*" Nick remembered Australia's proximity to Malaysia.

"No captain, I'm from California…American."

"America? You're very far from home then?"

"I am…" Nick smiled. "I was hoping you might be able to help me. My brother came here with the Peace Corps about fifteen years ago. You know… the American aid program?" Patong's expression barely changed. "Well… anyway, immigration records show him entering Malaysia in 1979…" Nick slid a copy under the plexiglass. "And you can see from this that he was never stamped back out."

An air of suspicion emanated from Patong as he studied the document. "I don't think I understand…?" he said, "You say it's been *twenty years*?"

"Since I've seen him, yes…" Nick thought it best to sidestep the complexities. "Here's his picture…when he was around seventeen."

He slid the photo under the plexiglass. "I thought you might be able to compare this photo with any missing persons or other records you may have…"

The captain studied the photo with what looked to be distaste. "Come with me, please," he motioned to Nick, buzzing a door open. Patong then led Nick down a corridor to an office where Patong opened the door and gestured for Nick to enter.

"Please, wait here," Patong said, pointing to a chair in front of the desk before disappearing back into the corridor.

After five or so minutes, a taller man in civilian clothes entered.

"Good morning, I am Inspector Kencuk," he said, taking the seat behind the desk. He wore a short-sleeve polo shirt, khaki pants and a pager of some sort on his belt. "I understand you are here about a missing person?"

"Yes, that's right, Inspector," Nick answered, then explained once more.

The inspector clasped his hands with index fingers to his lips as he listened. When Nick finished, Kencuk silently nodded to himself a moment before speaking.

"Patong said you're American?" he asked, and Nick confirmed the fact. "And, you have spoken to your embassy about this?"

Something in the inspector's tone mirrored Patong's wariness. "Well, yes… I have…" he replied, "They've promised to do what they can…"

"Uh-huh…" the inspector murmured, as Patong quietly returned to the office.

"How old did you say your brother would be now?" Kencuk asked.

"Well, he's a couple years older than me, so that'd make him forty."

Kencuk considered this a moment then spoke in Malay to Patong who curtly nodded and stepped out again.

"I asked Patong to search our records for any unidentified bodies that may have turned up over the last twenty years," Kencuk explained, "Caucasians, of course." At this, he leaned back from the desk. "Everything is on computers now… All the way back to 1957." This brought out a touch of disdain in his tone, suggesting an old-school skepticism toward technology.

"Are you married Mr. Hughes…?" Kencuk then asked.

The personal turn surprised Nick. "Uh, no, Inspector," he explained. "I live with a woman. We've talked about getting married at some point…" The response came off as defensive, as if he felt compelled to justify both living in sin and *not* being married at his age. He sensed a hint of disapproval in the inspector's mien: '*We love American fast food, innovation and consumer goods,*' Nick imagined him thinking, '*but your moral corruption is an abomination…*'

Just then, Patong returned with a couple of stapled sheets he handed to Kencuk, who briefly perused their contents before handing them to Nick.

"This goes all the way back to 1976," he said, "Twelve unidentified Caucasian bodies. None fit the age or description of your brother at the time they were found. They were never claimed and had no identification. When we get them, they've either washed ashore or have been picked over by people or animals. We go through the immigration records, looking for anyone who's overstayed their visas. If no identification is made, they end up here."

Nick looked the page over and agreed that none seemed to fit Evan's description. He had to cringe at the thought — anonymous corpses headed for a Potter's Field in some foreign country. No one to miss them or ask questions; forgotten lives, finally achieving a measure of peace in death of the sort that eluded them in life.

He handed the pages back to Kencuk. "I was wondering… Are the police here notified when someone overstays their visa?" he asked, adding, "After a certain amount of time?"

Kencuk considered this. "Generally, that only happens if someone is looking for them. Family or maybe the law. But I'll have Patong check to see if we've missed anything."

"That's great, thank you, Inspector…"

"What I think we should do first, is have Patong take your statement now so we can open an investigation," Kencuk suggested. "But…with the amount of time that's passed, I don't want to give you false hope."

"Of course," Nick agreed. "And please let me know if there's anyone else I should talk to. I plan on being here awhile." This last part he hoped would serve notice to Kencuk, et al., of his determination.

The Inspector stared silently at Nick, his mouth curled in an ambiguous twist.

"Your brother, Mr. Hughes…" he started to say, in a tone that sounded vaguely suspicious. "You say you have not seen him for many years?"

"Not since we were in high school," Nick answered.

Kencuk raised his eyebrows, then casually lit a cigarette and pondered.

"That's a very long time…" he remarked, leaning back in his chair, eyes on Nick. "People change…"

"True…" Nick agreed, wondering what Kencuk was up to. "Even so… My brother… We grew up together and…well, I'd like to think that doesn't change…"

Kencuk took a long draw on his cigarette. "Maybe not," he concurred, "Only…in my experience…" Now his piercing dark eyes narrowed as curling wisps of smoke wafted around his head. "…When people go missing like this, there's usually a reason…"

19.

Nick decided to walk back to his hotel, grateful for Kuala Lumpur's relaxed brand of Islam because he really needed a drink and a dose of something familiar. The hotel bar, with its business-friendly cocktail-hour vibe, fit the bill. A piano trio noodled around in the background while some scattered groups of upscale Asian and European business types lounged in booths over drinks and the bonhomie of global deal-making.

Finding a seat at the bar, Nick ordered a beer and mulled the day's encounters while absently fussing with his cocktail napkin. The general low-level din of conversation and tinkling piano notes were soothing. He considered calling Celeste, only to realize it was 2:00 in the morning in LA.

The unsatisfying encounter with the police had thrown him. Some of it could be written off to the peculiarities of culture, but then…*something* in his story had gotten the cops' attention.

At the opposite end of the bar, Nick noticed a man drinking alone. Something about him seemed vaguely familiar. Unlike the other business clientele, he dressed casual — an un-tucked polo shirt and dark slacks. He looked a bit restive, even anxious, and, after a few minutes, he drank up and left.

Turning back to his beer, Nick glimpsed his ragged reflection in the mirror behind the bar and winced. Tired and drawn, he looked like someone who'd washed up after a month at sea. As he stared at the strange face in the mirror, the piano trio took a break, leaving only the ambient hum of multiple conversations, unfamiliar languages, polite laughter, glasses on trays…

20.

Returning to his room, Nick tossed the key card on the table among scattered files, fliers, notepads and photos. A candid shot from one of Evan's yearbooks stood out from the pile, and he lingered a moment at the youthful face and wounded guardedness in the eyes. Nick lifted the photo and examined it as if something might reveal itself or perhaps draw out an insight, anything that might help explain his brother.

Exhausted, Nick put the picture down and removed his shoes to stretch out on the bed. He absently clicked through channels with the remote, stopping at a BBC news program. The mindless distraction brought welcome relief and, as his eyelids grew heavy, he noticed a tiny blinking red light on the telephone next to the nightstand — *a message.* He dialed the front desk where a clerk answered politely in English.

"Yes, hello," Nick said, "The red light on my phone is flashing…?"

"Ah, Mr. Hewjes, yes…" the clerk replied, "You had a phone call and the caller left a voice message. There are instructions near the phone on how you can listen to it."

Nick thanked him. Maybe the embassy, he thought, or Celeste.

He tapped the *9 combo on the phone's keypad and chose English from the menu. The automated voice reported one message. After pushing another combo, a male voice began to speak in accented English. Nick's eyes narrowed as he listened, then punched the keys to play it again: '*I know someone who can help you. He'll find you. Police can't help—don't talk to them.*'

That was it. He sat there a moment, the receiver frozen to his ear. Slowly, his arm came down and placed the phone back in its cradle. Then, he clasped his knees with both hands and considered. A minute or so passed before he once again dialed the front desk.

"Yes, Mr. Hewjes, how may I help you?" the clerk answered.

"Are you able to tell me the number of an incoming call? The message I received forgot to leave a call back number."

"I believe so, Mr. Hewjes," the clerk replied, "If you can give me a minute, I will ask the operations manager and get back to you."

"Of course," Nick said, thanking the clerk. He paced the room like a hungry cat until, a minute later, the phone rang.

"*Yes?*"

"Hello Mr. Hewjes, this is Mohammed at the front desk."

"Yes, Mohammed, what did you find?"

"That call came in at 4:49 this afternoon. But it was from a restricted number."

"*Restricted...?* Which means, what...? There's *no* number?"

"Yes, Mr. Hewjes, I'm sorry. No number. I apologize we couldn't be more helpful." Nick just stood there with the phone to his ear.

"Is there anything else I can do for you Mr. Hewjes?"

"No... No, thank you Mohammed. I appreciate your help."

21.

The phone rang again and again as someone on BBC International relayed the weather for various regions of the world. On the bed, Nick slept face down in his clothes as tropical sunlight spilled in from his window in slivery patches around him. He began to stir, rolling onto his back and reaching for the receiver — his wakeup call from the front desk. Thanking the clerk, he rose with a heaving motion and sat on the edge of the bed, rubbing bloodshot eyes and looking like he'd just come off a three-day bender.

Despite a lack of appetite, he had breakfast sent up. The coffee helped him focus as he replayed the phone message in his head: '*I know someone who can help you. He'll find you. Police can't help—don't talk to them.*'

With a slight tremor from the caffeine, he nibbled at the toast. The voice in the message was clearly a native English speaker, British maybe. *Don't talk to the police?* What was *that* about? Fear had not entered into it when wrangling with Lomax and Swarthout, or phoning and writing letters to evasive bureaucrats. But now, a sense of dread muscled in like a cold front. *Goddamn it*, he thought, *what am I doing?*

He'll find you.

Trying to distract himself, Nick scanned the English language *New Straits Times* delivered with breakfast, but couldn't focus. After figuring out the time difference — it was 5:30 the *previous* evening in LA, sixteen time zones away — he decided to call Celeste for what he hoped would be a friendly voice.

"Are you *okay?*" she asked, answering the call.

"Fine," he replied, self-consciously upbeat. "How about you?"

"Good…" she answered, somewhat guardedly. Still holding onto things, thought Nick. "Busy…" she added after a moment. "What's going on there?"

Nick sighed deeply. "Hard to say, really. It's only my second full day."

"Yeah? You sound exhausted… What day and time is it there?"

"About 9:30 in the morning. The *next* day. Tomorrow for you. I've entered the future."

The feeble attempt at levity missed its mark and the rest of the conversation continued in the same vein. He sensed a brittleness in her tone, a hint of simmering grievance underneath it. Normally, he'd try to smooth things over, but right now *he* was the one in need of soothing. They were still too far apart so he went right to his visit with the ambassador and the Malaysian police which softened Celeste. Then he shared the phone message.

"*What??* That's *all* he said…?"

"That's it," Nick answered. "In some flavor of an Anglo accent…"

Several seconds ticked by in silence.

"…I don't know, Nick…" she said at last. "…Something's really not right there…"

"I'll say…"

"I'm serious," she insisted, "'*Don't talk with police*'? Who tells someone that?? *Jesus!* Are you hearing this??"

Her concern was well-taken though Nick hardly needed the reminder.

"Look," he told her, "Of course I'm a bit rattled. But I can't buckle every time something makes me a little nervous. I'll give it a few more days to see if somebody really *does* come forward. In the meantime, I'll keep asking questions and poking around."

Again, the silence.

"Are you hearing yourself…?" Celeste asked, after a moment. "You sound like you're in one of those men's groups where they all sit around a fire and howl at the moon… Like this is some sort of 'inner warrior challenge'…

"Oh, for Christ's sake, Celeste," he moaned, "Give me some credit…"

"I'm trying," she objected, "And I get that you want me to understand why you need to do this, but I *can't*, Nick. I'm sorry… Whatever happened in your childhood with you and your brother that makes you think you *have* to do all this…" She stopped herself and took a breath. "I only hope this gets it out of your system…whatever it is. Because I'm worried about your judgment…that you won't know when it's time to quit."

Nick knew there was no point trying to convince her he had it under control, because they could both see that he didn't.

22.

The streets had come alive with people going about their business in the morning rush of Kuala Lumpur. From a table at a small street-side café, Nick sipped coffee and made notes hoping to clear his head. The call with Celeste had spun him around and he needed to refocus.

As he glanced out at the life of the city, he found himself intrigued by the way modernity and tradition found mutual accommodation here. At bus stops, women wearing head-to-toe coverings in a range of tropical hues, munched fast-food breakfast fare while men in traditional wide-brim straw hats piloted three-wheeled bicycle rickshaws carrying passengers and goods through traffic, dodging cars, trucks, scooters, vans and each other.

At barely past 10:00 in the morning, the heat and humidity already felt oppressive and tamped down what little appetite Nick had. Instead, it made him thirsty with a craving for cold fizzy drinks like Coke or *Schweppes Bitter Lemon*, a colonial era remnant.

A vague sense of dread lingered as he began to wonder if the voice message had actually been a *ploy* of some kind, an attempt to jangle restive nerves, perhaps in hopes he might turn back. If so, it meant he'd be waiting for a phantom contact. Of course, if it *were* for real, the caller surely wouldn't expect him to sit tight for very long.

Nick finished his coffee and, when the waiter arrived, pantomimed writing on his palm for the check. The waiter nodded and said something that ended with the word, '*ringgit*', the currency of Malaysia. Nick opened his travel wallet looking for the ringgit he'd bought at the airport only to realize he'd burned through it. Since the café didn't take credit cards, he offered a US ten dollar note to the waiter who immediately shook his head and again said '*ringgit*'. Nick then made a waving gesture suggesting he didn't expect any change, but the waiter just shook his head and said, '*ringgit.*'

Anxious to leave, Nick put the ten-dollar bill down on the table and started for the door. The waiter noticed and shouted something but Nick just waved as if he didn't understand, hoping the man would chalk it up to stupid American tourists.

Outside, he moved quickly down the street thinking he'd just had his most expensive cup of coffee ever and chastised himself for not changing more money at the hotel. He had to find a bank and not embarrass himself any further. Within several blocks, he found one and went inside, handing over his passport and $200 in signed traveler's checks to a clerk who took them to a man at a desk. Twenty minutes later, Nick's wallet was stuffed with Malaysian ringgit.

The episode at the café had a *clarifying* effect, so he decided to return to the hotel and consolidate his next steps. Nick threaded the late morning sidewalk traffic and, a half block from his hotel, he noticed a man leaning against a black Mercedes parked near the hotel's entrance. The sharp dark suit, equally dark sunglasses, and hands folded in front exuded a hint of menace, the kind usually associated with Secret Service agents and mob capos. As Nick neared the hotel entrance, the man straightened up and spoke to him.

"Mr. Hughes?" he said in English.

Nick stopped in his tracks.

"Could we speak with you a moment?" the man asked, reaching for the rear door of the Mercedes.

The tinted windows were opaque and Nick saw his own eyes reflected in them, nervously darting between the car and the man.

"What's this about?" he asked.

"Mr. Hughes, please, we'd just like to speak with you," came the chill reply as the man opened the rear door onto an empty seat. A man in the front passenger seat faced forward.

Nick's heart began to race and he felt sweat running down his face and neck while he tried to conceal the slight tremor in his hands.

"Who *are* you…?" he asked, his voice tinged with fear.

"Mr. Hughes, *please,*" the man insisted.

Somewhere in Nick's amygdala, an autonomic spark suddenly lit, triggering the fight or flight instinct and, before he knew it, he'd bolted several blocks. Stopping at last to catch his breath and gather his wits, he quickly realized neither the man nor the Mercedes were in pursuit.

Flush with adrenaline, he continued briskly around corners and down side streets until he came upon a large plaza. At a fountain near its center, people hung out by the cool splashing water. On the other side of the plaza, taxis queued up in front of another upscale hotel. Nick hurried over to one and opened the rear door.

"Can you take me to the downtown Marriott?" he asked, climbing in and shutting the door.

"*Where* you wanna go?" the driver answered in thickly accented English.

"You know the *Marriott* Hotel?" Nick elaborated between anxious breaths.

Puzzled, the driver repeated the hotel name, then shrugged and said, '*Okay*', before pulling into the scrum of traffic.

23.

Back at the hotel, Nick paced the room. What had he done? Why hadn't he taken a breath and thought about it? If they were police, why didn't they flash their ID? Only then did it occur to him that it might've been the contact: *He will find you.* The black Mercedes though, had spooked him given its association with various flavors of power, official, corporate *and* criminal. Even more disturbing…they knew *where* he was staying. They'd been waiting for him to return.

After splashing some water on his face then drying himself in the mirror, Nick froze at the reflection. Pale and gaunt, with dark circles under his eyes, he winced and quickly turned away. His mind swerved in one direction then another, unable to focus. Scattered on the room's coffee table were sections of the English language daily, '*The New Straits Times*'. He stared at the masthead then dialed the front desk.

"A taxi to where, sir?" the clerk inquired.

"To the main offices of *The New Straits Times.*"

Twenty minutes later, Nick stepped out of a taxi in front of a modern office tower housing *The New Straits Times*. At the security desk in the lobby, he asked the guard where the editorial offices were (…English being the newspaper's language, he *assumed* its use here…) The guard directed him to a bank of elevators and the eighth floor.

Taking one of the elevators as directed, Nick exited into a large waiting area fronting the editorial offices of the newspaper. A woman with a headset sat at a reception desk with the *New Straits Times* logo in raised silver letters filling the wall behind her. He caught a distorted glimpse of his own reflection in the letters and self-consciously ran a hand through his hair.

"Yes, how may I help you?" the receptionist asked in a formal tone while scrutinizing him.

He hesitated. "I… uh, I was hoping to speak with someone, one of your reporters maybe, regarding a potential story," he clumsily explained.

The receptionist, a bright-eyed Chinese-Malaysian woman with fine features, looked skeptical.

"And may I ask what this story is regarding?"

Nick shared the broad strokes of his brother's story as the receptionist listened and assessed his credibility.

"One moment please," she said, then picked up her phone and spoke quickly and perfunctorily in Malay. With a nod, she put the phone down and looked up at Nick.

"There's no one available right now. Can I get your name and contact information and someone will call when they're available?"

The brush. He had to think quickly.

"Please…" he pleaded, "I really need to speak with someone… My brother may be in trouble and I can't get anyone to help me. Not here *or* in the US. I've met with the American ambassador here as well as the national police and I think my poking around is making people nervous…"

The receptionist raised an eyebrow at this.

"I've come all the way from California," he continued. "I just need someone to hear my story. Ten minutes, that's all. Just give me ten minutes and if they don't think there's anything here, then okay, I'll be on my way."

Her expression softened slightly. "Can I have your name?" she asked.

"Hughes. Nick Hughes."

"Please sit down over there, Mr. Hughes and I'll see if I can find someone."

Nick thanked her and took a seat in the waiting area. The receptionist dialed an extension then spoke to someone in Malay. This time the conversation went back and forth as she tried to convey his story. He anxiously watched, trying to read the situation. On the table in front of him were several issues of the *New Straits Times,* so he picked one up and distractedly flipped through it.

After five minutes or so, a man emerged from a corridor behind the reception area, looking the part of harried reporter with unbuttoned collar and loosened tie. In his early thirties and also ethnically Chinese, he sported a fine mop of jet-black hair that was stylishly unruly — a reflection, Nick hoped, of a youthful tilt in the paper's editorial perspective. The man walked over and introduced himself as Ky Chap-Leong, a reporter here.

"Call me Ky," he said, shaking Nick's hand and explaining that it rhymed with '*key*'. He said he worked the international desk and Nick thanked him for hearing him out.

"So, you say your brother has gone missing?" Ky began, getting right to the point.

Nick understood this was a screening, so he gave Ky the condensed version: his brother's involvement with the Peace Corps back in the late 1970s, right up to the men with the black Mercedes today. The lucidity with which he described it all seemed to allay the reporter's skepticism.

"Do you have any pictures of your brother?" Ky asked.

Nick handed him one of the photocopies he'd brought. Ky cocked his head as he looked at the image, then asked Nick to follow him. They walked briskly past a clamoring newsroom with people typing, scribbling notes, cradling phones between cheek and shoulder and staring at computer screens. Ky led Nick to a glass-walled office just off the newsroom and had him take a seat. He picked up the phone and spoke briefly to someone in Malay. As he placed the phone back on its cradle, Ky asked Nick if he had his passport on him.

"Just need to be sure who we're talking to here," he said, noting Nick's crinkled brow. "You'd be surprised how many people come in with story ideas…"

Nick wasn't exactly sure how to take that last bit as he watched Ky flip the passport open to the identification page, make some notes then thumb through the visa pages. "You haven't got much use out of this," he commented.

"Yeah…" Nick agreed. "I renewed it about five years back for a trip to Mexico and haven't used it since. Until now…"

Ky reached across the desk and handed the passport back as the door swung open and another man entered, startling Nick.

"I have that effect on people…" the man said in a distinctly British accent as he extended a hand. "Derek Wolcott, colonial holdover."

Nick shook the offered hand and sized him up. Tall, middle-aged and clearly British, Wolcott had the disarming easiness of a Fleet Street veteran. "They keep me on here as language warden," he added, self-deprecatingly.

"Derek's actually one of our managing editors," Ky interjected. Wolcott certainly fit Nick's idea of a career newspaperman. The years and poor dietary habits had thickened his narrow frame in the middle, and his pooching belly lent him a kind of leaned-back posture. His salt-gray hair, while slightly unkempt and thinning, still had some curl, though the flesh of his jawline had begun to sag. Despite the veneer of roguish jocularity, Nick immediately understood that Wolcott was all sharpie here, a man who discretely used wit to probe a situation and its principals.

"Ky tells me you've got a story to tell," Wolcott said as he sat on the corner of the reporter's desk. "I'd like to hear it if you don't mind."

Once again, Nick related the entirety of his story, in more detail this time, as the two men listened. Wolcott occasionally interrupted for clarification in the manner of a prosecutor piecing together bits of a story and forcing the whole thing into an ever-narrower chute. When Nick finished, the editor pensively leaned back with arms folded and a finger pressed to his lips. He looked down in thought then turned to Ky.

"Ky, can you have Sammy Zhao check the archives from '83 on, for the Sarawak incidents?" With a quick nod, the reporter picked up the phone, while the last bit lingered in Nick's ear: *Sarawak incidents.*

"Malaysia's an unusual Muslim country," Wolcott went on, nodding toward the shiny glass and steel cityscape beyond their window. "Have you heard about these strongman contests they've been holding here? It's like a television show of some kind, I think. What do they call them, Ky?"

"I believe that's what they call them," Ky responded, "*Strongman Competitions.* Contestants from across the world compete. I know the American network ESPN was here covering it a few years ago."

"Right," Wolcott concurred. "Anyway, it's a hell of a thing to see. All these bull-necked men and women from Latvia, Poland, Bulgaria, even the US, throwing tractor tires around and heaving tree stumps and iron balls. Quite the spectacle, really."

Wolcott folded his arms. "You know, this part of the world's been a crossroads of trade for centuries. Arabs brought Islam in the fifteenth century and the indigenous Malays eventually preferred its monotheism over the more arcane tenets of the Hinduism and Buddhism brought by the Chinese and Indians. Probably a reflection of the racial divisions here. And it might've helped that the Arabs weren't intent on colonizing either…"

At that moment, a man stepped into the room with a stack of newspapers. Wolcott thanked him and spread them out on Ky's desk, sorting through them as he spoke.

"The Chinese and Indians that *did* plant themselves here, make up about a third of the country's population," he continued. "Hasn't always been smooth going — especially for the Chinese. Their business and political acumen has earned them disproportionate political power and whipped up resentment among the majority ethnic Malays who generally blame government crony-ism and corruption on the Chinese." He paused.

"For some time now, those in the Muslim majority have been clamoring for a more Islamic state, which as you may guess, hasn't gone down well with the minority Chinese and Indian communities."

Wolcott then picked up one of the newspapers and folded it to a specific article and handed it to Nick who noted the headline:

'*Dayak Group Protests Logging Operations*'

"*Dayaks…?*" he asked, glancing up. "I read something about them…"

"Catch-all term for the indigenous people of *Borneo*…" Wolcott explained, then asked, "Were you able to pick up a bit of the colonial history here?"

Nick shrugged. "The broad strokes, I think… Spice trade, British and Dutch colonialism, the basics."

"And the Portuguese," Wolcott added, "They briefly planted a flag here as well. Way back when Europeans thought of this as the *East Indies*…

"The British ruled the southern Malay peninsula up into Burma, while the Dutch took most of the Indonesian archipelago from the Portuguese. Soon enough, both the Dutch *and* the British claimed the island of Borneo though neither had much appetite for fighting over it, mainly because they didn't know what to do with it.

"Borneo's coast was well known to the outside world — the Chinese traded there for centuries — but its mountainous interior remained impene-trable well into the nineteenth century. The few hardy souls who *did* venture into Borneo's interior described impassable rivers, dense, overgrown jungles with massive trees along with tribes of headhunters and cannibals — none of which got in the way of the two powers carving it up among themselves.

"The Dutch took the southern two-thirds of the island for Indonesia, while the British got the northern third for Malaysia, which became the two states of *Sabah* and *Sarawak*. The Sultan of Brunei shrewdly played the Dutch and British against each other to keep an oil-rich sliver of the northern coast for himself, now the *Sultanate of Brunei*."

In Nick's mind, the word '*sultanate*' evoked images of Turkmen, of deserts, East Africa and Asia Minor, not the sweltering jungles of Maritime Southeast Asia.

"Fast forward to *today*," Wolcott went on, "This part of Asia's been in the throes of an economic boom for several years. There's a global hunger for raw materials and countries like Thailand, Taiwan, Japan, Vietnam, South Korea — they've used up most of their own natural resources, so they started looking elsewhere and *Borneo* became that *elsewhere*.

"Multinational corporations were soon tripping over each other trying to cultivate friends in the Malaysian and Indonesian governments. Most wanted to get in on the one-time bonanza of Borneo's tropical hardwood, while others wanted the cleared land for palm oil plantations. The Malaysians were eager for foreign exchange and ready to cut deals, while the Indonesians went a little slower..."

Walcott briefly hesitated.

"Our reporting discovered that some high-level officials in Kuala Lumpur obtained shares in these companies as gifts to help grease the bureaucracy's wheels, but we can't prove it. Besides, most of our readers probably think that's just the way things work in this part of the world... Even so, nobody asked the indigenous people of Borneo what *they* thought about any of this..." He lifted another issue from the papers strewn about the desk and silently handed it to Nick.

'*Troops Called in on Dayak Protests; Interior Minister Decries Agitators*'

Nick's eye immediately went to a photo in the center of the page. Taken from a distance, the picture wasn't especially clear, but had been framed in a way that emphasized a white man with a scruffy beard among a large group of indigenous tribesmen confronting a line of armed soldiers. Nick zeroed-in on the man's face and a vague unease began to grip him... The caption read:

'*Dayaks and unidentified foreigner confront interior minister in Sarawak*'

He stared a moment then lifted his eyes to Wolcott and Ky, about to ask something, but quickly turned back to the photo.

"I believe this may be the only photo anyone has of him…" Wolcott was saying. "One of our reporters had gotten a tip about this white man somewhere in the upper Baram River who'd been seen with an indigenous group protesting logging intrusions on their land. No one had any idea who he was or how he came to be there… We couldn't find anything on him, so I sent a photographer and reporter up there to check it out. They had to be careful as the whole area is off-limits for travel. This is the piece we ran as a result…

"Naturally, when Ky told me there was an American in his office who claimed his brother had gone missing in Malaysia, my ears perked up." Wolcott paused, trying to get a read on Nick, then nodded at the photo. "He look familiar…?"

Nick gazed at the photo.

"…I, uh…I'm not sure…" he muttered, "I was in high school the last time I saw him… But…yeah…*maybe*…?" He looked up, glancing between Wolcott and Ky.

"What *is* all this…?" he asked, trying to comprehend.

"Well, that's what we'd like to understand," Wolcott answered. "It would appear, this man — *possibly* your brother — he's put himself in the middle of a land rights squabble between the government and these indigenous people in Borneo, the *Penan*, who still live nomadically in the interior… They're notoriously difficult to contact and this particular group has resisted all attempts to settle them. It's thought they're only a few hundred, living way up near the source of the Baram River…" The editor let this register a moment.

"Not long after we ran these," he continued, "I got a call from the interior minister's office threatening to arrest the reporter and photographer for violating the travel ban and accusing us of biased reporting in the coverage." An ironic smirk curled the corners of his mouth. "Nothing new there…"

"No other pictures…?" Nick asked.

"None better than this…" Wolcott replied. He lifted another of the newspapers and placed it down in front of Nick while tapping a particular paragraph with a finger. "This was the official reaction from the minister after our story came out…"

Nick began reading the paragraph aloud: '*Interior Minister Wong described the protests as being instigated by outsiders trying to stand in the way of lawful operations. "This isn't about land rights," Wong said. "These people are acting outside the law...working for international organizations that want to keep Malaysia down. These outside agitators will be hunted down and arrested."*'

"That sort of pseudo-nationalistic blather," Wolcott continued, "...is the typical blustery response to any story critical of government actions. Blame it on outsiders, foreign interests, anything to distract from the government's own failures and corruption. Here on the Peninsula, it plays well because the people are ethnically and culturally *very* different from the indigenous people of Borneo. Most Malaysians, whether of Chinese ancestry like Ky, Tamil Indian ancestry or the '*bumiputra*' — the majority ethnic Malays, mainly Muslim — they can't understand why the Penan would want to live nomadically in the forest like they do rather than enjoy the benefits of civilization and progress like everyone else."

As Nick scanned the article, it occurred to him that, if the man in the photo was, in fact, Evan, his engaging in protests against the host government would most certainly have not gone down well with the Peace Corps.

"Any idea if he's still there...?" he asked, after a moment.

"That's an unknown," Wolcott sighed. "These articles are a few years old now... Since then, several NGOs have brought lawsuits to halt the logging while they build a case for Penan land rights. As you can imagine, this hasn't played well with the government, especially with men like the interior minister, a Malaysian Chinese named James Wong. He's used it to stoke nationalist outrage by labeling it 'foreign interference' and hoping everyone gets too riled up to notice any of the millions he and his cronies have quietly made by opening Borneo up to development."

Nick began rubbing his forehead, trying to piece it all together.

"Borneo..." he muttered, "...Is that where they sent him...the Peace Corps?"

Wolcott shrugged. "Well, it *is* part of Malaysia."

Nick mulled this a moment. "You said it's illegal to be up there..." he began, after some interval, "So, how did your reporters swing it?"

"Contacts and gonads," Wolcott answered, wryly.

"I'm guessing they weren't able to speak to him?" Nick asked.

"Not under those circumstances..." Wolcott told him, "They had to keep their heads down... But...I suspect our readers *would* be interested in what he has to say."

"Maybe he'd talk to *you?*" Ky suggested, leaning forward on his elbows. The question caught Nick off guard.

"I'd like to think so…" he told them, glancing between the two. "…Once he knew who I was."

Wolcott got up from the corner of Ky's desk, folded his arms and let his head hang a little before bringing a finger to his lip.

"Let's say we could get you in there…" he began, "If you're willing to try… We'll take care of the travel, arrange the contacts and all that and help you try to find him."

Nick glanced back and forth between the two newspapermen.

"*Okay*…" he said, clearly thrown by the offer. "And *you…?*" he continued, "…I take it you want a story…?"

"Of course…" Wolcott replied, "In *this* part of the world, journalists quickly develop a habit of self-censorship if they want to stay employed. They avoid stories that might contradict the country's idea of itself as this happy multi-ethnic state where the law applies equally to *everyone*." His eyebrows rose suggestively.

"But I still have a bit of that English cheek in me and I like to sell papers. And if we were to run a story about this enigmatic *American*, sent here through a foreign aid program, who somehow got involved with these indigenous people and their land rights squabble with the government, well, that just might sell a few papers. And if some of the government's unseemly business up there gets folded in as well, all the better. The increased ad revenue will make that little pill easier to swallow for all the government officials who own shares of the paper."

As he listened, Nick again felt that tidal force acting on him with its irresistible gravitational pull.

"I need to ask you, Nick," Wolcott then said, his tone ambiguous. "You say you haven't seen your brother since high school…?"

"That's right…" Nick answered, unsure where this was going.

"Was that by choice?" the editor pressed.

"Not mine…" Nick assured him, then added after a few beats, "Why, what are you after here?"

After another moment's hesitation, Wolcott continued.

"Look, forgive me if this seems impertinent…" he began, carefully. "… But, I'm curious… After so long without any contact…it's actually quite remarkable that you've come all this way and done all you have on your brother's behalf… I don't think many others with a similar history would've done the same… So, naturally, I'm curious… *Why…?*"

Nick exhaled deeply and leaned forward, elbows on his knees.

"…Doubt I could give you a satisfying answer…" he explained, "…Other than something inside telling me it's the *right* thing to do… And because, no one else is going to do it… We had a strange childhood…my brother and me. He was a couple years older and always looked out for me when we were kids…especially after our parents divorced. So…I suppose in a way, this is my time to look out for *him*. To make a payment on that old debt…"

"Fair enough," Wolcott concluded, folding his arms. "I ask," he went on, cautiously. "Because this man…who *may* or may *not* be your brother…well, he's run afoul of some very powerful interests…"

At this, the editor paused, removed his reading glasses and began rubbing his eyes. "Let's be clear, Nick. We're talking about *Borneo* here… It's nothing like Peninsular Malaysia. Beyond the few coastal cities there's very little in the way of civilization and infrastructure…" With reading glasses in his hand, Wolcott looked directly at Nick.

"Borneo's interior is essentially lawless," he added. "No police to call if you get into trouble, no hospitals or ambulances and no roads to speak of… Some of the indigenous people still resolve disputes with the blade of a machete. You'll be traveling by river and if something goes awry, well… you're on your own. People disappear in Borneo never to be heard from again. So it's important you understand what you'd be getting into…"

Wolcott waited as he folded his reading glasses. Nick rested his forehead on clasped hands. For a good half minute, he sat like that before lifting his eyes to Wolcott's gaze.

"…Okay…" he heard himself say, "…Where do we start?"

Satisfied, Wolcott took a breath. "I'll make some calls tonight," he answered.

24.

That night, despite his exhaustion, Nick couldn't sleep. He slouched on the sofa in his darkened room and stared at the lights of Kuala Lumpur while sipping a Scotch from room service. Relief that his brother might still be alive had been tempered by new revelations — what had Evan gotten himself involved in?

When his brother was around twelve, he told Nick that their parents had only married because of their mother's pregnancy with him. And while neither parent ever suggested as much, Evan knew this to be a fact. Nick couldn't forget the caustic pique his brother had carried around like a war wound. Even so, Evan never indulged in self-pity or melodrama. Instead, he developed an independent spirit and emotional self-sufficiency that further distanced him from their fractious parents, a walking testament to the power of resentment over love.

Hours passed in thoughts like this until the first light of morning squinted over the horizon. According to Nick's watch, it was a little before 6:00 am. He rubbed his eyes with the heels of his hands then let his head fall back on the sofa cushion, and in seconds, was sound asleep.

A phone began to ring somewhere in the distance. No one answered and it went on ringing. Eventually, Nick realized it was *his* phone and clumsily answered.

"Morning, Nick. I trust you slept well," said the voice on the other end — Wolcott, dry and cheerily British.

"…Not sure I'd call it sleep…" Nick drawled as he pulled himself up on the couch.

"Ah, well, what do those workout nuts say? You can sleep when you're dead…?" the editor quipped. "In any event, I called to tell you that I spoke with my ex-wife Carole who's a correspondent for the BBC here in Kuala Lumpur. We stay in touch and share story leads from time to time. She knows this corner of the world better than anyone."

"I see…" Nick muttered, still foggy. "And…?"

"She's interested," Wolcott explained. "Wants to meet and discuss putting something together."

Nick wasn't sure he heard correctly. "*Wait*... You mean something for the *BBC…?*"

"That's right," answered the editor. "And something for my paper. I'll explain on the way over to her office."

Nick sat up and ran a hand over his hair.

"…*okay*…" he murmured, "…wow… When?"

"In a couple hours," Wolcott answered. "I'll send a car for you. Say, half past twelve…"

As promised, a car waited in front of the hotel at 12:30 as Nick exited. Clean-shaven, with a change of clothes — tropic-weight blazer, a gift from Celeste which, he remembered joking at the time, made him look like a '*Banana Republican*' — and a pair of stylish sunglasses hiding baggy eyes, he awkwardly thanked the sharply dressed Sikh driver who politely greeted him and opened the rear passenger door. Twenty minutes later, they arrived at Wolcott's office complex where the editor waited out front. Before the driver could step out, Wolcott opened the rear door himself and slid in next to Nick.

"I thought we'd talk a bit further on the way over," he said, his tone vaguely conspiratorial as he nodded to the driver. "After sharing your story with Carole, including your visit to the police and the US embassy here, she suggested it's likely your inquiries stirred a hornet's nest. And that we should assume someone's keeping an eye on you."

Nick felt his chest tighten.

"She thought we might use an alias for you," the editor continued, "Just while traveling…"

"An *alias*…?" For Nick, the word had deceit in its bedrock, .

"Try not to overthink it, Nick…" Wolcott told him, with decidedly British equipoise. "You're in good hands with Carole."

Nick raised an eyebrow.

"…So says the ex-husband…?"

The guard at the BBC security gate bantered a moment with the editor as if he were a regular, then waved the car through. With instructions to the driver to return in an hour, Wolcott escorted Nick into the building and through another security station. Here too, the newspaperman was recognized and greeted by name.

"This way," he told Nick, leading him down a corridor past cubicles where people on phones busily scratched notes on yellow legal pads while others typed at computer terminals. They soon stopped outside an office with glass walls where Wolcott's ex-wife, Carole, stood cradling a phone between neck and shoulder.

"…Don't you have enough coverage there…?" she asked into the phone as Wolcott knocked gently on the open door. With a quick multi-tasking smile, she waved them in while continuing her conversation. "No, I can't spare anyone down here…. No. Steven is not available… No. Of course! I've tried several times. Who was that BBC stringer we used in '91? What was her name?"

Tall, stately, and probably in her early forties, Carole's stylish shoulder-length blonde hair was tinged with streaks of gray, her bearing akin to that of an athlete, a swimmer perhaps, upright and lean. Years working in the tropical sun had left some 'squinting' wrinkles around her eyes that otherwise didn't diminish a youthful vibrance. She exuded a kind of no-nonsense confidence that must have been an asset in the sharp-elbowed world of broadcast journalism. Framed awards lined a row of cabinets along with photos of Carole buddied up with political figures and celebrities.

With some closing words, she ended the call and stepped over to give her ex-husband a hug.

"Everybody wants *lifestyle* stories these days!" Carole declared, turning with outstretched hand to Nick. "*Carole Wolcott*," she said, beaming. Nick shook the offered hand and introduced himself.

"You guys hungry at all?" she asked. "I'm starving and thought we could go over things at lunch?"

"Sure," Nick answered agreeably, before turning to Wolcott, who nodded.

"Great!" Carole exclaimed, then took a breath and looked askance in her ex-husband's direction. "…Has he shared *our* history with you?" she asked, turning back to Nick who replied in the affirmative.

"Right, well… Derek, wasn't much of a husband," she ribbed, "But he's one hell of a features editor…"

Wolcott play-winced at the gibe/complement.

"In any case, given Derek's enthusiasm for your story," Carole went on, "I went ahead and chartered a flight to Kuching for later tonight. I hope that's okay? I know it's short notice, but it'll take a couple days to arrange things there and I thought, the sooner we started, the better."

"*Tonight…?*" Nick echoed, glancing over at Wolcott. "Okay…sure. I'll have to change my hotel reservation."

"Not to worry," Carole assured him. "We'll have a car take you after lunch."

25.

At lunch, Nick shared more background with the two journalists and fielded their questions. Carole then explained the cover story they'd use if questioned: they were doing a BBC travelogue on Malaysia, a 'puff-piece' she called it. "Government officials love that sort of thing…" she added, telling Nick, "You'll be our production *assistant* and we'll provide the proper credentials using a different name… on the chance ports and checkpoints may have been alerted to lookout for your name…"

On the ride back, Wolcott told Nick that a freelance reporter would join them to cover the story for his paper with the hope it might also be picked up by the wire services. Things were moving fast and Nick felt like he was being swept up in a whirlwind of his own making.

Later that evening, he checked out of his hotel and returned to the BBC offices in the car Carole sent. The tropical night once again came on quickly — no lingering dusk to ease the transition as in the temperate latitudes. He'd dithered about calling Celeste since it was the middle of the night, *yesterday*, Los Angeles time. Vetoing the idea brought a guilty sense of relief in that he could avoid Celeste's animus while putting it off on the time difference.

In the BBC's employee lounge area, Nick scribbled some notes regarding what he'd learned so far. A strangely exaggerated sense of time and distance resulted in the feeling that he'd been here *far* longer than a week. Los Angeles and his life back there began to seem more distant, like a peculiar twist on the dog-years/human-years ratio: a week here being equal to *six months* back in LA.

Earlier, the day's humidity had spawned a massive thunderstorm that called to mind the summer thunderstorms of his Pennsylvania youth. In late July, after several weeks of hot sticky weather where even the asphalt in the streets softened in the heat, the afternoon sky would haze-up, steadily darkening until thunder rumbled from somewhere within it. Eventually, a split-second flash would light-up the skies, followed by a rolling cracking and ripping that sounded like the heavens were being shredded. Nick and his brother would count the seconds between the lightning and thunder to see if the storm was moving toward them or away. They'd sit on the front porch of their father's house and watch the rain come down in sheets, splatting and sizzling on the blacktop and generating wisps of steam. Overloaded rain gutters became waterfalls and downspouts were like open hydrants. The storm's violence was usually brief and, afterward, the air had a distinct, *clean* smell, cool and refreshing with hints of earth, flora and ozone, a kind of renewal through cataclysm.

It then struck him that he'd now spent half his life in Southern California — long enough to forget the syrupy humidity that brought those summer thunderstorms in his childhood. Southern California had no such meteorological mood swings. Other than day length, seasonal shifts were generally marked by the need for a jacket and, on occasion, an umbrella. Of course, this topped the list when it came to LA's slippery seductions: its human-friendly climate tended to soften the harsher bits of contemporary life.

Around 8:00 PM, an Asian man in his mid-thirties arrived and began making coffee. Noticing Nick, he introduced himself as Antonio, Carole's videographer accompanying them to Sarawak. He had a calm, self-contained demeanor that Nick found refreshing. The *Hispanicized* first name pegged him as Filipino, but Antonio's features suggested Southeast Asian origins further west, possibly Vietnam.

"You doing okay?" Antonio asked in an English just barely tinged with an accent. Nick answered in the affirmative.

"Good," Antonio said. "We're supposed to leave for the airport in an hour or so. Carole wanted to make sure you'd eaten as we probably won't get a chance for dinner. I'm grabbing some take-out from the street carts. I can get something for you if you like?"

"Hey, that'd be great," Nick replied. "Noodles, dumplings, whatever you find."

About twenty minutes later, Antonio returned with take-out containers of Chinese food, declining Nick's money and spreading the containers out on a table. As they dug in with chopsticks, Nick had to smile at the ubiquity of Chinese take-out — he could just as easily have been eating the same food from similar containers in Los Angeles.

"Carole told me a little about what we're doing," Antonio offered by way of making conversation. "I usually try to get the outline of a story before we take off. Helps me know what I need to bring and how much. You know, extra batteries, solar generator, that sort of thing. But she's been kind of vague on this one." He shrugged.

Nick nodded in sympathetic agreement, unsure what he should or should not share with the cameraman.

"…She said we'd be traveling mostly by boat once we're there," Antonio continued. "That means water-tight cases, which take up space…"

How they would get around in Borneo had not crossed Nick's mind.

"Hadn't thought about that…" he confessed. "California reflex… We think the whole world gets around by car."

Antonio plucked a dumpling with his chopsticks and grinned enigmatically.

"Well," he observed, "You wouldn't get far in Borneo on wheels…"

26.

"Revelry, Nick!" Carole announced, cheerily. "We'll be leaving soon."

She stood gazing at him on the sofa where he'd nodded off. Disoriented and fuzzy, it took Nick a couple seconds to remember where he was. He pushed his hair back and asked her for the time.

"About half past nine," she replied, then asked how he was fixed for clothes. "Should've asked earlier as we'll likely be in the bush much of the time."

The *bush*. That Anglo term for those un-manicured reaches beyond the platted edges of civilization. For Nick, the bush conjured images of a sun-fried Australian crocodile hunter wearing khaki shorts and a wide-brimmed hat folded up on one side while holding a can of Foster's. The 'bush' in *this* rendering meant a spiny, scorching, arid place, awash in alkali glare and an abundance of biting, stinging, venomous creatures. While Sarawak was *anything* but arid, it apparently still qualified as *un-manicured.*

"I should be fine," he answered, "Got some lightweight pants and shirts at an outdoor store before I left Los Angeles."

"Perfect," Carole said, approvingly, as she placed a manila envelope on a table. "Here's your laminated I.D. and a lanyard if you want to use it. I never wear mine unless it's an official press event or something of the sort. We decided not to go with a cover identity for you after all since, once we're out of Kuching, it's not likely we'll encounter much in the way of anyone or anything 'official.' There's an immigration check at the airport even though it's still technically in Malaysia and there's always the possibility they've flagged your name…" She paused to see if this registered with him.

"But I doubt it," she went on. "You only made contact a couple days ago and it'll take some time to work through the bureaucracy. And flashing the BBC card usually zips us through check points."

Carole smiled in a way she hoped was reassuring.

"Right… well," she wrapped up, "The car should be here in an hour at the main entrance so I'll leave you to it."

A little over an hour later, Nick and company were packed into an SUV on route to the airport. In the front seat, Carole went over some notes while Nick and Antonio rode in the rear seat with Wolcott's freelancer, an Australian in his thirties who introduced himself as Ian. Thankfully for Nick, who had no appetite for fielding questions from the Aussie reporter, Antonio ended up between them. Not that it mattered since the ride to the airport went quickly and, in a rush of coordination from Carole, their bags were tagged and stowed and they were buckled-in for the short flight to Sarawak.

27.

Around twenty minutes after takeoff, a storm kicked up. Its enormous store of pent-up energy buffeted the plane and the pilots scrambled to climb above it. Nick clutched the armrest as the aircraft bounced and stuttered through the turbulence. Making matters worse, Ian had taken the seat next to him and, after introducing himself with some initial small talk, he began probing for some background.

"Derek said you haven't seen your brother since high school?" he said.

"That's right…" Nick answered in a weary tone he hoped would discourage the reporter.

"All this must've been quite a surprise, then?"

Nick nodded as the aircraft bounced.

"Anything in his history that might've inclined him toward something like this?" Ian asked.

Of course, Nick thought; Ian was fishing for a *hook* of some kind to hang the story on, something that would help *explain* Evan, as if the unfortunate tacks in a life could be traced back to a singular trauma. That myriad complex and often bewildering events were more consequential in such lives was far too subtle for quick-read journalism.

"I'm just trying to understand him," Ian added, when Nick didn't answer. "You know, some background to help get a sense of what makes him tick?"

"I don't know that I can help you there…" Nick told him. "It was half a lifetime ago…"

"Sure…" Ian remarked, "But maybe there's something you remember that could give readers a sense of your brother and how he came to this… Being wanted by the authorities in a foreign country…?"

The last bit stopped Nick. Somehow, he had not yet fully absorbed the fact that his brother — if the man in the photo *was* indeed Evan — had in fact, done something *illegal* in the eyes of a foreign government. Ian didn't miss the shift in Nick's expression.

"Sorry… Wasn't trying to make you uncomfortable…" he explained.

"Huh…?" Nick mumbled, returning to the moment. *"Uncomfortable…?"*

"Yeah…sorry."

"Forget it…" Nick answered, exhaling deeply and turning to his window.

"I think we passed *uncomfortable* a while ago…" he muttered, as the plane continued climbing above the storm.

28.

At such a late hour, the Kuching airport felt spectral, like an outpost gone to seed in some forgotten equatorial republic. A custodian listlessly mopped a floor and emptied ashtrays as if in a trance.

Nick noted the tourism posters here and there promoting Borneo's natural bounty. Dramatic scenes of lush jungles, surging rivers, fog-shrouded mountains, colorful birds and various indigenous people — images wildly out of character with the airport's utilitarian vibe.

Much to his relief, they all cleared the lethargic customs checkpoint without a fuss, then followed Carole to the airport's exit and out into Sarawak's humid and viscid night air. A couple of taxi drivers leaned against their cars, smoking and waiting for a fare. One called out but Antonio waved him off. Carole dragged her small rolling suitcase to the curb and looked to her left in the direction traffic would have approached had there been any at this hour.

The humidity felt more viscous here than in Kuala Lumpur. In the distance, Nick could see the dingy sodium vapor glow of nighttime Kuching in the overcast sky and thought it strange that his brother might be out there somewhere beyond those city lights. He knew Borneo was vast, the third largest island in the world. In terms of land area, Sarawak alone equaled *the entirety* of Peninsular Malaysia where eighty-percent of the country's population lived. The majority of Sarawak's population clustered near the coast, mainly in two cities, Miri and Kuching, leaving the rugged interior essentially wild.

As they waited for their transportation, Antonio spotted a police vehicle approaching, slowing as it passed them.

"They were obviously checking out the camera cases…" Carole remarked after it had disappeared. "Let's hope they've got other things to do."

Several minutes went by before a minivan similar to the tinny, narrow and ubiquitous passenger vans seen all over Kuala Lumpur approached from the same direction.

"That must be our driver," Carole said, pushing the telescoping handles of her luggage trolley back down.

The van pulled to the curb and stopped. "Hope I'm not late…" the driver said, as he stepped out to open the side door. "Have you been here long…?"

"Not at all," answered Carole. "Let's get moving, shall we?"

They were all anxious to be away from the airport and its empty nocturnal menace. As they pulled away from the curb, Carole made introductions from the front seat. The driver's name was 'Bedalaman', she explained, a native of Sarawak. After introducing Nick and the others, she directed the driver to the Crowne Plaza Hotel and thanked him.

"Very good," Bedalaman replied and changed lanes. He then turned the air conditioner up a notch to compensate for the added bodies. "Let me know if it's too cold," he added, looking into his rear-view mirror.

Away from the airport and its lights, the countryside became dark and empty. Seated behind the driver, Nick silently stared out the window. They were only a few kilometers from the airport when he glimpsed Bedalaman anxiously checking his rear-view mirror. Nick turned around to see that condensation had formed on the rear window from the AC, distorting the headlight beams of another vehicle not far behind them. Bedalaman backed off the accelerator and, no sooner had he done so, when a pulsating swirling red beacon lit up the glass.

"*Huh?* Already??" Antonio moaned, looking back.

"Probably the same guys who saw our camera gear deciding to take a look…" Carole guessed. "Remember…we're journalists here doing a story on travel opportunities in Sarawak…"

Bedalaman gave Carole a knowing nod as he pulled the van over. A policeman in military garb got out and cautiously walked up to the driver's window, shining a flashlight around inside. Another policeman followed on the opposite side of the van, an assault weapon hanging from his shoulder. With narrow eyes and humorless demeanor, the first policeman said something in Malay to Bedalaman, his face pinched into a scowl as if in response to some inner gastric distress.

The driver passed his papers to the officer who glanced about at the passengers. He grumbled something in Malay again and Bedalaman responded, gesturing in the direction in which they were headed.

"Di manaka pasport?" the officer snapped, shining his flashlight around the floor and dash.

Bedalaman turned to Carole. "He wants to see your passports..."

Carole calmly reached into a valise and produced four passports. "Kenapa anda membawa semua pasport?" the officer bleated. Bedalaman turned again to Carole. "He wants to know why *you* have all the passports."

"Tell him we're journalists with the BBC doing a story on travel opportunities in Sarawak and I'm the producer in charge. That's why I carry all the passports."

Bedalaman explained this in Malay as the policeman studied Carole with a skeptical gaze. The cop appeared to relish the effect he had on others, officiously examining each passport and glancing around suspiciously as he did. He thumbed through the pages of one passport in particular, noting the various visa stamps.

"You English?" he finally said to Carole, surprised to hear him speak her native tongue.

"I am," she replied, cool but polite.

The policeman handed the passports back to Bedalaman who returned them to Carole. Then, he muttered something to the driver, who briefly glanced at Carole before opening his door and stepping out. The police officer directed him toward the rear of the van. In the driver's mirror, Nick glimpsed the two men talking.

"What's going on...?" Antonio asked.

Carole shook her head. "I don't know..."

Just to the front of her window, the other policeman, weapon at the ready, watched them.

"Think he's looking for a bribe?" Ian asked in a hush.

"Maybe..." Carole answered, "It's another country over here..."

Nick anxiously tried to watch the driver and cop in the side mirror, but they had moved just out of view.

"They're probably going to want to search the gear..." Antonio muttered. "Should've folded a few bills in the camera case..."

Carole was about to say something when the discussion suddenly ended and Bedalaman returned.

"It's okay..." he said, climbing into his seat. "The police here...you know..."

"Oh, I *know*..." Carole agreed. "I *know*..."

Bedalaman turned and flashed an awkward smile at Nick and the others before starting the van. His sheepishness seemed to confirm it had been some sort of shakedown — the cost of doing business here, apparently. And with that, he shifted into gear and they were off again.

29.

Kuching was clearly not Kuala Lumpur, thought Nick, as he took in the view from his sixth-floor hotel window. In the hazy morning light, the city had the feel of a frontier boom town, raw and sprawling around the edges. After a fitful night's sleep, he wanted to linger a bit before breakfast and get his bearings after the last couple days.

On a table near the mini-bar, some glossy brochures promoted adventure tours in the wilds of Borneo: whitewater rafting, jungle tours, bird-watching, cave tours, hot-air balloon rides, longhouse tours, etc. His guidebooks said that Kuching was the largest city in Malaysian Borneo, the jumping-off point for trips into the interior. The city also had the distinction of being the administrative and business hub for the main industries here: timber, petroleum and palm oil.

As he mulled this, the room's phone rang — Carole reminding him of the time if he wanted breakfast.

"On my way," he told her.

The East Asian décor in the hotel dining room reflected the clientele, a mix of what looked to be Asian businessmen: Korean, Japanese, some Chinese. On the walls, framed reproductions depicted scenes of Eastern tranquility: minimalist bamboo landscapes, mountains, flowing streams, rice paddies.

"Nick! Over here," he heard someone say, then turned to see Ian waving from a booth. Across from him, Antonio scanned a newspaper over breakfast.

"Morning…" Nick said, pleasantly, as he slid in next to Antonio. "Carole not up yet?"

"Making some phone calls," Ian answered, tapping an ash from his cigarette.

"Said she needed to check a couple things," Antonio remarked, flipping another page.

"Cigarettes…?" Nick commented, glancing at Ian before scanning the menu. "Thought you Aussies were all surfers and sun worshipers?"

"Right! Just like all you Californians!" Ian countered, with a grin.

Nick nodded approvingly at the riposte, then eyed the open pack on the table.

"Hmm…mind if I have one?" he asked, with a slight nod at the pack. Ian slid the pack and lighter toward him.

"Closet smoker or only on occasion?" he chided.

As he took a cigarette from the pack, Nick nodded in gratitude and lit it with a moderate drag.

"I quit years ago…" he explained, exhaling a stream of blue smoke. "But every now and then I get a craving."

"Well, indulge it, mate. I doubt one or two every now and again's going to kill you," Ian assured him. "Hell, just breathing the bloody air in most cities is probably worse."

'*Certainly in LA*', thought Nick as Carole arrived trailing a server with coffee and tea decanters.

"Morning all," she said, sliding in next to Ian. "Everybody get a couple hours' sleep?"

The lines around her eyes and mouth suggested it was about *all* she got. Her blue-green irises had a touch less sparkle this morning, but she still had a convincing presence. Nick imagined her cultivating such a confident demeanor as part of a conscious effort to counter stodgy male resistance toward women in the world of broadcast journalism.

"I've set up a meeting with some contacts later this afternoon…" she reported, sipping coffee. "And I'd like Nick to go with me." Another server delivered baked items and a platter of fruit to the table, along with something that resembled porridge.

"Thank you," Carole said to the server, then turned back to the others. "Bedalaman left some detailed instructions for booking transport upriver along with some contacts."

"How long on the river?" Antonio asked, helping himself to some porridge.

She grabbed a pastry and took some slices of fruit from the platter.

"Not entirely sure… I'm hoping to have a better idea by this evening. *After* our appointment." This last bit she shaded with uncertainty.

In the borderline chill of the overdone air-conditioning, Nick wondered if the hotel's management had decided to provide a psychic bulwark against the steaming tropical heat beyond its walls. The charge from the caffeine/nicotine combo had given him a 'jacked-up' clarity and reminded him how preposterously unlikely this entire moment was. Two months ago, he'd been sleep-walking through the predictable outlines of his days, watching them pass with a slow, steady, and barely noticeable drift toward apathy. Each year, the faces of his students changed while little else did. He'd gone all-in on a career path that required an advanced degree and took almost eight years to complete, only to arrive at a place where doubt nibbled away at the certainties that once guided him.

"Nick, aren't you going to eat anything?" he heard Carole say after a couple minutes.

Returning to the present, he shook his head while stubbing the cigarette in an ashtray.

"Not right now," he said. "My stomach's kind of off…"

"Fair enough," she replied. "I'll put a couple of these pastries in my bag to snack on…" She held one up for him and wrapped it in a napkin. "So… They're *here*…"

30.

A young woman lectured a crying child upset that the upper half of his ice cream treat had melted and fallen to the pavement. Nick and Carole stepped around the pair as they approached a shop Bedalaman had directed them to. It was almost 2:00 in the afternoon, the warmest part of the day and Nick already looked wilted.

"In here…" Carole said, as they ducked under an awning across the street from the shop. "The sun can be *brutal* at this latitude… You learn to be a 'shade-spotter…'"

"…I'll bet…" Nick answered, wiping his brow with a shirtsleeve, "…if only shade could help with the humidity…"

The equatorial swelter had turned Nick into a sweaty, wheezing tourist while Carole appeared much better adapted.

"*Nothing* helps with that…" she smiled, "…We *are* only one degree north of the equator, after all…"

Nick smiled at the distinctly British unflappability — *'Keep calm and carry on!'*

"One degree…?" he repeated. "That's as close as I've ever been to the equator."

"Really?" she remarked, "Maybe you can make a stop there while you're in this part of the world. It's just over the border in Kalimantan. Get your picture snapped with a foot in each hemisphere."

"Oh, how many times have I wanted to be in two places at once…" Nick mused, earning a wry grin from Carole.

"Now, tell me again…" he continued after a moment, veering back to business, "Who are we supposed to meet here?"

"I'm not entirely sure…" she replied, glancing at her watch. "I was told to wait for *that* shop to open…" She nodded toward a storefront that looked to be a showroom or gallery for indigenous crafts and artwork.

"Bedalaman said to be here this afternoon when they reopen and someone will contact us."

"Really…? So, we just hang out until someone introduces themselves in hushed tones…?"

"Or, maybe not so hushed, but, yes," she told him, "That's the idea…"

Nick nodded vaguely, having never engaged in anything remotely like this before. They were in a grey zone now, operating outside the constructs, as well as the protections, of the law. It reminded him how oblivious we really were to the shadier business going on all around us at any given time.

"I see Ian's been busy looking for an inside line with you," she observed, making a stab at small talk. "Certainly bent your ear on the flight over…"

"…oof, that guy…!" Nick grumbled, "He could use some remedial work in learning how to read an audience."

This got a snigger out of Carole.

"Yes, he does seem to wield his curiosity like a blunt instrument…" she remarked. "Never worked with him before and my first thought was, subtlety isn't his strong suit. Kind of like a terrier nipping at your pant leg."

They chuckled at the analogy while, across the street, Carole noticed a woman unlocking the shop's door.

"I think that's our cue," she said, "Let's browse."

A chime announced their entry when they opened the door. Inside, the shop was tastefully appointed with what looked to be artisanal indigenous works. Buff-toned walls hung with paintings and woven mats, while carvings and woven baskets were carefully arranged on shelves, tables and in floor displays. Neatly folded textiles and large thatch mats were fanned out on long tables or hung from display trees.

As they took in the surroundings, a petite woman behind the register counter said 'hello' and smiled graciously. She had fine features that didn't seem entirely local, making her origins difficult to pinpoint. Streaks of gray randomly tinged shoulder-length hair pulled tightly back, while a restrained touch of liner provided a subtle accent to her eyes. Nick noticed a willowy, almost lissome quality to her carriage that set her apart from other local women.

"Such a lovely shop you have here," Carole said in her affable British manner as the woman approached.

"Thank you," the woman replied. "I have pieces from all over Borneo. You see here?" She stepped toward some striking wood carvings on a shelf and held one up for them. "These are done by the *Kayan* people," she continued, "They're known for their elaborate wood carving."

"Exquisite…" Carole murmured as she and Nick admired the piece.

The shopkeeper placed the carving back, then fussed at some dust she noticed.

"The indigenous people of Borneo," the woman went on, brushing dust with her fingers, "Their culture and traditions are not at like the peninsular Malays or the Javanese, you know. Malaysia and Indonesia have no meaning to them. Here, they are simply *Iban* or *Kenyah* or *Penan* or *whatever*. And their allegiance begins and ends with their people." She finished tidying and brushed off her hands. "You're *not* on a tour?" she queried, a vague hint of suspicion in the tone.

"No, we're traveling on our own," Carole told her, wondering if *she* might be the contact.

"We get many tour groups on their way to or from the interior," the woman went on. "They come to see the rainforest and the headhunters. Many Europeans come to bird watch or see the Orangutans."

The shopkeeper looked at Nick, who hovered distractedly. "You German?" she asked him.

"Uh, no…" he replied, a bit startled. "American, actually. But *she's* British." He gestured at Carole who smiled awkwardly, as if Britain's proximity to Germany were somehow germane to the woman's question.

The shopkeeper's brow noticeably wrinkled. "Are you two married?" she asked Nick as Carole smiled, pleased the question had been put to *him* rather than her.

"Married…? No, no," he assured her, glancing at Carole to chime in at any time. "We're just *colleagues,* actually. We sometimes travel together, you know…share expenses, that sort of thing."

"*You* are *not* married?" remarked the shopkeeper, incredulous that a man his age should be single. Nick muttered uncomfortably then began to restate his answer when she cut him off.

"No, not to *her*," the woman corrected, nodding toward Carole. "I mean *you*. Do *you* have a wife?"

Nick felt his face flush.

"Well…um…" he stammered, "I *do* live with someone back in California," further baffling the shopkeeper.

"What is *someone?*" she asked. "You don't like women?"

"No, no, that's not it," Nick protested, his face reddening, "I *do* like women—"

"How old?" the woman went on, cutting him off again. "*You*," she said, pointing at him. "How old are you?"

"Me…? I'm almost forty, but—" Before he could finish, the woman winced and turned her head with an exasperated cry of "*aaaow!*" as if she could barely express the difficulty of understanding such people.

Carole, though quite amused, finally sprang Nick by asking about another piece that caught her eye.

"*This* is incredible," she said, looking at an exquisitely carved bird-like creature on a display shelf.

The shopkeeper's attention snapped back to commerce.

"That is the *Kenyalang*," she explained. "In English, it's called '*the rhinoceros horn-bill.*' It is the national bird of Sarawak."

The woman reached up and brought the object down from the shelf, turning it carefully as she spoke.

"It is considered an omen by many people in Borneo…" She pointed to a second structure sprouting from the bird's toucan-like beak near its face.

"You see this?" she went on, "This is called the '*casque.*' It looks like a rhinoceros horn. That's how the bird got its name in English." She held it closer as Carole considered the unusual feature and Nick looked over her shoulder.

"The purpose of the casque is a mystery. No one really knows why it's there or what it does. I think only the bird really knows."

"I can live with that," Carole declared. "We need more mysteries."

"Yes, I think so too," the shopkeeper agreed, before abruptly shifting gears. "Now, where are you planning to go in Sarawak? What is it you want to see?"

"Well, we're actually here for work," Carole told her.

"*Work?*" The woman appeared startled by this.

"Yes, that's right. We're doing a travel story on Borneo for British television. You know, the BBC?"

"British?" the shopkeeper echoed, quizzically. "Do you know the National Geographic people were here last year and came to my shop? They were making a show on Borneo wildlife. When they come to my shop, I remind them there are people here, too. You see, all this…" she waved her arm at the store's contents, "This is also Borneo."

"Absolutely," Carole agreed. "And we intend to feature Borneo's culture in our program."

"That's good," the woman said, apparently reassured. "Come, look at this." She gestured toward another part of the shop as Carole and Nick followed, then stopped in front of an extraordinary woven mat hanging on a wall. "You see this," she said, holding up an edge of the mat. "This is woven by one of Sarawak's last nomadic tribes, the *Penan*. See? It is rattan from palm leaves."

The mat was in fact a work of intricacy and geometric detail that looked to Nick and Carole like an endeavor of heroic patience.

"*This* is from palm leaves?" Carole asked in disbelief. "Extraordinary…!!"

"Yes, of course," the woman continued. "Look at this weave. Look how fine, how watertight. You can't do this with machines. See these patterns…?"

She pointed out the intricate, linking geometric patterns that seemed to form different relationships as one's perspective moved in and out. Nick tried to imagine human fingers twisting and threading thousands of palm fibers into the object before them. In a world where machines made *things* and people made *money,* such manual skills had mostly vanished, destined for an eventual oblivion where they would one day be as lost to us as the techniques used to build Stonehenge. The interconnected global economy now taking shape demanded efficiency; driven by the pursuit of wealth and acquisition, it had no time for craft and the pride of manual skill. He reached down to feel the fiber and stitching.

"Incredible…" he muttered, running his fingers along it almost reverentially. He wanted to ask the woman how she had come upon it, but thought this might be interpreted as challenging the mat's provenance or the methods of its acquisition. Instead, he opted for a question less likely to cause offense.

"Can I ask how much?"

"*This?* This is *priceless*," the shopkeeper demurred. "It's not for sale. I keep it to show something about the people here. One day, I'll give it to a museum before I die, so people in the future can see what Borneo used to be..." She ran a finger thoughtfully along the mat's edge.

"You can't find these anymore," she went on, "The younger people, they're all in a hurry now. They want jobs, money to buy things..."

She paused, her words hanging there, suspended like dust in an afternoon sunbeam. Then, the spell was broken as the shop door chimed again. A man in pressed gray chinos and tucked-in polo shirt closed the door behind him.

"And you?" Carole asked, changing the subject. "Is your family from here?"

"My mother, yes, she was Iban," the woman replied, distracted. "She married a Japanese engineer who'd been working in the oil fields off Miri. He'd stayed here after the war."

"Is that right...?" Carole murmured, further intrigued. "Did he ever talk about his decision to stay here rather than return to Japan?"

The woman hesitated, absently fingering a spot on the mat. "He never spoke about it. His family was from Nagasaki..."

Nick cringed; his generation of Americans — those born in the years after the war — were the children of parents who had been alive when atomic bombs were dropped on Hiroshima and Nagasaki by the United States in 1945. A vague, lingering ambivalence would shadow many in his parent's generation, becoming an even vaguer psychic inheritance for their offspring.

"That must have been interesting growing up here...?" Carole delicately went on. "The Japanese...they had a reputation as occupiers..."

The shopkeeper sighed. "After the war, people mostly forget. My father opened this shop in 1949. It was a drug store then. He made sure people got whatever medicine they needed. Even if they couldn't pay. He wanted to show that not all Japanese were the same."

As she finished, the shop door opened again and what looked to be a Japanese tour group began filing in. "Excuse me..." the woman said, then walked toward the group, now dispersing into the shop, and greeted them in Japanese.

"Now there's a way to explain irony to my students..." Nick said, eyeing the Japanese tourists as Carole gave him a sidelong glance.

"The Japanese..." he clarified, nodding their way. "One-time conquerors returning as wealthy shoppers."

With their attention on the shopkeeper and Japanese tourists, Nick and Carole hadn't noticed that the man who'd entered a few moments prior had worked his way toward them. Casually examining the wall hangings, he inched nearer.

"*Carole...?*"

She turned in surprise and answered in the affirmative.

"I'm *Sendat*," he offered, somewhat hushed. "Bedalaman's friend..."

"Yes, of course..." she said, relieved.

They shook hands and Carole introduced Nick who noted the peculiar handshake again — more fingers and thumb, rather than the full-on, sturdy, whole-handed Western clasp. While the Western sensibility might misconstrue the local handshake as *weak*, Nick had learned from teaching in Los Angeles with its one-hundred-eighty or so different languages and ethnicities, that one culture's *weak* was another's *polite.*

Sendat looked to be in his twenties, with features that Nick thought might be *Melanesian.* He recalled reading something about coastal Borneo being an anthropological crossroads where Austronesian and Melanesian peoples overlapped.

"Would you care to walk?" Sendat asked, gesturing toward the street. His compact, wiry frame suggested a lean, nimble kind of strength, like an acrobat or gymnast, while his manner was circumspect.

They walked toward the chiming door where Carole thanked the shopkeeper before exiting. Sendat navigated pedestrian traffic while making small talk and polite inquiries about their stay so far. After several blocks, he spotted a bus coming their way.

"Do you mind riding the bus?" he asked, as it pulled into the stop. Nick and Carole did not and boarded the bus with him, sitting on opposite sides of the aisle. For several minutes, they rode in silence. Then, after a couple of stops, Sendat relaxed slightly and apologized for suggesting the bus.

"It's better this way," he told them. "Just to be safe. Sometimes...they watch us."

Carole remarked that they understood before getting down to business.

"Bedalaman thought you might be able to help us," she said, avoiding specifics.

"Yes, of course, he explained things and we are happy to help," Sendat answered, with the grace of a diplomat while turning to note the stop. "Two more stops," he added. "We have an office near the government district where I'd like to show you something."

He then went on to explain that he was with '*SAM*', an acronym for *Sahabat Alam Malaysia*, an environmental organization affiliated with *Friends of the Earth*. They had been in Sarawak since 1981 trying to help slow the rate of deforestation. Through that work, he had come to know a little about the Penan.

At the next stop, they exited the bus and Sendat led them toward a bland looking office complex where they followed him through a service entrance at the rear of a building, then up some stairs and down a corridor to an office suite with only a number on the door. Inside, the general disorganized mess reminded Nick of a college newspaper's office — cubicles and desks cluttered with papers, photos, coffee cups, maps, typewriters and computer terminals. Toward the rear, a freestanding counter was strewn with rolled and unrolled topographic maps and what looked to be aerial photos.

"This way, please," Sendat told them, gesturing toward a small conference table near the map counter. "Please, sit..." he went on, "Would you like something to drink? We have soda, water, some tea?"

"Water would be great, thanks," Carole answered, with Nick nodding in agreement. Sendat stepped over to a small refrigerator and returned with three bottles of water.

"I'm sorry for the detours," he went on, handing them each a bottle. "We try to be careful..."

A flicker of concern briefly flashed in Nick's eyes as he glanced at Carole.

"Of course," she said to Sendat while catching Nick's glance, "Always good to shake up routines..." She took a healthy sip of water, then returned to the point. "So, Bedalaman was able to give you an outline of what we're looking to do here?"

Sendat confirmed that he had, then turned to Nick.

"This man with the Penan...he's your brother...?"

Nick explained that he thought so based on the newspaper photo he'd seen in Kuala Lumpur, adding, "But...the last time I laid eyes on him...he was a teenager."

The idea of siblings being removed from each other's lives for decades seemed to disturb Sendat.

"I see..." he murmured, scratching his jaw in thought. "Well, I can tell you that no one knows the man's name. Maybe better that way. He started sending anonymous updates down on the boats alerting us to what was happening up there with the Atakun Dam project. You've heard of it?"

"A little..." Carole answered, briefly glancing Nick's way, "But maybe Nick hasn't?"

Sendat nodded. "Yes? Well, the Malaysian government, for a long time now, they've wanted to exploit Borneo's potential for hydro-power. About five years back, they finally came up with a plan and got funding from the IMF and World Bank. There's a lot of money involved and all sorts of interests got behind it. Engineering firms, contractors, construction workers, concrete and steel manufacturers, companies that make turbines, heavy equipment manufacturers, the list goes on. They all line up at the offices of government ministers who award the contracts and throw money at them…what do you call this…*kick-offs*?

"Kick*backs*," Carole corrected.

"Yes, that's it: *kickbacks*… Everybody gets something except the people whose land will be flooded by the dam.

"The Malaysian government passed laws in the 1970s to protect indigenous land rights and that's what we're using in court to stop the project." At this, he leaned forward and clasped his fingers together in front of him.

"But Sarawak is a long way from Kuala Lumpur," he continued. "For most Peninsular Malaysians, it might as well be another country. What goes on in Borneo has nothing to do with their lives and they have little interest in what happens to indigenous people like the Penan."

"Sendat, help me understand something," Nick interjected, "These people, the Penan — they don't want to live in longhouses like some of the other indigenous people?"

"This group of Penan, no…" Sendat replied, "Permanent settlement has never been part of their culture. They stay in one spot for a while, hunting, fishing, and taking whatever the forest offers, then they move on. In a few years, they might return to that same spot and start the cycle over again, the way they have for thousands of years.

"And that's exactly what the government is using against them…" he continued. "They say the Penan can't make claims to land they haven't settled. Now, it's in the hands of the courts to decide. They issued an injunction to halt work on the dam until a decision is reached, but there's really no way to enforce it up there.

"We're trying to get the story out to Western news outlets hoping to draw international attention to what's going on here. This sort of controversy generates negative publicity that makes the IMF nervous. The idea is to shame them into holding up further funding until all indigenous claims are resolved. If you stop the money, you stop the project."

"But has it made any difference so far?" Carole asked. "Like you said... work's still going on?"

Sendat sighed. "A thing like this..." he dolefully explained, "...can get easily lost when there's so much else going on in the world..."

For Carole, the statement was particularly pointed; as a journalist, she provided fuel for that noisy marketplace.

"Well, that's a large part of why I'm along on this," she assured Sendat. "The BBC has *reach* and I'd really like to shine a light on what's going on up there. While hopefully helping Nick find his brother, as well." She briefly paused then added, "Can you help us?"

"I think so..." he said, exhaling. "But keep in mind, the government has made it illegal to go up there. The whole area is off-limits. Here, let me show you something..." He rose and gestured for them to follow him toward the counter where maps and photos were spread out. On the wall behind it, Sendat pointed out the state's generally east-west orientation on a large map of Sarawak.

"We're here," Sendat went on, pointing at Kuching in the small handle of Sarawak's south-western corner. "And, the Penan lands are over here." He ran his finger in a loose circle around an area in Sarawak's north-eastern region near the border with North Kalimantan in Indonesia, its eastern edges pushing northward like a graph on the rise. Nick and Carole both noted the rugged and remote terrain where there looked to be almost nothing in the way of roads or settlements.

"Doesn't look like an easy place to get around in..." Nick commented, a note of apprehension in his tone.

"It *isn't*..." Sendat confirmed. "Borneo is very mountainous and very difficult to travel in. Not many places flat enough for an airstrip and the government controls what few there are. Just recently, they cut a dirt track for bringing heavy equipment up to the Atakun Dam project, but it's off-limits. Only vehicles working with the hydro project and the military are allowed to use it. So, everyone else still travels by river. Borneo's highways."

Sendat then pointed to a small city on the northeast coast. "Here...this is Miri, where business gets done and this is the port where all the oil, gas and raw logs get shipped. From here, you take an express boat up the Baram river to Marudi, then change to the smaller boats that go all the way to Long Akah. We'll give you some local contacts there who can help take you the rest of the way upriver into Penan territory where the dam is being built."

Carole gazed at the map as she contemplated this. "Great… And they can help us make contact with the Penan?"

Sendat's expression softened. "Yes, but keep in mind, with the Penan, you need to be patient. They are forest people and very suspicious of outsiders. Our contacts are known to the Penan and speak their language. Even so, finding them is not an exact science. You go where they might be and wait for them to contact you."

Carole glanced back at Nick. This sort of contingent arrangement was not unfamiliar to her: terrorist cells and other secretive groups she'd dealt with over the years were equally difficult to meet. But it wasn't just the open-ended unpredictability that troubled her; such difficult, inaccessible places always seemed to harbor a deep antipathy toward any human presence.

"You have equipment?" Sendat asked.

"Only the bare essentials," she told him. "A couple cases for the camera and recorder."

"I ask because you may need to carry it by foot at times."

Nick's eyes widened at the possibility — he had seen Antonio's substantial equipment cases. At the time, he wondered how they could possibly 'fly under the radar' with them. They certainly wouldn't be mistaken for amateur birdwatchers on a tour.

"Remember…" Sendat continued, pointing again at a spot on the map. "All this area beyond Long Akah is closed to travel. Technically, it's off-limits because of the Atakun Dam project…" He hesitated and his tone grew more serious. "That means, you would be there *illegally* and could be detained by the military." He glanced between them a moment.

"Also," he continued. "Little things can turn deadly up there. A tiny cut can become infected and spread through your bloodstream… Dehydration and heat stroke are a real possibility, and there are venomous snakes, leeches and biting insects. If something happens, you're several days from any medical care."

Sendat's litany of potential hazards and menace whirled around Nick's mind. He looked over at Carole to gauge her reaction — if any of this worried her, it didn't show.

"Okay…how soon could we start?" she asked him.

"Well, there are two flights daily to Miri, depending on weather," he replied. "Once there, you arrange a taxi to the Marudi Wharf where the Long Lama express boats leave from. You might even be able to do both in the same day."

"How about tomorrow?" Carole pressed.

"Hmm… Maybe better the day after…" Sendat explained. "We need to arrange those contacts in the upper Baram. There's no telephone up there, but we do have short-wave radio communication with some longhouse communities and missionaries…"

"Okay, the day after tomorrow," Carole agreed, glancing over at Nick who nodded his assent.

The activist provided further details about the area and told them he would leave a message at the hotel with the names of contacts in the Upper Baram.

On the ride back, Nick silently brooded. The encounter with Sendat had left him feeling a bit daunted as he mulled the reality of what they were about to undertake. Despite Carole's reassuring cool and seasoned competence, a pall of apprehension began to draw like a gauzy curtain around him.

31.

That evening, Nick had dinner in his room then called Celeste. With the time difference, he knew she'd be at work and he could leave a message. There was no point updating her on any of this as it would only lead to further debate, especially when he explained this latest development. For now, a message would do, duty met.

Hoping to clear his mind, Nick went for a stroll on the riverfront promenade. At half past nine, the evening was still a balmy seventy-two degrees. The Sarawak River lazily flowed toward the South China Sea as Kuching's lights shimmered in the ripples on its surface. The silty, mud-sad smell reminded him of the Mississippi in New Orleans. Strangely enough, Kuching had other things in common with the Crescent City, especially in summer when the best part of the day in New Orleans was the *night,* and the sultry air became more bearable, the pavement no longer glared, and people ventured back out into the streets.

And just like the *Big Easy,* Kuching felt like a human-scaled city. Along the waterfront, young and old alike looked revitalized in the evening air. People relaxed on benches along the promenade, smoking and talking, while others gathered at cafe tables to watch the world go by. Parents leisurely pushed children in strollers and young lovers snuggled against the rail gazing into the river's opaque mysteries.

At a kiosk, Nick impulsively purchased a pack of clove cigarettes and lit one. The morning's smoke with Ian had rekindled a weakness for the nicotine buzz, and the clove-tobacco mixture did not disappoint.

A slight breeze off the river blended with the pungent, smoky scent of spices and charcoal-grilled meat wafting in and out on the air. Boats called 'sampans' plied the nighttime waters, parting the reflected lights of the city rippling on the surface in their wake. A welcome moment of serenity began to lift Nick's spirits, helped in no small part by the mild nicotine buzz and a couple of beers he'd had in his room.

He stopped and leaned over the esplanade rail. For a relatively short river, (its total length a mere *seventy-five miles*), the Sarawak had enormous depth and volume. Compared to these deep silty waters, his paltry, concrete-lined Los Angeles River seemed a poor specimen indeed; barely flowing a good portion of the year, it was a stretch even *thinking* of it as a river. Much of its fifty-one miles were corralled in concrete and littered with trash. Most Angelenos rarely thought of it outside an especially rainy winter.

"Christ, those things are disgusting…"

The voice and accent were unmistakable: Ian had snuck up behind him.

"Mind if I bum one…?"

Nick smiled and, after a moment's hesitation, offered the pack.

"This is what you started this morning…" he playfully chided, striking a match for Ian.

"I'm ashamed," Ian replied, as he exhaled a bluish cloud and joined Nick at the rail. "If I'd known you'd sink this low…"

The shot of repartee had a disarming effect and Nick wondered if the Australian might not be so artless after all. Ian considered the clove cigarette in his fingers and the memory it apparently conjured.

"Haven't had one of *these* in years…" he recalled. "On holiday in Bali — that's where I first tried one. It's right next door. Bali, that is. You know, kind of like Mexico for you Yanks. A place close by where the local coin goes further. People there actually smoke these God-awful things. After a few lagers, I must've liked them, too."

Nick nodded, mildly amused, then wondered if it might give the Australian the wrong idea; he hadn't come here looking for conversation. A minute or so passed in silence.

"You play golf?" Ian inquired at last.

"Golf...?" Nick repeated, with a sidelong glance. "No, not really," he went on, curious what the reporter was after. "Took a couple lessons once, but didn't find it all that relaxing. Too regimented for something that's supposed to be enjoyed in your leisure-time. God help you if you're late for a tee time, or slice one into the rough and spend more than thirty seconds looking for your ball. The foursome behind gets irritated and wants to play through, catching up at the next tee just in time to watch you shank your drive..."

Ian grinned. "True enough..." he agreed. "It's a blood sport for some... Anyway, just wanted to toss that out, as there's this new course built by the Japanese. They're crazy about golf, and real estate in Japan is so expensive they've taken to building courses in less developed countries around Southeast Asia where they can play while traveling on business."

Nick took another drag on the clove cigarette as Ian went on.

"Since we've got another day here, Antonio and I thought we'd try to rent some clubs and get nine holes in tomorrow. Why don't you join us?"

"That's kind of you, thanks, but I think I'll pass. I'm a little too preoccupied to enjoy much right now."

"Understood..." Ian assured him, as he watched the ripples of light shimmering in the current. "By the way..." he continued, after a couple beats, "How'd the meeting go today? Carole didn't say much about it."

Nick bristled slightly — the man was nothing if not persistent.

"Fine, I guess," he answered, after a moment. "Spent a lot of time waiting around..."

Ian smiled at this. "Oh yeah, you get a lot of that in this part of the world..." he said, then shifted gears. "I'm only curious, that's all," he added. "Trying to get my head around various angles of the story..." At this, he began to pick tiny bits of clove and tobacco from his lip.

"Whew," he exclaimed, quickly pivoting. "Think I got a bit of a buzz from this thing... You suppose they're any worse for you...?"

Once more, Nick smiled. The reporter certainly had a touch for the subtle collar job.

"I hope so," he replied, deadpan, then decided to turn the tables. "So, tell me something. Are you and Derek *pals* or are you just a hired gun?"

The question surprised Ian. "By pals, you mean, do we go out boozing?" he asked. "No... but we've worked together in the past."

"I see... So, you weren't surprised he brought his ex-wife in?"

"Not at all," the Aussie answered. "Like I said, she's good. *Respected.* And as 'exes', they share leads all the time. Derek knows Carole can find her way into a story like nobody else. And for something like this, they can pool resources to cover costs, so it makes good business sense. Derek gets the story for print and Carole gets the broadcast version for the BBC. Win-win…"

"Yeah, it seems to work," Nick observed. "Guess I didn't expect such congeniality with ex-spouses who also happen to be colleagues…"

A sly smile curled on Ian's lips.

"Surprising…I know. But they've both been at this too long to let a failed marriage get in the way of professional advantage. Especially Derek. A story like this could be leverage for the transfer he's been after — a soft landing at the *New Straits Times'* office in Singapore, where both the restaurants and women are more plentiful."

"Savvy career move," Nick agreed, looking back out at the river.

"You know, I can't help but wonder, Nick…" Ian then began to say, "If that *is* your brother up there and we do find him… What then?"

Nick sighed, exasperated enough for a dose of candor. "Honestly…? I'm not really sure…" He considered a moment. "Part of me just wants to look at him again. Just to see his face… But then…there's all this other business. With whatever's going on up there…"

"Right…" Ian mumbled, thoughtfully. "If that's him, I'm thinking his involvement with these indigenous people against the government here wouldn't go down well back home." He fussed some more bits of clove and tobacco from his lips.

"Yeah, the thought did occur to me," Nick eventually replied. "After I saw the article Wolcott had… I can see how it would put the Peace Corps in an awkward spot…"

Ian drew on the clove cigarette then exhaled.

"Might help explain some of what you experienced," he added. "Pissing off the host country. Not exactly the kind of goodwill a foreign aid program is after."

For several seconds, Nick stared silently at the river. It was true, what he'd told Ian — he really had no idea what he was hoping for if the man upriver turned out to be his brother, other than addressing some vaguely understood inchoate yearning.

"Listen, I'm beat," he said. "You guys enjoy golfing tomorrow…" At that, he turned and started back for the hotel.

32.

The flight to Miri was fairly bumpy. Carole suggested a 'hide in plain sight' strategy which meant a short-hop commercial flight with Marudi Airlines so they'd blend in with the tourist crowd. Thunderstorms had been threatening since takeoff and turbulence bounced the small sixteen-seater about as the pilots tried to navigate around the storms, adding time to an already delayed flight.

Miri sat in an unusual patch of terrain on Borneo's northwest coast. Nick tried to square his guidebook's map with the view flying in. The meandering Miri River surrounded the city in a kind of oblong lasso shape before emptying into the South China Sea. The guidebook described this as something called, the '*Yazoo Effect*', where a tributary runs parallel to a river's main channel for some distance before joining it. In the Miri River's case, a strip of barrier sediment had built-up over time due to a southerly offshore current in the South China Sea, 'corralling' the river and causing it to run parallel to the sea for about eight kilometers before finally breaking through.

This part of Borneo, he'd also learned, was endowed with vast oil deposits, both onshore and off. The city had been founded in 1910 when Royal Dutch Shell drilled the first well here and it soon became the center of Malaysia's burgeoning petroleum industry. In late 1941, the Japanese Empire, in need of oil for its expansionist aims, made it ground zero for their invasion of Borneo a week after attacking Pearl Harbor. Postwar, Malaysia would work out an arrangement with Shell Oil that gave rise to the national oil company, Petronas.

Almost thirty kilometers to the north was the border with Brunei, a tiny Islamic sultanate made fantastically wealthy by its sizable share of those oil deposits. When Malaysia gained its independence in 1957, the Sultan of Brunei shrewdly chose to remain a British protectorate rather than become part of Malaysia. This calculus paid off when tiny Brunei achieved its own independence in 1984 to become the world's *fifth* wealthiest nation.

One of Nick's guidebooks said that Miri had recently become a major draw for backpackers and birdwatchers. While the eco-tourism cognoscenti had discovered this part of the world, he doubted most Americans could even find Borneo and Miri on a map, let alone muster the time and money to visit.

33.

With the weather delays, they landed in Miri later than scheduled and had to wait to catch the next day's express boat upriver, so Carole booked them into a hotel popular with Japanese and Australian tourists. That evening, rather than dine in the hotel's restaurant, which Carole felt too conspicuous, they ate at a Chinese restaurant in an older part of the city.

As they picked at a turntable of various dishes, Carole and Ian debated the most unlikely place they ever had Chinese food. Antonio stayed out of it, spinning the turntable and sampling the various dishes between sips of beer. Nick appreciated the cameraman's generally detached manner, a welcome counterpoint to his more voluble colleagues.

"Nick, I don't think you ever told us what you did in the States," Ian said at last, changing the subject.

"Ah," Nick replied. "Well… I teach English at several community colleges around Los Angeles. Hoping to impart some basic competency in the mother tongue."

"Are we talking literature?" Carole asked, working her chopsticks.

"If only…" he answered. "More like basic usage and composition, actually. Mostly, I try to get students to write a decent enough cover letter to get a job interview and then speak in complete sentences during it."

"In college…?" Antonio observed. "I thought that's what secondary school is supposed to do?"

"It used to be," said Nick. "But you'd be surprised by how many of these students are barely literate… These kids are from working-class families and educated in the public schools. The idea behind the community college is to shore up academic deficiencies where you can and offer programs in practical occupations that lead to a job. Things like accounting, computerized drafting and engineering, nursing, those sorts of careers."

"Sure…" Ian chimed in. "Why *shouldn't* higher education be more practical? Not everyone needs to understand Shakespeare."

"I don't know about understanding *Shakespeare*," Carole observed, while grabbing a dumpling with her chopsticks, "But I don't think a democracy can work very well if its citizens have little or no grasp of history and culture. Democracy *needs* an educated and informed citizenry or it gets hijacked by monied interests who know how to bamboozle the public."

"Agreed, but you can't just shove culture down people's throats if they don't want it," Ian countered. "What say you, Nick? Is a working knowledge of Shakespeare essential to being a good citizen?"

"It would be, if *I* ran things…" Nick answered dryly. "In fact, I'd have a law that said you can't vote unless you demonstrate a working knowledge of *Lear*."

This got a chuckle out of everyone.

"But seriously," Ian persisted, "Does anyone really think people need a grounding in the humanities to be responsible citizens? To succeed in life? Today, when technology's changing everything?"

"All the more reason we need the humanities," Carole insisted. "Technology might make us smarter, but it does nothing to make us wiser."

"Absolutely," Antonio added. "I was introduced to Shakespeare in high school."

"Funny, you don't look that old…" Ian joked, while stabbing at a dumpling.

"It's true," Antonio went on, ignoring the remark. "Everything you need to know about human nature…it's all there in Shakespeare."

"Now *that's* a fact…" Ian agreed, going for another dumpling. "But Nick…you must get restless teaching all that structural stuff, no? Wouldn't you rather be teaching literature somewhere? I mean, there must be more suitable opportunities out there?"

Nick smiled. "There are. Just not in California. I regularly check the job listings in the academic journals, and most of the tenure-track gigs on offer are in other states. In California, the majority of openings are similar to mine: teaching composition and patching holes in students' high school education, all part-time, what they call *adjunct* faculty. A fancy word meaning they don't offer benefits. The occasional full-time, tenure-track position that *does* come up in California, gets swamped with applicants like me. Bottom line is, there are plenty of jobs teaching remedial English and almost none teaching Shakespeare…"

"What about teaching English overseas?" Antonio wondered. "Like in Thailand or Korea? Pay's pretty good, I hear, and I *know* the students are well-behaved."

"Better food, too," Ian added, at which they all laughed.

"Will work for *Pad Thai!*" Nick joked.

In the momentary slack that followed this bonhomie, Carole tried to change direction.

"Look, we need to talk about tomorrow," she began. "I've been thinking it might not be wise for all of us to travel on the same boat. We've stayed under the radar so far, but the four of us together is sure to draw attention…"

"You think we should split up?" Nick asked, concerned.

"That's what my instinct tells me," she answered, pausing to gauge the reaction.

"Once we're upriver we'll be fine. But on the way up, this seems better. Four strangers traveling together stand out way more than two."

"Makes sense. So who goes when?" Ian asked.

"I think you and Antonio on the first morning boat," she suggested. "Nick and I on the next one out… We'll re-connect in Long Miri. That's the end of the line for express boats, so we'll have to find a private boat to take us from there."

"Listen, I trust your judgement," Nick countered, "But… What if there's a delay or an unscheduled stop or any *number* of things that could mess with the timing? This isn't the Swiss railway, you know? If something went wrong, how would one party contact the other…?"

"No question, that's a risk," Carole agreed, "Compared to attracting the wrong kind of attention though, it seems worth it. We're way out on our own here, and this far out, officials of any stripe are hyper-wary, generally unsupervised, and often corrupt. And if we assume your visit to the police has made the rounds…then we should also assume they don't want you up here."

"She's right, Nick," Ian volunteered. "The four of us together, it's just too conspicuous. Better to fly under the radar when we can."

Nick saw the sense in this, though he still had misgivings — they were nearing a point where backing away would no longer be an option should things go awry. After several seconds, he nodded his acquiescence.

34.

The sun had barely crossed the horizon and the air already felt thick with humidity. After several restless hours tossing in his room's heavy air-conditioning, Nick gave up on sleep and went for an early morning walk. His watch read a little past 4:00 AM so, with no particular destination in mind, he wandered toward a beach area where Miri met the South China Sea.

A rosé light tinted the eastern sky, fringing the tiny waves lapping at the sand. The mild offshore breeze had a salty-metallic tang to it as Nick tried to recall pieces of an aborted dream in which he drove a lonely stretch of road in what looked like the Mojave Desert, its featureless terrain and low scrub stretching to the horizon under a searing blue sky. He remembered a figure up ahead…someone stepping out from thick brush at the side of the road…a young boy in farmer's overalls.

The boy's red, wind-chapped face suggested a life spent outdoors. Nick turned to gaze at the boy as he slowly drove past. When he turned back to the road and glanced up at the rear-view mirror again, the boy now stood in the middle of the road watching him pull away. Minutes seemed to pass as Nick drove on, but the boy's image in the mirror remained fixed as if the car weren't moving. The car's speedometer needle moved to seventy, then eighty, ninety, a hundred miles an hour… Nick removed his foot from the accelerator but the engine still roared. He then looked back up at the mirror, but the boy had vanished.

A tern steeply swooped down to the water, snatching a small fish in its beak and returning Nick to the moment. He watched the bird land on a stretch of beach to enjoy its catch. Nearby, men with straw sun hats were prepping a fishing boat. Nick's watch said it was almost 5:30 and he realized he'd lost track of the time, so he started back to the hotel where he met Carole already returning from breakfast.

"You're up and out early," she remarked.

"…Ah, restless night…" he told her.

She studied him a moment. "Well, you can still catch breakfast, but the first boat leaves in about an hour and we need to get our tickets at the launch."

"Okay…but I probably need a shower more than breakfast…" Nick explained, running a hand along his stubbly jaw.

"Tell you what…" Carole suggested, a vague hint of concern in her tone, "I grabbed a couple croissants from the buffet for later. I'll save them for you."

Sensing her apprehension, Nick tried to put on some enthusiasm.

"That'd be great," he said, "Thanks…"

35.

In the back seat of a taxi, Nick nibbled one of the croissants Carole had taken from the buffet as they passed acres of what he assumed were palm oil plantations. Miri's reason for being was its proximity to the oil fields, but its location wasn't suitable for a deep water port to handle the prodigious shipments of palm oil and timber that now rivaled petroleum exports. Twenty kilometers north, at the actual mouth of the Baram River where it emptied into the South China Sea, the silt-laden river grew wider and deeper, far better suited for large tankers and log barges, as well as the plethora of express boats.

Soon, the palm oil plantations gave way to industrial operations: plywood mills and oil storage tanks, welding and fabricating operations, ship works and dry docks. A salty-oily smell lingered in the air, part New Jersey industrial maritime, and part steamy equatorial boom town. The river itself soon came into view and Nick peered out at hundreds of logs floating side-by-side, corralled by booms as they waited to be stacked on barges. Weathered wharves fronted the river where other barges were moored, many piled with tangles of drilling equipment like piping and casing. It was impossible to miss the fact that everything here flowed one-way — *outbound*, as if Borneo had become Asia's supermarket for natural resources.

The taxi dropped them near a dock wedged into the industrial waterfront that also served as the express boat terminal from which, earlier that morning, Ian and Antonio had departed. Now, a little past noon, groups of people milled about the docks, many hauling purchases from Miri — cookware, LP gas bottles, fuel cans, galvanized wash-tubs. Near the gangway, pushcart vendors sold grilled meat and fish and the air was thick with a smoky charcoal/ fat redolence blending with random wafts of silt, oil, salt and rusted metal. Occasionally, the breeze shifted and exhaust fumes blew in from diesel and two-stroke engines on the river. Suspended in the thick air were countless tiny particulates from incompletely combusted hydrocarbons that produced a gritty, greasy feel on exposed skin.

For Nick, it called to mind something out of Melville or Conrad, a chaotic and noisy former colonial frontier outpost overloading the senses with its jumble of human activity. At the express boat dock, he and Carole got in line for tickets with the other waiting passengers. Most were *Dayaks*, Borneo's native people, calling back and forth in their individual languages. Outsiders had ruled over their island in one way or another for the last five centuries, the Malaysians being only the latest. Despite this, much in these Dayak cultures persisted, especially when it came to personal ornamentation, evident in the variety of ornate tattoos and ritual-scarring on display. Especially fascinating for Nick, were the pierced and stretched earlobes — some drooping to seemingly impossible lengths, like strands of rolled dough, or a pretzel yet to be looped on itself. By piercing the lobes then continuously fitting the hole with increasingly larger plugs, many Dayak women had managed to stretch their earlobes to their shoulders. One woman even had lobes that drooped down to her chest.

While the skin art remained traditional, the clothing was more discount store summer wear. Tee-shirts with screened graphics were ubiquitous, many sporting cartoon characters or declarations like '*New York Girl*' and '*Let's Party!*' in stylish, sometimes glittery fonts. All the men and children wore gym shorts and flip-flops or, in many cases, bare feet. Some of the women wore tee-shirts, but many preferred some kind of wrap or sarong in place of gym shorts.

Nick's attention shot from one thing to another as he and Carole patiently waited their turn at the ticket window. With his height and very white complexion, Nick began to feel conspicuous and clumsy. In contrast, Carole maneuvered with precision and purpose; her shoulder-length hair barely bounced as she squeezed between people.

Near the ticket window, a small group of Japanese tourists clustered together to negotiate their purchase with a uniformed clerk who seemed overwhelmed. The scene appeared to bemuse Carole, which Nick found somehow beguiling. She had an air of casual confidence that he didn't often find in American women, especially in Los Angeles where *posturing* had become an art. As a colleague explained to him when he'd first arrived, LA was a world-class, multi-ethnic, polyglot city with a skin-deep soul.

When their turn finally arrived at the window, Carole raised two fingers and said '*Long Miri*.' The female clerk spoke enough English to ask if she wanted round-trip to which she answered, yes. The clerk punched in some numbers, took Carole's money and slid two tickets at her. "Dock seven," she said, pointing. "In ten minutes."

They hurried down a concrete pier toward the unusual craft they were about to board. Around ten to fifteen meters in length and quite narrow, it resembled an airplane fuselage without the wings. A thin deck with a rope-rail extended from the hull and wrapped around the craft just beneath the cabin windows. Panels of slightly tinted glass fronted the wheelhouse.

Cargo of all sorts had been lashed to the roof, secured to another steel rail about six inches high encircling it. It could've been a floating department store with all the stuff up there: portable generators, televisions in boxes lashed to other boxes with rope and twine, sections of PVC piping, rubber tubing, cases of motor oil, cook stoves and what looked like galvanized wash tubs.

Nick and Carole followed the line of passengers down the loading gangway while an attendant helped lash passenger's cargo to the boat's roof. Having nothing to stow, they sidestepped the queue and entered the cabin. Inside, a narrow aisle separated the interior's three-by-three seating scheme. Nick followed Carole and looked around for the exits, noting the orange life vests stuffed into slots on the ceiling.

"Here we are," Carole said, arriving at their seats near the boat's center. They settled in as the cabin filled and, after another ten minutes or so, a voice from a distorted loudspeaker announced something in Malay, then quickly repeated it in English: they were about to depart. The boat's engines began rumbling to life in the rear, rattling the floorboards. An oily petroleum smell like diesel hinted on the air while, across the aisle, a Dayak woman with deeply sun-wrinkled skin and stretched earlobes stared at them, clearly puzzled by their presence.

Then, a sudden movement startled Nick as the boat began to ease back from the pier and into the swirling reddish-brown current. With a noticeable heave, the air conditioning kicked on while video monitors hanging from the cabin's ceiling at the front and middle squelched to life with a tabloid news program in Malay. The audio blared at a volume the boat's pilots must have deemed necessary to overcome the engine noise.

Nick leaned toward Carole. "I don't suppose they'll be serving drinks…?" he quipped, barely above the din. This got a smile out of her.

"How many hours to Long Miri?" he then asked.

"Less than three, I think," she answered.

He scrunched his face at the thought of enduring this racket that long. Conversation and sleep both seemed out of the question, so Nick leaned back as Carole made some notes. On the monitors, a noisy commercial touted the miraculous capabilities of a household cleaning product, followed by another for a frozen dairy concoction that concluded with a montage of happy Malaysian kids and moms dancing and jump-cutting all over the place to a cloying pop soundtrack. The Dayak woman across the aisle had lost interest in them and was instead transfixed by the production on the monitor screens, despite the voice-over being in Malay, a language she may or may not have understood. Most of the other passengers looked to be equally fascinated by the commercials. Nick began to wonder if these Dayaks saw their own futures in the buoyant, middle-class Malaysian consumers on the screens.

When the boat reached cruising speed, Carole leaned in toward Nick.

"Mind if I ask you something?" she said, pulling him back from his thoughts. "I mean…" she added, "…Since we've got such a long ride anyway…"

Nick playfully raised his eyebrows for effect. "On the record or *off*…?" he asked, archly.

"Strictly *off*," she answered with a smile. "This has all been moving so fast… I thought I should check how you're holding up…?"

Nick shifted self-consciously in his seat. "Fine," he told her, "I'm fine…"

She searched his eyes for any hint of wavering.

"But now… *I'm* curious," he countered, "What's on your mind…?"

For a brief instant, he thought something flickered in her eyes.

"Just checking in…that's all…" she assured him. "I tend to forget most people don't live at *this* pace."

"I'm not about to change my mind if that's what you're worried about."

"No, I wasn't thinking that at all," she explained. "I don't doubt your commitment… But there's more hard travel ahead."

"I'm okay with that…" Nick reassured her, "…I may look a little frayed around the edges, but I'm all in."

A skeptical smile gradually lifted the corners of Carole's mouth as she weighed this.

"…Okay…" she said, her eyes narrowing slightly. "How about your… *partner* in Los Angeles? How is she doing with all this?"

The question amused Nick. "My *partner*…?" he repeated.

"That's the term du jour, no?" she asked, "For unmarried but otherwise involved adults? What do *you* use? *'Significant other?'* Sounds so…clinical… *Girlfriend* and *boyfriend* seem a bit juvenile after a certain age. An editor I know recently used the term *'fuck buddy'*… Coarse, and maybe a bit…reductive… But…accurate enough in some situations, I suppose."

He grinned appreciatively at her unabashed bluntness.

"Well…" he explained, "Her name's Celeste and she hasn't exactly been on board with this project…" The turn toward the confessional surprised him, but Carole's direct, earnest manner had lowered his guard and it was a relief to vent with another woman.

"She'll come around," Carole offered. "My first husband was like that. Not keen on my traveling all the time… I told myself he'd adjust, but he never did…"

"This was before Derek?" Nick asked.

She nodded. "Mmm… Afraid so…" she answered, ruefully. "Derek was actually my second time around. A kindred spirit, same line of work and all… He just didn't see why marriage should keep us from occasionally seeing other people." Carole exhaled deeply. "Can't blame him, really… This life… you're always on the go. Not the best career choice for domestic stability. Two years at this bureau, three at another and so on, until you have to think for a second when people ask where you're from."

They fell silent as a slightly less-blaring martial arts movie replaced the commercials on the video monitors.

"There *is* something else I've been wondering about…" Carole began again, somewhat tentatively. "…Have you considered the possibility that your brother — provided it's him with the Penan — that maybe…he might *not* line up with the person you remember? That you might be *disappointed…?*"

The question echoed Ian's earlier probing. Apparently, both journalists *had* considered the possibility.

"Eh…" he mumbled, mulling his answer, "Haven't really given it much thought. I'd like to think I'm way past expectations…" His brow wrinkled slightly. "But, I suppose…if he chose to take the heat from the Peace Corps and two governments to stand with these people, well… it's hard to be disappointed in someone like that." He hesitated, then added, "But, what is it you're *really* asking?"

Carole smiled disarmingly. "Just wondering, that's all. This story got me thinking about a woman I ran into not so long ago. We sat next to each other in grade school. *Waaayyy* back… One of those classroom buddies kids make at that age. I only knew her from school. We ate lunch together, studied together, talked girl stuff, that sort of thing. I must've been about ten when she moved away. Never saw her again…

"Some years back, when I was working in Sydney, I bumped into her. Didn't even recognize her at first! She'd gotten heavy and hadn't aged well.

We went for drinks at a place by the Harbor Bridge and it ended up being awkward. Her politics had taken a hard right turn and, as the drinks loosened her tongue, she said some fairly vile things. Afterward, I had to ask myself whether *she'd* changed or if I'd gotten her wrong way back when we were kids? I thought maybe she was just as appalled by the person *I'd* become. By the time the check arrived, I think we both wished we could've left it back at grade school..."

"I'll bet," Nick remarked. "At that age, the world hasn't gotten to us yet. We're just these newly minted little people with uncluttered minds. No baggage yet."

The comment seemed to resonate with Carole and her brow wrinkled briefly in thought.

"Anyway..." she continued, steering the conversation back to Nick's brother. "I guess I'm curious... Back then, could you ever have imagined, your brother doing something like this?"

Nick sighed. "Not really..." he told her, "Even though he was the kind of kid who'd stick up for someone being bullied or picked on. Always took the side of the underdog... So, I suppose in that way maybe, this business with the Penan isn't so surprising."

"Sure... Carole murmured, ponderous. "Tell me, *you* didn't happen to be one of those kids being bullied?"

He gave her a sidelong glance. "Are we still off the record?" he chided.

Taking the jibe in good humor, Carole leaned her head back on the headrest. "Completely," she said, duly checked.

"Uh-huh..." Nick muttered, holding her gaze for several seconds. "Well, in our neighborhood, it was tough going if you didn't have an older sibling. The first couple times some older kid picked on me, Evan warned them off. Then he told me I'd better learn to stand up to them myself. Get a backbone. So I did. Tried, at least. And that's the first thing I learned about bullies — they only go after the easy pickings." He shrugged and a wry smile hinted at the corners of his mouth. "Deep down we're just like those screaming apes in *2001: A Space Odyssey*. Scared little monkey people looking for an advantage."

Carole raised her eyebrows in mock surprise. "So says the professor?" she teased.

"Instructor," Nick corrected, "*Adjunct* instructor..."

As they bantered back and forth, a Hong Kong-style martial arts movie replaced the commercials on the video monitors. Soon, blaring music and shouts of 'YAH!' buzzed in the overdriven speakers with exaggerated sound effects for every slap, kick and punch. Other than the Japanese tour group, most of the passengers appeared to be riveted by the choreographed mayhem. The noise made conversation almost impossible and Nick's eyes began to wander the cabin.

"I'm guessing they have a restroom on this thing…" he remarked, glancing about.

"In the rear of the cabin, I think," Carole suggested, turning to look, while Nick quickly spotted the 'WC' sign toward the back of the boat.

"There it is…be right back."

Maneuvering down the aisle, Nick took in the faces of his fellow passengers. The Japanese tourists had clumped together in a couple rows, noses in guidebooks or snoozing with neck pillows. Some of the men looked old enough to have been in Borneo during the war.

Across the aisle from the Japanese sat two somewhat scruffy young European (…so Nick guessed…) backpackers who looked like they'd been traveling in Asia for months on the cheap. Both had deeply tanned faces and clothes that hung loosely from their bony frames, a combined result, he surmised, of multiple bouts of diarrhea along with constantly hauling packs on and off crowded buses, third-class railroad cars, and express boats in steamy climates. Ah, the glamour of travel.

Close to the rear of the boat, two men sat apart from everyone. They looked to be from the Peninsula, possibly businessmen, and Nick wondered what business brought them out this far. Perhaps they were associated with the hydro project or one of the big timber operations further up.

After finishing in the restroom, Nick thought he might catch a breath of fresh air to escape the heavy AC and martial arts squawking. Through the windows of a narrow door that exited onto the stern deck, he noticed more cargo lashed down. Surprisingly, the door's handle turned — it was unlocked. Glancing back quickly, he went through.

Beneath his feet, the planking vibrated with the engine's rumbling, while an acrid belt of diesel exhaust lingered in the slipstream. Taking care not to rouse suspicion, Nick avoided the door's skinny window. To its left on the port side, a narrow ladder went up to the roof. A metal sign had a warning in Malay and, after another quick look back, he started to climb until his head was above the roof line.

The mountain of cargo and luggage lashed to the steel rails circling the roof, recalled something out of '*The Grapes of Wrath*'. On both sides of the river, up and down, a riot of tangled vegetation ran to the water's edge, while thick woody vines coiled around trees, limbs and each other. A meter or two back from the riverbank, the forest fell into deep shadow.

After a couple minutes, Nick thought Carole might be worried and started back down. He opened the cabin door and had barely stepped in when the restroom door swung open, startling him.

"Excuse me!" said the man in the doorway, in English. "I didn't think anyone else was back here."

Nick recognized him as one of the businessmen sitting near the rear of the boat. The man's use of English tripped him up and he smiled awkwardly, nodding toward the stern deck.

"Just needed some fresh air," he explained.

"Out *there...?*" the man asked, as if everyone except Nick knew you'd only be drafting exhaust.

Nick shrugged. "Ah, well, I'm not so fussy..."

The man seemed puzzled and Nick excused himself then started back toward his seat. As he slid in next to Carole, he glanced over his shoulder toward the rear of the boat where the businessman was now peering out through the rear door's skinny window.

"Were you studying the plumbing?" Carole inquired good-naturedly.

"Wanted a little air, so I went out on the stern deck..." Nick confessed. "Stunk of diesel smoke."

"I see..." she murmured. "...Not sure that's keeping with the plan to stay *low-profile...*"

"Ah...right," Nick muttered, realizing the lapse. "*Sorry...* Totally blanked on it..."

"Forget it..." she told him, with the hint of a smile. "Just keep in mind... there's no telling who might be paying attention to us."

Nodding contritely, Nick told her it wouldn't happen again. He'd been careless, momentarily forgetting just how far out of his depth he really was.

36.

The boat's sudden movements startled Nick from a doze and he reflexively turned to see Carole craning her neck for a better view out the window.

"What's going on…?" he asked, "…Is this Long Miri?"

The boat was inching up to a short dock at a settlement of some sort. The video monitors were off and a few passengers had begun to stir and gather belongings.

"Not sure…" Carole answered, watching a crewman hop onto the dock to secure mooring lines. "Can't see much…just some longhouses."

"Unscheduled stop, maybe…?" Nick wondered, trying to look around her.

On shore, people gathered in anticipation. Then, a voice blared from the speakers, first in Malay then in English:

"*Long Akah!* This is Long Akah. Boat leaves in fifteen minutes."

Carole checked her watch. "Good chance to grab some fresh air," she said, "Feel like stretching your legs?"

Nick nodded and they joined the procession disembarking. As they stepped from the air-conditioned cabin, a wall of humidity enveloped them.

"Phew… Maybe we can find a cold beer?" Nick suggested, half-seriously, as they took in the surroundings.

Smaller boats of various types were tied here and there on the riverbank. A few were hand-hewn dugouts with small motors attached to the stern; a couple looked like rafts of lashed-together bamboo. Ragamuffin children played in the mud and dirt wearing filthy gym shorts or, in the case of the youngest, nothing at all. Further back from the river they noticed several wooden structures built on raised stilts that looked deeper in length than in width.

"Maybe this is all that's here…" Carole observed, checking her map for Long Akah.

"Looks like it…" Nick agreed, taking stock. "Just some kind of longhouse community… Probably communal except for sleeping quarters."

"Must be," Carole concurred, "With each family having their own little space."

They wandered down the length of a longhouse as chickens, dogs and children milled about. The structures had corrugated metal roofs and plank siding in which openings had been cut for windows and ventilation — a couple older women watched them from one of these openings while puffing on pipes. Smoke from cooking fires vented through sheet metal flues on the roof.

"Not that different from the Iroquois longhouses I visited once in upstate New York," Nick recalled.

"Is that right…?" Carole remarked, "What's the likelihood of that? Two different cultures on opposite sides of the planet coming up with this same kind of housing arrangement?"

At the far end of the longhouse, the distorted strains of television speakers poured from an open doorway where stairs led up. Carole climbed them and peeked inside. She had what a friend of Nick's liked to call, *moxie.* He cautiously followed her up, noting some boys playing pool on a table with torn felt. Window openings were the only light source beyond the glow of a lone television where young and old sat on the floor absorbed in what looked to be a Malaysian soap opera. A group of older men sat against a wall pensively drawing on their pipes and gently releasing curls of blue smoke into the haze. A couple of them noticed the two white people peering in from the doorway. One of the men with strands of white hair and teeth ground to nubs, smiled when Nick nodded his way.

After a couple minutes, Carole looked at her watch.

"Is it time already?" Nick asked, checking his.

"Not yet," she replied. "Just realized I should've used the loo on the boat…"

"We can go back…" he suggested, charmed by the Anglo slang for a toilet.

"Not necessary, thanks," she told him, "We still have almost ten minutes before we leave, so look around a bit more if you want. Just keep an eye on the *time.*"

Nick was quietly grateful — he was in no hurry to return to the cramped boat. They descended the stairs and she departed as he walked over to another wooden stairway and climbed to a landing leading to another open entryway. Inside, two older women were stretching and weaving a mat from palm fronds. The silent, harmonious interaction fascinated him. He smiled when they briefly looked up before turning back to their work.

It then dawned on him that this was somebody's *home*; that it lacked a door was *not* an open invitation to gawk. Feeling a bit awkward, he retreated down the steps, deciding to return to the boat. On the way, he thought it better to relieve himself in the abundant bush rather than deal with the boat's tiny bathroom. Stepping into the surrounding forest, he unzipped and let go behind a tree. As his stream spattered the ground, he observed the orgy of plant life around him. Vines coiled around trees and each other, some dangling from branches; ferns, mosses and other epiphytes sprouted in the crotches of limbs; plucky saplings pushed up wherever light broke through the canopy, and a single orchid with delicate creamy tones reclined languorously on a limb.

Life's unruly plenitude here amazed Nick. Wanting to relish it a bit longer, he lit a clove cigarette, took a deep drag and exhaled a mighty cloud of syrupy bluish smoke. A surge of nicotine rushed through his brain and brought a smile as he once again realized how absurd and unlikely this moment was; a reality so far removed from his own that he might as well have been on another planet.

As he finished and stepped out of the brush, a voice startled him.

"Quite something, isn't it…?"

Nick abruptly turned to his right where the Malaysian businessman from the boat smiled as he drew on a cigarette.

"…Oh…you again…" Nick said, warily sizing him up. "From the express boat, right?"

"That's right," the man answered, "I was waiting for the water closet when you came out."

Suddenly, Nick felt a bit uneasy.

"I stepped off for some air…" the man went on, "And I saw these."

He gestured at the longhouses. The man's polo shirt, neatly tucked into pressed khakis with sunglasses hanging from the shirt's unbuttoned 'V', gave him the appearance of a realtor or property developer. A sporty wristwatch and stylish shoes rounded out the presentation as Nick glanced at his watch and took a deep drag from the clove cigarette, hoping to conceal his discomfort.

"Right…" he muttered, agreeably. "Well…should probably start back…"

"Are you going up to Long Miri as well?" the man asked.

"I am," Nick replied, guardedly. "With my wife," he added, a misrepresentation intimating he wasn't here alone.

"Very nice," the man said, approvingly. "That's the woman you were sitting with?"

"Yes," Nick answered, "We're on our honeymoon here." The words were out before he could register the shock of speaking them.

"Oh yes, well, congratulations!" the man continued. "But this is an unusual place for a honeymoon, no...?"

Nick forced a little half-smile. Instinct told him to excuse himself and leave, but he thought it might come across wrong. Instead, he overplayed his hand.

"I know," he replied, piling it on. "It's all my wife's idea. Second time around for both of us and she wanted to do something out of the ordinary."

"Well, this *is* a special part of the world," the man agreed, gesturing toward the forest near the settlement's edge. "So many things here you won't find anywhere else."

"I believe it," Nick concurred, very conscious now of the time. "Anyhow, we should probably get back to the boat. Wouldn't want it to leave without us..."

As he took a final pull on his clove cigarette, Nick sensed the air being displaced behind him and turned to see the man's traveling companion.

"Oh...hi," Nick said, determined to stay cool and not overreact.

"Hello," the man replied, his tone flat.

Stockier and slightly shorter than his friend, he wore a button-down short-sleeved oxford shirt and a pair of olive-colored pants. His physique suggested ample time at a gym.

A few seconds of awkward silence followed when the first man spoke again.

"We were hoping we could to talk to you," he explained, then reached into a pocket to produce a leather identification holder he held open for Nick displaying a passport-sized head-shot with official looking details in Malay and a screened watermark for the background.

A deep chill ran down Nick's spine. "I'm sorry...who are you?" he asked, a noticeable quaver in his voice, "...And what's this about?"

"We're with the Malaysian Federal Police," the man calmly replied.

Nick glanced at the partner, still expressionless. "Really...? Okay, well... what can I help you with?"

"Would you have some identification?" the first man coolly asked.

Straining to keep a poker face, Nick produced his passport. The few encounters he'd had with police as an adult taught him the value of silence in such situations. The first man looked it over, comparing the photo with the man before him then thumbing through the blank visa pages.

"Los Angeles...?" he said, slowly flipping pages. "Where your passport was issued?"

"Yes, that's right," Nick answered. The man then flipped back to the only stamped visa page — *Malaysia*.

"This passport is new?" he asked, returning to the personal details page again. "You haven't used it much?"

"It is. I recently renewed it for this trip," Nick told him.

The man then closed the passport without handing it back.

"And what kind of work is it you do…Mr. Heewges?" he asked, phonetically voicing all the letters.

A tinge of irritation complicated Nick's low-simmering fear. "Hang on a second," he protested. "What's this about?"

The two men remained silent, their expressions flat and unreadable.

"I'm a teacher," Nick answered at last.

"In Los Angeles?"

"Yes, that's where I live…"

"But you are from '*Pennsylvania*' *USA?*" He pronounced it as 'Pen-sile-*vahn*-ya'.

It had to be a universal trait of cops, Nick thought, relishing their upper hand in the power dynamic, hoping to rattle something loose by drilling away at details, hanging on the silences and charging the air with suspicion. He could feel sweat soaking through the shirt on his back.

"Well, yes, I was *born* in Pennsylvania," he explained, "…and moved to Los Angeles as an adult."

This elicited nothing from the two men.

"Look," he continued, his mouth becoming dry with fear. "I don't know what you're after here, but, if you want to talk to me, I'd like to have my wife present. Now, can I have my passport back?"

Again, the two men were silent. Nick glanced back and forth between them, his fear rising.

"We'd like you to come with us," said the man doing all the talking. "Please…"

No one moved and Nick's breath stuck in his throat. Instinct told him to *run like hell* for the boat, but he resisted; it wasn't his country and he had no idea how these men would react. He tried to stay calm and *think* — Carole wouldn't let the boat wouldn't leave without him.

"I don't understand…" he said, stalling.

"We'll explain," the man told him. "But *not* here, please."

"Why *not* here??" Nick insisted. "Are you arresting me? Have I done something wrong?" He hoped to delay them long enough for Carole to get anxious and come looking for him.

The first man subtly shifted his weight in a menacing way while the other remained impassive.

"My wife's on *that* boat..." Nick continued, a nervous catch in his voice. "She won't let it leave without me..."

"Please," the first one repeated, "We can't talk here..." The two men began to nudge him forward by his elbows.

"Hey, hold on...wait a minute!" Nick objected, as they ushered him away.

37.

The wheelhouse door opened and the pilot scowled at Carole — she had been knocking insistently for several seconds.

"Yes??" he said, his tone brusque.

"I'm sorry to bother you..." Carole apologized, "Do you speak English?"

"Yes, little English," the pilot replied.

"Well..." she continued, explaining what had happened. When she finished, the pilot briefly sized her up and answered, "The boat stops *fifteen* minutes."

"Of course," she agreed. "And my friend *knew* that. I even reminded him before I returned."

This pilot had been here before, she thought. His expression seemed to say, "*Why do foreigners make such problems?*"

"I'm very sorry," he told her. "But I have to keep schedule."

She could see he had no intention of turning around.

"I understand..." she said, running through other possibilities in her head. "And there are no other boats coming up here today?"

"Next boat tomorrow morning," he answered.

Thanking him, Carole returned to her seat as the other passengers watched, obviously puzzled that her companion hadn't returned. What had happened? She couldn't imagine Nick losing track of the time — this was *his* project, after all. More disturbing possibilities began to emerge, the most likely being, they had been *followed.* Perhaps Nick's visit to the police *had* made someone nervous. This certainly lined up with her suspicion that there was far more to this story than they had imagined. Something else was at play here but she couldn't make out the various pieces and how Nick's brother fit. Even more, it baffled her why the authorities, if in fact, that's who they were, would wait until Nick had come this far from Kuala Lumpur to intervene.

38.

Nick walked with the two Malaysians who followed a path through the forest beyond the longhouse. Several times, he glanced back in the vain hope of seeing Carole until they finally arrived at a newly scraped dirt track where a black, mud-spattered SUV waited.

The quieter man opened the rear passenger door as Nick tried to stall.

"Look, you said you wanted to talk to me and I agreed," he objected, "You didn't say anything about taking me anywhere. If you want to talk, fine, let's do it right here. I'm an American citizen and the embassy here *knows* I'm in the country."

"We just need you to come with us, Mr. Hewgess," the first man said, "Please..."

"Come with you *where?* You still haven't told me what this is about and I'm not going anywhere until you do!"

"Please, Mr. Hewgess, don't make this more difficult. There's a plane waiting for us at the landing strip."

"A *plane?* What are you talking about?? No! No way! I'm not getting on any plane with you!"

"Mr. Hewgess, I'm not going to ask you again. Either you get in the car we'll have to *put* you in the car."

Nick glared bitterly at the man holding the door open. The thought of being restrained in any way terrified him and he could feel himself trembling with rage and fear, hoping it wasn't obvious. He would have to comply, finding thin consolation in the fact that, as long as his hands and feet were free, he was not entirely helpless. Soon enough, Carole would realize that he hadn't returned to the boat, though he had no idea what she would do about it. At this point, only a handful of people knew about their plans, but that much, at least, heartened him. Three of those people were here in Borneo and, hopefully, when Carole reunited with Ian and Antonio, they would mount an all-out effort to find him. Trying to conceal trembling hands, he climbed into the back seat of the SUV as the door shut behind him.

39.

Long Miri was the last stop for the express boat and the dock was congested with people disembarking and others looking to board for the return trip. Back from the main crush of activity, Ian and Antonio watched for Carole and Nick. They had taken an earlier boat as agreed, without incident. When Carole finally emerged onto the dock, Antonio waved to get her attention and when she started in their direction, he knew something wasn't right.

"Where's Nick…?" he muttered as the remaining passengers exited the boat.

As she drew near, Antonio noticed her grim visage and anxiously glanced at Ian.

"Let's walk," Carole said, tersely. She led them to a little stand selling drinks and snacks and took a seat at a small wood cable reel used as a table. A man came over with a one-sheet hand-written menu from which they ordered bottled water. When he was out of earshot, Antonio leaned forward and clasped his hands on the cable reel.

"You want to tell us what's going on…?" he asked, with evident alarm. "Where's Nick…?"

At this, Carole exhaled deeply. "I don't know…" she confessed, eyes seared with dread. "We stopped at Long Akah, probably like you did—"

"Not us…" Ian interrupted, "We didn't stop *anywhere* but here."

This surprised her.

"You *didn't* stop at Long Akah?"

"It wasn't on the schedule," Antonio explained, "Not for our boat, at least."

"Okay, so…you stopped at Long Akah, *and*…?" Ian prompted.

She gave them the broad strokes of what had happened, finishing with the boat's pilot refusing to turn back. For a minute or so, they sat in stunned silence.

"Maybe he was distracted?" Ian eventually suggested.

Antonio shook his head. "To the point of missing the boat? I can't see him doing that."

"No, probably not…" Ian agreed, "But it can happen. Even if you're paying attention… Someone speaks a little English and you engage with them, get caught up in the moment…"

"Not Nick," Carole countered, "Antonio's right — he's *not* frivolous. He put his life on hold to come all this way. He's not distracted by the novelty of the place "

"Then *what...?*" Ian asked, "You don't think somebody might've *grabbed* him? All the way up here...?"

"I don't know..." Carole muttered, pressing a knuckle to her lips in thought. "But it fits with this feeling I've had from the start...that there's more to this than we can see..."

Antonio's eyes widened. He knew that when Carole got a whiff of subterfuge, she rarely let go.

"When you got off the boat, did you see anything unusual or anyone official-looking?" he asked.

"No... Nothing. Certainly no one in any kind of uniform. Just people from that longhouse community."

She slowly shook her head as another thought came to her.

"There *is* the possibility..." she added, ominously, "...that someone might've followed us..."

Antonio leaned back while Ian stared in dismay. For several seconds, they each silently considered a range of darker possibilities in their heads, then Ian exhaled with a 'whoosh.'

"Okay..." he concluded, "What now?"

"There's no choice," Antonio asserted. "We go back."

"Of course..." Carole agreed. "We have to go back to Long Akah... If something happened...if Nick *is* in some kind of trouble, then *we're* the only ones who know about it..."

Her words underscored the point that Nick was no longer just their story, he had now become their *responsibility.*

"We'll have to ask around," she continued, "Somebody must've seen something."

"Let's hope," Antonio agreed. "But we're a long way from Kuching. Might not find many English speakers there."

"Then we'll find someone to interpret for us," she told him.

"I suppose enlisting the authorities' help is not an option...?" Ian wondered.

"Not until we know more..." Carole answered. "Let's just get back there first..."

"Wait, hold on a second," Ian interjected, "Maybe it would make sense... if *one* of us stayed here?" he suggested, careful not to challenge Carole's authority, "Just in case Nick *did* miss the boat departing and somehow found another way to get here? You said the pilot told you the next boat was tomorrow morning, but, what if he hired a private boat? Shouldn't *one* of us be here just in case?"

"Good point..." she agreed, "You volunteering?"

Ian shrugged. "Sure..."

"But how will we know?" Antonio asked. "It's not like we can pick up a phone and call each other."

Carole absently nibbled at her lower lip as she mulled the point.

"How about this," Ian proposed. "If you don't make it back by dusk, I'll figure it out...sleep in a longhouse or whatever. And if I *don't* hear from you by tomorrow mid-day, I'll catch the next boat to Long Akah. You can leave me a message at the dock somewhere and I'll do the same here in case we miss each other. Unless you've got a better idea."

"Makes sense," Antonio concurred, turning to Carole who nodded vaguely.

"Fine..." she agreed, angry with herself for leaving Nick alone out there as if they were in some holiday theme park.

"That'll work," she added. "And let's hope I'm making more of this than there really is..."

40.

In the back seat of the SUV, Nick's mind careened between terror and fury as the truck followed the dirt track upriver. According to his watch, they'd been driving more or less parallel to the Baram River for about fifteen minutes now, but it was impossible to gauge how far they'd traveled given the battered condition of the road. On straight stretches, the driver accelerated a few seconds before having to swerve and brake for an obstacle. Much of the track had been pummeled by all the heavy equipment going upriver, and the monsoon rains only made it worse, dislodging rocks, scouring ruts and gouging channels through the clay.

Still, the taciturn driver bashed on through. Each time the truck entered a curve too fast or skittered sideways, Nick would clutch the handle above his door and suck in a gasp while the driver tried to maintain control. At times, the track veered close to the river, its roiling waters just outside Nick's window. Making matters worse, storm clouds were piling up and the sky darkened toward quasi-twilight.

The man who'd first spoken to Nick had been largely silent in the front passenger seat. Sitting behind the driver on the SUV's right side, (…another British colonial vestige: *right-hand* drive…) Nick recalled a student who had once written that 'anger was more useful than fear,' as though we were in command of either. Such an observation could only come from someone familiar with fear, he concluded, because only someone in a protracted state of fear could see the superior utility of anger. At the moment, his anger was for himself, for not running when he had the chance.

Nick knew he had to focus his mind. Carole would soon join the others in Long Miri and he tried to imagine what they would do. With no idea what or with whom they were dealing, and knowing they were here illegally, enlisting help from official channels was not an option. But then…*what…?* What *could* they do…?

Whatever all this may have been about, Nick got the sense these men meant him no harm. Some flavor of federal police, they had probably been ordered to return him to Kuching or Kuala Lumpur, for reasons that clearly had to do with his brother. Obviously, his poking around at the embassy or with the police, possibly both, had stirred some kind of hornet's nest.

Just then, a thunderclap boomed overhead and vibrated through the entire SUV. Startled, the driver muttered something to his anxious partner. Seconds later, lightning flashed like a strobe, washing out the entire sky for a second or so. Another searing crack of thunder quickly followed and the driver accelerated as if thinking he could outrun the storm.

Within seconds, rain began to fall, lightly at first, then in steady, bloated drops that resoundingly splatted on the truck's body and windshield. The lightning flashes continued in multiple bursts that lit up the world outside like a highly overexposed photograph. A sharp tearing sound trailed each burst by a split-second, followed almost instantly by an explosive, booming electrical crack that rattled the SUV's window frames. Rain soon came down in sheets, pummeling the truck's exterior metal in a deafening roar. Visibility instantly went to zero, even with the wipers running at top speed. The driver slowed the vehicle to a crawl and Nick gripped the handle above the door frame so tightly his knuckles were white.

When the truck crawled to a stop, the Malaysians began shouting at each other over the din of the downpour. Nick anxiously peered out his window trying to gauge how close they'd come to the river, but the curtain of rain was like a waterfall you couldn't see through. As the two men argued, Nick discretely tested the up/down switch for his window, quickly lowering and raising it a couple inches, surprised and grateful it hadn't been disabled.

In that instant, he marveled at the stunning absurdity of the situation and the colossal foolishness that had brought him to this moment, further proof, as if any were necessary, that the chaotic and indifferent universe gave no quarter for human folly. This called to mind another gem from one of his students: we had fashioned God as a bulwark against the unbearable knowledge that ultimately, we are completely alone.

41.

After negotiating with a surly Dayak boatman, Carole and Antonio returned to Long Akah, having ridden out the deluge under the boat's canopy. The landing area was deserted, most likely cleared out by the storm. Carole helped Antonio carry the gear to a spot near the largest of the longhouses. In several of the window openings, people began to peer out at the two foreigners, giving Carole an idea.

"Let's set up the camera," she said, inspired. "C'mon…" she urged, noting Antonio's dubious reaction. "We'll get some B-roll."

"*Seriously?*" he asked.

"Sure! I'm thinking it will draw people out," she told him. "And hopefully, someone among them will speak a little English."

Antonio still seemed doubtful how this would help them with Nick.

"Look, we're on our own here…" she reminded him. "Even if there were some sort of authority here, which doesn't look to be the case, we couldn't go to them for help, so it's on us to do this. And the first thing we need is someone who can translate. We need help here, and if you've got something better, let's have it."

Conceding the point, Antonio set up the camera and tripod while Carole clipped the wireless lapel mic to her shirt.

"Stand-up first?" he asked, fussing with adjustments.

"Yeah," she replied. "Let's see what happens."

At this, Carole looked around for a decent background. "How about this?" she asked.

"Good," Antonio told her, glancing at the viewfinder. "The longhouse is framed over your right shoulder. Nice."

He focused and asked for a sound check. She jabbered some words as he watched the volume meters. "Okay," he said, then stood back from the eyepiece. "Whenever you're ready."

Carole took a deep breath and cleared her throat.

"Right," she said at last, and Antonio put his eye to the viewfinder.

"*Rolling...*" he said, while she counted off, 'Three, two, one...'

"*Far up the Baram River in Sarawak, Malaysia,*" she began, "*...is the longhouse community of Long Akah. Here, the Dayak people of Borneo live semi-communally. Over the last century, colonialism and Christianity have brought profound changes and, as the modern world continues its push into this part of Malaysian Borneo, the Dayaks here are likely to see even more dramatic change.*"

Her delivery and manner snapped with that world-wise, dignified tone peculiar to BBC journalists.

"*What will all this change mean to them?*" she asked, in a rhetorical challenge. "*What of their traditional culture can survive as technology and the cash economy alter reality on the ground? Indigenous people on both sides of the border here between Malaysian Borneo and Indonesian Borneo will continue to face these questions and others, asking themselves what will be gained and what will be lost as progress finds its way to this last wild corner of the Asian Pacific.*" She held it a couple seconds then relaxed her correspondent's posture. "How'd that play?" she asked.

"Beautiful..." Antonio told her, astonished as usual by her ability to improvise a compelling stand-up with little or no preparation. In less than a minute, she could wrap it up, provide context and a concise rendering of core issues while teasing out just a touch of drama.

"Interviews or more B-roll?" he asked.

Carole glanced about, noting the interest they'd drawn: the curious had come out onto porches and landings for a better look, while children clustered on stairs near doorways and men in t-shirts and shorts hovered nearby.

"An interview, I think..." she answered, scanning faces for potential subjects.

"Hello," she said to the gathering, in as disarming a tone as she could muster. "Anyone here speak English?" A low murmur began to stir.

"Yes...? Anyone...?" she continued, affably. "We're looking to speak with someone here, if possible."

"Are you the television lady?" asked a man from a group gathered near some wooden stairs. A faded silkscreen of the letters 'DKNY' was barely visible on the front of his worn t-shirt.

"Well… Yes, I *work* in television, yes," Carole replied, homing in on him. "I'm with the BBC. From the United Kingdom? The British Broadcasting Company?" The light of recognition she hoped for did not appear.

"Is it the television from Kuching…?" he asked.

"Well…yes…" she answered, in a harmless nod to expediency over truth. "We've worked with them. Could we talk with you?" She glanced quickly at Antonio who repositioned the camera and tripod.

The man resisted while others egged him on.

"Can you tell us your name?" Carole began, an encouraging note in her tone.

"*Seladang…*" he replied, self-consciously. "My name is Seladang." He looked over at the camera and its little red light as Carole nodded at Antonio to confirm sound level. She guessed the man to be somewhere in his forties and evidently a person of some esteem, given the reaction of the those around him.

"And how old you are, Seladang?" she asked, with a smile.

"Me, I am forty-three years."

"And you have family here?"

He nodded. "Yes, I have a wife and three children. My mother and my father, too."

As he spoke, people began squeezing tighter behind him.

"That's terrific!" Carole remarked, "Do you all share the same long-house?"

Seladang answered that yes, the family had their section of the longhouse.

"Can you tell us a little about life here in Long Akah?" she went on, "How people live and work? *You* for instance?"

"Me? I have my boat. I take people and goods up and down the river. Sometimes I take tourist groups to see the nature here."

"That sounds like good work," Carole commented.

"Yes, yes, very good work. A boatman is very good work here."

Holding her sense of urgency at bay required a delicate touch, as Carole knew she first had to elicit some goodwill and trust before inquiring about Nick.

"Is your family from here, Seladang?" she then asked.

"No," he told her, swinging an arm upriver, "My family comes from up there, where I was born. When I was fifteen, the government moved us here to Long Akah…"

Carole zeroed in on this. "I see… Did people not want to leave?"

"No…" he answered, hedging. "But I think people…most people, they're okay living here now."

"And you…? You like it here?"

Seladang smiled and scratched his temple. "Yes, I like it. With my boat, I can make money. Is better for my family."

By now, the crowd had swelled and Carole decided to get to the point.

"Seladang," she then said, switching gears, "Tell me…did you or anyone else happen to notice a white man from the express boat walking here earlier?"

The question brought some murmuring from the crowd and Seladang stiffened noticeably, averting his eyes and distractedly fussing a spot behind his ear.

"Yes…there was a white man…" he said at last. "Do you know him?"

"We do," Carole told him, "He's from America and came here looking for a brother who'd gone missing twenty years ago. He thinks this brother may be with the Penan people further upriver. We were going along with him to record the story for the BBC."

Seladang nodded thoughtfully and ran a hand over the stubble on the back of his head. Carole picked up on his discomfort and glanced over at Antonio with a subtle shake of her head. He stopped recording and lifted his eye from the viewfinder.

"…It's okay…" Carole reassured Seladang, "The camera's off…"

Noting the little red light's absence, the Dayak shifted his weight and, after a few beats, began to speak.

"Some other men…" he explained, haltingly, "From that same boat… They left with your friend…but not toward the boat."

Carole quietly sucked in a breath and momentarily felt like the air had been knocked out of her. "…I see… And those men? They probably weren't from around here?"

The boatman shook his head, avoiding her gaze. "No…not from around here…"

She nodded thoughtfully a couple times, then glanced briefly at Antonio, now resting an arm on the camera and tripod. They'd been in some tight spots together, but no one involved in a story had ever been kidnapped.

"Did anyone here see which way they went…?" Carole then asked, clearly hopeful.

Seladang made a soft 'whooshing' sound as he drew a breath through his teeth and another spate of low murmuring circled the crowd.

"Some people…" he began, "…saw these three men go toward the new track, the one they made for the dam construction…" Behind him, a younger man with a bowl haircut said something in the local tongue and the boatman turned to him.

"He says, one of those men from the boat," Seladang translated, turning back to Carole. "…he left a black jeep or lorry the other day… Like you see the government men drive around…"

The words kicked up a sour feeling in Carole's stomach. She instinctively looked over at Antonio whose distressed visage must have mirrored hers.

"This *track*…" she then continued, carefully. "It runs all the way from Miri to the dam site?"

The boatman nodded and she followed by asking if anyone had seen whether the vehicle went toward the dam or back toward Miri. For a minute or so, Seladang discussed this with the others gathered around him.

"This person says…" he translated, real-time, "…They go up *that* way…" He swung an arm in said direction. "Toward the construction site…upriver…"

"…The hydro project site…?" Carole repeated, making sure she heard correctly.

Seladang nodded. "…I think, maybe…" he explained, "…They take him for the airplanes… Like they do with government people and bank men… they come and go on airplanes…"

The two reporters fell silent for several seconds as each tried to apprehend this.

"They must've built a landing strip up there," Antonio concluded, at last. "To get the bigwigs in and out…"

Carole's mouth tightened. "Right…" she agreed. "So… You think they're taking him back to Kuala Lumpur…?"

"*We can hope…*" he answered.

The comment took a moment to register with Carole — until now, she hadn't considered the possibility that Nick could be in anything other than *legal* jeopardy. Antonio's remark served to remind them they had no idea who these men were or what their intentions might be. Out here, the law and its protections were non-existent; someone could disappear and never be found.

Given that Nick's abductors waited until he was alone to snatch him, suggested they were shadow operators likely doing the bidding of powerful unseen interests well-versed in the art of intentional obscurity. Still, the temerity of grabbing Nick like this and potentially harming him made little sense; the disappearance of an American citizen on foreign soil, especially one with a paper trail of recent pointed inquiries, would undoubtedly bring unwanted scrutiny of the sort that posed a far greater threat to such rarefied interests than whatever Nick's poking around might've stirred up. Or, so she thought. Steeling herself, she looked directly at Seladang.

"…Is it possible to go up there by boat?"

The Dayak stared as if he'd missed something, then said, yes, it was possible.

"Good…" she remarked, deliberating. "Then…could we hire you to take us up there? With your boat? We'll pay whatever you want…"

Seladang quickly demurred. "I don't know…" he muttered, suddenly unsure of these people and whatever they were involved in.

There was no misreading his reluctance and Carole immediately sought to blunt it.

"I understand your concern," she told him, "…But that man they took? I assure you he's done *nothing wrong.* As I said, he came here all the way from America hoping to find this brother who'd disappeared. He's not even certain that man up there *is* him, but he's hopeful. That's really *all* there is to it. When he came to us for help, we agreed in order to film their reunion for the BBC. It's important you believe me. He's done nothing wrong."

Antonio's mouth tightened in a slight frown. Carole had been known to *massage* the facts from time to time, and he usually looked the other way. 'Benign expedience', she called it, enlisted only as necessary in service to the story.

"…You say this man they took…?" Seladang then asked, "His brother is with the Penan…?"

"That's what we think," Carole answered. "A newspaper in Kuala Lumpur ran a story on protests against the proposed dam up there with a photo that showed a white man standing with the Penan. There's a good chance he's this man's brother."

A subtle change came to the boatman's expression as he mulled it.

"I *have* heard of a man…" he said, after a minute. "A white man living with the Penan in the forest… But no one here has ever seen him…"

"…Well, this man," Carole continued, "Whoever he is, it appears he's taken up the Penan cause." She worked it, hoping to enlist the boatman's sympathies. "Our friend, who those men took, he's got nothing to do with *any* of that. He only wants to know if that's his brother up there with the Penan."

At this, a low murmuring began to stir among the gathered crowd and Carole suspected others were getting the gist of her words.

"Please, Seladang," she implored, "All we're asking is that you drop us off up there. You can turn right around and come back. And we'll pay you a hundred US dollars…"

Seladang's eyes widened a bit and he absently rubbed his head in thought.

"…Yes, but it is dangerous up there…" he muttered, still uneasy. "The military people… If they stop you…"

"We can deal with that…" Carole assured him. "We're citizens of the United Kingdom, working journalists for the BBC, and the Malaysian government *has* to respect that. That includes anyone we hire to help us."

The boatman chewed it over, occasionally glancing about the crowd as the seconds passed.

"…Okay…" he said, surrendering at last. "I will take you."

Relieved, Carole glanced at Antonio then warmly thanked the boatman, hoping he nor anyone else could see the tiny cracks in her sheen of confidence.

42.

The rain had eased slightly as the SUV slammed and splashed through water-filled ruts. Gushing rivulets of reddish-brown to cocoa-colored slurry crossed the dirt road in their rush to the river, scouring and gouging uneven channels through the clay soil and loosening large rocks. Small mudslides left piles of debris here and there that the driver dodged, while in spots, runoff cleaved huge gashes in the roadbed near the river's edge, sending a slurry of loose rock and clay tumbling into the swirling current.

Undaunted, and apparently intent on making-up time, the driver sped the truck through and around such hazards, while in the back seat, Nick clutched the handle above his door ever tighter with each jarring crash of the truck's wheels. Agitated and helpless, he kept telling himself that he'd done nothing wrong, that these men, whatever their purpose, meant him no harm.

The thought quickly dissolved as he spotted something ahead — a large wash-out that cut across the entire dirt track. They were moving too fast for the driver to react and he held the steering wheel tightly as the SUV blasted through with such force that the vehicle shuddered and skidded sideways when it came out the other side. A cocoa/henna-colored slurry had splashed from the channel all over the SUV, coating the windshield and momentarily blinding the driver as they lurched to a stop.

After a very brief interval of stunned silence, the man in the passenger seat began shouting in Malay at the driver, who gave as good as he got before flipping the wipers on for a couple quick swipes.

They then started off as the two Malaysians continued swiping back and forth while Nick considered feigning sickness in order to open his window for a possible jump. That such a foolish idea could seem reasonable, attested to his desperation; even if he landed *without* breaking something, there was little chance of escaping these men. They would catch him and shackle him to his seat for the rest of the drive, a far more terrifying prospect given the condition of the road and the driver's recklessness. At least with hands and legs free, he had some illusion of a fighting chance.

Outside, the rain started picking up again, falling in steadier, thicker drops that loudly splatted on the windshield. Nick felt himself winding ever tighter — no sooner would the driver accelerate on a clear patch of track when he'd have to brake quickly and crawl through a slalom of debris with the SUV hewing dangerously close to the river's churning, swirling waters. The particular spot they were now passing through had recently been logged, leaving only scattered piles of half-burnt brush and limbs on one side and the river on the other.

In the front passenger seat, the other man suddenly groaned at something up ahead. Nick leaned around the driver for a better look and immediately sucked in a breath: a steeper section of logged-over land to their left had collapsed onto the road, burying it under a huge pile of muck and rock. The sheer volume of debris was impressive, sloping steeply over the dirt track and into the river leaving no path around it.

The driver slowed the truck to a crawl and the two Malaysians conferred in hushed, urgent tones. Nick assumed they would have to stop as the landslide looked completely impassable. Nervous seconds ticked off as the SUV edged closer. Then, with no warning, the driver impulsively stomped on the accelerator.

Nick heard himself gasp and, in an instant, the truck rolled up on the pile at a forty-five degree angle, leaning toward the river on its right. Without thinking, he instinctively pulled himself to the high side of the truck behind the passenger seat, clutching the handle above the door as the truck surged and bucked across the landslide. The vehicle tilted so far over to their right that Nick was looking *down* into the river.

It happened so fast — five seconds maybe — and the truck cleared the pile, once again rolling onto level ground. The shock took another second or so to release its grip, and when it did, the driver's partner lit into him in Malay with Nick right on his heels.

"What the fuck was *that?!*" Nick demanded, chiming in from behind the man in the passenger seat. "We could've been *killed!!* Are you fucking crazy?!"

In a flash, the man in the passenger seat turned angrily to Nick.

"Mr. Hewgas!! " he snapped, glaring at him. "That's *enough!*"

The severity in the man's eyes put Nick on his heels while the truck shuddered through another huge pothole, rattling the windows in the door frames.

After a brief silence, the man spoke again.

"You think we don't know about you, Mr. Hewgas…?" he said, cryptically. "You think you're smarter than we are?" He let this sit for several seconds, dividing his gaze between the road and Nick.

"We've known about your brother for some time. How he came here… Maybe now though, he needs help. And maybe we can help him. But first, you help us."

This baffled Nick who thought he'd misheard.

"What are you talking about?" he asked, just as the driver groaned: '*Ohhh…* ' In front of them, a torrent of muddy runoff had ripped through the roadbed, tearing loose a huge corrugated pipe that had been buried under the compacted soil and rock to channel drainage. The runoff's volume overwhelmed the pipe, crumpling it like so much tin foil and eventually collapsing the entire roadbed, scouring a channel four or five meters wide. Water and muck now surged unimpeded into the river with terrifying force. Chunks of roadbed kept falling away on each side of the torrent, its depth unknowable beneath the opaque slurry. Nick instinctively clutched tighter at the strap as the SUV slowed its approach and the two Malaysians heatedly debated their options.

Back and forth they went until the driver finally leaned back in his seat, both hands gripping the wheel and, without warning, began to accelerate.

"...Jesus, no...!" Nick blurted as the truck lurched forward, quickly dropping over the shorn edge of roadbed and slamming into the washout. Immediately, the vehicle began bogging down, its rear pushed faster by the surging runoff to spin the truck around so it faced upstream. The driver frantically tried to counter-steer while flooring the accelerator until they were once again pointing forward. Now though, current began to pile up like a pillow on the vehicle's upstream side where Nick held on while the SUV's wheels spun wildly in the slurry. In the passenger seat, the other man clutched his strap and screamed at the driver whose frantic efforts could not keep the torrent from pushing them right *toward* the river.

Instinctively, Nick pressed his window switch as the pillowing water lifted his side of the truck and, in a few chaotic seconds, it was up on two wheels, then over onto the driver's side and into the river.

Water surged into the vehicle, rolling the truck onto its roof. The cabin filled with the opaque, silty water, and visibility went to zero. Nick desperately felt around for the frame of his now open window and, when his fingers found an edge, he squeezed through and kicked free, bubbles circling him as water replaced all air pockets inside the cabin.

Gasping for breath, Nick poked his head through the river's surface and flailed while the current's power swept him away from the submerged SUV. It took everything he had just to keep his head above water, each desperate gulp of air less than the one before. Spotting the river's opposite bank to his left, he desperately started kicking toward it.

43.

Seladang's boat looked to be about six meters in length, maybe two meters across. A long, fairly slim craft designed to carry people and goods up and down the Baram River, its wooden construction gave it a swift, sturdy appearance.

Carole sat near the bow while Antonio took a seat behind her to distribute the weight according to Seladang's instructions. The video equipment had been stowed in the rear of the boat and covered with a canvas tarp to protect it from the spray. Antonio sat silently beside her, wearing what Carole had taken to calling his '*Bangkok blasé*' face, an expression that usually appeared when they were in trouble.

The boatman kept them close to the shore on river left with its vantage on the dirt track and, so far, they had seen nothing. Carole scanned the riverbank hoping to see a vehicle through the thick vegetation. She quietly seethed, upbraiding herself for letting her guard down.

"Maybe we missed them…?" she suggested, turning to Antonio and Seladang, the note of trepidation in her tone lost in the engine noise. "Maybe they're already there?"

Antonio inhaled deeply, his mouth tightening as he considered this while Seladang shook his head.

"With the monsoon, the road gets very bad," the boatman explained, swiveling a hand at the wrist for emphasis.

Then, as if to confirm this, rain began to spit and the boatman quickly assembled a canvas cover using support poles that fit into slots in the gunwales and gestured for Carole to move from the bow and join Antonio under it.

A few seconds later, the rain began to fall more steadily. Huddled beneath the canvas, Carole and Antonio watched as the dirt track emerged from the forest for a stretch, only to disappear once again behind the trees. Minutes passed in fraught silence as they gazed out, the rain coming down in curtains. Carole began to say something when Seladang suddenly cut the throttle. On their left, in an area where the forest had been cut, a considerable chunk of the bank and roadbed had been mangled by surging runoff. A crumpled corrugated culvert pipe stuck out of the rubble, apparently ripped from the roadbed by a torrent of mud, rocks and logging debris. Carole glanced over at Antonio — the alarm in his face mirrored in her own.

"…Maybe they got through before it came down…" Antonio suggested, reading her thoughts.

"Maybe…" Carole agreed, looking up at the clouds. "But how would we know…? Any tracks would be washed away by now…"

Antonio considered this and the dilemma it posed as Seladang gradually maneuvered the boat closer to the washout. The three of them gazed upon the devastation in grim silence.

"We'll have to make a best guess," Antonio finally answered. "And hope we're right… Because we won't get a second take."

44.

Nick kicked and stroked with everything he had trying to keep his head above water in the roiling current. Several times, an undertow dragged him down and sapped his adrenaline-fueled energy surge. Each time, he fought his way back to the surface and got a desperate gulp of air only to be slammed into submerged rocks or logging debris. At one point, a massive standing wave pummeled him like a giant washing machine and, for a moment, the world turned into a white froth without dimension.

Somehow, despite the terror firing in every cell of his body, Nick found enough presence of mind to realize the current was pushing him *toward* the opposite bank. With an inexplicable hyper-focus, he pointed himself toward it when a foot snagged in some tree branches just beneath the surface. He instinctively reached down and frantically struggled to free himself just as a piece of his shirt got hooked on something. In an instant, the current began pushing him under and he fought to keep his head up. Flailing wildly, he managed to free the snagged foot while his shirt stretched to the point of finally ripping loose.

Both arms and legs were now like lead and a thought quickly flashed: *Is this how it ends?* Then, just as quickly, it dissolved as Nick realized the opposite bank had somehow gotten much closer. A deep unconscious will enlisted some mysterious cellular reserve and he pushed toward it. Remembering something a rafting guide had once said about keeping a forty-five-degree angle to the current if forced to swim, he did so, kicking and flailing until he felt the break of a strong eddy line around five meters from the bank. A vine dangled down over the water and he thrust an arm up, clutching the vine and hanging on for a minute or so to catch his breath.

With one more surge of effort, he let go of the vine and kicked toward the muddy bank. Clawing with his fingernails dug into mud, Nick pulled himself up and immediately fell face down on the ground, coughing water from his lungs. As the hacking subsided, he rolled onto his back, laying there as the monsoon rains continued pouring down.

The adrenaline drained away and his situation gradually began to register: dark impenetrable forest on one side, the raging flood of the Baram on the other, with only this sliver of muddy bank separating them. Rain splattered on leaves and the ground, providing a counterpoint to the river's thundering waters. A few meters into the forest, Nick glimpsed orchids and other epiphytes sprouting from tree limbs and growing in the crotches of branches, all now thoroughly drenched by the deluge.

It wasn't long before his thoughts returned to the men who'd grabbed him. Whatever their intentions may have been, the thought of them trapped in the truck as it sank into the river's opaque depths, horrified him. He could only hope they too managed to escape and survive the river's churning waters.

Shaking the thought away, he tried to focus on the reality in front of him. Obviously, he'd washed up somewhere between Long Akah and the hydro project upriver, though he had no idea which was closer. They'd traveled the dirt track for maybe a half-hour or so and had seen no other settlements, boats or vehicles. His only option now was to follow the river — either *upstream* to the hydro project, or back *downstream* to Long Akah.

Glancing at his wrist for the time, Nick realized his watch had been a casualty of the river. He looked up at the sky but the monsoon's cloud cover made it impossible to gauge how much daylight remained. The prospect of spending the night out here alone and exposed terrified him; not only were his clothes soaked, torn and filthy, he had no way to start a fire and zero food or water. Worse still, the night out here came with a full array of unseen menace: biting insects, poison plants, feral creatures, venomous reptiles.

Despair now began to overwhelm him and he told himself to stay focused, concluding his chances were likely better going *upriver.* With that, he got to his feet and started to follow the riverbank upstream toward the hydro project. Within minutes, all the anger and fear finally broke in a salty bouillon of tears and sweat. A low point came when, avoiding some roots along a narrow stretch of bank, he slipped and fell, clutching at vegetation to stop himself before almost sliding into the river again.

For several minutes, Nick lay there trembling. While rolling into a ball might've been a momentary salve, he knew it wouldn't alter the facts of his situation. And so, he pulled himself upright and pushed on, his soaked hiking shoes slip-sliding on the greasy saturated clay of the riverbank which, at times, narrowed to less than a meter in width.

After ten or so nerve-wracking minutes of this, he stopped to catch his breath and gather his wits. Up ahead was more of the same — the thundering swollen river winding around one bend after another. There could be several more miles of this and, at this rate, it looked doubtful he'd reach the hydro site before dark.

As this grim reckoning registered, Nick glimpsed a huge tree just inside the forest. Inexplicably, he moved toward it. Where it met the ground, the massive trunk spread out in large 'fans' that called to mind the flying buttresses of a Gothic cathedral or the tail fins of a rocket. An adaptation to its environment, he'd read that these fans evolved as a way for these shallow-rooted trees to gain height *with* stability in the thin clay soil. They could also serve as shelter, for the cove-like notches these fans created were large enough for a person to hide in. Nick stepped into one and ran a hand along the bark. Turning to face out, he leaned back against the trunk. Gradually, his entire body went limp and he slid down into a sitting position.

All the spent adrenaline, terror, and emotional drain, along with inadequate food and sleep, had hollowed him out. He *needed* to rest, just for a few minutes. Despite the urgency of the situation, his eyelids involuntarily closed...

Scattered flakes of snow floated in the air. A familiar place, a street... Yes... Davis Street, a three-block walk from his mother's apartment to A.W. Booth School. No wind today and, in the air, a peculiar clean smell, a tang like frozen steel in early March when spring was still a month or more away. Cutting through Johnny Santoro's back yard now, footfalls lightly crunching on the frozen grass to the compact back yard then onto the stoop of his mother's apartment, second of four attached working-class brick row houses in the style of the old Erie-Lackawanna station down the street. No need to remove sneakers at the back door since the ground was too frozen for mud. A tuna sandwich on a hard roll and a glass of chocolate milk waited in the refrigerator. At noon, the 'Hollywood Squares' came on so he could watch while eating lunch from a folding metal TV tray.

Fishing for the key and opening the door into the kitchen now, but something isn't right. A bag of groceries sits on the table, a couple items taken out as if someone became distracted. His mother's keys were there...the rubber fob with 'James V. Clune Insurance' printed on it, her purse open on the chair.

In the dining room between the kitchen and living room, a stale smell... human breath with after-notes of booze and cigarette smoke. From the living room, a gasping, snoring sound like someone with sleep apnea. And there, on the sofa, curled up asleep in her coat...his mother. Circling her, she's startled by a light gurgling rattle in her upper throat.

Don't wake her — she'd only mumble something about 'needing to rest'. Just watch her chest move with the labored breathing, then switch on the television, volume low…

45.

At the Long Miri boat landing, Ian watched as Seladang secured the lines. Carole and Antonio had already disembarked and were sharing what they'd discovered.

"…I don't get it…" Ian said, clearly troubled by their report. "You think those guys were following him — *us,* all the way up here?"

"Looks that way…" Carole answered.

"But…how does that make any sense…?" Ian continued, "I mean, why wait until we got *this* far to snatch him? If they were cops of some sort, they could've done it anytime. Back in Miri or Kuching, even. Why play it like this?"

Carole glanced at the ground, her lips curling inward as she considered the question.

"That's assuming they *were* some sort of police…" Antonio offered.

Ian frowned. "Right, but…who else would be using the dirt track?" he asked. "You said it's off-limits except for officials and construction traffic."

For several seconds, no one spoke.

"I don't know…" Carole finally answered, "Maybe the order came down late, after we'd already left."

"But they followed us, right?" Antonio again chimed in. "And *planned* it by leaving the truck at Long Akah. Then waited until Nick was alone."

This cast things in a more sinister light: if the men who took Nick *weren't* police, then who were they and what did they want?

"Well, let's not forget…" Ian reminded them, "There's a huge amount of money involved in this hydro project. It's not a stretch to imagine some high flyers on either end of the deal getting nervous over this American asking about his brother up here. They wouldn't be too keen on the possibility he might talk to the press about what's going on up here, about the shabby deal the indigenous people are getting…? Could make the big funding sources skittish."

"True…" Carole agreed. "But since when have the IMF and World Bank been swayed by public opinion…? Particularly when they stand to make *millions* on these loans. I don't see them walking away from that kind of return over a land squabble with some indigenous tribe in a place most westerners have never heard of."

"Not necessarily…" Antonio added, "Remember, they're both funded by wealthy nations, mostly the Americans, with educated citizens who get worked up over this kind of thing. They can make the kind of noise that politicians notice."

"Point taken," said Ian, "Even so…I could count on one hand the number of projects the World Bank ever pulled out of over some controversy."

Carole nodded vaguely and nibbled at her lower lip.

"Okay, so…" she began, refocusing, "Setting all that aside, there's still that huge washout we came across. We don't know if they got through before it happened…"

This framed their essential dilemma: they would have to make a calculated and consequential decision based on very limited information.

"They might've turned back," Antonio speculated, "And we could've missed them."

"It's possible," Carole concurred. "But my gut says no."

"I'd have to go with Carole on that," Ian remarked. "If I had to bet on it, I'd say they got through before that landslide happened."

As they debated their next move, the pressure squeezed Carole tighter. While she couldn't back away from this, Ian the freelancer could. If he wanted out, now was the time.

"Listen Ian, you're the freelancer here," Carole told him, "This is on the BBC and *me* specifically, so there's no hard feelings if you want to turn back."

Ian sighed. "It's not the possibility of arrest that worries me," he answered after a couple beats, "Derek can fix that… It's the remoteness that concerns me. Should concern you too. *Anything* can happen up there and who's to know? There's no civil authority, no law, and no accountability. Just soldiers. Men and boys barely out of high school with automatic weapons and jacked on power…"

"True…" she agreed. "But we do have the imprimatur of the BBC. For what it's worth."

Ian nodded vaguely, considering. "Right, well…" he muttered. "I signed on for the long haul. Just making sure we know what we're walking into."

For a brief interval, they fell silent as the mood darkened along with the afternoon sky. Seladang noted the gathering clouds and suggested they get moving. As if to emphasize the point, lightning flashed in the distance, followed by rumbling, and the three journalists arranged themselves under the boat's canopy.

Seladang untied his lines and they were off again. Visibility soon shrank to a few meters as he cautiously piloted the craft upstream. Initially, the canvas tarp offered some cover from the downpour, but sagging patches soon began pooling water that the boatman relieved by pushing up with his hands to expel.

After another ten minutes or so, the rain let up a bit and visibility improved.

"How much further do you think, Seladang?" Carole asked over the din of engine noise.

The boatman turned his hand a couple times in a 'more or less' gesture. "Ten…maybe twenty minutes…"

He kept the boat closer to the right side of the river to avoid a pile of submerged logging debris washed into the main channel. Various rapids had formed and he skillfully navigated the boat through them while the three journalists anxiously clutched at the gunwales. Having cleared the hazard, the boatman steered them back toward the main current. In an eddy to their right as they motored past, no one noticed a hand swaying lifelessly just beneath the surface. Nor did they see further down to the lifeless body the hand belonged to: a man in a polo shirt who, in his final terrified moments, had strained to reach up from the water's deadly grasp.

The terrain soon began to open up as they rounded a bend in the river, arriving at a massive area that had recently been logged.

"Here…" Seladang said, searching for a spot to land.

The whole scene offered a jarring contrast to the verdant forest they'd just passed through. On both sides of the river, the trees had been cleared as far as the eye could see with only scattered piles of brush smoldering here and there among the ruts and churned-up earth. As the boat neared the river's left bank, Carole spotted several construction trailers in the distance. Near the trailers, an armada of heavy equipment — bulldozers, graders and front loaders — stood at the ready. The entire setting had a strange 'end of the line' quality about it, a queasy sense that beyond *here,* the world was unknown and inhospitable.

Seladang nosed the boat into an eddy, cut the engine and secured the bowline to an upturned rock. Carole and Ian helped Antonio offload his gear onto the bank. Carole then shook the dampness from her hair and watched Antonio wiping water from the tripod legs.

"All the rain…?" she asked, noting his more than usual fussiness.

"Yeah…got into the locking knobs," he told her. "Makes them less grippy…"

Using the same towel, Antonio dabbed at the perspiration beading on his forehead. "I'm more concerned about the camera's electronics," he added. "With this humidity…"

Despite all the rain, the humidity hadn't eased and everything felt damp. Antonio set the tripod aside and opened the camera case while Seladang curiously peeked over his shoulder and Ian hovered.

"It's off the scale," Ian observed, wiping his forehead with a bandana, "Even for this part of the world."

Unfazed, Carole surveyed the surroundings.

"What do you think about getting some B-roll…?" she asked Antonio.

"Uh, okay…" he answered, somewhat puzzled. "But isn't Nick still the priority?"

"Of *course,* he is," she affirmed, "But we're *here* and you might as well get some B-roll while Ian and I go see what we can find out at those trailers. No point all of us going up there."

Antonio saw the sense in this and began readying the camera.

"You know, I'm still not sure…" he added after a few beats, "What if we have it wrong? About those men who took Nick?"

The comment threw Carole.

"What do you mean…?" she asked.

Antonio hedged a moment.

"You must've thought it, too…" he told her, "I mean, if you wanted to lose someone… It'd be easy out here…"

For some seconds, no one spoke.

"Well, let's not get ahead of ourselves," Carole finally said. "Let's say we meet back here in an hour?" With that, she turned to Ian and they started toward the construction trailers.

46.

Shadows along the riverbank signaled evening's approach and life began to stir in the heavily shadowed forest as unseen birds called out and the occasional monkey leapt between branches. The river's swirling waters and insistent rhythm began to rouse Nick who had dozed off in the 'vee' of the tree trunk. Slowly, his eyes blinked open and his mind registered the reality. For a brief moment, he despaired it hadn't been a dream.

The facts were not on his side; night would fall quickly and he had no idea how much further to the hydro site. With the night he could expect an abundance of biological menace, from mosquitoes with their litany of parasites, to venomous snakes homing in on body heat, along with whatever other stinging, biting arthropods were out there.

He told himself this couldn't be happening, that only a few weeks earlier he'd been having dinner with Celeste at a Thai restaurant in Los Angeles. The despair wasn't helped by his tattered and filthy condition. *Keep it together*, he thought, just keep it *together*... Carole and the others *had* to be looking for him. Sitting up, he noticed a dribble of dried blood near the bottom of a pant leg and leaned in for a closer look. Reaching down, he slowly pulled the pant leg up and an involuntary gasp squeaked from his throat — several small worm-like creatures were attached to his skin trailing dribbles of blood: *Leeches*...

Moaning in revulsion, Nick tried to pick them off. One in particular looked especially horrific, as long as his thumb and engorged with *his* blood. He kept at it, pulling the creatures one-by-one from his shin and calf with sticky red fingers and flinging them, each time wiping the bloody, mucous-like slime on his grubby pants.

He gagged several times, before shoes, socks and pants came off and he immersed his lower legs in the river. Picking off the last of the leeches, he rinsed his legs with river water the color of creamed coffee. Disgusted, wincing, and trembling, he fought back tears and cursed the universe. Leeches were *everywhere* out here, hiding in leaves and clinging to vegetation.

Gazing out at the swollen river, Nick tried to steady himself. Where would the others even begin to look for him out here? Steadily, reality narrowed to a single inescapable conclusion: he'd have to spend the night out here. *Alone*...

As this realization set in, he clutched his head with both hands, telling himself to stay rational. The river was right there and a boat *had* to appear at some point tomorrow. For tonight though, he'd have to get by out here on his own, doing something, *anything*, to make the situation bearable. As his heart sank at the thought, he tried to steel himself, remembering what a Little League baseball coach once told him after he'd been called out on strikes: better to go down swinging than looking.

47.

Antonio looked through the viewfinder as he panned the video camera across the logged-over land. Shooting this 'B-roll' footage gave him more say over a project's visual feel, as an editor would use it for cutaways, so he took care panning the tripod. Seladang stood close-by, having surprised them with his insistence on providing return transport to Long Akah and, noting the boatman's interest in the camera, Antonio had enlisted his help carrying the tripod. While he appreciated the extra set of hands, Antonio felt uneasy about pulling Seladang into all this. In his experience, the remoteness of such places is what made them especially dangerous, far more so than insurgencies or active combat zones. Out here, you were a long way from civil society and its mitigations — medical care, communication, the law. As if Nick's abduction hadn't been enough, they were now putting another 'civilian' in the cross-hairs.

He'd become acquainted with journalism's occupational hazards early on. Over the years, he and Carole had been detained, deported, shot at a couple times, and once, he'd even gotten a minor beating from police in China. Carole's poise and command of the facts generally helped them through such scrapes, and working for the BBC didn't hurt; the sun may have finally set on the overseas British Empire but it had yet to go down on the BBC. Despite CNN's gains in television news, and Rupert Murdoch's *Sky TV's* international presence, the BBC still ruled the global market in English language broadcasting.

And yet, Antonio understood that the imprimatur of the BBC offered little protection to the locals who'd worked with them once the BBC's crew left the country. These facilitators were largely forgotten and often faced repercussions after the fact.

Satisfied with the B-roll footage, Antonio disconnected the camera from the tripod, set it down and retracted the tripod's legs before handing it to Seladang. They then started back toward the boat and hadn't gotten far when both men picked-up the distant thwack-thwack-thwacking of helicopter blades. Stopping in their tracks, they anxiously watched the sky as what looked to be a huge green military helicopter emerged from the cloud cover.

Antonio instinctively readied his camera as the helicopter circled then slowed to hover above a patch of open ground before starting to descend, sending standing puddles of brownish water spraying upward as Antonio framed a long-shot and rolled tape. Through his zoom lens, he could see the saturated soil rippling from the force of the rotor blades. No sooner had the chopper landed when a rear hatch opened and a ramp came down, quickly followed by a squad of soldiers in combat gear.

A knot tightened in the cameraman's stomach as he continued taping.

At the construction site, Carole and Ian paused at the sound of a large diesel loader being fired up nearby, its exhaust spewing clouds of oily blue-black smoke. They agreed this was as good a place as any to split up, with Ian going ahead to look for the airstrip while Carole went on to the construction trailers. There was no discussion of what to do should either encounter Nick and his abductors — things would be improvised from here on.

As she drew near the trailers, Carole noticed a couple men loading gasoline cans onto the back of a truck and approached them.

"*Office…?*" she asked, hoping the English word might register. The men's faces were dark and weathered from a life spent outside. Obviously some version of Dayak, one had a cigarette dangling from his lips despite all the gasoline cans.

"*Office…?*" she repeated, adding, "*…Bosses?*" with a deferential smile.

The two workers stared at the strange white woman who'd appeared out of nowhere. The man with the cigarette muttered something in his native tongue and swung an arm toward the trailers. There were three of them and one in particular, a 'double-wide', as an American colleague called them, looked to be the apparent nucleus of the operation with its various antennae poking out from the roof. Carole cautiously approached a side door near the back where a diesel generator hummed nearby. Peering through the door's thin window, she glimpsed several cots and a row of lockers. Further in, a couple of rectangular fold-up tables had been brought together and cluttered with rolled-out plans and blueprints currently being examined by several men who were likely project engineers and/or managers.

As she opened the door and gingerly stepped inside, a wave of super-cooled air engulfed her. The dampness in her clothes suddenly felt heavy and cold against her skin. Around the table, the men looked up in astonishment.

"*…Hello…*" she said graciously, "*…Do any of you speak English…?*"

For a good twenty seconds, they stared at the white woman with reddish-blond hair standing before them.

"Yes… I speak some English," the tallest of them finally said. He looked to be of Indian descent while the other two were likely bumiputra Malaysian.

"Wonderful…" Carole answered, "Thank you…" She reflexively clutched her arms in the excessive air-conditioning.

"…My friend and I…" she continued, "…we were caught in the storm out on the river…"

The tall man said something to the others in Malay and one of them quickly disappeared into a back room. Seconds later, he returned with a blanket for Carole.

"Oh how kind, thank you…!" she preened graciously, while wrapping the blanket around her; no harm playing the more delicate sex in such moments.

"Are you lost…?" the tall man asked.

"Um…not entirely," she said, choosing her words carefully. "We're with a guide who has a boat…"

This puzzled the man further. "But…this is a construction area…?"

"Yes, of course, only that wasn't what brought us here," she explained, forcing a smile.

The tall man tried to read her facial cues while his colleagues, excluded from the conversation, watched intently. Carole then went on to explain that they were looking for a friend who had been taken by some men in a black vehicle said to be coming this way. At this, the man's brow furrowed and he glanced over at his colleagues.

"Who are these men?" he asked, "Only people with authorization can be up here."

With authorization, indeed, Carole thought. She then provided a brief summary of the brother's story, hoping the honesty might elicit some sympathy. The tall man stared thoughtfully as she finished.

"There's been no man brought here," he then explained, glancing again at the others as if to confirm. "We received a radio call that a plane was coming from Kuala Lumpur this afternoon, but nothing more…"

This threw Carole. "How long ago was that?" she asked, and the man shrugged, guessing maybe an hour or two.

"Could they have gone to some other place…?" she continued.

"There is nothing else out here," he told her, "Only that dirt track… It's possible the rains slowed them down, or…sometimes, a landslide blocks the road. During the monsoon season."

"I see… And no one radioed in anything like that?"

The man shook his head. "Nothing," he said, adding, "All vehicles on that road must have two-way radio to contact us if they see a problem."

This little wrinkle put Carole back on her heels: If the vehicle had two-way radio and had run into a problem, why hadn't they used it? Various scenarios quickly flashed through her mind, all horrifying, and she felt her stomach tighten.

When Antonio and Seladang arrived back at the boat, Carole was sitting under the canvas tarp making notes. She looked up as they approached and Antonio immediately read the distress in her eyes.

"Where's Ian...?" he asked.

"Looking for the landing strip..."

Carole then shared what she'd learned at the trailers.

"...*Phew*..." he muttered, when she finished. "So, the plane never showed...? And those guys in the trailer knew nothing more about it?"

Carole sighed. "Nothing..." she answered. "They *did* tell me there are constant problems with that dirt track. Like that washout we came across... Happens all the time, apparently." She then bit her lower lip in thought. "But anything like that...they would've radioed it in."

Antonio's eyes narrowed. "Unless they lost the ability to make radio contact. Or, if they never intended to in the first place..."

Both scenarios had crossed Carole's mind. She had yet to encounter a situation where shortwave radios just stopped working without something catastrophic happening. That they had seen no vehicles, disabled or otherwise, along the way, apparently eliminated this possibility. The second scenario came with far more sinister implications and she had avoided considering it — until now.

"What are you saying...?" she asked, "That this may have been some kind of off-the-books operation?"

Antonio absently rubbed at the back of his head.

"It's possible..." he surmised. "No radio contact, no records... A perfect setup for plausible deniability."

If this actually proved to be the case, thought Carole, then they were, without a doubt, in over their heads.

"Okay..." she began, after a moment. "But then...if that's what we're looking at, where are they? That dirt track only goes up and back. They were headed here and never showed up? They didn't go back to Long Akah, so... what happened?"

Here was the essence of the dilemma, and it had potentially dire implications for Nick.

"Right…" Carole finally resolved, "We need to go back… Somewhere between here and Long Akah, something must've happened."

The subdued anguish in her eyes was unmistakable as Antonio waited for more.

"We have to try *something*," she insisted. "One of us should wait here for Ian and the possibility those men with Nick might still show up. You and Seladang go back, look up and down both sides of the river, especially downstream from that washout, and I'll go back to the construction trailers."

"Hold on," Antonio objected. "I'm not about to leave you here by yourself!"

Carole waved him off. "No, you're better with Seladang and the boat, and you've got better eyes. Besides, I've already met the men in the trailer. I'll be fine."

Antonio hesitated, not at all comfortable with this. He also knew the pointlessness of arguing with her. Ultimately, he capitulated, agreeing to meet her back here in an hour. As he prepared to leave with Seladang, Carole resisted an impulse to tell him how sick she felt over all this, that she now wished she'd said 'no' when Derek first approached her about the story. Such confessional urges, however, usually went nowhere. Early in her career, she'd cultivated a prodigious ability to tamp down anything that could be seen by her male colleagues as weakness. In their eyes, any sign of emotional ambivalence simply confirmed that women were inherently incapable of handling the thorny ethical conundrums journalists routinely faced. Time had hardened this reflex in Carole, despite its corrosive effects on other aspects of her life.

48.

Nick's eyes had taken on a distant glassy sheen as he navigated the riverbank. On the opposite side of the swollen river, the dirt track had vanished behind a screen of dense, uncut forest.

Every step felt labored now and an unnerving sense of a some other vague presence hinted on the air, almost as if he were being stalked. It may have been his state of mind, which was anything but sound given his overwhelming fatigue. Still, the feeling persisted, resisting all attempts to brush it away.

Then, from inside the forest, a branch snapped and Nick instantly turned and squinted into its murky depths. His fingers reflexively curled, balling into fists as he strained to subdue his anxious breathing. The fight or flight instinct that had earlier failed him was now on high-alert, and he scanned the riverbank for anything that could be used as a weapon. Every creature in the forest probably sensed his heart pounding and smelled his fear. '*Make yourself more intimidating, more fearsome,*' he thought, remembering something he'd read while hiking in the Santa Monica mountains: if you should encounter a cougar or bear, stand your ground and try to appear *bigger*…

Trying not to make a sound, he watched for any sign of movement. Whatever was out there, it felt closer now…hovering, waiting, patient; a presence so completely in its element, it was as if the entire forest were a single mind that had decided he didn't belong there.

Taking slow, deliberate steps, Nick continued. On his left, the river rumbled with the distinct gurgling sound of voluminous water moving fast, a sound that reminded him of the Susquehanna River before it swamped Wilkes-Barre during the 1972 flood when he was just a kid. To his right, the brooding forest waited, seemingly charged with sinister purpose. '*Get a grip…*' he told himself, trying to stay rational. Then, from within the forest's depths, a twig snapped and he froze.

"*Who's there??*" Nick shouted, "*I can hear you…*" His hands trembled from fear and physical depletion as he desperately scanned the forest.

"*I know you're there… What do you want?? Show yourself…*"

Suddenly, a thin whooshing sound sliced the air and Nick felt a sharp sting in his back. With a reflexive yelp, he grabbed at the spot and felt something there, stuck in his flesh. He frantically pawed at it.

"*Shit!!*" he blurted, finally yanking it out. In his hand he held what looked to be a thin, sharpened twig with some tiny feather fluting on one end, like an arrow… "*What the hell…??*"

As he examined the object, an odd physical sensation began to wash over him. His limbs tingled and suddenly felt leaden. He gazed at his hand and it seemed to belong to someone else. A lag in the circuitry between brain and muscles gave him the shambling movement of a sloppily controlled marionette. Within seconds, his motor control had been become more like that of a clumsy toddler.

Focusing his will on a tree within reach, Nick strained to extend an arm but could barely lift it. Slowly, he began crumpling to his knees, moaning low like an inchoate drunk about to nod off. He then fell onto his side, eyes wide with incomprehension as he realized he had the ambulatory capability of a helpless mollusk hoping for the tide. Several indistinct figures soon began to hover around the hole he now sank ever deeper in. The paltry daylight darkened to a gauzy deep gray, as if ever denser veils were being layered over his eyes. He tried to scream out but his tongue and lips were numb and unresponsive. A barely audible '*Wait...!*' gurgled in his throat just as the world went black.

PART III

49.

The sky was January blue, a brilliant diamond-sharp hue familiar to those in the northeastern part of the US in early winter when the sun barely climbed above the southern horizon. Such skies often appeared the first couple of weeks of the new year, resulting from what weather reports referred to as, Canadian high-pressure systems. These *'Canadian Highs'* would stall over the Great Lakes and Northeast in a trough of crystalline clarity that brought frigid temperatures and intensely blue skies and, for a few brief hours each day, from late morning until mid-afternoon, the new year seemed bright and flush with promise. The auspicious timing of these dazzling azure skies helped offset the post-holiday season gloom of early January when curbsides were lined with tossed-out Christmas trees.

There were few sadder sights than those spent firs and spruces laying in the gutter. Only a week or so before, these trees inspired abundant joy and hope; now their brittle skeletons sat forlorn and spindly atop patches of dirty snow and frozen grass, needles mostly shed with a few stray mylar icicles still clinging here and there. Wilkes-Barre had a two- to three-week window in early January when the city collected these trees so, every year around that time, gutters all over town were lined with scraggly dead conifers, pointed reminders of life's essential transience.

Behind a row of attached brick homes, near the rear fence of its compact yard, a child swings back and forth on a badly weathered swing-set. Its painted surfaces, long since oxidized into coarse, brick-red tones, now looked incandescent in the warm light of the low winter sun. Bundled up against the biting cold, the child flies higher with each kick, the rusty chains keeping time with their loud squeaking.

Nick *knows* this child…

Suddenly, there's a thin metallic *smack,* cold sheet-aluminum against stone as a storm door is violently thrust open, its dangling chain clattering from a broken pneumatic damper. The child looks up from the rusty swing set toward a rear brick stoop and an open doorway into a darkened entrance where a woman will appear… Angry, she's shouting at someone… *'Don't you turn away when I'm talking to you!!'*

Nick *knows* this voice, too. His *mother's* voice. And he knows what will happen next. She grips his brother's shirt as he tries to yank free from her, bringing them both closer to the concrete steps leading down from the stoop. In a blurry instant, the two bodies spin with one crashing head-first onto those steps…

The child's swing slows to a halt. Voices shout, *'Call an ambulance!'* and *'Someone call the cops!'*. Windows fly open and people emerge onto other stoops. Nick watches the child rise from the swing's seat, just as *he* himself had done that January day. And just as he had also done that day, his brother rushes down the steps past his mother's crumpled body to intercept the child as another man (…her boyfriend, *Strycker*…?) splays out on the steps beside the lifeless body, sobbing in anguish and cradling its bloody head.

Sirens wail, accompanied by urgent-sounding voices. Ambulance attendants quickly wheel a gurney into the scene, police shoo people away, the air crackles with two-way radio chatter. Evan wraps his arms around the child who strains to watch as a sheet is pulled over their mother's head.

Then…a sterile room with long rectangular fluorescent light fixtures hanging down from a high ceiling…a man in a nylon wind-breaker asking questions: *'Are you okay' 'Do you need anything?'* of two boys. Evan and… *him*…? Both boys shake their heads, *'No'*…

Another man appears, their *father*, younger now, and sits across the table from the boys with his wife Sylvia at his side. Behind them, vending machines and more tables… Smells of aging plastered walls, old burnt coffee, stale cigarettes stubbed out in Bakelite ashtrays… Oversized institutional windows are spaced evenly along one wall, shades still up. Outside, the January daylight has edged toward evening. A voice says something about Strycker pulling their mother away from Evan, that she *lost her footing*. But that's not what he remembers…

Different, fainter sounds intrude at the edges now, logy and distant, as if emerging from the viscid mire of an opiate dream. Soon, the sounds distill into…*voices*… Hushed, liquid, on the edge of emptiness… Then, other sensations — smells, air moving over skin, the dryness of a throat — an ongoing aggregation of senses gradually merging into an *'I'*…

Like someone coming to after a surgical procedure, the basic facts began to line up for Nick, now on his back in…a confined space, dark and indistinct, with a few thin shafts of anemic daylight cutting through a smoky bluish haze. *'What's all this…?'* he wondered as fragments of memory returned: the river, forest, walking, and then…*what*…? Somewhere in the surrounding darkness, he could hear voices softly murmuring.

A dull ache radiated in waves from the center of his skull. Grimacing, Nick tried lifting himself up on his elbows only to go back down. In the air, he could sense tiny perturbations, like the breath of another person observing him. As he attempted to lift just his head, a voice began uttering strange, unrecognizable words full of glottal contortions and complex tongue-and-tooth sounds. The high-throated raspy voice belonged to an older woman who, at that moment, leaned over him, her form barely discernible in the darkness. Lifting his head with one hand, she raised a cup to his lips with the other. Cool water ran over his thick tongue and down his parched, constricted throat. When finished, the woman gently let his head down to fill the cup again.

His eyes began to adjust as the woman returned and again lifted his head for another sip of water. In the faintly glowing coals of a small cooking fire, he could just make out the contours of her face: prominent cheekbones, withered skin retreating with age; weary, rheumy eyes and pewter-gray shoulder-length hair pulled back tightly.

When she let Nick's head down again, he glimpsed her earlobes, each stretched into two noodle-like strands like tiny jump-ropes of flesh. He then tried to prop himself up again, only to be scolded with another barrage of unintelligible words until he went back down.

Satisfied he'd gotten the message, the woman disappeared through some sort of flap where, for a brief second or two, anemic light spilled in on the surroundings, revealing palm thatch walls of bamboo framing and floors of lashed bamboo lengths covered with thatch mats.

Outside, muffled voices made unfamiliar sounds. Nick began to recall the 'stinging' sensation just before the world went black. Had *this woman* brought him here, wherever and whatever this was? As the pieces started lining up, the flap again flew open, briefly casting the space in dingy daylight. Nick swiveled his head to glimpse someone entering before the flap came down.

"*...Hello...?*" he squeaked into the returned darkness. "*Hello...?*"

The new visitor silently blended into the shadows.

"*...Who's there...?*" Nick called out, "*Where'd you go...?*"

He was about to call out again when a voice spoke to him in English: "*Are you feeling better?*"

It was the voice of a young boy and Nick pulled himself up on his elbows.

"You speak *English?*" he said, part-question, part-statement, as the boy leaned in closer.

In the meager glow from the coals, Nick noted the boy's 'bowl-style' haircut, similar to that of the children on the express boat. What he could make out of the face had a sad, big-eyed quality that suggested a tough existence.

"Yes…" the boy answered. Then after a couple beats, he warily asked a question:

"What were you doing out there in the forest…?"

Nick didn't miss the slight challenge in the boy's tone.

"…I got lost…" he heard himself say, hoping it seemed self-evident.

The boy didn't immediately respond and it occurred to Nick that the kid might never have seen a white person before.

"Do you think I could get some more water, please…?" he then asked, his voice still brittle.

Silently, the boy filled the cup again. As he brought it to Nick's lips, the flap flipped open and the older woman entered with a bowl of something. The boy slid over for her and she looked at Nick and pantomimed eating with her fingers. He understood as she helped him slide back and upright against the thatch wall. Using fingers as instructed, he gathered a dollop of the doughy mixture in the bowl and tasted it; bland and starchy, the paste-like consistency reminded him of cold mashed potatoes.

When he finished, the woman took the empty bowl and muttered something in her native tongue before exiting through the flap.

"Thank you for that…" Nick said to the boy. *"What was it?"*

Slightly puzzled by the question, the boy hesitated.

"That was sago," he replied.

"Say-go?" Nick repeated, the word starchy like the gruel it described.

"Yes," the boy affirmed, "From inside the tree…?"

Nick shook his head, having no idea what he meant.

"Where do you come from?" the boy then cautiously asked.

"I come from California," Nick answered, "In America…?" He thought he saw a momentary flicker in the boy's eyes.

"Yes…I know of California," the boy told him, then hesitated, trying to stay focused.

"What is your name…?" he asked.

"Nick. My name is Nick. And you? What's your name?"

At this, the boy looked down self-consciously. "I am *Phillip…*" he said, suddenly shy.

"*Phillip?* That's a great name," Nick assured him. "I like it." His voice was returning.

"Other people..." the boy continued, "Like that woman... They call me *Andak*."

"Ah... An-*dak*..." Nick repeated, phonetically. "Well... that's a nice name, too. Which one do *you* prefer?"

In the murky darkness, Phillip fidgeted with a toe, considering the question. "...My father calls me Phillip..." he explained, "My mother...she calls me Andak... But I like *Phillip*."

"Phillip it is, then," Nick smiled agreeably. "You speak English very well," he continued. "Where did you learn it?"

The compliment brought a smile to the boy's face as he continued fussing at a toe in the un-self-conscious way of children. "I learned it here..." he replied at last.

"I see..." Nick said. "And where is '*here*'...? What do you call this place?"

Phillip stopped his toe-fussing and looked up.

"This is the upper *Baram River*," he replied, surprised that Nick didn't already know this.

Nick nodded, understanding this was as specific as it would get.

"And how old are you, Phillip?" he then asked.

"Me, I am eight-years-old," the boy answered, clearly pleased with the fact.

"Well, that's a great age," Nick assured him. "Everything's still ahead of you."

The last bit didn't quite register with Phillip who squinted.

"Ahead...*?*" Phillip echoed, slightly confused.

Nick smiled. "What I mean is..." he explained, "You have a lot of wonderful things to look forward to. So many new experiences on the way."

The boy twisted his mouth, not sure what to make of this.

"Like what...?" he asked.

"Oh, you know..." Nick fumbled, wondering why he'd strayed into this topic. "Stuff like falling in love...new people you haven't met yet, places you haven't seen..."

This clarified nothing and he sensed the boy's eight-year-old mind yearning for more.

"How did you come here?" Phillip eventually asked, trying to re-focus on the task he'd apparently been given.

"Ah well…" Nick began, "I was in a truck with some men out on that dirt road…on the other side of the river…?" He wasn't sure the boy knew what trucks were or anything pertaining to the hydro project.

"And all the monsoon rain caused a mudslide that swept the truck into the river…" He paused. "…I don't know what happened to the other men…"

Nick thought he detected a subtle change in the boy's demeanor, like he might have imagined himself being swept along in a rain-swollen river.

"Where were you and those men going…?" Phillip then pointedly asked.

"Well, the truth is," Nick answered, tentatively. "I'm not sure *where* they were taking me. They said they were police…" He paused, wondering if people living out here understood what police were.

"…Could I have some more water?" he asked, hoping to change the subject.

Phillip dipped the cup in the water bowl and held it for Nick to drink.

"And your people?" Nick probed, as he sipped, "…What do they call themselves?"

"My people…?" Phillip repeated. "We are *Penan,*" he answered, as if this were plainly self-evident.

Nick leaned forward.

"*Penan…?*" he echoed back, stunned. "You're *Penan…?*" His reaction further baffled Phillip who set the cup down.

"…Unbelievable…" Nick muttered, "…I was traveling on an express boat with a news crew from the BBC. Before those men took me…" He stopped himself. "The BBC people wanted to do a story on the Penan… For television, you know?"

The reference likely meant nothing to the boy, Nick realized.

"You've heard of television…?" he asked.

"I think so," Phillip answered, tentatively. "My father knows about it…"

This made Nick grin — at that age, a boy's father seemed like an oracle, a font of knowledge concerning the world and its ways, spinning gnomic observations that could bedazzle a hungry young mind.

"Anyway…" he continued, feeling foolish. "…It's not important."

Just then, someone spoke outside and the boy reacted.

"I have to go now," he hurriedly explained, betraying a hint of disappointment.

"Okay…sure…" Nick said, trying to sit up but still weak. "…Ahh…" he grumbled, as his head fell back.

The boy began to rise and he looked sympathetically at Nick. "Don't worry…" he said, "The poison will be gone soon."

"*Poison??*" Nick blurted, startled. "*What* poison??"

Phillip smiled; it was *his* turn to own the knowledge.

"The poison from the dart…" he answered, matter-of-factly. "But it's okay… It's not enough to kill a monkey or a man…"

"*A dart…??*" Nick asked, taken aback. "…You mean, like for *hunting*? With a blowpipe or…?"

The boy nodded, his expression seeming to say, '*Isn't that obvious?*'

Nick stammered in confusion. "What *the…? Really…??* I was *darted??*"

This amused Phillip and Nick suddenly understood why everything felt so sluggish. '*That thing in my back,*' he realized.

"You rest now…" Phillip said, reaching for the flap. "I'll come back soon…"

A momentary flush of outrage roiled Nick; he clenched his jaw and exhaled deeply through his nose. Then, he reminded himself what was happening up here; these people had *every* reason to mistrust foreigners wandering around the forest. '*…I'd have darted me, too…*' he thought.

The boy pushed the flap open as Nick called out.

"Hey, tell me…" he asked, "You said you learned to speak English *here*… Was that in some kind of school…?"

Phillip paused, then shook his head. "No…" he answered, "My father taught me…" With that, he exited and the flap fall shut.

50.

From the riverbank, Carole watched as Seladang pointed the boat downstream and skillfully used the current to drift into faster water at the center of the river. She fixed her gaze on Antonio, who anxiously gripped a gunwale with one hand while the boatman squared them into the main current and throttled the engine until they disappeared from view.

What Carole hadn't told Antonio, what she would likely *never* tell him, was how all this had shaken her to the core. She'd let her guard down, underestimated the scope of whatever shadowy interests were at work here. The men who had taken Nick were merely the visible tip of an unseen iceberg.

Whatever this was about, she had walked them right into it, putting the entire project in jeopardy and all of them quite likely in serious danger.

Angry with herself, Carole started for the construction office. Hopefully, Ian would be back by now, bringing her record down to only *one* lost person so far. At the trailer's side door she once again knocked then entered. Inside, the men looked up from what they were doing as she approached, apologizing for bothering them again. She asked if they minded her waiting there while her friends went back downriver to look for any sign of their companion. The man who spoke English nodded and, after some hesitation, gestured toward the long table strewn with maps.

"Please..." he said, politely, though with little enthusiasm. "...Sit *here*..."

Thanking him, she took a spot at the table that afforded a view out a window onto the construction site. Warming slightly, the lead man asked if she'd like some tea.

"How kind of you!" Carole answered, hoping a sunnier disposition might ease the edginess in her hosts.

Out on the swollen river, the racing current swept Seladang's boat back downstream. Antonio kept his eyes on the dirt road whenever it emerged from behind the trees, hoping for some sign of the truck or its occupants. Feeling a need to do *something* more to steady his mind, he decided to shoot some hand-held B-roll.

Mounting the camera on his shoulder, he panned around, slowly swiveling in his seat. He readied for another pass when Seladang suddenly throttled in reverse to slow them. Unprepared for the change of momentum, Antonio grabbed at the bench seat to steady himself.

"What's going on...?" he asked, noting the boatman's grim expression as he fixed on something near the right bank.

Smoothly turning the boat upstream, Seladang then throttled forward just enough to keep their place in the river. Working the tiller and throttle together, he edged them closer to an area a few meters upstream and to their left now. Antonio tried to get a fix on whatever had caught the boatman's attention as they nudged closer to a huge tangle of fallen trees with their limbs stuck on submerged boulders. Seladang eased up on the throttle and skillfully placed them in an eddy.

The portion of the mess poking up through the river's surface suggested a much larger one hidden beneath its opaque waters. As the two men gazed upon the pile, Antonio thought he glimpsed something reflective as Seladang pointed to a particular spot in the snarl of submerged timber. There, poking up through a tangle of branches, the crumpled and scraped rear end of an SUV bobbed with the surging current.

Out of habit, Antonio put the camera on his shoulder and began recording. As he zoomed in for a tighter shot, part of a man's face gradually appeared inside the flooded compartment and bumped against the rear window. The lifeless eyes eerily seemed to stare accusingly, the face frozen in a rictus of unimaginable horror that must have marked his final moments pinned against the locked rear door.

Antonio had seen death in his viewfinder before, but something in the expression on the man's face proved especially haunting. It could've been the open eyes, bulging and distorted, veins burst from the pressure as the man's lungs filled with water. Or that he had held his breath until the very last second, knowing full well this was how he would die. A shudder jolted through Antonio as he ran tape for a minute or two, then removed his eye from the viewfinder and gently let the camera down…

51.

No one returned through the flap for some time and Nick eventually dozed off again. Then, as his eyelids twitched open, he realized he'd been out and a sudden pang of dread nipped at him — how long had it *been?* There was a nagging sense of having missed something, like taking a nap in the afternoon and waking up to find it's dark outside. He lifted his head and glanced around, but nothing had changed.

Flexing his fingers, he then tried to stretch his arms and noted the returning motor control. Sitting upright against the wall, it had somehow previously escaped Nick's notice that he'd been adorned in a pair of gym shorts a couple sizes too small and too tight. A flush of embarrassment came over him and he cringed, realizing the Penan had undressed his darted carcass.

With some effort, Nick tried sliding himself over to the water bowl near the tiny, barely smoldering cooking fire. He filled the cup and drank several times while watching the flap over the opening. At last, he slid over and lifted the flap, wincing at the daylight like some mole peeking out from its subterranean lair. Several rungs of bamboo step-ladder led down to the ground. Squinting and sticking his head out further, he saw maybe a dozen similar structures laid out in a semi-circular pattern around a central area where several small fires burned. Here and there, women engaged in various workaday activities: some pounded at piles of what looked to be pith (perhaps the sago starch?), while others wove mats and stripped fibers from bark and palm leaves. Small children darted about giggling and playing as a few scruffy dogs sniffed around or snoozed. Nick felt like he had wandered into a National Geographic pictorial.

Beyond the huts, the surrounding forest rolled away, its interior a realm of perpetual twilight. Nick stretched a leg out onto the several bamboo steps and was startled by his own filth, now visible in the daylight. Welts and scabs from leech and insect bites peppered his lower legs, while his feet still had a crust of grayish silt and dried mud caked between the toes. He unconsciously ran a hand along a cheek with several day's scruffy beard stubble and imagined how appalling he must have looked. His hair felt crusty and matted with an earthy mix of sebaceous oils, river silt and grime. Glancing down at his groin and the too-small gym shorts, he took some solace that neither bowels nor bladder had added to the embarrassment.

At the bottom of the bamboo steps he spotted his hiking shoes, apparently left there to dry. At least he could have *one* item of his own clothing, he thought, putting them on. Slowly, he then got to his feet, steadying himself on the hut. Standing there, he now saw that the gym shorts barely covered his crotch, while also emphasizing the pasty, scratched-up white flesh of his legs and ankles. *Quite the fashion statement...* he thought.

Feeling steady enough, Nick began to walk. Nearby, several young children tossing sticks and gobs of muck into a puddle, immediately froze as they saw him approach. They stared in amused astonishment and he felt even *more* self-conscious; the over-tight gym shorts had the effect of *exaggerating* his anatomy with what his college pals used to call the 'disco bulge.' Like some creepy middle-aged weeny-wagger, here he was, a grown man, virtually naked among small children. A discrete brush with his hand confirmed nothing 'hanging' out down there.

Smiling sheepishly, he moved on to a spot where some older Penan women were working away at what he assumed to be the sago starch he'd had. The women spread out on a large rattan mat near several piles of mounded pulp. A few of them tore and shredded the pith with what looked like small machetes, while the rest pounded and pulverized it with various implements.

As Nick drew near, several of them looked up and momentarily ceased their labors. All wore their graying hair pulled tightly back and sported the now familiar stretched earlobes. Hoping to spare himself close-up humiliation, he kept a respectful distance and smiled apologetically. The women stared for half a minute or so then went back to pounding and shredding, as if tall, unkempt, pale-skinned white men wearing only children's gym shorts and hiking shoes were a regular feature here.

"Excuse me…" he muttered awkwardly, "*Phillip…?*" He hoped they might recognize the boy's English name.

The older of the women swung an arm in the direction Nick had been walking and spoke in her native tongue. He smiled politely, gesturing with a palms-up shrug that he didn't understand. The woman tried again, speaking slower and louder this time, still waving her arm in the same direction. The absurdity of the situation reminded Nick of the white Angelenos he'd occasionally see speaking loudly in English to the Hispanic gardener or housekeeper, as if volume were the only obstacle to communication.

By now, more children had taken an interest and were shadowing him. Again, Nick self-consciously fussed at the too-small gym shorts. The whole scene could hardly have been more ludicrous, so he simply smiled and said '*Hello.*' Several of the children giggled while others stared dumbfounded, as if a dog had just spoken. One of the youngest boys, naked as the rest and with filthy fingers in his mouth, was so transfixed he began peeing on the ground in front of him.

"…Does anyone know *Phillip…?*" Nick asked, to a chorus of giggles. "*Phillip…?*" he repeated, slower this time. This resulted in more giggling and screechy kid gibberish. He then tried the boy's *Penan* name.

"*Andak?*" he said to peals of squealing laughter. "An-*Dak?*" he said again, drawing it out to more snorts and giggles. *This is going well…* he thought, smiling at the absurdity of the situation.

While the elderly women continued working away at the sago, the children hovered, anticipating the next antic gag from this strange visitor. There was a dreamy, somewhat surreal quality to everything — probably part of the poison dart hangover, Nick surmised. He felt a bit like an anthropologist who'd just made contact with an undiscovered people. Between his weakened state and the unexpected exhilaration of realizing where he was, Nick had forgotten the bigger picture: Were *these* the same Penan with the man in the newspaper photo? What if they *weren't?* And what about Carole and the others? If they came upon the wreckage of the SUV, would they assume the worst? Then, there were the men who'd grabbed him; if they'd survived, would they come for him? If they hadn't, would others follow? It all made his head spin.

Waving 'goodbye' to the children, Nick started off in the direction the woman had pointed out, but soon succumbed to fatigue. Bending over with hands on knees, he caught his breath, then sensed a subtle change in the air pressure, as if something with *mass* had displaced many molecules of humid air. Turning around, he immediately sucked in a gasp: several Penan men stood there staring at him.

Nick's pulse raced in his ear as he met their gaze. One of the men in particular had an air of authority about him, a bearing that said, '*leader among equals*.' The man had a lean, sinewy frame, his bare feet and thick meaty toes were splayed from years in the forest. Randomly woven into strands of grayish hair were various arrangements of small bones, feathers and beads.

A couple of the men wore shorts, while others had a kind of loincloth wrapped around their waists then threaded between their legs and back around like a codpiece. Each sported twined fiber bracelets on their wrists and just below their knees, which Nick took to be both ornamental and practical. All wore their hair in the bowl haircut style with the younger men growing out the back in a kind of Penan '*mullet*'. To a man, they proudly displayed machete-like implements on their waists while a couple shouldered long blowpipes.

In what he hoped would be seen as a universal gesture, Nick bent his head in a slight, deferential bow. He then scanned their faces hoping for a reaction but saw no change. The 'leader' shifted his weight, trying to read Nick. As they stared silently, Nick recalled the boy saying he'd learned English from his father, possibly one of these men.

"Hello…" he said, with an awkward frozen smile.

Their general fitness stood in sharp contrast with his own soft fleshiness. The sheer physicality of life as *they* experienced it belonged to another era of human development. For the most part, work in the modern world emphasized brain over back. Our cognitive prowess had mechanized much of the drudgery and physicality of everyday life, freeing us from our toil so that we could spend our leisure hours in gyms using more machines in hopes of looking like these men. It recalled a favorite episode of his from the original *Star-Trek* TV series that conjectured an advanced civilization of beings who had evolved massive skulls on stunted bodies with ever-shrinking extremities from lack of use.

In the anxious silence, Nick imagined how preposterous he must've looked standing there in children's gym shorts and hiking shoes — an absurd, essentially naked, pale and soft-fleshed white man, whose only visible advantage was height; despite their obvious fitness, the tallest of the Penan men looked to be only five and a half feet in height.

Placing a hand on his chest, Nick spoke his name. This too brought no response from the Penan. He self-consciously repeated the gesture to more silence. Then, with a suddenness that startled him, the 'leader' spoke and pointed toward Nick's waist. Like someone being reminded to check his fly, Nick reflexively looked down, despite knowing the gym shorts lacked a zipper. Cringing with embarrassment at the excessively snug fit highlighting the contours of his anatomy in such striking detail, he shrugged with a clumsy grin.

The 'leader' again muttered something before turning into the forest, the others following. Baffled but relieved, Nick watched them quickly disappear from view. Apparently headed in the same general direction the woman had pointed out to him, he decided to follow.

Beneath the forest canopy, the diffuse daylight rolled off so quickly it was impossible to distinguish much beyond thirty meters or so. After a couple minutes, Nick stopped, having lost the Penan. In the hush of the forest, he noted a faint burbling sound like the trickle of a stream. Homing in on it, he came upon a tiny brook and followed downstream to where it joined a larger stream on its way to the river.

Little more than a couple meters wide, the stream had a pristine, primeval feeling, surrounded by ferns and vines hanging down from somewhere above. Moss-covered rocks sat half-submerged in the clear running water and the air smelled vaguely of dried silt on stone. The coolness of the water with its hint of damp earth and wet rock reminded Nick of childhood summers and the hot sticky days of late July and August when friends' parents would invite him along on day trips to the cool streams of the nearby Appalachians.

Crouching to splash some water on his face, he silently took in the surroundings. The stillness felt almost unnerving, a reminder how inured we'd become to the ambient noise of everyday life. Our paleolithic ancestors living on the savanna must have evolved with a keen sense of hearing, both in order to hear prey and, to avoid becoming prey themselves. Having evolved in such primal silence, our prodigious otological sensitivity was now often overwhelmed by the cacophonous noisiness of contemporary life, leading to jagged nerves and lingering anxiousness.

The cool water revived Nick and he got to his feet, then followed the stream to a spot where it widened in a confused jumble of boulders. Picking his way through, he heard what sounded like splashing in the distance. He crouched behind a boulder and peered over it. Up ahead, maybe fifty or so meters away, a group of Penan men, women and children were bathing in the stream.

Mesmerized, he silently observed as if watching an anthropological documentary on Public Television. It struck him to think that, as the second millennium of the so-called Common Era was winding down, these people and their way of life had barely changed the entire time.

"You should join them…" a voice said in English, startling Nick from his reverie.

He abruptly turned to see a white man clad only in a pair of threadbare khaki shorts.

"Do you a world of good…" the man continued. "You may feel some *sebarau* brush up against your legs, but they're harmless. Might nibble at the hairs on your leg, but otherwise, nothing to worry about."

Nick's stomach tightened and he stretched an arm out to steady himself on the boulder. Time had marked its passage in the man's features but the eyes were unmistakable.

"…*Evan*…?" he feebly muttered at last, his mind swirling.

The sandy hair, once thick and unruly, had thinned with the years and showed patches of dullish gray; a blondish-gray stubble framed his cheeks and thin lips, while crow's feet at the temples suggested a life spent outdoors.

For what seemed like minutes, the two men stood in silent regard of each other, reckoning the chasm of years where a shared history might otherwise have been.

"Didn't mean to startle you…" his brother explained.

Staring mutely in stunned disbelief, Nick tried to reconcile the boy from memory with the man standing before him. After all he'd been through, it astonished him to realize that dumb luck had somehow brought him to his brother's doorstep. Of all the ways he had imagined this moment, standing there in a pair of too-tight kid's gym shorts and hiking shoes, had not been among them.

"You look good, Nick…" Evan continued. A tiny smirk hinted on his lips as he noted Nick's surprise and the ill-fitting gym shorts. "Sorry about the shorts…your clothes were soaked and that's all they could find. Leftover donations from Christian missionaries…"

Nick blinked several times, his mouth open in a stalled attempt at speech.

"Why don't we walk…?" Evan suggested, noting his brother's bemusement. "There's a smaller pool further downstream. It's quiet there."

52.

Banks of cumulus clouds moved across the sky, the daylight waxing and waning with them. One moment, the day would be brightly gleaming, the river's surface dappled with shifting highlights, and an instant later, it would turn dull, soft and flat like an overcast day. Seladang held the boat to a moderate speed as Antonio sat against the camera case in the bow — the humidity had built up again and the moving air up front offered some relief. They each appeared to be weighed down by their grim discovery.

At a slight bend in the river just shy of the spot they'd previously landed, Seladang let up on the throttle and nudged them into an eddy near the shore. He cut the engine then jumped onto the riverbank with the bow line, securing it to a tree.

"Better here," he explained, as Antonio climbed out of the boat. Out of caution, the boatman had drawn up downstream of their original landing spot.

"Should go find Carole…" Antonio said at last.

With a somber nod from Seladang, he started off and hadn't gotten far when the boatman called out.

"Your friend…" Seladang said, perhaps to reassure himself as much as Antonio, "Maybe…he got out…"

Occasional bursts of chatter had gone back and forth on the two-way radio, mostly in Malay, with an occasional word or two in English. The project managers essentially ignored it while poring over plans and print-outs scattered about on the joined tables.

Carole stared out the window and fidgeted. Her mind skittered between poles of guilt and dread. The way Nick had been taken — following them and waiting for him to be alone — more and more it looked to be an 'off-the-books' operation.

Such extralegal tactics, she knew, were the purview of state actors need-ing cover for unsavory activities. Antonio had it right: whatever the *interests* behind Nick's abduction might be, they seemed to be after *plausible deniabil-ity*, that strange twisting of legal doctrine into, '*innocent because our finger-prints are nowhere to be found.*' It worked because most people were content *not* to know the nasty things governments routinely did in their name, while it also assuaged a need to believe that wiser minds than theirs had deemed such actions necessary .

Still, something about it all didn't add up. How could a part-time English professor from America warrant the use of such shadowy tactics? She kept returning to the essential conundrum: if the aim had been to keep Nick from his brother, why do it this way?

She was about to check her watch when, in the distance, she spotted Anto-nio approaching from a different direction. Thanking her hosts, she exited the trailer and started toward him, quickly picking up on the grim set of his jaw.

"You okay…?" she asked as they met.

"Fine…" he answered, a bit furtively. "Anything here?"

"Nothing… Some routine chatter on the two-way…but not much else. No *Ian* either…" Her eyes narrowed and she felt her stomach clench. "…Any sightings…?"

At this, Antonio averted his gaze and hesitated.

"…We found the truck… In the river… Wrecked…"

The color drained from Carole's face.

"One of the Malaysians was trapped inside…" Antonio continued, "Only him as far as we could tell… It probably went in at that washout…and he must've gotten trapped in the truck's rear compartment with the door locked from up front…"

"…Oh, *shit*…" Carole muttered, devastated. She was about to add some-thing further but the words seemed were checked in her throat.

"And Nick…?" she finally asked.

Antonio mustered a vague, uncertain shrug. "He probably made it out…" he said, "But then, he'd have to survive the river…"

Carole's jaw tightened as she imagined Nick flailing in the churning opaque waters of the Baram River.

"Jesus…" she muttered, after some time, "Well, that's it then. We have to find him…"

Antonio nodded solemnly at the foregone conclusion.

"And Ian...?" he asked.

"I left a message with them," Carole nodded toward the trailers. "Telling him to wait there..."

With that, they fell silent and started back toward the river.

53.

"Through here," Evan said, as he zig-zagged between rocks. Nick tried to keep up, occasionally losing his balance and splashing a foot. They gave a wide berth to the other Penan bathers and soon arrived at a smaller pool where Evan stepped into water up to his thighs.

"Come on in..." he called to Nick, "Scrub some of that river silt off..."

He then slid under as Nick watched from the pool's edge. A couple seconds later, Evan popped back up, pushing his thinning wet hair back with both hands. Somehow, he seemed older than his years; beneath the gray eyes, his pouchy skin had begun to sag, and the sunken cheeks called to mind some hardscrabble Depression-era migrant.

Still barely able to speak, Nick crouched lower and shimmied into the water, slowly dunking himself. When he came up and wiped his eyes, Evan had seated himself on a rock shelf, his legs still in the water.

"There's a little ledge right here," he explained, "Plenty of room for another scrawny white butt..."

This got a smile out of Nick who waded toward him, feeling for the ledge with his hands. Finding it, he pulled himself into a comfortable sitting position an arm's length or so from his brother. An awkward minute or two passed as they silently watched the rippling water flatten out. A vague note of melancholy nipped at Nick, a reminder how little he had thought about such a moment over the years. By choosing to view Evan's silence as a tacit rejection, the confused jumble of hurt had, over time, softened into indifference. In that moment, Nick understood that some degree of their mother's mulish stubbornness lived on in him; when she felt wronged by someone, they were excised from her life, as if they'd never existed in the first place.

Words eluded him as he stared at his reflection in the water, clearly troubled by what he saw.

"...oooofff..." he groaned, at the rough character staring back at him. "...I look like *hell*... Like I've been on a bender for the last month..."

He ran a hand over the stubble on his face while Evan gave him a sidelong glance.

"You *are* looking a bit feral…" he agreed, adding, "To the Penan, I mean."

Nick turned to him with a raised eyebrow.

"The body hair and pale skin," Evan explained.

"*Body hair…?*" Nick objected. "I'm hardly *hirsute.*"

"…True…but maybe you've noticed that men in this part of the world generally have almost no body hair. The Chinese, Malays, and Dayaks, other than the crotch, the head, and a little on the face, they're essentially hairless. Probably an evolutionary adaptation to the climate, but who knows…"

As he listened, Nick pushed his wet hair back just as Evan produced a hotel-sized soap bar from a pocket in his shorts.

"I've got a secret stash of these," he said, tossing it to Nick, who held the bar as if it were the rarest of luxuries.

"*…Whoa…*" he cooed, "*Real soap…*"

He began to lather his face and upper body as Evan watched.

"…I'll bet…" Nick continued while scrubbing, "The last time I was this filthy, I still believed in the trifecta of Santa, the Easter Bunny and the Tooth Fairy…"

A knowing smile curled Evan's lips and he splashed some water on his shoulders.

"You *did* love the dirt," he remarked. "Remember when we were little and mom made us take baths together…? I must've been in first grade and you hadn't started kindergarten yet. You'd spend all day out back in that patch of ground where the burn barrels used to sit… The only part of the yard she let you dig in."

Nick warmed to the memory. "*Whoa…* Hadn't thought about *that* in years…"

"Yeah…" Evan went on, "You'd be filthy from digging holes and moving piles of dirt around with your *Tonka* trucks like you were building a subdivision. I didn't want to be in the same water with you!"

As he listened to his brother's recollection, Nick quietly shuddered at how little any of this remained in his own memory.

"Wow…" he began, "I don't have many solid memories from that time. Mostly just some bits and pieces… Like the fireflies at dusk in summer, or the way the light looked somewhere, that sort of thing. Really short clips and fuzzy snapshots from ground-level, like a tike's POV."

Bemused and vaguely unsettled by his patchwork memory, Nick slid under to rinse. As he popped back up and wiped the water from his eyes, the facts of the current moment had begun to settle and were stunning in their sheer unlikelihood. That he and his brother should reunite in *this* remote corner of the world after decades without any contact, felt nothing less than surreal.

"I come here to get quiet," Evan offered, after a bit. "Soaking helps clear my head. Suppose it's as close as I'll ever get to real meditation…"

The words and Evan's surprisingly diminished appearance underscored the extent to which time had rendered them strangers.

"The ancient Romans," Evan went on, "They really understood the value of a good soak. That it served both body *and* soul and was essential to civic order. Everywhere they ruled, the Romans built elaborate public baths. It's no wonder Europe slid into the Dark Ages after the Empire fell…"

Immersed to the shoulders, Nick quietly listened to his brother.

"All those Germanic tribes," Evan went on, "Too busy fighting among themselves to do anything on the scale of the Romans. With no central authority to collect taxes, the public baths, like everything else, fell into ruins. For the next fourteen-hundred years, give or take a century, regular bathing was a luxury only the nobility could afford…right up to the early twentieth century. Most people washed their *clothes* more frequently than they washed themselves… Made for a thriving market in perfumes and other concoctions to help mask the stink."

"Now *there's* something you never get in the history books," Nick observed, "The *stink* of history…"

Evan smiled appreciatively; they both seemed to understand this banter as a means of deferring more difficult discussions to come. It also served to probe the chasm time had left between them, to gauge how wide and deep the years had cut and whether or not the bonds of blood and a shared childhood could surmount it.

"Wow…" Evan said, assessing his brother, now standing in the water. "Look at you, all grown up… You know, for a long time, whenever I couldn't sleep at night, I'd lay there trying to imagine what *you* might be doing at that very moment. I'd try to *age* you in my head, imagine you as an adult… How you looked, where you might be living, what kind of work you did, wife, kids, even how you *voted*…"

Nick smiled then lightly harrumphed.

"Not to disappoint you," he remarked, "But I haven't voted in years… Nothing to be proud of, I know, and I'm *not*… No wife or kids, either." He hesitated. "Figured it would just happen on its own…when the timing was right…" He hesitated, plainly discomfited. "Anyhow, I've been in Los Angeles almost fifteen years now. And for the last five, I've lived with this woman, Celeste… It's still a work in progress…"

"Los Angeles…?" Evan asked in mock bewilderment. "Really…? Don't tell me you're in the entertainment business?"

"Hah!" Nick laughed, "Some of my students might think so… But no, I teach English as an adjunct at different colleges around LA county. Everything from remedial English, to comp courses… Even the occasional lit course, when I'm lucky. It was supposed to be temporary. Until the right tenure-track gig came along."

"An *adjunct?* Meaning, what…freelance? No tenure?"

"No *anything*…" Nick carped. "It's all part of this new push to make education more 'entrepreneurial.' That's the word they toss around now. *Entrepreneurial.* All those MBAs and bean-counters who really run things. They talk about education as a 'product' and students as the 'market'. They're all about finding 'inefficiencies' to fix so they can justify their inflated salaries. And the biggest inefficiency of all, of course, is the bloat of full-time tenured faculty. Some VP of Finance is hired and convinces the administration that adjuncts are a bargain, a fraction of the cost of full-time tenure-track hires. No benefits to pay, no commitments, no baggage."

Evan's eyes hardened a bit. "And they go for that? Administrations?"

"They have been…" Nick answered. "All those sweet retirement and benefits packages for faculty always end up costing more down the road than originally planned. So the bean-counters come up with ways to cut costs that never touch the sweetheart deals the president and deans get.

"I *could* improve the odds by looking out-of-state…" he continued, "But Celeste is determined to stay in LA…she was born there and her family's all there. So for now, I'm in the crush with every other PhD in California." He stared into the water. "Sounds like I'm bitching about it but I don't mean to. After all, the weather's great and…if you have to be stuck in your life somewhere, you could probably do a lot worse than LA…"

He stared at his fingers, now slightly pruned from the water.

"It creeps up on you, though…" he added. "Time. One term ends and another begins before you've had a chance to catch your breath… The years pile up and it's not long before the young man who once thought he had the world by the balls, is now a middle-aged man who's learned it's the *other* way around, and the world's got *him* by the balls…"

Evan raised an eyebrow. "Interesting… And, have you shared this hard-won wisdom with your students…?"

Nick snorted. "Now *there*'s a course that should be required for *all students*: '*Remedial Reality!*'…"

Both men briefly chuckled before falling silent again. A minute or so passed and Nick absently began to run his hand back and forth across the water's surface, barely touching it in slow sweeping motions.

"…I, uh…" he carefully began, "…I've been wondering…when you're going to ask me just what the hell I'm doing here…"

He let the question dangle, glancing between his hand skimming the water and his brother. Given the decades of silence, Nick had absolutely no idea how Evan might react upon seeing him again. He certainly had to be the *last* person in the world his brother would have expected to see out here and yet, strangely, Evan appeared unsurprised.

"Well… It *had* crossed my mind," his brother answered after a moment.

The cool equanimity threw Nick. As young boys, Evan always itched to *get on* with whatever it was — a baseball game, bike outing, newspaper delivery, snow shoveling or lawn mowing — as if the world was holding him up.

Nick exhaled deeply and began with their father's death, then paused to let his brother respond. Evan's eyes narrowed as he gazed into the water.

"Didn't think Sylvia would go first…" he remarked, after a moment. "She was way more active. I thought for sure she'd outlive him…"

"Same here," Nick agreed. "But remember how much she loved the sun… Spent all day on the tennis court or golf course or working in the yard. Always in those sleeveless tops with the thin shoulder straps. Finally caught up with her. Skin cancer…" He shook his head. "Life's never short on irony…The thing she loved most in life — other than our father — ends up killing her. Awful…"

Evan's relationship with their father's second wife had been fraught at best. Sylvia's affection for their father had not entirely extended to them, Evan in particular, with whom she maintained something closer to detente.

"Anyway," Nick went on, "When the call came from the old man's lawyer, Celeste and I flew back east. Dad had already taken care of his own arrangements, services, obituary, burial… The '*Good Hands*' insurance guy to the end…

"We got the house ready for sale. Went through all the personal stuff, like his files and plaques and whatever else wasn't going in the estate sale. It all looked so insignificant when we packed it up for the dump… The entirety of a man's life. Just a bunch of boxes bound for the landfill…" He stared off into the forest on the stream's opposite bank.

"Anything worth saving…?" Evan quietly asked, after a moment.

"Not really…" Nick replied, "Why?"

"I don't know…just thinking, there must've been *some* photos of us as kids, maybe?"

"There were, but not many… You remember the old man's thing about living in the past. Sylvia was his *second* chance… A way to get it right this time. He wanted a fresh start and that's what he got. We didn't really figure into it.

"Anyway, I did find a few tucked away…" Nick continued. "Brought some with me, but…well, they're back in my travel bag…still on that express boat as far as I know…"

The middle-age reflex for nostalgia had little hold on either of them, attributable perhaps to the thin catalogue of happy childhood memories.

"The house sold for eighty thousand," Nick went on, staying with practical matters. "*Reverse* sticker shock for me, living in California where you couldn't buy a taco cart for eighty thousand!" He sighed and shifted his weight on the rock shelf. "Hardly a surprise, but small-town, *Rust Belt* Pennsylvania isn't exactly in the midst of a real estate boom… It's a place people move *away* from, not *to*…"

He paused a few seconds.

"You should know…" he explained, "Half the proceeds are yours. From the house. According to the will… After the broker's cut, clearing dad's debt, deferred property taxes, legal fees, etcetera, we ended up with about twenty grand each."

Nick waited but this didn't get much reaction from his brother.

"That's about it…" he added, the words dangling in the humid air. "Dad actually sold the insurance business about seven years ago, not long after Sylvia passed. You might remember Stan? Can't think of his last name… Started working for the old man right out of high school, probably only a couple years older than you… Anyway, that's who bought it." At this, he hesitated. "Apparently our father *financed* the purchase. And the will stipulated the loan be considered satisfied upon his passing."

Evan pursed his lips in thought. "Hmm… Probably the right thing to do. Don't you think?"

Nick agreed. They both knew that Stan had spent more time with their father over the years than either of them had.

"I also found out that he ended up going through most of his savings paying off the debt that piled up when Sylvia got sick," Nick explained. "He took her to Sloan-Kettering in New York and they lived out of a hotel near the hospital for a couple months. Those expenses and whatever insurance didn't pay for her treatment really added up…"

He paused for Evan to digest all this.

"*Sylvia*…" Evan muttered, his tone ambiguous. "She was something else… As soon as she entered the picture, it became *her* house and *her* rules. Treated us like a couple of boarders she had to house and feed."

Just then, something distracted Evan in the forest's edge on the stream's opposite side. He squinted in its direction a second or two then called out in Penan. His facility with the language impressed Nick and he called out again, louder this time. They waited and eventually, a small boy reluctantly stepped out from behind a tree: *Phillip*.

The boy grudgingly came toward them, crossing the stream with his head hanging. As he reached their side, he awkwardly faced Evan, who spoke sternly to the boy in Penan. Nick watched, puzzled by the dynamic between them as Phillip stood silently in that 'hangdog' way common to the age, while fidgeting at the hem of his shorts. When Evan finished, the boy nodded and, after a slight hesitation, Evan returned to English.

"Nick, I believe you've met Phillip," he said, eyeing the boy.

"I have," Nick replied, with a warm smile in Phillip's direction. "He speaks English very well and he's been really helpful."

"It's not like him to eavesdrop on adult conversations," Evan continued, "He's really an honorable boy. But…he's still a boy." Evan's expression softened and a slight smile curled at the corners of his mouth as he watched Phillip.

"You remember how hard it was at that age to contain your excitement…" Evan went on, directing the comment at Nick. "Always wanting to be in on everything?"

"I do indeed," Nick replied, playing along. "It's the sign of a curious mind," he added, with a wink in the boy's direction.

"…You don't say…?" Evan mused, an eyebrow raised. "Well… Can't blame him for being curious. It's not everyday you get to meet an uncle from the other side of the world…"

At first, Nick thought he misheard and some seconds went by as he processed. Then, his eyes gradually widened. '*Of course…!*' he realized. Hadn't the boy said, '*…he'd learned English from his father…?*'

Suddenly mute, Nick stared at Phillip, trying to get his mind around what he'd just learned. In the daylight, he could see some resemblance: the luminous, penetrating eyes, deeply set and wary; the slight upturn of the narrow nose, the bony shoulders and long, skinny arms — Phillip could have been a darker-skinned clone of his brother at that age.

"He didn't know who you were when he looked in on you earlier," Evan continued. "Then I told him you were his uncle who'd come from the United States to visit…and he's been wound-up ever since."

Dumbstruck, Nick gazed upon his nephew and an initial burst of bloodline pride was quickly tempered by the inescapable complexity of the context. He merely stared in amazement as Evan spoke in Penan and the boy stepped closer.

"Hello…" Phillip said, looking down at his feet.

Still a bit nonplussed, Nick steadied himself and smiled affectionately. "Well…hello again, Phillip."

Evan went on, clearly pleased.

"We talked about a name from the land of his father's birth," he explained, "To go with his Penan name. I shared the story of *Metacomet* with him, the Wampanoag chief known as 'King Phillip', who led his people through difficult times. He really liked the story and chose the name himself."

"A wise man, indeed," Nick concurred, "And a great name."

Phillip squinched his eyes. "*Why's…?*" he repeated, mis-hearing the contraction as '*why is*'.

Amused, Evan clarified: "He thinks you're saying, 'why is'… We're still learning to listen for *context…*"

"Ah, sure," Nick said, jauntily now. "English is a confusing language to learn. So many words that sound alike. Like the one I just used: '*wise*', W-I-S-E, which sounds like 'why-is' when you say it quickly. It's how you might describe someone who's smart and sensible."

The boy looked to his father then back at Nick as if checking their agreement. Evan then spoke again in Penan and Phillip's shoulders drooped —

the universal body language of a child frustrated by parental authority. Evan added something and Phillip grudgingly said goodbye to his uncle in English, then turned on his heels and left. When he was out of earshot, Evan exhaled deeply.

"Always afraid he's going to miss something," he remarked. "I was the only white man he'd ever seen until you. And the fact that you're also my brother *and* his uncle…well, the kid can hardly contain himself."

Nick nodded, still in shock, "… *Wow* …"

Apparently satisfied, Evan stood up.

"C'mon Nick, let me show you around," he said.

Nick rose and fussed with the too-small and now soaked gym shorts awkwardly clinging to the contours of his anatomy. Evan silently led them back to the settlement where a dozen or so Penan now stoked a fire in the central area. Evan approached and spoke in Penan, as all eyes turned to Nick.

Uncomfortably self-conscious in the skin-tight gym shorts, Nick's face flushed and he pulled at the shorts trying to stretch the paltry fabric down further on his pasty un-athletic thighs.

A general murmuring ensued, as the men, women and children stared. Nick forced a smile while awkwardly clasping hands over the 'fire-hydrant' outline of his penis. Just then, one of the Penan men offered up a comment that got them all chortling.

The forced smile dissipated as Nick understood the joke was on him; here he was, a pale, fleshy white man in soaking wet children's swim trunks clinging to the crack of his ass while outlining everything else. The man who'd just commented, now pointed directly at Nick's crotch.

"*What…??*" Nick asked, turning to his brother. "The *shorts?*"

Evan shook his head, clearly in on the joke. "No…not the shorts," he explained. "It's… Your *apparatus*…"

Nick winced. "Jesus, Evan…!" he yelped, clumsily cupping hands over his crotch. "What the *hell?!*"

He squirmed, self-consciously fussing his hands this way and that, noting the amused glint in his brother's eye.

"They're puzzled…" Evan explained, "That you're *cut*…"

"*Cut??*"

"You know…your, um…*circumcision*. They find it strange. Don't understand why we do it."

"*Why* we do it...?" Nick repeated, glancing back and forth. "Well... we do it because... I mean...the hospital does it. When we're born...right?"

Evan raised an eyebrow, deliberating how best to translate this for the benefit of the Penan.

"It's a hygiene thing..." Nick went on, "From the *Old Testament*...?"

His protestations only increased the giggling and murmuring.

"Well...what about *you??*" he asked his brother. "We were born in the *same* hospital!"

"True," Evan replied with a smile, "But *my* dick isn't the one announcing itself right now."

"*Shit!*" Nick blurted, red-faced and fussing at the shorts. "Whoever put these on me must have been blind... They're *kid's* shorts...!"

"Ah, probably *Mama Senji*," Evan told him. "Your clothes were a mess when they brought you in and she must've changed you. Of course, she's almost *blind*..." He pointedly paused a second or two. "My wife washed your clothes and I thought they'd be dry before you came to..."

Nick anxiously shifted from one foot to the other, unsure what to do with his hands and smiling self-consciously as the Penan studied him.

"They're very curious about you," Evan explained. At this, he turned and spoke to the assembled Penan in their language. Watching, Nick again found his brother's fluency with the language and attention given him by the Penan somewhat astonishing.

"I told them who you were," Evan said in English to Nick. "I had to modify a little..." he added, cryptically.

The high spirits of the Penan were attenuated by curiosity and many of them stared at Nick as if he had just crawled from a ghastly freeway pileup. Several of the men stepped closer to inspect him. Their powerful compact bodies were impressive; with limbs that might have been formed from some elastic mineral-like compound, they could have been a sculptor's anatomic ideal. Compared to them, Nick's own loose-limbed fleshiness suggested the possibility that a strong wind might pop an arm from a shoulder socket. '*This is what happens when a species no longer worked for its food,*' he thought. '*Like an animal provided for in captivity, we get soft to the point of throwing a disk just by getting out of bed in the morning!*'

As the Penan hovered uncomfortably close to Nick, he brought his arms up and folded them over his bare chest while awkwardly smiling.

54.

The evening humidity thickened as the sun, now a squat, plump ball of blood-orange in a pale hazy sky, edged closer to the horizon. Beneath the forest canopy, visibility began to dwindle as a twilight gloom settled in. Within the forest's shadowy depths, insects trilled and unseen birds occasionally called out, while monkeys randomly leapt between tree branches.

Nick returned to the little hut to find his clothes waiting for him. He immediately changed into them, relieved to be done with the ridiculous children's shorts. It surprised him how clean the clothes looked. Having earlier caught a glimpse of Penan women scrubbing and slapping their wash on rocks, he was doubly thankful they survived. His hiking shoes, however, were still a bit damp and, given the humidity, were likely to stay that way.

The faintly glowing embers of the tiny cook fire barely illuminated the hut's murky darkness, which at the moment, Nick found comforting as he needed time to collect his thoughts. Of all the scenarios he'd imagined for his brother, having a family and living among a group of nomadic people in a tropical rain forest had certainly *not* been among them. In just two days, Nick had gone from having *no* family to now having an *extended* family. It was both exciting and a bit daunting to think their bloodline, that vexed amalgam from their parents' ill-fated union, would continue in a way no one could have imagined. And while this was an undeniably auspicious development, it did little to ease the vague sense of dread still nibbling at him.

An hour or so passed as Nick turned these new facts over in his mind. Evan told him he'd return soon but had yet to show. Unsure what to do, Nick slid over to the entry and pushed the flap open. Evening had come on quickly and he noticed some Penan gathered near a central fire. Out of habit, he once again glanced down at his wrist for the watch that was somewhere in the South China Sea by now.

His curiosity piqued, Nick descended the several rungs of bamboo and started toward the fire. As he drew near, he noticed that the assembled Penan around the fire were largely seniors. Each sported some version of the pierced and stretched earlobes fashionable here: moderately stretched lobes were fitted with disks or rings ranging in size from coins to small pancakes, while others had been stretched to the shoulders or beyond. Men *and* women alike pensively puffed on homemade pipes.

Evan was nowhere to be seen in the mix as Nick tentatively stepped toward several women tending a large kettle of simmering liquid. Fascinated, he smiled and watched as they stirred and sampled, the glow of firelight reflecting from their bodies onto the frothy liquid. One of the women appeared to offer a critique which resulted in a lively discussion until another woman barked something that probably meant, '*you think you can do better, go ahead!*'

One of the pipe-smoking men noticed Nick and began speaking to him in Penan. He waved a hand at the kettle and continued speaking as Nick smiled helplessly. The man gestured toward the brew again, speaking more loudly as if volume once again was their only problem with communication.

He finished and stared, apparently waiting for a response. Nick anxiously looked about, hoping to spot his brother to rescue him. Sweat beaded on his forehead as he nodded and smiled. One of the women stirring called out and waved Nick over — saved! She pantomimed drinking and Nick realized they wanted him to taste their brew. Somewhat relieved, he bowed slightly and thanked her. Before he knew it, another of the women handed him a hollowed-out coconut shell filled with the brew. The woman stirring now held her own coconut shell of brew as if for a toast; she had clearly taken it upon herself to be Nick's guide in the endeavor and, after a moment, threw back the shell and its contents.

Nick understood they expected him to do the same and, with a 'here's looking at you' gesture, he downed the brew with a calculated flourish, much to the crowd's approval. Whatever the stuff was made from, the liquid had a starchy, slightly bitter taste, an astringent alcohol varnish and a small touch of fizziness. Nick wiped the foamy dribble from his lips with the back of an arm, which brought more spirited murmuring, while children began to gather and cluster tighter to the fun.

In no time, the drinking circle expanded. Two other Penan men stepped up with shells extended to toast as Nick's cup was filled again. He could do little more than smile and throw back each toast like the new village idiot. After tipping back three or so shells of the brew, an unfamiliar tingling sensation began to buff away the sharper edges of his self-consciousness. The bonhomie began to flow despite the lack of a common tongue.

With each brew he downed, Nick's hosts cheered their approval and he played along, gesturing to the crowd with an arm raised, nodding like some beneficent *Caesar* in the Forum. Normally, this sort of behavior would have made him cringe — the caricatured, too-buzzed tourist '*wah-hooing!*' it with the locals over drinks, shedding both inhibitions and good sense. The home brew, however, had obliterated all such restraint and good judgment.

Two parts alcohol buzz and one part something else, the brew had a delayed kick. Nick's face felt flush, warm, and slightly numb to the touch. Nearby, a couple of younger Penan men started to bang on a hollowed-out log of some sort suspended by rattan vines at each end. A couple meters in length with the diameter of a steering wheel, the log produced syrupy percussive sounds with every strike of the blunt wooden batons. The men played at opposite ends *and* opposite sides of the log. A range of notes could be achieved by moving up and down the log like a vibraphone, which they somehow did simultaneously without ever smacking each other's batons. As Nick listened, an image came to him in the firelight of some primitive microscopic organism moving in time with the unfamiliar harmonic tones and rhythms.

Another of the older Penan men then pointed at Nick with his pipe, apparently asking a question. Nick stared and the man went on, gesturing with the pipe like a neighbor discussing the latest municipal tax levy. That Nick had no idea what he was saying did nothing to diminish the man's enthusiasm.

"*I don't understand...*" Nick mumbled, shaking his head. The man just went on, untroubled by the one-way nature of the conversation.

The strangely beguiling music being coaxed from the log began to take on a weird reverb effect while notes from something with a higher register like a flute, now floated into the mix. Circling the log's percussive sounds, the flute music used the same unfamiliar tonal scale. Nick turned in its direction and thought his eyes were playing tricks on him — an older Penan woman sat cross-legged holding a flute-like instrument to her *nose.* He squinted and shook his head, but there it was: a woman making music with her nose.

When he turned back to the man still jabbering at him, he felt a bit wobbly on his feet. One of the women stirring took note and grabbed his arm. She then led him to a spot near the fire where some other geriatric Penan sat on mats watching the flames. Finding an empty spot between two shriveled-looking old men, the woman gestured for Nick to sit. He complied, wavering slightly as she held his arm and helped him stick the landing. The two men looked on in amusement as Nick plopped ass-first right between them.

Feeling a bit like a foolish teenager who'd overdone it, Nick smiled sheepishly, thankful to be away from the home brew. He turned to the man on his right, who nodded in commiseration and muttered something that sounded like '...*ahhhh...*', his open mouth revealing a few remaining stumps of what had once been teeth.

Nick gazed at the fire and tried to get hold of himself. He'd apparently been placed with the Penan version of the 'early-bird' set. So be it, he thought, relieved just to sit and avoid another round of home brew. Hopefully, he could still find his way back to the little hut once the wobbling stopped. Be patient, he told himself, and *don't* vomit on your neighbors. The liquid sloshing around in his otherwise empty stomach had made him a little queasy and he tried to let the fire and the music tune it out. This endeavor was aided by the introduction of another instrument: a harp-like device made of bamboo and strung with fibers probably twined from a vine. A younger man played it using a pluck-and-strum technique to fill spaces between the other instruments. Here were four players and three instruments, an asymmetrical setup mirrored in the asymmetrical tonality of the resulting music, a hypnotic aural experience that, helped along by the brew, had begun to make Nick dizzy.

His 'early-bird' neighbors appeared equally transfixed by the sounds. The man to his left stared at him as if he'd belched. Firelight flickering across the man's face kept changing his expression; a clown one minute and a madman the next. Things were getting stranger and Nick desperately hoped Evan would show soon and rescue him. He began turning back to the fire when the wild-eyed man thrust an arm out at him. In his palm he held a package wrapped in neatly folded leaves as he nodded: *take it.*

Gazing at the little bundle, Nick smiled graciously and shook his head. The man's expression didn't change; he simply thrust the offering closer. Nick anxiously glanced about for his brother once more. When he turned to his right, the other ancient Penan with the nubs of remaining teeth smiled and went, '...ahhhh...' again. Not wanting to offend anyone, Nick mumbled '*thank you*' in English to the man holding the offering and took it. The old man then mimed placing the contents in his mouth, jabbering words to the effect of, '*Now you!*'

Buzzed and feeling cornered, Nick put the leaf bundle in his mouth and began to chew slowly. Thankfully, the flavor at least didn't offend. In a matter of seconds though, his tongue and mouth grew numb and copious amounts of saliva began to collect, much like the time he tried chewing tobacco in high school. Worried about drooling all over himself, Nick reached his fingers to his lips which were also numb.

With the abundance of saliva pooling in his jowls, he didn't know whether to spit or swallow. Better to spit, he thought, clumsily leaning toward the fire to heave a poorly formed gob at the coals. When he reached a hand to wipe his mouth, he realized most of the ejected spittle had ended up on his chin and shirt. His geriatric neighbors chuckled as he winced at the mess. Nearby, one of the older women hawked a perfect stream that sizzled when it hit the coals. She looked in Nick's direction and said something he took to mean, 'Like *that*...'

Once again, he glanced around for his brother but, beyond the fire's glow, the world had become a blur of shadowy forms moving about. Pleasantly woozy now, Nick puckered his mouth and drooled the poultice-like remains into a palm, noting its unappetizing hue in the firelight. In an attempt to wipe the drool from his chin, he instead managed to smudge it, giving him the appearance of a clumsy drunken clown who'd smeared his makeup.

His neighbors watched in growing amusement as Nick gawped helplessly at the masticated contents in his hand. Lifting his head to the fire, he stared into the flames that now dipped and swayed in time with the music's trance-like rhythms. Like a snake being charmed, Nick felt lighter and lighter, thinking he might just float away...

55.

The boat drifted closer in the eddy until the half-submerged wreck of the SUV and its grim cargo came into view. Clutching at the gunwales, Carole and Antonio stared silently at the ghastly site for what seemed like minutes.

"...Those people at Long Akah..." Carole said, gazing at the wreck, "... They said there were *two* men..."

"The other one must've gotten out in time..." Antonio surmised, "Like Nick..."

Carole looked out over the river's churning waters and tried to imagine the unseen dangers beneath its surface.

"One thing in their favor..." Antonio continued, trying for a hopeful note, "...The water's not *cold* enough for hypothermia..."

This wasn't much solace for Carole.

"I doubt water temperature is at the top of the list when it comes to things to worry about out there," she bleakly observed. "...Let's hope Nick's a good swimmer after living in California all these years..."

While neither said it, both she and Antonio implicitly understood the likelihood of panic for anyone having to swim such a deluge. The roaring current and opaque waters were terrifying, inducing a wave of nausea in Carole. *How could anyone survive that?* she wondered. Antonio didn't miss the ashen look on her face and turned to the boatman.

"Seladang, what do you think…?" he asked, trying to keep them focused, "Someone in the river out there…which side do you think they'd try for?"

The boatman thoughtfully studied the currents for several seconds.

"…Hmm… The current…it pushes to *that* side," he told them, swinging an arm toward the left side of the river.

The comment jostled Carole from her dire thoughts.

"*Okay…*" she said, with a whooshing exhale. "Let's say Nick makes it to the bank on that side of the river… *Then* what? What would he do next…? Wait there? Try to walk?"

"Phew…" Antonio murmured. "…Well, it wouldn't take him long to figure out there aren't many boats this far upriver… And I doubt he'd sit still and wait for help, either… Not out here…"

"Yeah…" Carole agreed. "I'm guessing he'd try to keep moving, staying close to the river… But, which way? Up or down?"

Antonio scratched his head. "After all he's been through…the safe bet, would probably be back downriver to Long Akah."

"Sure, but what if he decides the hydro project is closer?"

The cameraman shrugged. "He might… But that assumes he's thinking clearly and somehow figured that out. I'm just guessing most people would probably go with the devil they knew…back to Long Akah."

Carole pressed her lips together tightly as another thought came to her.

"There's possibly the other guy, too…" she reminded him, "From the truck…if he made it out as well."

Whether Nick would consider any of this in his deliberations or not was little more than an academic luxury at the moment. Right now, they had to bet on one or the other and she had to make the final call.

"Right…" Carole decided at last, with a mix of resolve and dread. "Back toward Long Akah then, staying close to the *left* side of the river."

56.

"*Uncle!...*" Phillip exhorted as he tried to rouse Nick, passed out face down on a mat in the hut. "*Please uncle!... You wake up now...*" the boy went on, shaking him by the shoulder.

A string of drool trailed down Nick's mouth and chin, both stained a reddish hue from whatever he'd been chewing, while a '*snorfling*' sound burbled from the netherworld of his sinus cavities. Slowly, he began to stir, moaning as his eyes blinked open.

"...*wha*...?" he muttered, squinting to focus in the meager light.

"Uncle, you wake up now!..." Philip urged, as Nick rolled over on his back.

"...*where*...?" eked from his lips.

"Are you *okay*, uncle?" Philip anxiously pressed.

"...*oh*...*am I?*... *how?*..." Nick mumbled in fragments of thought. "...*what did I*...? Ohh...!! My *head*..."

"You fell asleep at the fire," his nephew explained. "Father had to bring you here."

As the facts slowly began to coalesce, Nick lifted himself up on his elbows, looking like a man fresh from a three-day bender. He rubbed his puffy bloodshot eyes and swiped a hand at the drool still dangling from his chin.

"...oh *man*..." he moaned, "...what the *hell happened*...?"

Philip studied his uncle as if he were a puzzling exotic creature of some sort.

"What is '*the hell*', uncle?" Philip asked, confused.

Nick's dry mouth and tongue felt swollen and he smacked his crusty lips, grimacing at the awful taste stirred up.

"...*eckkkk*..." he winced, the onomatopoeia needing no translation. Philip lifted a cup of water to his uncle's lips and Nick slowly drank.

"Thank you..." Nick said when finished. "Better think twice the next time the Penan offer me something to drink..."

This further puzzled the boy. "You want more to drink...?" he asked.

Nick smiled in amusement. Obviously, the little dab of understated irony fell short of the mark.

"No, sorry…" he apologized. "I was just being a wise-ass… What I meant to say was, those drinks I had last night…You know…that stuff they were drinking…? It's got some *kick*…"

Phillip squinched his eyes. "You were kicked?" he asked, perplexed.

"No, no, I mean the stuff in the kettle, that home brew… It's really *strong*."

"You *don't* like burak?" his nephew probed.

"*Boo*-rak…?" Nick repeated, exaggerating the pronunciation and accent. "Is *that* what they call that stuff…? oof…"

"I don't like it," Philip remarked, a tinge of guilt in his eyes.

"Well, between you and me, Philip," Nick observed, "I didn't much care for it either. I was just being *polite*…"

The playful conspiratorial tone suggested their mutual distaste for burak remain secret, and Phillip nodded tentatively, not sure if this was okay.

"Wait a minute," Nick said, his still-fuzzy mind lagging. "Don't tell me you actually *drink* that stuff?"

The question further baffled his nephew who shrugged.

"Ah, well, no big deal," Nick conceded, walking it back. "It's a *cultural* thing, right? Like the French having wine with every meal."

The clumsy exchange underscored how little experience Nick had with children, especially those his nephew's age; as if a seven-year-old boy living in a tropical rain forest understood French gustatory sensibilities.

"Anyway, you know what I mean…" he continued, deciding he should keep quiet until his head cleared. He sipped some more water and felt his empty stomach churn with the liquid, emitting an embarrassingly loud gurgling sound. Grinning mischievously, he glanced over at Philip as the water noisily worked its way through his internal plumbing. The boy looked wary at first, but his uncle's smile suggested that amusement with awkward digestive noise was okay. As another loud series of gurgles rumbled and squealed in Nick's alimentary tract, he hung his head to scrutinize his belly, holding it like that a moment before gradually looking up with an expression of theatrically exaggerated alarm.

Philip wasn't sure how to respond. Noting this, Nick widened his eyes and puffed out his cheeks as if he might blow up from within. His nephew's jaw dropped and Nick finally lost it and cracked up at his own silliness. Phillip instantly joined in and the two of them were soon howling with laughter.

Their shared hilarity quickly ceased as the hut's flap swung open.

"Good to see you're no worse for the wear," Evan commented, sticking his head in while leaning on his elbows in the opening. The bonhomie between his brother and son clearly pleased him. "Probably should've given you a heads-up on the burak…sorry… The potency varies with every batch. You never know what you're going to get."

"*Eeesh*…" Nick groaned, "Is that a nightly occurrence?"

Evan grinned. "Not for me," he answered, "I don't try to keep up with the Penan."

"Ah, well… apparently, *I do*…" Nick declared, rubbing his eyes. "Must've made quite the impression…"

"Oh, you did. Vomiting, passing out, drooling on yourself — did the family name proud."

Nick half-stifled a snicker then absently scratched at the back of his head.

"…I'm told you were kind enough to bring me here, thank you…" he said. "Now if you'd only shown up *before* I made a complete ass of myself."

"On the contrary, I think you made some friends. The burak notwithstanding."

"*Jesus*…" Nick grumbled. "…Phillip told me about that stuff… That '*Boo-rak*…?' Named for the sound you make when puking it up? What is it, exactly?"

"More like 'boo-*rok*'…but, that's close enough. Most indigenous people brew some version of it. At the longhouse communities, they tend to make it from rice now. Nomadic people like the Penan still use sago palm mash. It's the main source of starch in their diet. Like wheat is for us or rice for the Japanese. Since they don't clear land and plant crops, the Penan use what the forest provides, like the sago palm. They've got elaborate ways to squeeze everything they can from it. The leaves, the bark, and especially the pith."

"*Pith*…that about describes the taste," Nick teased. "And what the hell was that stuff in the folded leaves that had me drooling like I just had a lobotomy?"

Evan raised his eyebrows. "*That*…" he explained, "…is the *betel* nut. Kind of like chaw with a kick… Technically, it's the fruit of the *areca* palm, found all over this part of the world. It's dried then sliced or ground up and wrapped in leaves from the *betel* vine, a completely *different* plant. Hence the name, *betel-nut*. People have used it for centuries to keep a little buzz going. And, just like chaw, it makes you spit a lot and stains your teeth and mouth this awful reddish hue."

Nick self-consciously ran his hand up to his lips as if to feel the staining. "Nice…" he muttered.

"It'll wear off," his brother assured him, "…if you lay off betel nut."

"Too bad," Nick mused with an obvious touch of irony, "It's such an appealing habit…"

It heartened Evan to see his brother's mordant wit still intact. Stifling a grin, he looked at Phillip and spoke in Penan to the boy, who then slid obediently past his father through the flap.

"He's off to get some broth and sago for you. Breakfast in bed…"

"*Sago…?*" Nick asked. "Like the stuff I was drinking last night??"

Evan shook his head. "No… Just the pith. *Un*-fermented."

For a good half a minute or so, he studied Nick from the entry.

"You know…the kid's really taken a shine to you," he said, with obvious delight.

"Goes both ways," Nick told him, then dodged any potential sentimentality with some '*aw shucks*' humility. "Probably just the novelty… Am I the only other white guy he's ever seen?"

"You are," Evan assured him. "*And* the only kin he's ever met on his father's side…"

The allusion to family lingered awkwardly between them, throwing Nick, who had long since determined he'd have to make do without it. This uncomfortable aside quickly vaporized when Evan nudged over in the entry to make room for a Penan woman holding what looked to be some sort of gruel served on a banana leaf.

"Nick, this is my wife," Evan said by way of introduction, "*Kelesau…*"

With a shy smile, the woman crawled over and placed the leaf near Nick, who suddenly felt self-conscious.

"Phillip's been teaching her some English but she's still not comfortable using it…" Evan explained.

Nick thanked her and Kelesau gracefully bowed her head. Despite the brevity of the encounter, Nick caught the grace and intelligence in her eyes as she turned on her knees toward the entry. Evan leaned back from the opening for her to pass and prepared to depart as well.

"Anyway…" he continued, "…I dropped by to let you know I'm going on a hunt this morning. Thought you might be interested in tagging along. If you're up for it."

"*A hunt...?*" Nick repeated, trying to visualize his brother stalking and killing an animal. "Really?... Okay, sure...of course..."

"Good. I'll be back after you've eaten."

57.

Nick counted six men, some he thought he'd seen last night. All had the stretched earlobes to some degree, most fitted with ornamental disks. Each also sported tiny arrangements of beads and small feathers twined into their hair along with some sort of dried vines wrapped like bracelets above elbows and just below knees. Nick thought they must have some practical purpose as his brother wore these twined bracelets as well — his only outward adaptation of Penan adornment.

Nearby, two of the men held a thin, straight tree limb almost two meters in length upright and taut by coiling some ropey vines around it. Standing on opposite sides of the limb, they alternately pulled on the coiled vines, much the way loggers once worked two-man saws. This rotated the limb back and forth like a washing machine agitator, while another man on bamboo scaffolding leaned over the top with a tool that sank into the pith, hollowing out the limb as it turned.

"That's how you make a blowpipe," Evan remarked, noticing his brother's fascination with the process.

"Really?" Nick replied, impressed. "I got the impression they made them from some kind of reed that was already hollow?"

"Oh no, for a blowpipe, you need something really rigid and durable," Evan explained.

"Makes sense," Nick acknowledged. "And the length?"

"For velocity and accuracy, the same way a rifle barrel works. The Penan call it a '*keleput.*' When they finish hollowing it out, they'll use a *poeh* — a machete — to whittle away the bark and round out the surface."

"Are they planning on using it today?" Nick asked.

"Those men aren't going today," Evan told him. "These guys are, though."

He turned toward three other men. "Nick, this is Ngang, Angit, and Luwak," he continued. "They're honored to have you accompany them today. And hope your presence will ensure a good hunt."

"Thank you," said Nick, meeting their gaze with a vague nodding bow. "Please tell them I'm grateful for their generosity in allowing me to tag along. And that I'll do my best to stay out of the way."

The Penan men listened as Evan translated, looking slightly amused by the last bit about staying out of their way. Nick noted their lean, taut muscularity compared with his own pale fleshiness. *Their* bodies were well-adapted to life in the rainforest — short, sturdy, compact. In comparison, he and his brother were too tall and rangy for life out here, their height perfect for smacking into low-hanging branches and vines.

Luwak, whom Nick took to be the eldest of the three, reached for a finished blowpipe leaning against a tree. He then took a rattan strap with loops at each end and attached it to the device so he could sling it over his shoulder. Like the others, he wore a *poeh* sheathed on a woven waist belt hanging to one side. When finished, he spoke to the other men who started into the forest while Evan adjusted his own belt and poeh before turning to his brother.

"You okay for a bit of walking…?" he asked, concerned with Nick's condition.

"Of course," Nick answered, with a hint of defensiveness. "You might be shocked, but this isn't my first hangover."

While he may have been no stranger to what their mother had called, '*a big head*', he *did* feel somewhat 'green around the gills', broth and sago notwithstanding. Even so, the chance to tag along on a hunt thrilled him.

"Good," Evan told him. "Try to stay close and step *gently*... Like the Penan."

With this, he started in the direction of the hunters, Nick close behind. Within minutes, Nick's hair and shirt were sopping with sweat and he felt as though he might vomit. They soon arrived at a small meandering stream and the hunters altered course, following its edge. Several times along the way, Nick tripped on hidden roots, stifling an impulse to curse. The Penan, he noted, never stumbled, their bare, splayed feet landed each step softly and precisely. His brother had acquired some of this agility as well, though he wisely wore a pair of tatty old running shoes on his feet.

After some time following the stream, the hunters stopped. They stood stone-still in the silence broken only by the occasional fluttering of leaves or the distant call of some unseen bird. In every direction, the trees were massive, their trunks spreading out in huge buttress-like fans, many of them taller than a person. High above, the dense canopy concealed the sun and sky while diffusing the daylight that reached the forest floor.

In the stillness, Nick's labored breathing stood out. The hunters had barely broken a sweat, while he could feel his heart pounding in his ears. Surprisingly, he noticed his brother looked a bit winded as well, which didn't quite fit given the physicality of life here and Evan's rather spindly frame.

With a finger to his lips, Evan waved him closer. The oldest of the three hunters, Luwak, began to move with slow deliberate steps while the other two flanked him in an ever-widening arc. They moved without so much as stirring a twig or leaf, every step precise, controlled and disciplined in the manner of ballet dancers and tight-rope walkers.

After another minute or so, Luwak halted and, in one fluid motion, brought his blowpipe around. Holding it steady against his chest with one arm outstretched, he reached for a dart on his waist belt with the other. Fascinated, Nick watched as the hunter cupped his tongue and placed the feathered end of the dart in the 'U' it formed. Holding the blowpipe steady, he lifted it to his mouth. Breathing through his nose, Luwak puffed his cheeks with air several times, inflating and deflating them as if priming the pump. Then, in one smooth motion, he aimed the pipe up toward some higher branches in a nearby tree and let loose. A distinctive 'whooshing' sound sliced the air, followed immediately by a horrific screeching and chaotic, frenzied flailing among the branches.

From a rational standpoint, Nick understood predation as nature's highly effective and often brutal means of energy exchange; something had to die so that something else might live. Even so, and despite growing up in Pennsylvania, he'd never hunted a day in his life. Meat, as he and his fellow Americans had come to know it, came in sanitized, shrink-wrapped, foam-tray packaging that kept the gore of the slaughterhouse at a safe remove.

The desperate flailing began to slow and the hunters carefully moved in. A hushed tension hung like static in the air as Nick gazed up at the branches. Then, a crashing sound jolted him and he glimpsed a dark object tumbling through leaves and limbs before landing with a muffled thud on the forest floor. Luwak quickly pushed through the brush to retrieve it. Reaching the spot, he crouched down to grab a carcass he then held by the leg for everyone to see: a monkey of some sort, not much larger than a garbage-raiding raccoon, with reddish, rust-colored fur and a smooth hairless face ringed by a distinct edge where fur again sprouted on its head.

As the hunter returned holding the monkey by a leg, Nick unexpectedly found the analogous *human* form of the felled primate a bit unsettling. It was one thing to hunt and kill creatures with hooves and beaks, creatures that didn't *look* like *us*, but *this* was a primate, its digits mirrored ours, right down to the opposable thumbs. The monkey's death mask had frozen in a startled, shocked anguish, a kind of terminal astonishment that it should meet with such a fate on this otherwise unremarkable day. Evan sensed his brother's unease.

"You okay…?" he gently probed.

Nick nodded, gazing at the dead monkey. "What kind is it…?" he asked, tepidly, "…the monkey…"

"A *red langur*," Evan told him. "Also known as the 'maroon leaf' monkey."

Luwak and one of the other men held the monkey up by its ankles while the third hunter removed a smaller *poeh* from his waist and sliced into the creature's carotid artery. Blood streamed onto the forest floor, spattering leaves and the men's bare feet and shins. Nick resisted an urge to turn away. The slaughter and butchering of animals, he once again reminded himself, had long since been sanitized away in the developed world where the factory abattoir remained hidden from view. A lifelong omnivore, he had come to believe the modern world had placed us at too far a remove from the harsh reality that put animal protein on our plates, and that he, like most, would find it difficult, if not impossible, to kill and butcher an animal. By veiling the process that turned a living creature into marbled cuts of flesh under cellophane, we had lost sight of the unappealing fact that the spilling of blood was essential to our success as a species. Nick was reminded of his students' reaction whenever he assigned the Ray Bradbury short story, '*To Serve Man*', in which human beings were used as 'livestock' by an extraterrestrial race that saw *us* as edible protein. Some of his students found it shocking, while others appreciated the darkly ironic take, but none could forget it.

It took about a minute for the langur's blood to drain, then Luwak jabbed his poeh into the monkey's chest right beneath the breastbone and sliced it open down to its pelvis. Nick's stomach heaved slightly at the smell, a mix of blood, fat, urine and feces. Luwak then spread the incision with one hand and began slicing at connective tissue with the poeh, while glistening veined intestines, fat and other stringy viscera fell from the cavity. Nick watched, repulsed yet fascinated, as the hunter's bloody, greasy hands yanked and trimmed at the monkey's insides until the last of its steaming entrails lay in a pile on the ground.

Evan noted with amusement his brother's pallor and the sweat beading on his forehead.

"He has to drain the blood and remove the organs immediately…" he explained, in a vaguely clinical tone. "Before rigor sets in…"

"Right…" Nick agreed, nodding vaguely. "You do all this too…? The blowpipe and the butchering…?"

"Sure…" Evan replied. "I've tried to learn whatever I could from the Penan, and hunting tops the list. The real skill is tracking… Listening, observing, learning to spot tiny differences on the ground or in the brush." He paused a moment. "I get by, but… I'll never be like these guys. They started when they were Phillip's age. It's like skiing or learning a language — the younger you start the better."

"And the actual darting?" Nick asked.

A brief grin flashed on his brother's lips.

"Ah, well… I might starve if I had to live off my *darting* technique. I'm not bad at the tracking, though. And, even more surprising, I have a knack for the butchering… Can you imagine the old man's reaction if I'd told him I wanted to be a *butcher?!*"

Nick chuckled. "He'd have told you to be the *owner* of the business and hire *other* guys for the dirty work… Lifelong Republican that he was."

"No doubt…" Evan agreed, "He *loved* reminding us about the generations that busted their asses in mines, mills, and factories so *we* wouldn't have to. That we at least *owed* them the respect of graduating to the white-collar world."

The brothers shared a subdued laugh while the hunters began trussing up the langur carcass with bamboo and lashing. The image it presented was a little creepy, like some animistic fetish intended to appease an angry, blood-lusting spirit. In no time, the hunters finished the task and started off again. Tagging along behind Evan, Nick tried to recall the last time he'd felt *this* alive and in tune with life. For years now, he'd been sleep-walking through his days, hurrying from one teaching assignment to another, oblivious to little more than the relevant freeway exits and on-ramps germane to the destination.

The few minutes of necessary gore notwithstanding, Nick's senses were on high-alert. All around, life was vivid and abundant: orchids apparently growing from thin air; pitcher plants with surreal and vaguely sensual forms luring insects into their liquid death chambers; green bladed epiphytes sprouting from the sides and crotches of trees; strangler vines tangled in impossible contortions around trees and each other. All of it, a stunning and intricate choreography of life and death evolved over millennia.

Up ahead, Nick saw that his brother and the hunters had stopped to crouch over something. He caught up and squinted in disbelief — a *gargantuan flower* the size of a man-hole cover had sprouted from the earth, its surreal petals and bold coloring like some psychedelic phantasm from the mind of Lewis Carroll.

"…*What the hell…??*" Nick muttered in astonishment.

The flower had five huge reddish-orange petals with white blotchy spots, all surrounding a center orifice you could drop a soccer ball into. Inside were beguiling little cone-shaped protuberances poking up like some terrestrial anemone.

Luwak spoke, then smiled and pointed at Nick.

"He wants you to smell it," Evan translated.

Nick suspected a prank, maybe some hidden creature that would jump out like a jack-in-the-box as soon as he bent down to take a whiff. He skeptically glanced over at Evan, then cautiously leaned toward the gigantic flower. When nothing jumped, he looked up at his brother.

"It's okay," Evan assured him, "Go ahead…"

Wanting to be a good sport, Nick brought his face closer to the orifice and hesitantly stuck his nose in before instantly recoiling in disgust.

"Oh Jesus, that's *awful!!*" he blurted, leaning back and wincing in revulsion. "There's something *dead* in there…"

His brother and the Penan hunters were clearly amused. "That's possible…" Evan told him, "But I guarantee that's *not* what you're smelling… *That* delightful aroma is what the plant emits to attract insects for pollination."

"No *way…?!*" Nick blurted, waving a hand in front of his nose. "What kind of miserable creature would want to dip into *that?*"

"The kind that likes dead things and shit…" Evan explained, "…Flies mostly… People here call this the "*corpse* flower" or the "*meat* flower" because it smells like rotten meat. Its scientific name is '*Rafflesia arnoldii*', officially the world's *largest* flower." He crouched closer and gently lifted a petal. "…You know, you're incredibly lucky to see one of these," he continued. "They only grow alongside one particular vine found here and just a couple other places in the world. They're *extremely* rare and only bloom like this for a few days."

Nick stared in stunned amazement. "...*Phew*... All that for such a *brief* show...?"

"True..." Evan agreed, inspecting the petal. "Each flower needs to be pollinated by an insect that's already visited *another Rafflesia* of the opposite sex. It's a reproductive strategy based on deception. Flies looking for a meal and something dead to lay their eggs on are tricked into landing. They fumble around until they figure out there's nothing actually dead in the flower and take off, hopefully to find another Rafflesia. But the odds of that happening are pretty thin. You could spend years in the forest and never see another one."

"No one's tried to cultivate it yet?" Nick asked.

"Some have tried, but no..." Evan answered, "Like I said, Rafflesias are so fussy, they'll *only* parasitize this *one* particular species of vine — a vine that also requires specific *trees* to parasitize. Big old grand-daddys like this."

Evan gazed up at the layers of growth upon growth, rot upon rot, and the perpetual, invisible energy exchange running from the tip of the canopy all the way down into the soil where countless bacteria, fungi, and other micro-organisms completed the cycle.

"Can't exist without all this..." Evan added for emphasis, "An intact, ancient ecosystem..."

As Nick listened, he observed the Penan hunters reacting to his brother's words; they may not have understood their meaning but certainly picked up on the tone.

"Know how it got its name...?" Evan then asked.   t45

"Its *name*...?"

"'*Rafflesia,*'" he clarified as Nick shook his head. "Named for Sir Stamford Raffles, the British colonial who founded modern Singapore. There's a famous hotel there with his name: '*Raffles*'... A vestige from those long ago days when the sun never set on the British Empire. The *Singapore Sling* was invented there. You know, the *cocktail*...? Created by a bartender in the 'Long Bar' where guys like Graham Greene and Somerset Maugham once hung out."

An image came to Nick of two dapper colonials in white linen suits kibitzing over gin and tonics among potted palms and brass rails as ceiling fans spun languidly overhead. It seemed an unlikely, even strange, association with the gigantic flower in front of him and it quickly dissolved as the Penan hunters started off again. Nick moved to join them when Evan grabbed his arm.

"Let them go ahead…" he insisted in a hush.

Puzzled, Nick eyed his brother and complied as the hunters soon vanished into the forest.

58.

For a minute or so, the brothers waited in silence, Nick trying to divine Evan's intent. Then, with a slight jerk of his head in the direction the others had taken, Evan started off and Nick followed. After walking for some time, he noticed the Penan hunters were nowhere in sight and suspected that just might be the point.

"Hey," he called, as Evan turned without stopping, "I could really use some water…"

"Oh…sure," Evan answered, "Right up here."

He diverted slightly from the direction they'd been heading and started toward a tangle of spindly vines with large spade-shaped leaves.

"Here we go…" Evan said, carefully pulling a leaf toward him. Using his parang, he sliced along the upper stem, then cupped the leaf below to form a channel.

"Tilt your head back…" he instructed, lifting the cupped leaf to his brother's lips; tilting it just so, a teaspoon's worth of water trickled down into Nick's mouth.

"That's quite the trick," Nick observed afterward as Evan prepared another leaf.

"It could save your life out here," his brother assured him. "Dehydration comes on faster than you realize."

After several more sips, they started off again, Nick trailing Evan who hacked at vines and brush with his parang. They soon arrived at a bluff where the forest fell away and opened up to an expanse of unbroken green stretching to the horizon with a ribbon of flowing water slicing through its length. The light and open sky were startling after the twilight claustrophobia of the forest.

"This is what I wanted to show you…" Evan explained, as Nick shaded his eyes with a hand. Taking a seat on some exposed rock to catch his breath, his brother went on. "One of the few vantage points out here. You can actually get a sense of how vast this place really is…"

Nick gazed out appreciatively at the expanse before him. The adrenaline from the hunt had long since petered out and he was dragging his ass.

"I'll say…" he agreed, wiping sweat from his brow. That Evan appeared to be equally drained, added to the vague and nagging sense that something wasn't right with his brother.

"All this," Evan went on, thrusting an arm at the vista, "For as far as you can see…it's been Penan territory for millennia… *Long* before the Dutch and the British ever dreamed about a thing called the *East Indies*."

Grateful for the break, Nick joined his brother on the exposed rock.

"Might surprise you," Evan added, "But Borneo's interior wasn't unexplored by Europeans until the middle of the nineteenth century. Didn't take long for the Christian missionary groups to show up after that… They were hoping to get a jump on Islam here since Arab traders had already converted most of the populace in what would become Indonesia and Malaysia.

"And they did. By the 1950s, a majority of the indigenous people of Sarawak had accepted Jesus and were settled in longhouse communities like the ones you saw on the way up here. That included almost ten-thousand Penan. A small number held out, refusing to give up the nomadic life. They're still out there in small bands like this one, living off the forest as they always have…"

Evan then paused, gazing out at the vista as if it held some vague distant memory.

"For years, those Penan kept one step ahead of the chainsaws," he continued. "But now…there's nowhere left to go," His mouth tightened in a grimace.

"Only about *ten-percent* of Borneo's original forest remains. That's not much. Like this right here…" Jutting his jaw toward the vista, he spat in disgust. "It'll soon enough be buried under fifty meters of water…"

Nick frowned. "You mean the *reservoir?* For the *dam…?*"

"The future Lake *Bamaku…*" Evan answered, as if the words had a bitter aftertaste. He pointed to a spot where the forest had been logged.

"You see over there?" he asked, as Nick squinted with a hand shading his brow.

"They're taking the timber first," Evan explained, "The official line is, the revenue will help defray the costs of the dam… But it's no secret that a good chunk of that money's going to end up in offshore bank accounts."

This sort of complex money shuffling was notoriously hard to unravel, Nick knew, even for law enforcement. How had his brother, living out *here,* been able to glean such information?

"We're talking nearly 200,000 hectares that'll be flooded…" Evan continued, "About *half a million acres* for us metrically-challenged Yanks. That's just under *781 square miles*…

"If that's too abstract," he added, after a couple of beats. "Try this — y*our* city, Los Angeles, sprawls over almost 470 square miles of southern California. I still remember that from a course in California history at Berkeley… Meaning, this 781 square-mile patch set to be flooded is almost *twice* the size of LA."

The example hit its mark, as Nick tried to imagine the vista before him submerged beneath a man-made lake.

"And the Penan…they don't get a say in this?" he asked.

The corners of Evan's mouth curled in a bitter smirk.

"…Ah, well, there's the rub…" he explained, "According to Malaysian law, land rights automatically accrue to indigenous people *if* they can prove an 'established historical record' of settlement. Of course, the Penan, being nomadic, have *never* settled permanently in any one spot. They follow the monsoon cycle, much like everthing else in the forest, living for a time in their '*selaps*'— those bamboo huts — then, moving on. So, in the eyes of the government, without *permanent settlement*, they have *no* legal standing to the land…"

"*Really…?*" Nick said, clearly dismayed. "Why hasn't that been challenged? Legally, I mean. Like you said, these people, the Penan — *they're* not the newcomers here."

Evan shrugged. "Some NGOs *are* trying to help, filing briefs on the Penan's behalf. But the judicial system here moves at a glacial pace and it usually comes down on the side of power anyway. Like in much of the world. You end up with men like the interior minister, James Wong, who hands out logging contracts and other sweetheart deals to companies he has ownership stakes in…

"These guys are smart," he sneered, "And well-insulated. Wong and his fellow cronies keep their interests buried under layers of complex, arcane legal constructs like LLCs, blind trusts, that sort of thing. The money winds up in overseas banks with opaque financial secrecy laws; places like Switzerland, Bermuda, Grand Cayman."

"I don't get it…" Nick remarked. "The public must have some idea this stuff's going on, don't they?"

"To some extent, yeah, I suppose they always have," his brother answered. "Most working people in Peninsular Malaysia — like working people anywhere, really — they're just trying to pay their bills and attain something like a middle-class life. It's a given that politics and politicians are corrupt, that the kind of people who elbow their way into positions of power are the kind of people who'll skim some cream from the public trough. And the people in those positions who run things, they know they just have to keep it arcane enough so people don't give much of a shit about it."

At this, he exhaled deeply, clasping his fingers together and leaning forward, elbows on knees.

"What about the press?" Nick asked, "Where are they in all this?"

Evan hissed dismissively. "The *press*..." he repeated, "Feckless toadies, afraid to rock the boat... More concerned with ad sales than doing actual journalism. And no wonder — when you look beneath the surface of these media concerns, you'll find people working at the highest level of government having ownership stakes. That's how things get done in this part of the world — good old-fashioned cronyism. You do me right, I'll do you right.

"That's what the Penan are up against," Evan went on, a brittle note in his tone. "The government sticks to its line that this small group of people are standing in the way of progress for all. Better to settle them in longhouses like all the other indigenous groups in Borneo. The media generally echo whatever they say and the public shrugs, baffled why *anyone* would want to live as hunter-gatherers anyway."

As he reflected on all this, Nick couldn't argue, in theory at least, with the Penan desire to live in better alignment with the natural world. At the same time, he could also understand why the rest of Malaysia's citizens would find the Penan way of life incomprehensible. Mostly though, he found it astonishing that these forest people were determined to live as they did despite the obvious hardships. That their desire to remain *apart*, to be free and disconnected from the developed world meant far more to them than the soft seductions of physical comfort and material abundance, seemed both crazy and somehow heroic. The Penan were easy to admire, he thought, but a whole lot harder to envy.

"The enlightened minds who want to domesticate the Penan," Evan went on, his tone biting. "They're the same kind of people who established the old Carlisle Indian school in Pennsylvania. Remember that saying from one of its founders? You had to 'kill the Indian to save the man'? Wipe out all vestiges of language and culture. Turn the savages into citizens and consumers. In two or three generations, they'll forget who they are and what was once *theirs*..." He coughed and spat in disgust.

"Anyway… If the world sees what's happening here, there's still a chance to stop this. That means calling out the World Bank and the IMF. Make it known far and wide that it's *their* money financing the dam and driving these indigenous people to the brink. Let people in the nations funding these development banks see what this project is going to do to the people that actually live here…"

While Nick's sympathies were decidedly with the Penan, he also knew they were swimming against the tide and the juggernaut of human progress. Evan surely must have understood that time wasn't on the Penan's side; by the time their case worked its way through the courts, the dam would likely be a *fait accompli*. As the legal process dragged on, public attention would inevitably drift, emotions would cool, and little by little, enough work would be done on the project to make turning back impossible. Evan clearly had one thing right: power listens only to money. But money also *bestows* power, and recent history had shown that the exceedingly deep pockets of post-war institutions, like the World Bank and International Monetary Fund, usually prevailed.

"Well…that's playing the long game…" Nick commented, with a hopeful note. His brother, however, now appeared to be elsewhere, as if the subject had run its course.

"You know," Evan eventually began to say, "I've been thinking lately how these people, the Penan… how they have a lot in common with the wolf…"

Nick wasn't sure he heard correctly. "...The *wolf...?*" he repeated.

"Yeah…you know… The way there's something deep down in the wolf's DNA that *resists* domestication… When dogs split from the wolf's bloodline tens of thousands of years ago, they learned to live with us, submit to us, fear us. On the other hand, wolves remained stubbornly wild, refusing our table scraps and our dominance. So we persecuted them to the point where they're now found only in extreme northern latitudes, in places people can't live. Virtually eradicated in the lower forty-eight, even though a handful remain in northern Minnesota near the Canadian border…"

As he listened, Nick once more recalled how his brother had held onto the notion that he was *cursed,* the original sin of their misbegotten nuclear family, the unexpected, unwanted pregnancy that bound two very incompatible people together in a doomed marriage destined to create a genetic dead-end on a stunted and withered branch of their larger family tree.

"I get what you're saying…" Nick eventually replied. "But in the end, doesn't everything under the sun have its time…? You, me, wolves…cultures, entire civilizations…? The way dinosaurs eventually became birds, or the way the Etruscans dissolved into the Romans, the Aztecs into Mexicans, Druids into Celts, Mongols into Kazakhs… Like those German and Italian neighborhoods where we grew up that are mostly Hispanic now… In another hundred or two-hundred years, they'll be something else, something we can't even imagine."

At this, he hesitated.

"What I'm trying to say is, the Penan had a good run… for millennia, they avoided the upheavals of the outside world, of history…" He let it trail off, feeling like he'd lost his point.

"…*History*…" Evan sneered after a moment, his tone astringent. "Like the history of indigenous people back where we come from? Like the Cherokee, the Navajo, or the Sioux — especially the Sioux… Two centuries ago, the master horsemen-hunters of the North American plains. And now? Where are they? Confined to reservations blighted by alcoholism, despair and suicide…That's s*ome* history…"

Nick unconsciously bit his lower lip; this wasn't the direction he'd hoped for.

"Look," Evan continued after a moment, softening a bit. "I'm not delusional. I know what the Penan are up against. And I know we live on a crowded planet where each year there's less and less room for people like them. Or for wild places…places like this where you still have a chance of seeing a corpse flower… And no matter how many ways I run it over in my head, it always comes up the same: That's not a future I want to live in…"

A tinge of remorse singed Nick's mood and he regretted the clumsy attempt at perspective. On top of this, he now felt foolish for harboring a vague, probably jejune and certainly naive yearning that, somehow, he and Evan might once again be a part of each other's lives.

Several minutes passed in silence and he gazed up at the high-altitude wind-smeared clouds in the eastern sky. Evan had noted their approach as well and appeared to be divining some meaning from them.

"High clouds in the east..." he observed, at last. "Monsoon's gathering steam..."

"Hey, look..." Nick began to say, contritely, "I wasn't trying to wash over what's happening here. Force of habit, I guess... Like urging my students to consider all sides of an argument..."

He let this float without further comment. It seemed increasingly clear to him that a shared childhood would not, in itself, be sufficient to bridge the two decades of silence between them.

"You know..." Evan eventually started to say, "None of this was planned. Kelesau, Phillip... Being a parent just wasn't in the cards. I didn't think someone like me had any business having kids. But then, I started working with the Penan and, well...one thing led to another..."

"I'm glad it did..." Nick observed, "You always had better parental instincts than our parents. The way you looked after me when we were kids, taking the heat whenever our mother or Strycker flew off the handle. You never let them take a swing at me."

A hint of mischief flashed in Evan's eyes. "True...if anyone took a swing at you, it was going to be *me...* "

The disarming playfulness briefly amused Nick, a bittersweet echo of their one-time familiarity.

"*Strycker*..." Evan then murmured, "Hadn't thought about him in *years*..."

The name of their mother's boyfriend brought a subtle shift in mood. She and Strycker had met at a bar she visited when their father was at work. After the divorce, Strycker became a regular at their mother's apartment in her old neighborhood. To both boy's dismay and disappointment, their father acquiesced to their mother's insistence they live with *her* so that she would agree to the divorce. The decision left Nick and Evan squarely in the maelstrom of their mother's self-destructiveness which would tragically and profoundly alter the course of their lives.

Nick could still see it as if it were yesterday. He had just turned eleven and watched from a rusty swing-set in their narrow patch of backyard as their mother argued with Evan about something on the rear stoop of her rented brick row house. The crisp, frigid clarity of the late January morning contrasted sharply with their mother's black mood; she had been drinking and, when his brother turned to leave, she angrily grabbed at him just as he reached the edge of the concrete steps leading down from the stoop. It happened in an instant — Evan reflexively jerked away and, unsteady from the booze, their mother lost her grip and fell head-first onto the concrete steps. The sickening dull thud of hair and bone hitting concrete haunted Nick for years. Everything came to a stop until Strycker, who'd been standing in the doorway, rushed out to their mother's inert body on the steps as Evan looked on in shock.

The fall proved fatal and, for reasons Nick would only come to understand years later, the police eventually chose to lay blame for their mother's death at Strycker's feet. While the brothers had little affection for Strycker, both knew he had nothing to do with it. And yet, when questioned by police, Evan maintained it had all happened so fast that he couldn't be sure about anything, a slippery misrepresentation which Nick essentially went along with.

Further confusing things, Strycker didn't protest the accusation, instead claiming he had been trying to separate mother and son when the fall occurred. The district attorney decided to pursue an 'involuntary manslaughter' charge and Strycker chose not to fight it. Apparently, he understood what everyone other than Nick and Evan did at the time: that the police, the city's leaders, the press, and the community as a whole, needed a way to explain this tragedy that would let *them* off the hook. At the time, the story captured the public's attention; for the next week or so, newspaper editorials cited a 'shared collective failure' and pressure grew to hold someone accountable, and that someone could *only* be *Strycker.* As the sole male adult in the whole mess, he became the explanation that assuaged the community's collective hand-wringing. Even Strycker himself seemed to agree, eventually pleading 'no-contest' to a lesser charge and sentenced to a year in the county jail. Released after three months, he moved downstate, never to be heard from again.

Years later as an adult, Nick would come to realize that, given the times, this was how it had to be. Such a self-inflicted family tragedy did not at all comport with the way the good citizens of Wilkes-Barre saw themselves in those days; theirs was not the kind of town where a teenage boy accidentally kills his neglectful alcoholic mother during an argument.

From then on, Nick and Evan lived with their father and his second wife, and neither spoke of the incident again. In truth, neither knew how to approach the subject or explain their silence as to what really happened.

"That *day...*" Evan started to say in a doleful tone. He vaguely shook his head a couple times and frowned. "In just a couple seconds...the whole world changed.

"For years, I couldn't shake it…" he went on, "…That look on her face just before she lost her balance…" He grimaced at the memory.

"No question, a part of me was relieved that it was finally over…that we wouldn't have to live like that anymore. At the same time, I felt like some kind of monster for feeling that way… She was our *mother* for Chrissakes… Didn't matter that it was just a matter of time, that with her drinking, it could've been a car wreck, or passing out in bed with a cigarette… I remember praying at night in silence so you wouldn't hear me, that however it happened, we wouldn't be there with her…" The thought briefly hung in silence.

"Being knocked-up at seventeen with me put her in a cage she couldn't escape from, locking her up with a man she'd never love. I felt it every time she looked at me…"

Nick couldn't dispute this. Their mother had grown ever bitter with each passing year and, in ways both subtle and otherwise, she never let Evan forget it had started with him. And while both brothers absorbed the psychic blows of life in a fractious household, Nick knew Evan bore the lion's share of the animus.

"Anyway…" Evan continued, sighing deeply, "Before Phillip interrupted us in the soaking pool, you were telling me how you came to be washed up on that riverbank."

"*Ah…*" Nick replied, welcoming the change of subject. "…Yes, *well…*"

He picked up where he'd left off when they were soaking, recounting the past six months, *all* of it, from the meetings with Lomax and Swarthout, to all the misdirections, dead-ends and contradictions. Evan listened, arms on knees, fingers clasped, as Nick told him how he'd decided to come to Malaysia, finishing with his enlistment of the BBC reporters, the journey upriver, the two Malaysians taking him and, finally, the SUV washing into the river.

In the silence that followed, Nick waited for a reaction. Seconds ticked away and finally, Evan sucked in a deep breath and silently shook his head.

"…Jesus, Nick… I'm sorry about all that…" he said, clearly distressed.

Nick waited as Evan seemed to be searching for something to add.

"Listen…" Nick began, seeing no further response was coming. "Maybe you can help me with some things *I've* been trying to understand…"

Evan shifted his weight on the rock and looked over at his brother. Hesitating, Nick chose his words carefully. "For instance," he began, "I can understand how your involvement with the Penan might've been at *odds* with the Peace Corps and its mission — I'm guessing they make it clear up front that you guys aren't supposed to get involved in a host country's internal politics, right? That you're volunteers in a respected foreign aid program, representatives of the US government with strict guidelines for conduct. Then, you go off-script by getting involved with the Penan and their protests and you're dismissed, kicked out of the country. That should be all there is to it, right? But it *isn't*... And that's what I can't get my mind around. How does something like this, a *personnel* issue, really...how does *that* warrant all these contortions from official Washington to scratch your name from the books? I get that your involvement with the Penan may have caused a minor diplomatic shit storm, but it hardly rises to the level of high-crimes and misdemeanors. I mean, you can't be the first Peace Corps' volunteer that ever got too close to the people you're supposed to be helping...?"

He watched his brother, waiting for a reaction, but Evan's expression revealed nothing.

"...Is there a question in there somewhere?" Evan finally asked, a wisp of mirth in the tone.

"...*Several*..." Nick answered with a half-smile.

59.

After a few fitful hours sleep on a longhouse floor, thankfully arranged by Seladang, daylight found Carole and Antonio again loading their gear onto the boat. The detour back to Long Akah had offered a shard of hope in that they came upon no bodies in the river, allowing for the possibility that Nick survived the swim. As Seladang tinkered with the motor's fuel line, Antonio finished arranging their gear and Carole leaned over the boat's gunwales to splash some river water on her face.

"...What I wouldn't give for a decent cup of coffee..." she muttered.

"Seladang might have some betel nut to chew," Antonio cracked, "That'll get you on your feet."

This got a thin snicker from Carole, now drying her face with a small hand towel she carried.

"If it weren't for the staining, spitting and rotten teeth, I'd consider it..." she retorted.

These dashes of levity did little to relieve the enormity of what lay ahead and it visibly weighed on them, especially Carole. As senior producer on the story, she knew this mess was on her; *she'd* brought them here and *she'd* let her guard down with Nick. And now she had to reckon with what went unspoken: the odds of finding Nick out here were bleak. Picking up on Carole's mood, Antonio tried to keep them focused.

"I've been thinking…" he began to say, "*If* Nick made it out of the river, and it's looking like he did, he'd have to spend the night out *here…*" He nodded toward the dense forest on the opposite bank. "And, I'm trying to imagine what he'd do…?"

"Well…" Carole began, "What would *you* do?"

Antonio gazed out at the forest on both sides of the river.

"Not sure," he answered, pondering. "I'd probably try to find a spot out of harm's way as much as possible to ride out the night."

"*Out* of harm's way…? And *where* might that be out here?"

"Back from the river for starters," Antonio suggested. "And out of the rain."

"That *would* make sense…" she agreed, "Assuming Nick still had his wits about him. But let's not forget, he's probably terrified and possibly injured. Who knows how he'd handle it — how *any* of us would handle it? I doubt I'd be thinking clearly and out here, you make a couple bad decisions and things suddenly get ten times worse. He's got no food or water, it's getting dark and he knows he's going to spend the night out here. It'd take a seriously disciplined mind to keep it together with all that…"

The implications were plainly daunting and Antonio tried to stay methodical.

"Look," he urged, "Seladang says the river's current would've pushed Nick toward the left side. So why don't we ask him to make an educated guess where he thinks Nick could've landed. Then we look for signs along the bank, narrow the range…"

Carole had nothing better, so she nodded her assent, though she kept her doubts to herself, feeling that *anything* they tried at this point would be little more than a long shot.

60.

Night had begun to fall over the Penan camp when Evan and Nick finally returned. Most of the Penan had assembled in the central area where the carcass of the red langur and a small deer were each impaled on a bamboo spit to slow roast over a fire. Phillip spotted his uncle and made room for him on the mat.

"Here uncle!" he called, "I have your place!"

Evan went to speak with Kelesau while Nick joined his nephew. A minute or so later, he returned, seeming preoccupied. He smiled at Phillip then spoke to Nick.

"I need to take care of something," he said, adding, "You're in good hands…" With that, he tousled his son's hair then disappeared into the deepening darkness.

It puzzled Nick that his brother could skip a meal after all the walking they'd done; a habit like that, he thought, could help explain Evan's withered frame.

Phillip placed a banana leaf containing some sago and charred meat in front of his uncle. "Now you can eat!" he said, pleased with himself.

"Oh…well, thank you, Phillip…" Nick muttered, looking over the charred fatty meat and sago mush; thankfully, the firelight revealed little detail as he picked up a hacked end of bone.

"What is this…?" he asked, nibbling.

"The langur from today," Phillip told him. "Here," he added, placing another stringy chunk of meat on the leaf. "This is some deer they also killed…"

"Mmmm…." Nick murmured, gnawing at the greasy and bony piece of monkey while trying not to think about its previous sentient form. "This… is… *interesting*…" He smiled, raising his eyebrows in an exaggerated way, then declared, "Tastes like *chicken!*"

The little stab at humor completely missed its mark and Phillip scrunched his eyes.

"It's a joke…" Nick explained, awkwardly, "…Back where your father and I grew up…" he continued, chewing, "When people try some sort of meat they've never had before, they often joke that it, '*tastes like chicken*'." The boy just stared and Nick realized the absurdity of trying to explain the ubiquity of chicken as a dietary staple to a eight-year-old boy living in a rain forest.

"…Because they eat chicken all the time, right…?" he added, clarifying. "So *everything* else starts to taste like chicken, you see…?" This didn't help.

"Never mind," he concluded. "Not important. Let's try the deer…"

At this, he reached down and swapped the bony piece of monkey for the less bony but stringier chunk of deer. Holding it with both hands like a sandwich, he took a bite, but the gristly meat just stretched as he tugged and yanked at it with his teeth. It felt a bit like playing tug of war with a dog and its rubber chew toy. After struggling for a minute or so, he gave up and played it for laughs while his nephew grinned with delight at his uncle's antics.

"You're enjoying this, eh…?" Nick teased, as Phillip put a hand to his mouth to stifle a giggle. Along with the fun, Nick tried to maintain some avuncular responsibility.

"Aren't you hungry?" he asked, observing that his nephew hadn't touched his food.

Phillip glanced down and reluctantly began nibbling on a greasy piece of monkey meat.

"Hey, you don't have to eat on my account," Nick assured him, girding himself for another go at the deer. "But, you know…" he added with mock gravity, "There are kids in China who would *love* to have a good piece of monkey to gnaw on…" The boy's eyes scrunched again in bafflement.

"Just messing with you!" Nick confessed with a wink. "It was something my mother — your *grandmother* — used to say when your father and I were about your age." he explained. "Whenever we left food on our plates, she'd try to make us feel guilty by reminding us there were children starving in other parts of the world."

 Of course, the explanation fell flat.

"Anyway," Nick continued, back-pedaling. "The point is, your dad and I were once *your* age too. And just like you, we didn't always like what our parents made us eat."

Phillip squinted while Nick continued nibbling at the stringy deer meat. "Uncle…" the boy asked, after a moment, "Do you have any children…?"

Nick froze in mid-chomp at the question.

"Uh…no…" he answered.

"You have *no* sons?" Phillip persisted, in the un-self-conscious way of children.

"Nope…" replied Nick, nibbling again. "…Not yet, at least…"

"You don't want children??" the boy pressed.

'*...From the mouths of babes...* ' thought Nick. "Well, it's not that I don't *want* children..." he explained, setting the meat down and licking the char and grease from his fingers. "...It's just that...well... It hasn't happened yet..."

"It *hasn't...?* " echoed Phillip. "How does it *happen...?* "

Nick grinned; he was cornered, remembering that vagueness only made things worse when trying to explain life's thornier bits to children.

"Well... between you and me..." he said, in a mock confidential tone, "I don't think anyone really *knows* how such things happen... "

His nephew blinked and frowned.

"Now, how about you, Phillip?" Nick deftly pivoted. "What kind of things do *you* like to do? You know, for fun, with the other kids?"

The boy's mouth tightened and he looked down at his food. "I help mother a lot..." he answered.

Nick raised an eyebrow. "Oh sure," he agreed, "But... You must have *some* time for play?"

Phillip absently fussed a spot on his leg. "...Sometimes..."

As he pretended to nibble the fatty meat, Nick wondered what he'd waded into.

"And your father?" he then asked. "Do you do things with him?"

The question hit a nerve and Phillip distractedly began pulling at a toe.

"...My father is different... Like *me*..."

This stopped Nick in mid-nibble. Apparently, the subject of his nephew's mixed blood had come up before.

"I see..." he mused. "*You're* different because your father is a white man and that makes you *half* white...?"

Phillip weakly nodded without looking up.

"...And the other children...They say things to you about being different?"

At this, his nephew began to squirrel his lips around and scratch at the thatch mat. "Sometimes..." he murmured, "...They say things to tease me... for speaking English..."

"Is that right...?" Nick mused. "Well, I think I know *why* they do that," he sagely reassured the boy who now met his gaze. "It's because you speak *two* languages while they can only speak *one*." He leaned in closer. "I had a similar thing happen when I was around your age... My classmates at school would tease me because I was a good reader…I could read faster than most. The teacher told me they were just *jealous*. You know what that means?"

The boy shook his head.

"Well…" Nick continued, "Jealous is the way some people feel when they don't have what someone else has. Or when someone does a thing better than they do it. Like those kids at my school…they were *jealous* I could *read* better… So they made fun of me." He paused a moment to gauge his nephew's reaction.

"Maybe…" he added, confidently. "Those other children are jealous that *you* can speak another language and *they* can't."

This only seemed to confuse Phillip further.

"But…" the boy muttered, "They don't *want* to speak English…?"

"Oh sure, that's what they may *say*," Nick countered, "But inside, I bet they wish they *could* speak English. They just don't know how to ask you." His eyes narrowed conspiratorially as he met his nephew's gaze.

"How about this…?" he suggested, "You tell them, if they learn English, you'll all have a secret language the adults can't understand. Except for your father, of course…"

This prospect appeared to brighten the boy's outlook and Nick again started at the piece of deer meat and winked, "Stick with me, kid…"

They each silently poked at their food as another thought came to Nick.

"Hey…maybe we should save some of this…*meat*…for your father?"

Something in the suggestion distressed Phillip and he hung his head.

"*Hey…?*" said Nick, concerned, "What's this…?"

The boy vaguely shook his head then glanced in the direction of his mother sitting with some Penan women.

"It's okay…" Nick assured him, taking note. "Whatever we talk about, it's just between us, right?"

Phillip briefly looked at his uncle and Nick inferred the child's concern about betraying an adult confidence.

"…I don't think father wants to eat…" the boy said, at last.

Not expecting this, Nick leaned back.

"Is that right…?" he gently remarked. "What makes you say that, Phillip…?"

Seconds ticked by and Nick noted the boy's increasing discomfort.

"Listen," he then suggested, disarmingly, "We don't have to talk about this now… Another time, okay?"

His nephew poked at the fatty deer meat.

"I think he's sick…" Phillip finally said with obvious hesitance.

Nick wasn't sure he heard correctly.

"*Sick…?*" he repeated. "Why do you think that…?"

The boy squirmed. "Because…where he goes…"

"Oh…? And where is that…? Where he goes?"

As he waited for a response, Nick sensed the boy wrestling with his conscience.

"To the *dayung…*" Phillip answered without looking up.

"I see…" Nick murmured, pondering. He let this sit a moment. "And what is that…? This *dayung…?*" he then asked, but the boy didn't answer.

"Tell you what…" he continued, "Maybe you could just show me? You know? Take me there when we're done eating?"

Phillip noticeably flinched at the suggestion and Nick deduced that he'd likely been warned off by his father. The request now presented a dilemma, confusing his nephew's loyalties and his conscience. Still, the genie was out of the bottle and Nick persisted.

"*Phillip…?*" he gently prodded as the boy fidgeted.

61.

With the heat and humidity it felt as if they'd been walking all day, but Carole's watch said it had only been about fifteen minutes.

Seladang had spotted a patch of riverbank where the soil looked scuffed up and pulled the boat over to investigate. There he noticed some footprint fragments from the tread of a hiking boot in the soaked clay soil. The boatman carefully began tracking the print remnants while Carole and Antonio trailed behind. It didn't take long for the thick, viscid air to overwhelm the two reporters. Perspiration dripped into their eyes, soaked their clothing and pooled on skin. Unable to evaporate in such high humidity, sweat merely collected on itself.

Carole kept about a dozen paces behind Seladang, Antonio trailing her. He carried the camera in one hand with the recorder slung over a shoulder, and looked just *slightly* less wilted — an advantage, she concluded, of his age and Thai genetics. Seladang forged ahead unimpeded by the heat as he slashed at vines and undergrowth with a machete while carrying Antonio's tripod on his shoulder.

Despite her discomfort and fatigue, Carole stubbornly tried to maintain an unflappable demeanor, what she liked to think of as one of the more desirable of British traits, that *keep calm and carry on* thing. Time and her career path had been hardening agents in the determination to counter the belief among her male colleagues that women were ill-suited to the rigors of reporting from war zones, insurrections and other flavors of global chaos. Initially, it startled her how easily she could tamp down emotions, ride out discomfort, and yes, even shit in a hole if necessary. With time, such qualms dissolved away as she gained respect and earned accolades in a profession traditionally dominated by men with outsize egos.

Still, Borneo appeared determined to put her stoicism to the test. In her younger days, a frenetic schedule and infrequent meals were enough to maintain a reasonable degree of fitness. Now in her forties, she'd learned that being *thin* did not necessarily equate with being *fit.*

"You doing okay?" she asked between breaths, glancing back toward Antonio.

"Fine..." he replied. Ten years her junior, he was capable and fairly fit, yet now looked almost as wilted and withered.

"You know... I could carry something..." she offered, "Like the recorder...?"

"...Thanks... I've got it," he answered, waving her off with his free hand.

The monsoon rains had saturated the clay soil, making for greasy footing. Carole's shoes, while practical, comfortable, and Euro-stylish, offered little in the way of traction. Several times she thrust her arms out anticipating a fall. Antonio's shorter stature and lower center of gravity offered some slight advantage, while Seladang's bare feet and splayed toes helped him move with ease over wet soil, bare rocks and rotting logs.

Soon, the trio arrived at a small rise and Seladang stopped. He pointed out a spot some distance ahead where logging operations had begun to cut into the forest. A small brigade of heavy equipment — bulldozers, graders, front loaders, dump trucks — all sat idle nearby. Smoky haze from smoldering piles of logging debris lingered in the heavy air, fixing the scene in a bluish pall.

"On other side..." Seladang said in a hush, waving a hand in said direction. "...the Penan blocking..."

Carole took '*blocking*' to mean '*blockade*'.

"Over there?" she asked. "The Penan have a blockade...?"

"Yes..." the boatman answered, nodding at the idle machinery. "They stop cutting. Because the Penan blocking..."

Surprised, Carole turned to Antonio, now anxiously fretting over the camera with a piece of cloth.

"Please tell me everything's working?" she said, watching him fuss.

Antonio wiped the sweat from his brow on a shirtsleeve.

"This damn humidity..." he muttered, "Plays hell with the electronics... But we're okay. For now..."

The assurance offered little comfort and Carole quickly turned back to Seladang.

"Wasn't expecting to run into this..." she muttered, gazing in the direction of the blockade site. The hard-bitten reporter in her knew they'd stumbled upon TV gold: a potentially explosive confrontation tailor-made for the camera. Even better, *they* were the only camera on the scene. At the same time, finding Nick *had* to be the priority, and now, the possibility of an unlikely convergence teased some hope out of her. If in fact, Nick had come this way as Seladang believed, he most likely would've noticed blockade as well and, despite the potential danger of seeking help there, in his state, he'd have no choice but to approach.

Noting Carole's attention to the blockade, Seladang went on. "When the dam project started...these blockings, they happen anytime now... "

She heard the words but her mind was elsewhere.

"Nick would've come upon this, too..."she observed, "If he made it this far..."

Antonio busily switched tapes. "Let's hope," he said. "But it must've also crossed his mind that there could be some people down connected to the men who grabbed him."

"True, but what's his alternative? Spend another night out here with no food or water?"

"Point taken," Antonio agreed, finishing up with the camera. "Meaning that's our next stop..."

He got to his feet and rested his hands on his hips.

"But let's be clear," he added, "We go in there, we'll be detained and probably have our tapes and equipment confiscated. And if it turns out we got it wrong and he's not there...well, too bad, that's it. We're done looking for him and the story's finished."

"Understood…" Carole replied, "But what else can we do? If Nick came this way, as Seladang thinks, then he would've seen this. And with what he's been through, he'd take any help he could get…"

62.

The glow of the settlement's fire receded in the darkness as Phillip led Nick along the stream. Overhead, a thin break in the canopy revealed a sliver of sky in which a full moon had risen, casting a faint ribbon of light on the trickling water. After several minutes, they arrived at a break in the vegetation where Phillip detoured from the stream and soon stopped, pointing out the faint orange glow of a cooking fire.

They cautiously inched closer and, in the meager light of the fire, Nick could just make out a thatch structure, open at the front like a lean-to. A gaunt, withered-looking old man squatted on his haunches and fussed with something in the fire's faint glimmer. Wrinkled skin drooped from the old man's skeletal frame that looked like it might blow apart in a stiff breeze.

Phillip softly tapped his uncle's arm and pointed to a supine body on a woven mat near the old man — *Evan*, his eyes closed in an apparent state of meditation. Nick noticed what appeared to be pieces of shriveled roots and stalks placed on Evan's torso. As his brother lay there motionless, the elderly man muttered and occasionally ran a frond over him, then dipped a finger into one of several small bowls to daub some sort of liquid on Evan's forehead, letting it dribble down his temples. At one point, he threw a pinch of what looked like crushed leaves into the fire and fanned the billowing smoke. All the while, Evan didn't move a muscle as the smoke produced hazy little shafts in the firelight.

Nick hadn't noticed the elderly man before — at least not with the other Penan. Elaborate tattoos adorned the man's arms and torso and his earlobes were stretched like noodle strands to the collar bone, making him hard to miss. A small headdress fitted with tiny feathers anchored the top and sides of his thin gray hair. Nick suspected the man to be some sort of *shaman* or *healer* who chose to live apart from the others in the forest where he could divine nature's deeper secrets.

Edging closer, Nick picked up tiny rivulets of sweat glistening on his brother's forehead. Perhaps his nephew was right, he thought, and Evan *had* fallen ill, which might explain the wheezing and weight loss. Life out here in the forest carried a litany of potential diseases that Nick learned about at UCLA's travel medicine clinic. Malaria, dengue fever, schistosomiasis, lymphatic filariasis, river blindness; a litany of horrific illnesses that would have convinced most reasonable people to stay home.

Just then, the shaman bellowed loudly, startling Nick and Phillip.

"*Jesus...!*" Nick inadvertently blurted, his heart thumping in his ear. "*What the hell is that...?*"

Phillip bit his lower lip then spoke in a hushed voice: "He says to stop hiding like a deer..."

Once again, the old man thundered, an insistence in the tone.

"He wants to know," the boy continued, "Why we are here..."

Nick took a deep breath and clasped the boy's shoulder reassuringly. An unfamiliar impulse told him to take the lead.

"Okay..." he said, "You wait here..."

Nick started toward the shaman who didn't look up from his ministration. When he was a few meters from the hut, Nick stopped. The old man then softly began murmuring incantations. An ineffable, unnerving energy imbued the surrounding darkness with menace, as if some banished medieval coven lived in the forest. An awkward minute or so passed before Nick spoke.

"...I uh..." he mumbled, "...don't um...speak *Penan*..."

The old man ignored this, continuing his intonations while Nick waited, unsure what he should do. Then, another voice startled him.

"He doesn't understand why a grown man like you is sneaking around in the forest at night." The voice belonged to his brother, eyes closed, still supine on the mat. "...I might wonder too, except I already have a pretty good idea."

Evan then spoke loudly in Penan for Phillip's benefit. At this, a rustling began to stir in the brush where the boy was hiding, and Nick surmised his brother had shooed the boy off.

"It wasn't his fault," he quickly insisted, in his nephew's defense. "I *asked* him to bring me here..."

A thin smile hinted on Evan's lips, but before Nick could say anything further, the shaman spoke.

"He says to come closer," Evan translated.

Puzzled, Nick took a few tentative steps toward the old Penan who spoke again with what Nick took to be disapproval in his tone.

"He thinks you don't look well…" Evan explained.

Nick frowned. "Well, sure…" he replied, a sardonic note in his tone, adding, "My routine's a little off…"

The shaman snorted and muttered something else.

"He says your color's not good," Evan again translated.

"My *color?*" Nick objected. "How can he tell in this light?"

"He knows," Evan assured him. "He's virtually blind, but…he can tell…"

Somewhat irritated by this, Nick frowned at the old man. People who believed they had some sort of clairvoyance usually made him uncomfortable, as if they were undressing his soul.

"What are you saying?" he asked. "…That he's what, some kind of *medicine man* or *shaman?*"

"The Penan call them '*dayung*'," Evan answered. "His name's *Galong Selah.*"

Nick watched the shaman now pinch dried bits of something into the fire as he muttered.

"He's preparing a tonic for you," explained Evan.

"For *me?*" Nick asked, still wary from the *burak* episode. "Well, tell him thanks, but my stomach's a little off…"

Evan's expression lightened at this and he slid over on the thatch mat.

"…C'mon, sit down…" he beckoned, patting the spot next to him.

Hesitating, Nick moved closer, carefully edging around Galong Selah to the mat, where he sat down next to his brother, legs pulled to chest with arms clasped around them. A smoky, gossamer haze hung in the air, barely back-lit by the fire's faint glow while the old shaman softly murmured his incantations, the tones evaporating into the empty night.

Some time passed in silence and Nick could have easily convinced himself he'd been transported back into the primal night of early hominids. He could barely make out the figure of his brother next to him on the mat. An arm's-length or so to his right, the shaman hunched over the tiny fire, his features ill-defined in its anemic cast. As his eyes adjusted, Nick found himself once again troubled by his brother's physical state; muscle appeared withered beneath sagging flesh in his arms and legs while, around his joints, skin stretched over little more than bone and connective tissue.

"Did you know…?" Evan began to say, "That almost half a billion people chew that Betel nut you tried?"

"…*I'm sorry…?*" Nick responded, not understanding.

Evan placed a hand under his head. "It's true," he went on, "You can find it all over the Asian Pacific. Extremely popular even though it's been linked to cancers of the mouth and throat."

"Yeah…?" Nick uttered, wondering where Evan was going with this.

"The only kind the Penan are even remotely familiar with."

At this, Nick's eyes narrowed and he began to suspect his brother wasn't looking to engage in a discussion on the epidemiology of cancer among indigenous peoples.

"You know…" Evan emphasized, pausing a beat, " *Cancer…* "

He voiced the word as if it left a foul taste on the tongue. Nick stared at his brother laying supine on the mat.

"…*Wait…*" he finally said, a note of dread in his tone. "…Are you *saying…?*"

The question went unfinished as Nick fell silent and a faint nausea began to roil him.

"…*Jesus…*" he muttered, his voice thin, brittle. "…Is that *what this is…? You're not saying that…that you…*" The thought fell away and he simply stared in stunned disbelief. Of all the things troubling his sleep the last few months, his brother's mortality had *not* been among them.

"I… I don't *understand…?*" he stammered, "Where did this come from…?" He shot a quick glance Galong Selah's way. "…From *him…?*"

The words had barely left his lips when the shaman spoke and produced a half coconut shell holding some sort of liquid. Nodding, he thrust it toward Nick.

"…*Wha…?*" Nick blurted, confused.

"That's what Galong Selah prepared for you," Evan explained, opening his eyes. "Based on what he sees… Go on, take it."

Nick took the shell and stared at the contents while the ancient shaman pointed a finger at him and began to speak.

"…Ah…sure…of course…" Evan commented as he listened, closing his eyes in thought.

"What the *hell…?*" Nick muttered, confused and agitated as his brother's news had barely registered.

"I don't want to do this now," he protested.

"Go ahead…" Evan urged, rubbing his temple. "You don't want to offend this old man, do you? It's fine… I promise. *Burak-free.*"

The slight whiff of burlesque in his brother's tone had Nick thinking that the shaman might've given him some sort of herbal concoction for pain relief and it brought on a mild inebriation. So be it, he thought; few maladies could compete with the wallop of a cancer diagnosis. Of all the horrific diseases life might throw at you, none terrified like the body consuming itself.

"Seriously," Evan continued, "Galong Selah will keep all your medical information strictly confidential…"

Thoroughly flummoxed, Nick swirled the mixture around in the shell. If drinking it meant not offending the old Penan and getting back to his brother, then drink he would.

"…Okay…" he said dryly and downed the shell's contents. The earthy, almost *moldy* taste, and chalky, gritty texture made Nick think of some 'fiber-in-a-beverage' product for seniors. He scrunched his lips and wiped them on the back of an arm. Then, with a bow of his head, he handed the shell back to Galong Selah who blurted something at him.

"*What now…?*" Nick anxiously asked.

"…Well…" Evan began to explain, a gravitas in his tone. "…I…uh… well… He *says* …you have too many wrinkles on your forehead."

"*Wrinkles??*" Nick repeated, incredulously. "He thinks I have too many *wrinkles??*"

Evan shrugged. "I'm just the messenger…"

"Tell him I'll have it fixed in LA like everyone else…" Nick complained. "Anyway, forget that and tell me…tell me why you think it's…" At this, he faltered.

"*…Cancer?*" Evan said, finishing for him. He gently rubbed his eyes and girded himself for an explanation.

"…Last year…" he went on, "An NGO brought a portable x-ray machine upriver on a converted tourist boat to some of the longhouse communities… There'd been some concern about tuberculosis after a couple cases were discovered in the lower Baram. The authorities in Kuching worried that all the river traffic up and down might bring it to more remote communities with no prior history of infection and, obviously, no immunity…

"I'd been having trouble keeping up on longer hunts… And, I'd sometimes get these dry coughing fits. So, when I heard about this portable x-ray unit, I thought I'd take advantage of it…"

As Nick listened, a throbbing sensation started lightly pulsing in his temples.

"The pictures showed a mass in my left lung. About eight centimeters…"

The words 'mass' and 'left lung' were all Nick heard.

"From my smoking days, maybe…" his brother continued, pinching the bridge of his nose with two fingers. "A pack-and-a-half-a-day since high school…" At this, he smiled briefly. "Gotta admit, though… I still miss it."

The two brothers fell silent as the shaman's low murmuring intonations floated in the heavy night air.

"…The doctors…" Evan then began to say, "They said all the things they're supposed to… *'You should get this looked at by someone.' 'Might still be early enough…' Lung cancers metastasize easily…*"

Nick began to feel numb and somewhat wobbly. He glanced over at the muttering shaman, then turned to his brother.

"So…*what?* You decided *this* would be the extent of your treatment?"

"Don't underestimate Galong Selah…" Evan admonished. "He comes from a long line of dayungs with an encyclopedic knowledge of the forest."

"I'm sure," Nick agreed. "I don't *doubt* Galong Selah can do *all* sorts of things. But I don't think he's going to cut a tumor out of someone…"

The throbbing, wobbly sensation in Nick's head now produced a weird spatial distortion that made nearby objects appear as if being viewed through a wide-angle lens.

"What about *Phillip?*" he asked, trying to focus. "And your *wife…?* Do *they* know??"

Again, no response.

"No…" Nick bleakly concluded, "Were you planning on telling them at some point?"

"Of course," Evan finally answered, hands clasped on his stomach, eyes still shut.

"You have to understand," he went on, "This culture… The Penan…their take on the world is way different from ours. To them, the spirit and the physical body are two sides of the same coin, and disease is the manifestation of some deeper *spiritual* deficiency." He opened his eyes and glanced at Nick, now looking a bit woozy.

"Here," Evan suggested, patting the thatch mat next to him. "Why don't you lay down? Pretend it's the floor of our bedroom when we were kids. Remember…? In autumn, when trees started losing their leaves and the streetlights cast shadows of bare limbs and branches on the walls and ceiling.

We'd lay there at night watching those changing shadows and making up stories to scare each other… "

A rueful little smile turned the corners of Nick's mouth. This had been one of the ways they distracted themselves from their parent's noisy quarreling downstairs, taking turns visualizing things in the shadows and concocting little yarns over their parent's muffled shouts and slamming of things.

"I remember…" Nick eventually said, laying down next to his brother on the mat. "We'd have the radio on low…listening to all those far-off AM stations we could pick up at night… "

He let his eyes fall shut, recalling the inexplicable sense of largeness and possibility those distant radio signals brought. Now, laying there with his brother once more as if half their lives hadn't already passed, those memories seemed like a dream, like someone else's history.

"Oh man, the whole world opened up…" Evan waxed. "Stations from the Midwest and the South. Even some French-speaking stations from Montreal… In the dark, I imagined being transported to those far-off places, traveling through the night with those signals while the rest of the world slept…"

Nick warmed to the memory; the records spun by DJs with different accents and the occasional foreign language hinted at a world far larger and more promising than the insular one they knew in Wilkes-Barre.

"We traveled in our minds…" Evan went on, "Science'll tell you it's all just neurons, synapses and electrochemical signals swirling around this gelatinous mass in our skulls. And, in an empirical, 'Joe Friday-ish' way, that's true. It's all just a theatre in our heads, nothing but chemicals and electricity. But that can't be *all* it is. This animating force that can love, create, think in the abstract and imagine things that never were — how can all that be explained by physics, chemistry and math?"

A familiar note flickered in Nick's mind as he recalled his brother's talent for heaving a load at you whenever he wanted to change the subject.

"It's not your *spirit* I'm worried about…" he reminded Evan. "Right now, I'm more concerned why you're not on the way to a hospital somewhere that can deal with this."

As he heard himself speak, Nick realized that his aural faculties had taken on an 'echoey' effect and a vaguely '*syrupy*' quality, like coming to after a medical procedure. *The shaman's concoction…*

Evan smiled at this. "What was it Nanette Frank's mother used to call you?" he asked, "Whenever you wouldn't let something go and just kept pressing on with questions. One of those Yiddish terms…something like '*noodge*'…"

"Not sure it was really Yiddish," Nick told him. "I think she made it up."

"Even better…" Evan declared.

While the dodge irritated Nick, it also heartened him that time had apparently not diminished his brother's irreverent sensibility and abundant talent for evading discomfiting questions. The quivery feeling in his head began to come on stronger and a few seconds passed as he tried to shake it off.

"Tell me something, Nick…" Evan eventually said, his tone different somehow, "All that business you came upon cleaning out the old man's house… That file and everything in it… Why not just let it go? No one would've blamed you…"

Of course, Nick thought. Even as a boy, his brother had mastered the art of changing the subject by throwing out a distracting question with layers of unsatisfying answers.

"I don't know…" Nick replied, "…Maybe I should have… Celeste kept insisting I 'didn't owe you anything.' But this, it wasn't about keeping some scorecard. That never entered into it…" At this he paused, considering.

"When I learned dad had hired these investigators to look for you," he went on, "I didn't know what to think…especially why he decided to do that after all these years.

"He wasn't there and I had all these questions, so I paid a visit to that investigation firm and found out they'd gotten pushback from the State Department to back off. From then on, everything just got messier. The more I dug, the stranger it all got. Like all that effort to wipe away any hint of your association with the Peace Corps… Just because you crossed a line by getting involved in a host country's domestic politics? Like that's *never* happened before in the history of the Peace Corps?" He paused to wipe the sweat beading on his brow with a forearm: *That damn shaman's concoction…*

"I just couldn't let it go," Nick went on, "Got under my skin, I guess… Somehow it started to feel…*personal*… Besides, if I didn't track this down, who would? Nobody else was going to do it. Only family would, and that meant me…"

He let this hang for an awkward minute or so. His brother's question had touched upon the raw nerve that went unsoothed. Evan's evident rejection of his past and his family ties, had obviously included *Nick*. Little wonder that most people found it difficult to understand why he would put himself through so much trouble to learn what happened to a sibling who had unambiguously rebuffed him.

"Listen…" Evan said at last, "No one has to remind me how much I fucked up in this life… I've lost count of the nights I'd lay awake wishing I could do things over…make 'em right. Make up for letting you down…" The words appeared to run aground, stranding him in mid-thought.

"But I knew, *nothing* could ever set things right," he continued, "Nothing… I didn't know how to live with that shame, that *guilt*. The only way to do that was to lose that part of me. To reinvent myself, I guess. To forget what I couldn't change, what I could never take back…"

Nick found himself surprisingly moved by his brother's candor. An unfamiliar emotional malleability had softened him and he suspected the shaman's cocktail. Still, he could understand how a man might try to escape his past with physical distance. His own move west had been driven by a similar desire to reinvent himself. The years, however, had shown the fallacy in such thinking; there weren't enough miles on earth to put distance between a man and himself.

"You know," Evan began once more, his tone reflective, "Early on, I'd convinced myself I had no business being a parent. I mean, what did *I* know about parenting? It's not like we had the greatest role models… Even so, it found me anyway, and I became a father, with this tiny life entrusted to me… A blank slate to shepherd into adulthood. I understood that, from now on, everything I did and said would be scrutinized by this little person…would imprint on him in some indelible way. It's a hell of a thing to get your mind around… That *my* example would help shape a kid's life. Powerful stuff."

In the scant light of the shaman's fire, Nick thought he could almost see his brother's words manifest in the air, emerging from the bluish haze to float there. Everything had taken on a dreamy quality and he felt like a sleepy child teetering on the edge of consciousness while being read a bedtime story.

"…As time went on and Phillip grew," Evan continued, "I had this secret hope that, maybe, while still possible…he would one day get a chance to meet his *uncle*. I told him all about you, of course… That there was this place on the other side of the world, a long, long way from here, where I had once been *his* age, with parents and a younger brother… Thought he should know his roots on his father's side, to understand why his father looked so different from the other Penan and why *he* himself looked different. That being different was a *strength,* something to be proud of… "

At this, he fell silent, reflective, and a vague melancholy settled over them both. For Nick, his brother's words brought a kind of confirmation that the parameters of our lives could be found in the circumstances of our birth; that fate's arcane caste system determined the trajectory of our lives at birth, outlining the range of our social and economic mobility in ways that could only be understood in retrospect. The man on the mat next to him had once been a little boy in '*Bugs Bunny*' pajamas who ran his orange plastic '*Hot Wheels*' tracks from the kitchen through the dining room and on into the living room; a boy who insisted that his action figures like '*GI Joe*' and '*Johnny West*' actually be buried in the back yard when they met their end in his conjured narratives. That these facts of their childhood would somehow lead to the current moment seemed beyond comprehension: two sons of America, half a world removed from their small-town, working-class Pennsylvania origins, laying side-by-side under a thatch roof lean-to in the equatorial night while a mad indigenous man invoked animist spirits.

Laying there, Nick's mind grew increasingly 'spongy,' his thoughts more obtuse and labored. A sour acrid taste leached into his throat and he rubbed his eyes with the heels of both palms.

"…I'm not thinking straight…" he murmured, "…must be that stuff I drank…"

Evan opened an eye and turned toward him.

"Or maybe you're just flat-out exhausted…" he suggested. "Why don't you take a nap for a while…?"

"…yeah… Maybe…" Nick agreed, "Just for a couple minutes…" And within seconds, he fell sound asleep.

63.

Antonio struggled along the sloping terrain as it descended toward the hydro project site. The camera in his right hand counterbalanced the recording deck hanging from a shoulder strap. Several paces ahead, Seladang carried the tripod, with Carole in the gap between them. At a particularly steep patch, the tape deck swung out ahead of Antonio and, attempting to counter the momentum, he lost his footing on the slick clay. Out of habit, he cradled the camera in one arm while blunting the impact of the fall with the other.

Carole heard him hit the ground and instantly turned, stifling an instinct to call out. Instead, she started back toward him.

"*You okay??*" she said in a fretful hush as she rushed toward him.

Splayed out on his back, Antonio winced and nodded with a muffled groan.

"Let me take the camera," Carole said, lifting it from his grip.

Antonio flexed his fingers and rubbed the wrist he'd fallen on. The possibility that one of them could be injured out here had been shoved to the back of Carole's mind where she'd hoped to keep it.

"*I'm* carrying the deck," she insisted, her tone preempting any debate. "Here…" she said, pulling a couple of pens from her pockets. "We can use these as a makeshift splint." Rifling through flaps of the recorder's case, she located a small roll of tape used to re-mark the videotape cases and taped the two pens together, placing them under Antonio's wrist and running more tape around the entire arrangement to hold everything in place.

"That's enough," Antonio objected, waving her off.

"Will you stop, already?" she snapped, finishing.

"My wrist got yanked, that's all…" he complained.

Carole gave him what she liked to think of as the 'eye of opprobrium.' As seasoned journalists on the East Asian beat, they'd survived numerous tight spots — arrests and detainments, passports lost, deportations, intimidation, etc. But they were *not* 'expedition' journalists. The BBC had a deep roster of *those* types, the ones that produced long-form nature documentaries and films about mountain climbers and other mad adventurers.

As she finished the improvised splint, Seladang appeared.

"Very close now," he said, hushed but urgent. He swung an arm toward a spot further down the slope in the direction they'd been heading.

"You can *see*…" he continued, "The army men, the Penan… Down there."

"Any sign of our friend…?" Carole asked.

Seladang shook his head. "I don't see…"

Carole then turned to Antonio and mulled their dwindling options. The tiny glimmer of hope that had sustained them so far had begun to diminish with Antonio's mishap and the lingering uncertainty that Nick had escaped the river.

"We can't do this on our own…" she grimly concluded. "I think we have to go in there and take our chances with the military."

Antonio offered no resistance as he reached for the camera.

"Maybe so,' he agreed, reluctantly. The fall had underscored the enormity of their endeavor and how out of their element they were. "I'll at least get some footage… Try to salvage what we can of this…"

Self-recrimination and second-guessing had quietly nicked away at Carole's confidence. It was one thing to be cavalier about her own safety, but it veered into recklessness to do so with others — Antonio had a young family to think about, children who saw her as an 'auntie'.

"Listen," she said, a stoniness in her tone, "I *have* to do this… This happened to Nick because of *me*… And now, *you're* hurt."

Antonio looked askance at her. "Forget whatever it is you're thinking," he told her. "No one twisted my arm into doing this. Nick's either…"

She sighed, acknowledging the point.

"Look," he continued, "I'll be fine. I *want* to see this through. So let's drop it, okay…?"

For half a minute, she searched his eyes gauging his sincerity. Then, with a deep sigh, she acquiesced.

"Right…" she concluded, in that distinctly British way that meant 'okay' as Antonio got to his feet.

"Moment," Seladang interrupted, extending a hand. "I can carry," he said, eyeing the camera and the splint on Antonio's wrist. The cameraman hesitated but, much to Carole's surprise, finally nodded and handed the camera to the boatman.

"He's much better on his feet out here…" Antonio explained as Carole raised an eyebrow.

So resigned, they started off again and it didn't take long before the unrelenting humidity and demanding terrain began to weigh on them. Carole wiped her brow on a sleeve, feeling like a wrung-out dish rag. She then realized Seladang had disappeared from sight. Antonio caught up and asked what was wrong.

Carole shook her head. "I can't see him…" she answered, "Or hear him…" For a minute or so, they listened for the sound of machete chops, but heard nothing.

"He must've stopped…" Antonio eventually surmised. "…Or maybe he's already *there*…?"

They waited, but the only sounds upon the languid air were the clicking and whirring of unseen insects, or the occasional call of a distant bird. But then, they heard something rustle the brush up ahead. Neither dared breathe as they gazed around at the dense forest enclosing them. At last, some nearby branches and vines parted and Seladang emerged.

"Over *here!*" he said, his tone anxious but hushed. "The *blocking...*"

With palpable relief, the two journalists started toward him, assuming he meant, 'blockade'.

"...How close?" Carole asked as she approached.

"A hundred meters this way, maybe," the boatman told her, jutting his head in its direction.

64.

An otherworldly orange sky glared over a desolate high-desert landscape. If not for occasional spikes of bristled grass randomly poking up between outcrops of basalt-like rock, it could have been high noon on Venus or Mars.

A thin, wobbly-pitched wind wheezed in the distance and the entire scene slowly began to rotate, revealing an endless wasteland of scrub and rock running to the horizon. In the near distance, a crumpled gray mass lay in a heap. Spasms of movement rippled on one side of it, gradually resolving into meaty, leathery legs quivering to life. Thrashing and kicking up dust, it struggled to right itself and, after several fitful attempts, it finally got to its feet to reveal a freakish rhinoceros-like creature.

Distressed and agitated, the rhino-like beast heaved and gasped at the air, its eyes wide and its head reeling back and forth as if trying to expel something stuck in its throat. With every heave, the beast snorted and shrieked, froth forming at the corners of its mouth. All the kicking and flailing coated the animal in a thin, gauzy veil of red dust. As it steadied itself and took in its surroundings, a massive shadow began to cast the entire expanse in gloom. Breathing heavily, the strange creature gradually started to slump, eventually leaning over to one side until it finally crashed to the ground in a plume of dust. A single eye stared out while its now slower, shallow breaths grew further and further apart before ceasing entirely.

Patterns of light and shadow rapidly alternated across the animal's lifeless head, mirroring different densities of clouds passing overhead. Moving across the sky with unnatural speed, as if the day itself had been sped-up, they soon vanished completely, leaving in their wake an empty fire-orange sky.

A single tear collected in a corner of the beast's eye then flowed down the wrinkled skin of its cheek. Seconds later, a stream of glistening, pallid gray viscera began spooling from the animal's nether regions and onto the ground, piling up like a tangle of garden hose. The spewing entrails terminated in a pale, gelatinous sac at the top of the pile with blue veins encasing it and wispy plumes of steam rising upward.

The distant howling of wind inexplicably ceased while the sac's elastic surface throbbed with random bulges as if something inside were pushing out. Each pulse stretched the sac further until the membrane finally ruptured, and what looked to be a yellow-orange beak pushed through.

As the beak rose up through the opening, it appeared to widen and curve like a Yemeni dagger, finally revealing its attachment to the head of a creature that appeared to be part-bird and part-reptile. Atop the widest section of the beak where it joined the face, another structure curled upward in a slight-ly theatrical flourish reminiscent of a Conquistador's helmet. The net effect made it look as if the creature had *two* mouths.

Large wings began flapping awkwardly as the thing tried to stand, even-tually pulling itself upright then falling to the ground and hurling sand with the impact. Shaking the grit from its body and wings, the beast made another attempt and, at last, found its footing. With several clunky robotic turns of its head, it surveyed the surroundings. Where plumage might have covered the body, the creature instead had a wrinkled, leathery hide, much like that of the thing that birthed it. On each side of its gray-black head, a single red eye peered out upon the world.

Summoning its strength, the thing clumsily hopped atop the inert carcass of the rhino and glowered at the sprawling wasteland. Then, with a heave of its chest, the winged beast let loose a screech as harsh and forsaken as the world stretching out before it.

65.

Nick woke disoriented and trembling. The night's darkness had given way to morning's pale light and he found himself alone. His brother and the shaman were nowhere to be seen while only a few smoldering embers remained from the fire. Nick lifted himself to a sitting position on the mat, brought his knees to his chest and wrapped his arms around them to steady the shaking. With a throbbing head and parched throat, he soon got to his feet and started retracing his steps back to the settlement. As he walked, the disjointed fragments of a disturbing dream haunted him — a thrashing, dying rhino-like creature and its grotesque spawn in a surreal furnace-fire waste-land, a by-product, he assumed, of the shaman's cocktail.

Back at the Penan settlement, Nick sensed something amiss. An eerie stillness had settled over everything and no one was up and about. Near his brother's hut, he noticed an elderly woman squatting and puffing a pipe. She watched him approach and, with arms raised palms up, Nick shrugged and looked about, hoping to convey the question, '*Where is everybody?*'

The woman's expression barely changed. He then spoke his brother's name on the chance she might recognize it. Her eyes narrowed ever so subtly and she began gabbling in Penan. Gesturing toward the forest several times with the pipe, he surmised the woman was pointing him in the direction everyone had gone. Nick nodded and pointed, "...*this way...?*" to which the woman nodded.

"...*ya, ya, ya,*' she muttered, swinging an arm out for emphasis.

He thanked her with a polite bow of his head and started off, stopping briefly to grab some of the strung-up bits of smoked bush meat. The woman had gestured, more or less, in the direction he and Evan had returned from yesterday, and Nick guessed everyone had gone to protest the hydro project, though his brother had made no mention of any such thing. Gnawing at the stringy, greasy bush meat, he picked his way through the forest, miffed that he'd been left behind. Apparently, Evan had concluded he shouldn't be there.

Nick allowed that this might've been his brother's way of protecting him in the event of trouble, a hard-wired vestigial instinct perhaps, that had apparently remained un-dimmed by the years. Once again, the fathomless, incomprehensible mysteries of blood proved far more durable than the slights we held onto.

At this, his thoughts returned to his brother's cancer. The news had shaken him to the core and his emotions careened from anger to sorrow to dismay. Why had Evan relied on the ministrations of an indigenous healer rather than proper medical treatment? This completely baffled Nick. His brother *must* have understood the ramifications of such a decision and what it meant for his wife and son. Flummoxed, Nick resolved then and there that he had to get his brother out of this forest.

66.

Carole and Antonio crouched and peered over the top of a rotting log. Behind them, Seladang sat full-squat with arms on knees, ass just off the ground. He drew pensively on a western-style pipe that might have been left by a tourist in his boat.

From here they looked over a wide forested valley with a tributary of the Baram running its length. Seladang explained that this would be the future reservoir behind the dam. At one end, loggers had begun cutting trees, trailed by heavy equipment scraping a new track. A sizable group of Penan, however, had gathered to block their way, having arranged logging debris and large rocks in a huge pile fronted by their bodies. Nearby, log trucks and other heavy equipment now sat idle while a small company of soldiers with batons and sidearms lined up to face the protesters.

Carole and Antonio had both worked the Asian circuit long enough to know what usually happened when the military went up against civilian protesters in this part of the world. As they took in the scene before them, neither had spotted Nick. If he *had* made it there, Carole worried, what would the military do with him, especially if they were in league with the interests behind his abduction. Further muddling things from her perspective was the very news-worthiness of the situation — soldiers lined up against unarmed civilians, ready to wield asymmetrical violence. Here was a breaking story impossible to ignore.

"Listen…" Carole started to say, "Maybe you and Seladang should go back. Get to a place where you can radio for help." She glanced toward the blockade. "This is too volatile…"

Antonio arched an eyebrow.

"No way," he told her, with a shake of the head. "There's not a chance in hell you're going down there alone…"

Carole half-expected as much; after seven years working together, often in dicey situations, they'd developed a kind of *'got your back'* soldier's ethic with each other. She briefly held his gaze then turned to the boatman who released little puffs of smoke from his pipe as he listened.

"Seladang…" she began, "…We can't ask any more of you. But…you understand we *have* to go down there… I can give you most of your money now and get you the rest when we're back in Kuching… You have my word."

With an appreciative and vaguely forlorn smile, Carole rooted in her sling-bag while the boatman continued puffing in the ponderous manner of pipe smokers. She gathered a handful of US bills, always a reliable exchange currency, and handed them to Seladang. He gazed at her outreached hand for a number of seconds, then calmly took the cash, nodding gratefully. Carole thanked him, then tore a page from her notebook to write down the name of their hotel in Kuching.

The boatman drew on his pipe while stuffing the bills in a shirt pocket. Carole finished and folded the sheet for Seladang but, instead of taking it, he rose from his squat and reached for Antonio's tripod.

"We should keep moving…" he said, shouldering the tripod before starting in the direction of the blockade.

Carole glanced over at Antonio.

"Well," he said, sighing, "You heard him…"

67.

After walking twenty minutes or so, Nick realized he'd gotten himself lost. Adrenaline and exhaustion had clouded his judgment and he'd underestimated the difficulty of navigating a rainforest. Everywhere he turned, it all looked the same; without obvious landmarks for reference points and with the sky obscured by the canopy, he had no idea how far he'd gone. His stomach tightened as he considered the unappealing options: continue on and risk becoming further lost, or, try to find his way back…and *also* risk becoming further lost.

Trying not to panic, Nick told himself to *think*. He thought of the old saying, 'fortune favored the bold' which, in this situation, meant continuing forward. Boldness though. could also veer into hubris. History, he knew, was littered with examples of audaciousness ending badly: lost expeditions, wrecked ships, starvation, death and financial ruin. Nick generally leaned toward caution in most things, and here that meant turning back, easier said than done since he couldn't be sure which direction he'd come from. Chances were, he'd just end up going in circles whatever he did.

At this, he helplessly spun about looking for a sign, anything to suggest one way over another. A paralysis of indecision gripped him and his breathing grew rapid and shallow. Unable to move, a nearby dull *honking* sound startled him as it suddenly intruded upon the still of the forest. Nick instantly turned and scanned the surroundings. A few seconds later, the dull honking started again, its low-pitched droning suggesting a corpulent duck with a decent baritone. Strangely, he thought the honking somehow directed at *him*, more like an attempt to communicate rather than a warning.

That he would even consider such an absurd notion further confirmed his shaky mental state. He took a few cautious steps forward and, within seconds, three distinct honks came in quick succession. Nick froze in his tracks and glanced around until something caught his eye — a small indistinct patch of orange/yellow on a tree branch some twenty or so meters ahead.

Cautiously, he went toward it and soon realized the patch of color was actually a beak belonging to some sort of bird. As he moved closer, the bird's body came into view. Its feathers had a bluish-black sheen with a smattering of ice-blue streaks in the tail feathers dangling down. The impressive beak appeared to be almost as long as the bird's body With its head turned in profile, the creature kept one red eye fixed on Nick, who now stopped a few meters away.

At first glance, the bird called to mind, 'Toucan Sam,' the cartoon toucan fronting the box of Nick's favorite childhood breakfast cereal, Kellogg's '*Froot Loops*'. When it came to embellishment though, this bird had gone *Sam* one better. The golden straw color at the beak's tip gradually transitioned to deep reddish-orange where it joined the bird's head and here, things got a bit strange. There atop the main beak, sat another beak-like growth. With the same deep reddish-orange coloring, it curled upward with a martial flourish, calling to mind the helmet of some avian conquistador. Evolution had at least set the creature's eyes on the sides of its head where this bulky ornament wouldn't interfere with its sight. The net effect gave the bird a vaguely clownish aspect.

More vexing still, though, Nick sensed something *familiar* about this bird. Then it hit him: the *thing* in his dream last night... His skin suddenly felt prickly. '*What the hell...??*' he thought, dumbstruck. Strange coincidences came and went, but *this?* Could a person actually dream of what they hadn't yet seen? The shaman's concoction must have something to do with it, he thought, but *how?* A chill traveled up his spine and he recalled Hamlet's words to Horatio: '*...there are more things in heaven and Earth than are dreamt of in your philosophy...*'

Just then, the bird impulsively launched upward, flapping powerful wings that carried it twenty or so meters further ahead where it landed on the limb of a smaller tree. Nick watched as the creature gripped and released its talons several times on the branch before finally settling into a regal bearing.

As he stood there mystified, Nick began to think it some sort of delirium probably brought on by exhaustion. From its new perch, the bird fixed its gaze on him and called out twice with what sounded to Nick like an *insistence*, or *urgency*, in its tone. He took this as further confirmation of a deteriorating mental state — hungry, lost and very likely dehydrated, he was attaching *meaning* to the behavior of a bird!

A rising swirl of panic started overtaking him and he chided himself for getting lost, for acting as if this were little more than a day hike in the Santa Monica Mountains. For its part, the bird kept its head in profile, one eye again fixed on Nick, who began to think it somehow sensed his helplessness. Maybe it was it waiting for him to die, hoping for first dibs on the carcass? He knew that, by the time Evan realized he'd gone missing, darkness would likely have fallen and he'd have to spend the night out here alone, a prospect that terrified him. He suddenly felt light-headed, reaching an arm out to steady himself against a tree.

At this, the bird honked once more with what Nick now took to be a note of disapproval in its tone. It then lurched upward and, with a couple flaps of its huge wings, swooped to another tree further on, landing once more on yet another branch where it squawked several times.

"*…What is this…?*" Nick muttered, gazing at the bird. "*…What the hell does this thing want…?*"

Never in his life had he experienced anything this bizarre and thought he may have crossed some sort of physical line where the intricate functions regulating the body's systems started to short-circuit. His last proper meal had been days ago and sleep had been fitful at best. Brain and body were in mutiny and no one was coming to help him.

Inexplicably, he began moving toward the bird, and as he did, the creature fell silent. Was *that* it? he thought. Did this thing actually *want* him to come closer? He shook his head — this must be his starving brain playing tricks on him. Still, he kept moving, gradually narrowing the gap between them. With its head in profile, one eye warily watching Nick draw near, the bird once again lurched upward and flew to another limb.

As ludicrous as it seemed, Nick thought the bird might be playing some kind of *game* with him. He stopped short of the bird's perch, physical weakness overtaking him. Leaning his back against a large tree choked with woody strangler vines, he let a minute or two pass as he watched the bird watching *him.* Gradually, an unfamiliar sense of calm came over him and Nick just let go, sliding down the tree with his back against it until his butt hit the ground.

From its latest perch, the bird showed no reaction, its single red eye still fixed on Nick who now realized that something else about the creature troubled him, something *other* than the unlikely coincidence. He just needed a moment to *think*, to clear the layers of haze from his mind. This must be some kind of delirium, he thought, never having experienced one. His eyelids had grown so heavy that he wanted nothing more in the whole world than to close them, if only for a minute or so…

With his eyes shut, shadows lightened and darkened across Nick's face, moving with the passing of time until eventually, his eyes gradually opened. Something on the air had stirred him from his doze, an acrid hint of burning wood peppered with the charred sap smell of smoldering green timber…

Realizing he'd dozed off, Nick instinctively looked down at his wrist for the watch no longer there, wondering how long he'd been out. Anxious and disoriented, he glanced about his surroundings and found the limb where the bird had been, now empty. How could he have missed its takeoff — the flapping of those huge wings would have rousted someone in a coma?

Getting to his feet, Nick went toward the tree and gazed at the empty branch. Somehow, things felt different, as if he'd been asleep for a very long time. Standing there, he thought he heard a faint, distant rumbling he hadn't noticed before, the sound of…*machinery.* Leaning an ear toward it, he listened, detecting an alternating pattern, a rising and falling like that of heavy equipment moving back and forth.

It appeared to be coming from the general direction the bird had been tree-hopping, suggesting a completely preposterous possibility: had the bird been *leading* him this way? *Stop it,* he told himself, shaking it off. Now he was finding meaning in coincidence, anthropomorphizing animal behavior to explain the inexplicable!

Once again, he faced his dilemma and rubbed the back of his neck, no more capable than he'd been before his snooze. Then, something else on the air got his attention, something vaguely familiar — the oily, charred signature scent of incompletely combusted hydrocarbons …*diesel exhaust.*

68.

The man speaking had a severe, officious countenance. His hands were on his hips in the imperious manner of an authority figure waiting on a forthcoming explanation. Unlike the couple dozen soldiers in uniform flanking him, his outfit appeared to come from an adventure clothing catalog: olive drab safari-type shirt worn un-tucked; epaulet flaps on the shoulders with sleeves rolled up above the elbows and buttoned in place; beige khakis complemented by a pair of Gore-Tex hiking shoes. He looked to be in his mid- to late-forties, his body thickened by middle age, a rich diet, and lack of physical activity. Ethnically, his features were more Han Chinese than Malaysian. Thinning strands of black hair combed over a balding pate exaggerated the roundness of his face and, together with the epicanthic fold of his eyelids, produced a cumulative effect akin to a 'Fat Buddha' statue, albeit an unsmiling one.

In a patch of still-standing forest, Nick peered out from behind a giant meranti tree. After following the sound of the heavy equipment for around twenty minutes, he'd found his way here. It appeared that the entire Penan settlement had shown up, standing before piles of rocks and logging debris arranged to block the access road. The 'Buddha-man' had apparently been fulminating for some time now about the ersatz barrier to Evan, who stood at the head of the gathered Penan.

His brother wore a threadbare short-sleeved buttoned-down shirt and cargo shorts — chosen, Nick surmised, to bolster his credibility. Even as a kid, Evan showed a keen awareness of the effect *appearance* had on a person's credibility. Perhaps his brother had concluded that looking too much like the Penan would make it easy for those in the outside world to dismiss him as some kind of 'crank' in the throes of a prelapsarian reverie, a white guy gone native.

A visceral sense of dread rattled Nick as he watched the standoff, unsure what he should do. The swagger in the Buddha-like man's demeanor smacked of authority, like an office holder unaccustomed to having his will thwarted, and he seethed with a barely contained rage that threatened to uncork at any moment. Behind him, the soldiers, batons at the ready, looked prepared to dole out some serious asymmetrical violence.

Seeing his brother on the front lines of a potential riot stirred some oblique associations in Nick's mind. It was with Evan that he had first been exposed to humanity's penchant for brutality. As children in the 1960s, he and his brother would usually retreat from their parent's heated dinner arguments to watch the evening news on one of the three channels their TV received. Each night, the news brought the tumult of the wider world into their living room — race riots, student riots, the war in Vietnam. Nick could recall thinking at the time that the world was losing its mind and coming apart at the seams, a painful echo of the discord at home. Whenever, it all got to be too much, he would retreat to their room and listen to a 'Top 40' radio station in the dark. Later, Evan would remind him that the world had both good and bad in it, just as people have both good and bad in them. Years passed before Nick truly grasped his brother's observation.

Suddenly, the agitated man angrily barked at Evan in accented English suggesting it wasn't his native tongue. Nick could almost see the spittle flying with each consonant.

"You have *no rights* in this country!" the man fumed. "*You* are here *illegally!*" As he bellowed, the man's eyes bulged and droplets of sweat flowed from his temples down a fleshy jawline onto neck and shoulders. He glared at Evan, allowing the point to sink in before letting loose again.

"I can have you arrested *right now*!" he railed. "You and *all* these people! This is an *illegal* action! Stopping these men from their *work!*" He swung an arm toward the idle workers and machinery.

Evan's *sang-froid* in the face of the man's bluster gave Nick an unfamiliar surge of familial pride. His brother merely listened to the attack with hands on hips, apparently unfazed by all the sound and fury. After a couple beats, he responded.

"You, of all people, Mr. Wong," Evan began, "…should know that this is *Penan* ancestral land." He spoke calmly and clearly, in a judicious volume for all within range to hear. "And yet, their rights have been consistently ignored and trampled on by *your* government."

The name '*Wong*' rang a bell for Nick. Both his brother and Derek Wolcott had cited the name and he recalled something about the man being a government operative of some sort, which would certainly explain the vitriolic harangue. Clearly, this Mr. Wong was *not* accustomed to such blatant challenges to his authority. Nick knew the type — the megalomaniacal bully with official power cowing others into submission. In his view, men like Wong embodied the heedless brutishness of human nature, specifically, the unbri-dled appetites of the 'alpha' male that took *whatever* it wanted *whenever* it wanted, much like an oaf trampling an entire garden for a handful of potatoes.

"If they have a claim, let them make it in a court of law!" Wong snapped. "They are citizens of Malaysia with the same rights and subject to the same laws as everyone else!"

"Well they do, in fact, have *several* claims before the courts…" Evan observed, his tone measured. "…But you know as well as I that those claims are being held up over a lack of documentation supporting the Penan's long history on these lands. Because, as you know, these people have no written language and instead have had to rely on the written records of early explor-ers who first encountered them here in the nineteenth century. Based on that, the courts have issued an injunction halting any further work here until this is sorted out and we've come here today to enforce it."

"Enforce it?!" Wong roared. "You can't enforce *anything!* You're not the law here! *I am!!* And I *demand* you end this illegal activity right now or I'll have you and everyone here arrested!" He then leaned closer to Evan's face and thrust a pudgy finger at his chest.

"And I'll see that YOU, *especially*, spend the rest of your life in a Malay-sian jail!" he seethed.

Evan remained unbowed. The Penan surrounding him were likewise steely and resolute; they may not have understood Wong's words, but they took the meaning.

"You can threaten all you want, Mr. Wong," Evan told him, "But when all is said and done, the law *will* still come down on the Penan's side. And that's why you want to get this done in a hurry…" He let this linger a moment before continuing.

"Everyone knows these people were here *long before* the British and Dutch carved up Borneo for themselves. They've been here for *centuries.* And as a member of the current government, you must know that the Aborigi-nal Peoples Act of 1954 entitles the Penan to *all* the rights of citizenship. And they're exercising those rights today."

Wong silently fumed at the legal citation.

"You don't tell me the law of this land!" he thundered, "You're an outsid-er! An agitator! An American shit!!"

Terrified and confused, Nick anguished over what to do. An uncanny ves-tigial sense worried his brother might overplay his hand. Evan must have understood that statutes on the books in Kuala Lumpur mattered little out here. In practical terms, he had to know it was pointless to argue with Wong — out here at least, Wong *was* the law and justice and due process were what *he* said they were. Given the intensity of the man's bile, Nick thought his brother's provocative tactics veered on the reckless.

An unfamiliar but potent clannish impulse began to rise in Nick, urging him to do *something*. But *what?* He could step forward and show himself, his presence possibly acting as a 'cooler' to deflect the tension and hopefully engender some restraint in Wong. Of course, it also meant he'd be detained and probably taken back to Kuala Lumpur to face jail and/or deportation, meaning his time with Evan would be finished and he wasn't ready for that.

"There are plenty of people who'd agree with you on that last part, Mr. Wong…" Evan concurred, "But what would those same people say about a man who uses his office for personal gain? A man who awards contracts to companies he has financial interests in…?"

Nick cringed at his brother's push-back.

"Like the shell company, *J&J Golden Associates*, that your brother-in-law happens to be one of the principle shareholders in…" Evan continued, "The company you awarded logging concessions to for most of Sarawak." He let the statement hang a moment. "I suspect the courts would see that as a clear violation of section SB dash 230C of the Anti-Corruption Act…"

Wong's face grew flush with contempt, his nostrils flaring. Nick could almost see the muscles clenching in the man's jaw. The air crackled with tension now and the Penan flanking Evan tightened their ranks. Behind Wong, soldiers gripped their batons tighter. Then, Wong leaned in closer to Evan and muttered something only the two of them could hear.

69.

"What's *he* doing out here…?" Carole said, as she, Antonio and Seladang, observed the blockade from within a nearby patch of forest. "Men like James Wong usually delegate this sort of grubby business to a deputy."

She had immediately spotted Wong, known to most in the media as Malaysia's Minister of the Interior and an enthusiastic proponent of this massive hydro-electric project. His name had crossed her desk several times over the years, mostly in the context of various ethics inquiries involving financial improprieties. Wong proved masterful at deflecting any criticism and his ability to work the international capital markets, where he'd been able to secure funding for the dam, had won over critics. Still, questions around his personal finances lingered, continuing to fuel long-simmering anti-Chinese sentiment among the bumiputra and bringing renewed scrutiny from the political opposition.

Carole knew that, as interior minister, Wong had the last word when it came to the disposition of Malaysia's natural resources, whether in the ground, on top of it, or beneath its territorial waters. A master of political patronage, Wong's style and methods were part Tammany Hall cronyism and part 'Robber Baron' wheel-greasing, with a touch of Randolph Hearst-like megalomania. He represented a wider political current in Malaysian politics, one that embraced economic freedom while at the same time eschewing political freedom in an unwritten compact that meant citizens were free to get rich, as long as they submitted to the ultimate authority of the central government. A colleague of hers had referred to this distinctly Asian flavor of democracy as, '*authoritarianism lite.*'

Wong's presence now took on new significance as Carole recognized the man arguing with him on behalf of the Penan.

"Isn't that *him…?*" she asked, glancing briefly at Antonio, "Nick's brother…?"

"I think you're right…" he answered, readying his camera.

They watched and listened anxiously as Wong frothed. Carole understood that men like Wong usually dealt harshly with those who challenged his will. In peninsular Malaysia, where eighty percent of the population lived, civil disobedience was rare. Coming from this world of compliant citizenry, Borneo must have confounded a man like Wong, who likely viewed it as more of a *colony* rather than another part of the same country. To Wong and others like him, Borneo was merely a steamy, overgrown bonanza of resource wealth inhabited by backward indigenous peoples impossible to understand.

For a minute or so, Antonio recorded some establishing shots with the camera on the tripod. When finished, he removed the camera with the quick-release lever and turned to Carole.

"Okay," he said, placing the recorder over his shoulder. "It's gotta be a walking stand-up. Let me worry about the tapes if we get stopped…"

"You sure about this?" she asked, as he tightened straps.

"Very," he answered, "Power up your mic, let's check levels…"

Carole switched on the power pack for the wireless transmitter in her pocket and adjusted the position of her lapel microphone, then counted off.

"…Stand-up, one-two…" she said, "…One-two…"

Antonio fiddled a couple of knobs with his injured hand.

"Good enough…" he said. "…Just don't get too far ahead of me…"

Carole nodded, her mouth tightening; there would be no time for fussing with technical issues once they stepped into the open.

"Avoid turning from the camera too much," Antonio reminded her. "And try to keep the transmitter pointed toward me."

The words had barely left his mouth when a commotion startled them — the soldiers had begun moving on the Penan.

"GO!!" Antonio shouted instinctively, "*NOW!! JUST **GO**!!*"

70.

Wong glared at Evan with utter contempt, then turned with a slight nod to the soldier in charge before starting away. The soldiers parted as he walked through them toward a waiting SUV where the driver held the passenger door open for him. As they drove off, the commander barked an order and his men closed ranks and moved on the Penan.

Nick sucked in a gasp of air, watching in horror as soldiers wildly swung truncheons and pushed protesters back. In the furor of crashing bodies, flailing limbs and swinging batons, women screamed and ran for cover, grabbing children on the fly. The soldiers made no distinctions in doling out their brutality — men and women were both indiscriminately beaten, the sickening 'thwack' of batons striking bare flesh blending with the cacophony of screaming and shouting. Nick caught a glimpse of his brother being rushed away by several Penan, and made a mental note of the patch of forest they disappeared into. A wave of nausea washed over him and he extended an arm to steady himself on a tree. With a hateful rage boiling up, he helplessly looked on, desperate to do *something*. But *what*, exactly? Go in there and get beaten and arrested in solidarity with the Penan? While it might help with his self-esteem, it would be the end of his time with Evan, and that couldn't happen. And yets, it felt unconscionable and cowardly to do nothing while innocent people were being subjected to unhinged violence at the hands of uniformed brutes.

Everything was happening so fast, he grabbed at his head as if it were about to explode. Then, something on the periphery of the melee caught his eye — a forty-something Caucasian woman followed by an Asian man with a video camera.

71.

"Behind me, as you can see…" Carole explained for the camera in an urgent, harried tone, "…The military has begun clearing these indigenous protesters by force…" She turned to look back every few seconds as Antonio kept up.

"…These people, the *Penan*, are blockading operations here at the site of this massive hydro project, the Atakun Dam… They maintain that this is *their* traditional land, and Malaysia's interior minister, James Wong, had come here to meet personally with the protesters…" Her voice bounced and jarred with the cadence of her steps as the words poured out extemporaneously.

"…But, those discussions have apparently failed…" she continued. "And Mr. Wong has now sent the military in to remove the protesters…"

She stopped a prudent distance from the actual fracas and observed many Penan face down in the dirt, wrists zip-tied behind their backs. Many were men, but there were also quite a few women and teenaged children similarly bound, some with welts and raw stripes on their bare backs, arms, and shoulders from the truncheons.

"…Here, you can see the results of the military's actions…" Carole said to the camera, gesturing toward the Penan on the ground. "…Men, women and children all bearing marks from the soldier's batons…" Her decidedly British knack for understatement felt wrong somehow; the wounds she saw had broken through skin and cracked heads.

As she turned back to the camera, a man shouted frantically at her and Antonio in English — it was the soldier in command, now racing toward them waving his right arm, hand flapping rapidly up and down.

"HEY!!" he barked, "You *stop*! You *stop NOW*!!"

Antonio was about to comply but Carole told him to keep going. He hesitated, but experience had taught him to trust her instincts.

"*Sir!*" Carole said, in a deferential tone as the soldier approached.

"How did you get in here??" he squawked in accented English, with a tinny, back of throat voice. "*No filming!!*" he commanded, waving his hand at Antonio. "*No filming!!*"

This time, Antonio pretended to comply by taking the camera from his shoulder and holding it at his side. Rather than turn it off though, he let it continue recording while discretely peeking at the viewfinder, turned to face upward.

Carole explained that they were with the BBC and had been filming a documentary in the upper Baram when they'd inadvertently gotten separated from the rest of the crew and become lost.

"We heard what sounded like people's voices coming from this direction," she told the commander, "…So, we found our way here."

Antonio let her do the talking — her uncanny gift for spontaneous fabrication *always* produced something fairly plausible. The commander however, would have none of it.

"This area *prohibited!*" he bellowed, "You can't *be* here! *No* media! *No* cameras!"

"Of course, we understand that now…" she contritely explained, noting the stitched-on name tag over the man's breast pocket. "And we're terribly sorry… *Lt. Satem.*"

The lieutenant glared at the two journalists while behind him, things were spiraling out of control.

72.

Seconds ticked away and Nick brooded over what to do. The surprise and relief at seeing Antonio and Carole quickly ricocheted back into an amalgam of anger, terror and revulsion at the violence being unleashed on the Penan. Instinct insisted he join his brother, while a sense of moral obligation told him to help the two reporters who had obviously been searching for him.

Decency ultimately tipped the scales and he started down for Carole and Antonio. He'd made it about halfway when he spotted the soldier's commander charging them, waving his arms and shouting. Hesitating, Nick watched the commander rush up and begin upbraiding the two journalists, his angry words unintelligible in the surrounding cacophony.

The ethical calculus suddenly changed as it appeared Carole and Antonio were about to be arrested. His being detained and deported with them wouldn't help anything, so Nick turned around. While it felt cowardly to abandon them like this, he told himself they had the BBC in their corner.

He'd only taken a few steps when an explosive, percussive crack rang out from within the melee.

In an instant, the commotion ceased, followed by an eerie, preternatural silence, as if all earthly sound had suddenly been vacuumed into the ether.

Then, a horrific shrieking ripped through the air and Nick's heart skipped a beat as he watched several soldiers run toward a spot where a Penan boy lay bleeding atop a soldier. Nick thought he recognized the boy, a teenager he'd seen at the Penan camp. With shaking hands, the young soldier pushed the lifeless body away and got to his feet as other soldiers began to gather around, hovering in dismay. The boy's body now lay face-up in a bulldozer track in the saturated clay soil, blood pooling with the water in its ruts as a Penan woman rushed over and threw herself on top of the boy, wailing in grief.

The commanding soldier who'd stopped Antonio and Carole instantly forgot about them and bolted toward the shooting while barking frantic orders in Malay. The young soldier, not much older than the boy who'd been shot, trembled with shock, the pistol dangling at his side, his muddy, torn uniform stained with the boy's blood. The commander stood over the dead boy a moment, then turned and physically moved the young soldier back while signaling for the others to get him out of there.

73.

"...*Jesus...!!*" Antonio blurted, as he and Carole flinched from the gunfire. Lt. Satem quickly spun around to see wisps of bluish smoke lingering in the air not far from where they stood. He began shouting in Malay and instantly started off.

Momentarily stunned, Carole and the cameraman stared in disbelief for several seconds. When a grief-stricken Penan woman screamed and threw herself on the young man, Antonio instinctively shouldered his camera, put the viewfinder to his eye and started recording as Carole followed closely, describing the scene for the benefit of the wireless microphone.

"...It appears that a young Penan protester has been shot..." she reported, a grim urgency in her tone, "...by a soldier here..."

The gunfire brought everything to a stop, with soldiers and Penan alike staring in dismay at the body crumpled in the bulldozer track. Lt. Satem immediately took charge, barking terse orders that startled his men into action. With Satem so consumed, Carole and Antonio continued filming the chaotic scene and pushing their luck.

"...From our position, we can't be sure what happened or why the soldier drew his weapon on an unarmed protester..." she intoned, stepping out ahead of the camera.

"Hey…!" Antonio called as she moved ever closer to the scene, mindful of the fuzzy line between *getting* the footage and getting *out* with it. "…Don't *push it*…"

Carole stopped herself and turned to the camera.

"The military seems to be standing down now…" she continued, briefly glancing over her shoulder. "…And a woman, possibly the mother of the young man who's been shot, has now just collapsed in grief on top of him…"

74.

Nick stood there dumbstruck. The Penan boy had not moved a twitch and, with his blood pooling in the bulldozer's tracks, it looked like he never would again. For the second time in his life, Nick found himself present at the moment of another's violent, untimely death and, in a freakish sort of irony, so had his brother.

With the soldier in command now focused on the shooting, Nick watched as Antonio and Carole sprang into action and immediately started recording again. In that instant, an impulse seized him and he went toward them, calling out Carole's name when he was within earshot.

"*My god!!*" Carole blurted, and Antonio lifted his eye from the viewfinder.

"*Nick!*" he called out.

Shocked but delighted to see him, they noted his bedraggled state with some alarm as Nick insisted they get out of there.

"My brother escaped that way with some Penan…" he told them, head tilting toward a spot of forest.

"Right," Carole agreed, quickly assessing the situation. "Then, let's go."

"Hold on," Antonio interrupted, "What about Seladang?"

Carole briefly filled Nick in on the boatman, who, Antonio reminded them, still had the tripod.

"I'd lay odds," Nick assured them, "That *he'll* find *us*…"

With that, they were off, Nick continuously glancing back, fearful they'd draw attention. Noting this, Carole hoped he wouldn't stray off course. Given his ragged appearance, she could only imagine what he'd been through the last couple days.

They soon arrived at the patch of forest and, once inside, Nick paused to get his bearings. In the frantic retreat, he hadn't considered which way they went after entering.

"There should be some signs..." he explained, looking about. "Broken branches, that sort of thing..."

The three scanned the surrounding forest for anything helpful, but immediately realized they had no chance of reading its subtleties.

"...It looks the same in every direction..." Antonio muttered.

Carole began to worry Nick might have gotten it wrong. Seladang's flawless guidance had made navigating the forest look deceptively easy, which she knew of course, was anything *but.*

"This is where they came in," Nick assured them, eyes darting about the undergrowth. "I'm positive..."

The anguished howling back at the blockade, though muted by the forest, could still be heard. Carole was about to suggest they should just move when something stirred the brush nearby. They spun in its direction, not daring to move a muscle or speak. Seconds later, another patch of brush rustled, closer this time. The humid air grew brittle with tension and Nick thought he glimpsed a flash of something move. His eyes darted about when, from within a dense tangle of understory, a man emerged, tripod on his shoulder — *Seladang.*

Relieved, Carole greeted him warmly and introduced Nick, explaining the situation.

"Nick saw the Penan bring his brother this way," Carole told the boatman.

Seladang's eyes had a glassy, sorrowful cast to them; clearly, events had horrified him as well. Carole wanted to assure the boatman that, even thick-skinned journalists like her and Antonio were not immune to the soul-crushing effects of witnessing such brutality. But, she assumed he probably already had a pretty good idea that nothing could ever inure us to the darker impulses of human nature.

In the space that followed, Nick again proffered that he was certain his brother and the Penan had entered the forest at this spot, but couldn't be sure which way they went next. The boatman listened, absently rubbing the back of his neck. Then, after a few seconds, he began turning this way and that, surveying the forest around them. Nick and the others watched, not sure what he might be looking for. At one particular spot, he lingered a moment before calmly shouldering the tripod.

"I think this way..." he remarked, then, with a nod, started off as they all fell in behind him.

75.

Seladang moved carefully through the forest, picking up tiny clues that betrayed the Penan's movement — a footprint fragment here, a bent branch there. Nick and the others followed, fascinated by the boatman's ability to spot these subtle signs of human disturbance.

They hadn't gone far when Seladang caught the faint scent of something on the air and stopped, placing a finger to his lips for quiet. Peering into the forest's depths, Seladang spotted the barely noticeable glow of a fire. Without a word, he started in its direction. The forest darkened as evening approached and, when they were about thirty meters or so from the fire, Seladang halted again, crouching down in the brush. Nick and the others followed his lead, unsure what he'd noticed. No one said a word as they waited for instruction from Seladang, who suddenly let go a sound like the call of a bird. Nick recalled his brother's words about 'announcing' your presence to the Penan. Seconds ticked by with no response and the boatman tried again. After several attempts, a faint bird-like call finally returned. Seladang turned to the others and nodded.

The diffuse light filtering down through the canopy continued to dim, deepening the shadows as Nick and his companions bunched tighter behind the boatman who carefully moved in the direction of the fire. They were soon able to make out some stilted thatched dwellings through the trees. The tension thickened and Nick turned to Carole and Antonio, speaking in a hush:

"…After all that's happened…" he cautioned, "I'm not sure how they'll react…"

The two journalists nodded their understanding.

Some distance ahead, Seladang at last emerged from the forest into the opening of the Penan camp and quietly greeted an older man among a group of grim and sullen Penan gathered near the fire. Nick emerged a half minute behind Seladang and several of the Penan somberly acknowledged him. A few seconds later, Carole and Antonio followed and stood in respectful silence as they noted the gloomy, almost sepulchral mood. Nick turned to them.

"Can you hold off any taping until I've had a chance to speak with my brother…?" he asked, his voice hushed.

"Of course," Carole assured him.

As her eyes adjusted to the firelight, she got a better look at Nick's ragged state; his disheveled, matted hair and several days of scraggly beard called to mind a man returning from a drunken jag, while his tattered, grimy clothes had him looking like the caricature of a skinny castaway.

Nick didn't miss the hint of alarm in her eyes.

"Listen…" she quietly began, trying to imagine what he'd been through. "Haven't had a chance to ask yet…you doing okay…?"

Nick self-consciously ran a hand along his stubble-covered cheek, then brightened ever so slightly.

"Never better," he said, an obviously ironic note in his tone. "Back down to my high school weight."

Carole smiled appreciatively.

"Anyway," he continued, serious again, "While I'm looking in on my brother, you might as well relax and have something to eat. There's usually this stuff called *sago* and there might also be some sort of smoked meat…" He hesitated, deciding not to expand on this. "Seladang can probably help with that…"

"Sure, sure," she told him, "We'll figure it out." They held each other's gaze for an awkward second or so before Nick turned to leave.

76.

"*…Hello…?*" Nick softly called, announcing himself at the selap's entry. For most siblings, the prerogatives of bloodline would've trumped protocol and the necessity of waiting for a response. But the reality of their fraternal history no longer afforded such familiarity. He was about to call out again when Phillip pushed the flap up. Even in the dim light, Nick couldn't miss the tell-tale glisten in his nephew's eyes.

As he crawled in and the flap closed, Nick's own eyes adjusted to the deeper darkness. Kelesau squatted near what remained of a small cooking fire, its reddish-orange glow the only ambient light. She too had a glassiness about the eyes and didn't look up. Sitting across from her with his back against the thatch wall, Evan looked to be the picture of a soul hollowed-out. The deep set of his eyes and drawn, lined visage suggested a lifetime of accumulated sorrow.

Nick had absolutely *no* idea what to say to his brother — the shock of the day's events had barely sunk in. Without a word, he quietly situated himself near his brother and leaned back. Kelesau continued fussing with the fire for another minute or so, then spoke to Phillip and started for the selap's entry. The boy scurried over and held the flap for his mother. Before turning to follow her, he glanced back at his uncle. Nick resisted an urge to go and hug the boy, to assure him that he too had once been a child swept up in the tumult of the adult world. Instead, he mustered what he could of a reassuring smile as the flap fell shut.

For what felt like minutes, the two brothers silently gazed into the glowing coals of the cooking fire. Nick assumed his brother wasn't aware that he'd found his way to the blockade.

"…I was there…" he said at last, "…Just inside the forest… I saw it all… You and Wong…the soldiers…"

His brother nodded vaguely without looking up. After a respectful interval, he expressed his horror and sorrow over the killing of the young Penan. While it had shaken *him* to the core, for Evan, it must have felt cataclysmic. Evan offered another detached nod as Nick fell silent. A part of him wished he could assure his brother that what happened was a crime, that there were witnesses and that justice would ultimately prevail. Only he now understood, as Evan certainly must have, that justice had little say out here.

For some time, Nick stared at the coals. Once again he thought about how foolish it had been to hope that he and Evan might unpack the years and make sense of how they had arrived at this moment. But, like the senseless killing of an indigenous boy, their years of silence could not be fathomed.

"Tell me something…" Nick eventually began to say, trying a different tack, "That stuff the shaman gave me last night…? Was it meant to keep me from being there today?"

The question appeared to hit the right note and Evan exhaled deeply.

"Not at all…" he answered, dryly, then paused. "It's true… I didn't think you should be there… For *several* reasons… But no. Whatever Galong Selah prepared for you, that's all on him. It's what *he* thought you needed…"

While not entirely convinced, Nick concluded it didn't matter. He preferred to believe that a 'hardwired' instinct in Evan for protecting his younger brother had not been diminished by the years, and the shamanic business merely served as cover.

"Those reporters from the BBC out there…" Nick continued, after a minute, "They're the ones I started up here with, who I told you about. Apparently, after those guys from the boat grabbed me, they hired a guide and started looking for me. I don't know how, but they found their way to the blockade this afternoon." At this, he paused for emphasis. "And I *think* they got some of it on tape…"

If this news heartened his brother in any way, it didn't show. Another interval passed in silence until Evan finally leaned forward and rifled around under some mats, producing a small greenish bottle. He unscrewed the cap and took a healthy quaff of the bottle's contents, wincing slightly as it went down.

"…Not very good…" he remarked, wiping his lips on an arm and looking at the bottle. "But good *enough.*" He threw back another. "Palm wine…" he added, "More like palm *liquor*… I know some Iban downriver who distill it." He offered the bottle to Nick who took a tentative sip, grimaced and handed it back.

The secret stash of alcohol surprised Nick. It had been their mother's abuse of alcohol that fueled her litany of bad decisions and ultimately led to that long ago January afternoon in Wilkes-Barre. '*Alcohol was a devil to some…*' their mother once said, on the verge of a mid-day nap. '*…But just one* more *devil to most…*'

Back then, Nick found this confusing and asked how many devils there actually were. His mother's heavy-lidded eyes fell shut as she sighed, '*…Too many…*'

Like some pithy Zen *koan*, it stayed with him, shifting meaning through the years and further acquaintance with his *own* devils. Hidden like 'Easter Eggs' in our DNA, they were enmeshed in our being and it often took the better part of a lifetime to understand their surreptitious ways.

As he stared into the coals of the cooking fire, Nick's mind wandered and he thought how time essentially felt irrelevant here in this eddy removed from the wider world. Barely a week or so, he'd left Kuching and yet, in many ways, it seemed like *years*. Time gave us no quarter and cared little how we might account for ourselves with its passage; false starts, missteps, slow learners and the like received no do-overs. Surely, Evan had to be aware of the hour and its lateness — both for him *and* the Penan. Without science-based medical intervention, his cancer would spread to other organs, if in fact it hadn't already. To Nick's complete dismay, his brother appeared to be untroubled by this. It made no sense, especially given that he had a wife and young child to think about. It was as if Evan had concluded that he could no more hope to bring his own renegade cells to heel than the Penan could hope to live forever in splendid isolation.

"You know…" Evan eventually began to say, the liquor loosening him, "…It didn't take Phillip long to figure out that his father looked *very* different from everyone else. And that *he* must somehow be different, too…"

He paused for another nip at the bottle as Nick wondered why his nephew had come up.

"I tried to explain," his brother continued, capping the bottle, "…that the hard thing about being different…is how long it takes to realize you should *embrace* it, not resist it. Phillip got that early. The kid's far more sensible than I ever was. More like the old man, really…"

The reference to their father added to Nick's confusion. To his way of thinking, their father's memory would forever be clouded by ambivalence. Emotionally distant, he'd never been certain if their father's opaque interior had been a veneer of protection or a cover for a shallow, troubled soul. That he was Phillip's grandfather now added a further layer of complexity to the mix. Nick recalled another class discussion some years back on parents and children, where one of his students suggested that we inherited more of our grandparent's traits than we did of our parents, an idea he'd found intriguing.

"I can still see him at the kitchen table…" Evan remembered, "Listening to Paul Harvey on the radio, flipping through the sports pages in the paper…"

Nick lightened at the memory. There had been moments like this in the early days before it all began coming apart, moments when it felt like a real family.

"I remember," he mused. "He was a real booster when it came to the American Dream, convinced that things always got better for the next generation…"

"Yeah, him and all his pals at the country club," Evan agreed. "That generation, they didn't overthink it. Born during Prohibition, reared in the Great Depression and shipped off to war as they came of age. After all *that,* life must've seemed pretty straightforward — to those that came back, at least. You put things together, a business or a trade, maybe a union job in a factory, or college on the GI Bill. You married your sweetheart, had kids, hung out at the Legion or the country club where you drank and played cards with people just like you."

Again, Evan raised the bottle to his lips and it struck Nick that his brother might be using the booze as a palliative, that the pain from his cancer was worse than he let on.

"It's funny…" Evan then remarked, "At first, Phillip saw being different as a badge of honor. Decided he wanted to learn English and it became *our thing*. It's all we spoke with each other… But even out here, there's peer pressure…

"Anyway, I came across some old textbooks the missionaries left at one of the longhouses. Most of your basic subjects, all taught in English. So we started having these improvised school sessions, just the two of us. He loved it. Loved learning and had forty questions for everything! '*The world is round and it spins…?*' '*How can it keep spinning…?*' '*How come I don't feel it…?*' *Why doesn't it run out…?*'

"When we got to geography and covered the part of the world his father came from, I really got the third degree! '*Did I have parents there? Sisters and brothers? Were they going to come visit?*'"

As Nick listened, he couldn't miss the weary but genuine sentiment in Evan's voice, unable to imagine the immensity bearing down on him. Having become the de facto spokesman for the Penan in their dispute with the government, had his brother considered himself co-author of the day's tragic events?

"How the hell…" Evan went on, "…Could I possibly explain *our* little family saga to a six-year old…? How do I tell him Grandpa and Grandma should've never married? That they were *forced* into it because his grandmother had become pregnant with *me*…?" He took a breath, exhaled deeply and stared at the coals.

"Like I said the other day, I never saw myself as a father…" he continued, letting this linger for several seconds.

"But then I met Kelesau and…it happened anyway. And I thought, how hard could it be *not* to fuck it up the way our parents did…? I may be a lot of things, but I'm not *them*."

Nick had to agree — we were not the people that brought us into the world. Clearly, his brother was proof of this, having become an exemplary parent in spite of their upbringing and any genetic predisposition.

"Well, you've got the knack, man," Nick told him. "That kid is *something else*…"

Evan poked at the coals and a minute or so passed in silence. Nick had the feeling his brother knew Phillip had clocked on to something being wrong with his father and decided to broach the subject.

"…He knows…" he then said. "Phillip…" he clarified, "He knows something's not right with you. That's why I asked him to take me there last night…"

Evan leaned back and gazed at the embers. In their anemic glow, Nick could see something of the rangy boy his brother had once been still present in the diminished man next to him. Only forty, his brother's withered body called to mind Yeats' biting characterization of an 'aged' man as *'a tattered coat upon a stick.'* He had to wonder if his brother's devotion to the Penan cause distracted him from the urgency of his own condition? Despite the day's traumatic events, Nick felt compelled to address the matter.

"Listen," he began, "I've been thinking… Those BBC reporters? They can help get you out of here. You know…to a hospital or a clinic, somewhere you can get *real* medical care. And I'll stick around to help any way I can…"

Evan's lips began to move as if to reply, but he hesitated. Nick waited expectantly.

"There's another thing I always admired about you," Evan eventually said, "Your ability to be self-contained when everything around you started going to hell… Especially when you were little… You would entertain yourself for hours on end in some little world in your imagination."

The unexpected turn jarred Nick. Only fragments of these memories remaiined, but Evan basically had it right. To escape the generally rancorous atmosphere of their parent's household, Nick learned to find refuge in his imagination. In the warmer months, he'd sequester himself in that bare patch of ground in the back yard near the rusty old burn barrel with his Tonka trucks; in winter, he'd hole up in his room or under their mother's massive dining room table with his 'GI Joe' and 'Johnny West' action figures.

"You didn't need anybody," his brother went on, "You figured out how to be alone, a really useful thing in this world." He then fell silent again, as if taken by another thought.

"Hold on," Nick objected, "Don't change the subject. I'm talking about trying to get you out of here for proper medical treatment."

At this, his brother dithered, several seconds passing before he spoke.

"I know, Nick," Evan answered, "And I appreciate it…"

He hesitated, about to add something.

"But the truth is… I *can't* leave… Not now, not ever…"

The words hit Nick like a bolt and he stared at his brother.

"*What...??*" he asked, dismayed, "I don't understand... What do you mean, you *can't* leave...?"

Evan gazed at the coals. "I can't, Nick... I just can't..."

Nick frowned and shook his head in disbelief.

"What are you saying? Is this about the Penan? Are you worried the Malaysians will arrest you if you try to leave? Because of all *this...?*"

The seconds ticked by, but Evan remained silent. He then sucked in a deep breath.

"It's not that simple..." he replied at last. Leaning forward, he lightly blew on the graying coals.

"Remember how in school, I had a knack for languages?" he continued, "The French club, Spanish club, all that? Well, that language background helped get me into Berkeley once I landed in California. Had to wait a year to get in-state tuition rates... Anyway, had no idea what to do with the languages and eventually decided to major in political science with a minor in Romance languages. During my senior year, I started thinking about foreign service and attended a recruiting event where I met some people from the US State Department. They're always looking for people with language skills — big surprise, right?" He paused to let this register.

"One of these recruiters took an interest in me and talked about all the opportunities in foreign service. At that point, I'd been toying with the idea of law school even though I wasn't that keen on being a lawyer. So this guy suggested I do a stint in the Peace Corps before committing to anything. Thought it'd give me some perspective. And, really, what kid in his early twenties couldn't use some of that? Told him I'd think on it and, well, he must've seen something he liked because, a few weeks later, he offered to fly me and several other students of interest to DC to tour the State Department.

"Gave us a private tour of the Capitol and we met with a bunch of undersecretaries of this and that, eeven rode the senate subway. Pretty heady stuff for a kid from Wilkes-Barre, Pennsylvania..."

At this, Evan paused, eyes narrowing.

"Only...something about the guy didn't add up," he went on. "He'd use this vernacular that sounded more like the kind of stuff the military conjures up. Things like '*operational discretion*' and '*strategic capabilities.*' Not what you'd expect from the diplomatic corps...

"I began to get the feeling the guy was vetting us. Floating certain questions and situations to see how we'd react… Like he was trying to get a sense of how comfortable each of us were with deception…"

Nick's brow wrinkled as he struggled to understand. "I'm not sure I'm following… You thought this guy might be ex-military and working for the State Department? But… Don't we use active and ex-military at our embassies and consulates overseas? For security, that sort of thing? Not the diplomacy part, of course."

In the silence that followed, Nick thought he noticed a subtle shift in the cast of his brother's eyes. As he waited for his brother to respond, different hazy threads began to coalesce in his mind.

"…*Hold on…*" he muttered, "You thought he was *vetting* you? Are you telling me this guy was…what…? Some sort of intelligence player…? Like a *spook* of some kind…??"

The words hung in the air and the blood slowly drained from Nick's face. He opened his mouth to speak but the words were stillborn.

"…*oh shit*…" he finally murmured.

Evan gazed at the dwindling embers and softly cleared his throat.

"…Is *that* it…?" Nick asked, leaning back, "They *recruited* you…?"

His brother once again blew on the coals as Nick stared, completely dumbfounded.

"Not in the way you might think…" Evan assured him after a moment.

"Not in the way I might *think*…?" Nick echoed, feeling like he'd just been sucker-punched. He pushed the hair back on his head with both hands. "*Christ,* Evan! What *other* way *is* there to think about it??"

Evan exhaled deeply, poking at the coals with a tiny stick.

"Wait until you hear me out…" he said, "Because I need you to understand…" He paused in the pointed manner of a prosecutor summarizing for a jury.

"I *was,* in fact, a Peace Corps volunteer…" he explained. "That was the whole point. At the time, the Agency was scouting potential Peace Corps volunteers in the Bay Area — Stanford and Berkeley mostly — for this new classified program under development."

'*The Agency*' needed no clarification. Nick understood it to be insider's shorthand, a way of reducing the formal to the familiar by invoking the essential identity in an organization's name, much the way FBI agents used '*the Bureau*' as shorthand when speaking of the mother ship.

"I found out a month or so after that trip to Washington, " Evan went on, "The recruiter called and said he thought I'd be a good fit for it — this new experimental program. No details, but he assured me it would *dovetail nicely* — that's the phrase he used — if I ended up taking an assignment with the Peace Corps. He then made it crystal clear I was *not* to discuss this with anyone. '*Not even your priest*', he told me..."

He let this float briefly before continuing.

"They liked my ability with foreign languages..." he explained. "I was thrilled, of course, who wouldn't be? But at the same time, I felt a little conflicted... Remember, this wasn't that long after the Church Committee hearings in the Senate had aired the CIA's dirty laundry... And the stink of Watergate still fouled people's minds when it came to all things governmental.

"Anyway, weeks passed and I didn't hear from the guy, so I just got on with life. The Peace Corps *did* interest me and felt like a good idea anyway, so I applied. About a week before Christmas my senior year, I got the acceptance letter with an assignment in Malaysia, starting that June.

"Then, around the end of January, the recruiter called again. Told me I'd been chosen for the experimental program. I figured he'd been testing me further, watching to see if I could keep my mouth shut, which I had. A month or so later, a small group of us met with him and another guy over a weekend at this hotel in Oakland, where we got the broad strokes of the program... Learned we'd be *hybrid* operatives — both legitimate Peace Corps volunteers *and* covert '*observers*'... That's how he described it. *Observers*... Eyes and ears on the ground in remote places of strategic interest, places notoriously difficult to keep an operative in..."

Evan paused a few seconds so that Nick could digest.

"It's no secret that every country on earth has spies embedded in its foreign embassies. That's just the way it works. They travel on diplomatic passports like all embassy personnel, carrying unscrutinized pouches in and out of the country. But this experimental program...it felt like a sketchy twist on that idea. Embedding covert operatives in a highly-regarded foreign aid program with volunteers all over the globe... Wasn't sure how I felt about it..."

Nick had yet to catch his breath. He'd been in high school when the Church Committee hearings had taken place in the US Senate in the wake of Watergate. For the first time, Americans learned the extent of their nation's covert activities around the world, especially the involvement of their most prominent intelligence agency in assassination attempts and inciting civil unrest in countries with left-leaning governments. They learned that the CIA had provided material support for right-wing coups, backed oppressive regimes that tortured and murdered the opposition, and secretly helped tyrannical despots cling to power, all on the US taxpayer's nickel.

The predictable result had been outrage and hand-wringing as politicians and pundits fretted that the CIA had, in effect, become a *de facto* separate branch of government — unelected, unaccountable, and uncontrollable. It mattered little that elections changed the cast of political players every few years; the CIA continued to do America's covert dirty work, its power institutionally entrenched and unaffected by any shift in the political winds.

"...*Jesus,* Evan..." Nick murmured at last, reeling from it all. Many things now began to line up; all the stonewalling, the forged records, contradictions and misdirections. It had never been about a policy violation by a volunteer in a foreign aid program who offended the host country, though Evan had certainly done *that.*

"...At the end of the day, I shelved my reservations because I wanted in," Evan went on. "I wanted to work for the State Department and this could be a way in. So I signed on. Became a Peace Corps volunteer and somehow this guy fixed it so I got assigned to the Upper Baram. Started working with other indigenous groups and eventually made contact with the Penan. All the while I kept notes on what I observed — surveyors, military movements, business or government people coming upriver — that sort of thing. Dispatches were sent on the express boats with information on what I should be on the lookout for.

"At first, the Peace Corps supported my contact with the Penan. But, when survey crews started showing up out here for the hydro project...things changed. A Penan hunting party ambushed one of these crews early on. Brought the two surveyors in just like they did with you. By then, I'd learned a bit of Penan and helped translate. They were young, these two, and spoke English, explaining that the ground we were standing on would eventually be the bottom of a lake behind Atakun dam. *Thousands* of hectares of forest drowned...

"I translated all this for the Penan but they didn't believe it. Just couldn't get their minds around the idea that men could do such things. I convinced them to free the surveyors, then demonstrated how the dam would work using a stream and some rocks. They'd already seen how heavy logging equipment could build roads and clear out entire forests in no time, so it wasn't a leap to convince them they had a fight on their hands.

"When the Malaysians got wind of an American in the Upper Baram helping the Penan fight the dam, they were furious. They lit into the American ambassador, since replaced by the woman you met with. Soon after, I received notice that I'd violated Peace Corps' policy and got the boot. The Malaysians revoked my visa and gave me seventy-two hours to leave the country. Of course, I'd already met Kelesau, so that wasn't going to happen. When I didn't show for deportation, they labeled me an illegal alien and issued a warrant for my arrest…

"Eventually, word got upriver that I'd be made an example…that they were lining up enough charges to throw me in one of their prisons for years. The folks back in Langley were *not* happy. The guy who vetted me got raked over the coals by his superiors who worried I might trade information to save my skin… If that were to happen, it would bring on a shit-storm of epic proportions. Revealing the intelligence gathering methods of the nation is a mortal sin with these people. I'd become a liability, putting the experimental program in jeopardy and potentially exposing US strategic interests in the region. Even worse, the whole episode would give the Agency another black eye leading to further congressional scrutiny."

He leaned forward and lightly blew once more on the coals.

"That could *not* happen," he went on. "Damage control went into overdrive. Heads had to roll in Washington and the problem over *here* contained…"

He paused a couple beats and sighed.

"You might think that, as long as I stayed here in the forest, who would care…? But these folks…they don't leave things to chance…" A thin, caustic smile hinted in the gloom. "There's no second act with them…"

By now, Nick had begun to think his skull might explode. The hut's enveloping darkness might as well have been the eternally empty night of space. Stupefied, he let himself fall back against the thatch wall of the hut.

"I… I don't know what to say…" he muttered helplessly, at last.

For several minutes, the two sat in silence.

"Sometimes," Evan eventually began to say, "I think how crazy all of this really is. I try to remember that kid from Pennsylvania…that other life. But it feels so remote now… Like I'm remembering someone else's life, not mine."

His head hung a little lower.

"A month or so ago," he went on, "I couldn't sleep, and I started to think about the passenger pigeon… Never saw one because they went extinct long before we were born. Used to be billions of them darkeing the skies over North America, but by the early twentieth century, they were gone. We blasted them out of the sky for sport and cut down the forest habitat they relied on. I tried to imagine what it must've felt like to be zookeeper at the Cincinnati Zoo in 1914, where they had the last remaining passenger pigeon in existence. Try to get your head around *that*. The *last* one! An entire species reduced to this *one* bird in Cincinnati. We did that. Wiped them out in a single century… "

Evan's words dissolved into the surrounding blackness as Nick sat there numb.

"These people…" Evan then continued, "The Penan… They don't understand the men who come here with their machines to rip down the forest and leave behind a wasteland. To take a place so full of life and lay waste to it… As if life itself were the problem…"

He shook his head and made a soft hissing sound through clenched teeth.

"I have a hard time seeing these people confined to some longhouse community, working for pocket change on palm oil plantations, or dressing up as 'wild men' for the tourists. Living on canned food and packaged shit brought upriver on the express boats…"

Completely nonplussed, Nick leaned against the thatch wall unable to speak. He recalled something their mother used to say of Evan — that he was a boy out to '*save the world.*' It had been her standard response whenever Nick asked why she and Evan argued about her drinking. All these years later, he could still see the grudging glint of admiration in the way she said it.

"…*For Christ's sake, Evan...*" Nick finally said, as he hung his head and held it with both hands.

"What about the boy…?" he eventually asked, "What happens to him…?"

His brother poked at the now dying embers with a stick.

"Ah, well…" Evan answered, an oblique note in his tone, "One of the first things I discovered about being a parent is that it rearranges your priorities. The universe has a new center and it's not *you*. Every decision from that moment on gets passed through that prism… And one of the hardest things to accept is this: what you might *want* for your child, and what might actually be *best* for that child…they don't always line up…"

He let this float a moment, fussing at the coals.

"Of course, I'd be flat-out lying," he went on, "If I said I'd never thought about a different life for Phillip. I have. And I do. At times I'll imagine him skateboarding or hanging out with pals after school... Or learning to drive and having his first broken heart, discovering he hates math... Just being a kid... Not having to grow up so goddamned fast..."

"That could still happen..." Nick heard himself say, "He could come to California with me..."

The words seemed to emerge of their own volition. Not that they were impulsive or ill-considered — *of course* he meant this. It was the *spontaneity* of the instinct that surprised him.

"Just putting that out there..." he quickly added.

The offer briefly eased the sullen note of heaviness weighing on them, and Evan leaned forward as if to blow on the coals again. Instead, he took a breath, conscious of a sheen in his eyes.

"I know that, Nick... Thank you... Though I suspect Phillip's mother would have an opinion on that..."

Sitting there in the lugubrious, enveloping darkness, Nick felt completely wrung-out, drained of all strength and will.

"One thing is certain..." Evan remarked, "Everyone gets acquainted with disappointment sooner or later in life... What parent wouldn't want to keep their kid from that as long as possible? Childhood's just this blink of an eye in the bigger picture, ten, maybe fifteen years of your life. So, maybe that's the right idea... Let children be kids for as long as possible, keep them at a distance from life's harsher truths... Think of it as the grace period before the long haul on life's choppy waters."

As the thought lingered, Nick sensed something shift in his brother.

"Maybe that's doing a disservice to a child, I don't know..." Evan went on. "They might be really out of sorts when they get to the real thing, maybe even unable to adjust."

He mulled this for a few seconds while still listlessly poking at the coals with the tip of the stick.

"While a part of me would love to see Phillip have the luxury of an American childhood, I know it would be a rejection of *everything* I've learned from the Penan. Letting Phillip enjoy an advantage none of the others could ever share in...? That's not their way..."

A faint hint of orange from the coals fringed the grim set of Evan's mouth.

"Phillip is half-Penan and has what most rarely find: A place where he belongs…"

77.

High clouds were gathering in the night sky, passing in front of the moon's fuzzy visage while distant rumblings hinted at the approach of another storm. Seated on a woven mat near the fire, Carole, Antonio and Seladang each picked at helpings of sago gruel dolloped onto banana leaves. They ate with their hands as Seladang had shown them. With the tips of their fingertips and thumb, they squeezed together clumps and brought them to their mouths. Carole and Antonio hadn't quite gotten the knack yet, but, what they lacked in technique, they made up for with enthusiasm.

"…Hard to believe something so bland could be so satisfying," Carole mumbled between mouthfuls.

"This, from someone reared on British food," Antonio remarked, chewing.

"…mmm…well…" she answered, "We've had centuries to master the art of *bland*… We Brits know how to cook the flavor and texture out of *anything*…"

Antonio wiped his mouth with the back of an arm. "True. The Anglo contribution to world cuisine — food that doesn't require teeth *or* taste buds…"

Carole smiled at the mordant wit. "How about that bottle of hot sauce you keep in your gear bag?"

The cameraman shook his head. "Left it behind in the interest of traveling light. Big mistake."

As he said this, Nick reappeared and, with an ambiguous nod, silently slid into a spot on the mat near Carole. He bunched some sago on the banana leaf set for him without making eye contact. Carole noted the change in his demeanor and glanced over at Antonio who also picked up on it. She cautiously began to probe.

"How's he doing…?" she asked, gingerly.

"Umm…" Nick murmured vaguely, "Not sure. He's rattled…like everyone, I suppose…"

"And you…?" she added, working some sago with her fingers.

Nick shrugged. "*Me...?* " he answered, eyeing the uneaten clump of sago on the banana leaf. It had been little more than seventy-two hours or so since he'd last seen her and Antonio, but it too felt somehow much longer. "I'm okay..." he added, "...considering..."

Sensing his reticence, Carole thought to change the subject.

"Listen, Nick..." she began, "I haven't had a chance yet to tell you how *awful* I feel about what happened back on that express boat. I shouldn't have left you alone out there."

"Nonsense," he replied, waving it off. "No one could have seen that coming."

"Maybe..." she admitted. "But I know this part of the world and should've been more vigilant..."

Still reeling from the shock of his brother's revelations, Nick wondered what, if anything, he could possibly share with her. If he explained that his brother was dying of cancer and had made up his mind to remain here with his family and the Penan rather than seek treatment, would she accept it without trying to dig deeper? Unlikely, he thought. Carole already had her suspicions that there was more to all this and he knew she'd keep at it.

Confused, conflicted, and with no idea how to proceed, Nick quietly listened to Carole recap what happened after they discovered he'd been taken.

"When we found out some men had grabbed you," she continued, "I knew they must've been watching us for some time, waiting for their chance..."

Nick had all but forgotten the two Malaysians; that too, had begun to seem like months ago.

Carole finished with how they'd found the wrecked truck in the river with one of the men inside, a development Nick took no pleasure in learning. As she finished, Antonio briefly glanced up between bites of sago and shared another thought.

"You know..." he remarked, "It's still not clear if those guys were really who and what they claimed..."

"True," Carole agreed, "And we considered that."

"Sort of," the cameraman countered, "We considered their possible range of intentions, *not* their affiliation."

This brought another uncomfortable silence as he clumped a ball of sago on the banana leaf.

"Meaning...? What, exactly?" Carole asked, "They might've been using *counterfeit ID?*"

Antonio shrugged. "It's possible, isn't it?" he suggested, between chews. "People in the intelligence game use fake credentials all the time."

"...*Whoa*..." Carole replied, slowly leaning back. "*That's* quite a turn into the weeds..."

If only she knew... Nick thought to himself, trying to imagine the myriad troublesome ways all this could turn were she to learn the truth about his brother.

In the distance, a low thunder rumbled.

"The monsoon..." Antonio observed, looking up at the sky.

An ominous hush fell over them as they gazed upward. Antonio wiped his fingers and began to fuss with the video gear before the rain hit.

"Wish I had some more of these silica packets..." he muttered, moving them around in the recorder's shoulder sling bag. Then, he spotted something.

"What the *hell*...?" he mumbled, his fingers prying free a disk about the size and thickness of a coin that was stuck to the underside of the bag's flap. The others suddenly stopped eating and watched as he examined it; the disk's deep charcoal-black made for easy camouflage in the flap's dark tones, and one side had an extremely sticky adhesive coating.

"...What is *that* thing...?" Carole asked, leaning closer.

Antonio shook his head. "No idea..." he answered, retrieving a mini screwdriver from the deck's pouch and prying the disk apart to reveal its insides: a wafer of printed circuitry.

"Looks like some kind of high-end electronics..." he observed, turning it over and back. "...*Very* sophisticated... Not the sort of thing you'd find at Radio Shack..."

As the cameraman studied the disk in the firelight, Nick felt the breath stick in his throat.

"...*Unbelievable*..." Antonio went on, tilting it this way and that. "You know what? I think this is a...a transmitter of some sort... Like a...*tracking* device..."

Carole's jaw dropped. "*What*...?"

For several seconds, they stared in shocked silence at the sinister implications.

"Are you saying *someone's* been using this to track our movements?" Carole finally asked.

Antonio sighed in dismay.

"Looks that way..." he answered, holding the disk between two fingers.

Neither journalist had ever come across anything like this before and it leveled a psychic blow that left them reeling. For Carole, it further validated her suspicions that there was far more going on here than they could possibly imagine.

"Bloody *hell*..." she said, "...How long you think it's been there...?"

Antonio shrugged. "No telling, really."

As Nick listened to the back and forth, he started to feel queasy. Antonio had it right — this wasn't an amateur job. The sophistication of the device they discovered and the finesse necessary to place it right under their noses had all the hallmarks of a state-sponsored entity with global reach. Unwittingly, it appeared they had led his brother's adversaries right to his door.

78.

The night sky briefly lit up with flashes of lightning. Moments later, thunder boomed and clattered across the heavens like a celestial bowling alley, and rain began crashing to earth in increasingly steady streams, as if the universe had determined the Earth needed a good washing.

Nick leaned back against the wall of a selap the Penan had vacated for him and his colleagues. Unable to sleep, he stared blankly into the darkness, noting the lightning flashes through tiny gaps in the thatch. Carole sat next to him, while Antonio and Seladang lay sleeping on their sides closer to the fading coals of a small cooking fire.

Carole quietly scratched some notes on a pad using Antonio's compact flashlight to see. That someone had been tracking their movements all this time and she completely missed it again, again pointed up her failings in the whole endeavor. Even more disturbing, the stealth used to plant a sophisticated transmitter with such advanced technology just didn't fit with what had already taken place. If they had been physically followed by the men who grabbed Nick, why the transmitter? On the surface, it made no sense. It suggested the likelihood that different interests with different agendas were at work here. After a minute or so, she put the pen down and glanced over at Nick.

"I must be getting sloppy with age," she began to say, an obvious chagrin in her voice, "This business with the tracking device... And those men following us on the boat. I didn't pick up on any of it... I'm really off my game."

Nick gave her a soothing glance. "*C'mon*... You need to let it go..." For the briefest of moments, he considered confiding in her, but held off, unsure where he'd even begin.

A short interlude passed in silence as they leaned their heads back against the thatch wall and Carole gazed up at the roof.

"...*Thatch*..." she murmured as the rains began picking up. "My parent's house had a thatch roof... In the Cotswolds... Couple hours west of London. Famous for its 'quaintness' and the local Cotswolds stone. And thatched roofs, of course... Still can't understand how they keep the rain out, but they do. That roof *never* leaked..." She edged herself up a bit higher and pulled a cigarette from her pocket.

"You mind?" she asked before lighting it.

Nick softly shook his head. "Think I could mooch one?" he asked, as she produced another and held the lighter for him. He thanked her, adding, "... My clove cigarettes didn't survive the river..."

"No great loss, I suspect?" she archly suggested, putting the lighter away.

They sat like that for some time, smoking and listening to the rain on the thatch. Nick found Carole's physical proximity somehow comforting and hoped it might be mutual. He suspected that the determined, steely persona she presented to the world probably fronted a vulnerable interior. Her savvy perspective and worldliness were a sharp contrast with the prevailing prosperity-driven fixations common in southern California, the sort that occupied the waking thoughts of someone like Celeste. She and Carole could not have been more different; a weekend spent darting between home-improvement stores seemed as unlikely to excite Carole, as sleeping in the same grimy clothes ripe with your own baked-in sweat would for Celeste.

"You know..." Carole began, quietly, "I never asked how much you witnessed out there today. At the blockade. We arrived minutes before the soldiers moved in..."

"I must've shown up not long before you did," Nick replied. "That's *another* story..."

"Hmm..." she murmured, "Worth sharing?"

He flashed a thin smile. "Maybe... But then you'd think I'm crazy..."

"Maybe I already do...?" she teased, taking a drag on her cigarette and exhaling smoke toward the hut's roof. "Tell me something, though..." she continued, pivoting. "Were you at all surprised to find your brother had become so...so involved with these people, the Penan?"

"*Surprised...?*" Nick answered, "I don't know if that's the right word..." He pondered this a moment.

"As a kid...Evan always had a self-righteous streak. Taking the side of the underdog and standing up for anyone being picked on, that kind of thing. So, as regards the Penan, not so much. But marriage and a kid...? No, didn't see that coming..."

Carole did a double-take. "*Marriage?*" she repeated.

Sighing deeply, he filled her in about Kelesau and Phillip, then paused, thinking to add one more thing.

"I doubt he wants this known, but..." he hesitated, avoiding her gaze. "Turns out...he has cancer. In his lungs."

"...Oh, Nick..." Carole muttered, "I... I'm so sorry..."

Her voice fell away and Nick quietly hoped this news might dampen her enthusiasm for any further turning of stones. For now, it at least offered a reprieve from the ambivalence over what to share of his brother's revelations. He glanced down at the cigarette in his fingers.

"These goddamn things..." he mumbled before taking a drag.

Carole then reached over and placed a hand on his forearm consolingly. Nick's eyes met hers and, as men tend to do, he saw what he wanted to. Several awkward seconds passed as thunder rumbled closer. Then, outside the selap's entry, a clamoring startled them. Nick moved toward the flap just as his soaking wet nephew pushed it up.

"*Uncle...!*" the boy said, wiping rainwater from his face and struggling mightily to contain himself.

"*Phillip...?* What is it...?" Nick asked, clearly alarmed. He quickly introduced Carole who anxiously leaned forward.

His nephew's large brown eyes were wide with distress as he breathlessly tried to explain.

"It's *father!*" he said, "He heard something...and went out to look... And he hasn't come back yet!"

Nick tensed visibly, then glanced over at Carole. "Okay, let's slow down," he suggested, trying to calm his nephew. "And start over...he *heard* something?"

Phillip nodded and continued. "Yes, outside... Something scratching. Then he went out to see..."

"Did you hear it too?" Nick asked, and the boy nodded again.

"Right… And your father didn't say anything else before going out?"

Phillip shook his head as Antonio and Seladang began to stir from the commotion.

"Well, maybe it was just something digging around…" Nick posited, "A dog or some other animal. And your father followed it, lost track of the time…"

Seconds after saying this, Nick realized his nephew would never buy such a facile explanation — why would his brother go chasing after some roaming animal in the middle of the night in torrential rain?

"Or it's possible…" he then suggested, trying to contain his own apprehension now, "…He decided to visit that medicine guy, you know?"

Nick gently squeezed his nephew's tiny shoulder reassuringly.

"So, why don't I go take a look, okay?" he told the boy, doing his best to sound calm and avuncular.

"…*What's going on…?*" Antonio moaned, still half-asleep, while Seladang had rolled to his side to listen.

"How about we do *this*…" Nick went on, "…You go back and take care of your mother and make sure she's okay until I return…will you do that for me?"

The boy nodded gravely, the trust in his eyes almost crushing. He reluctantly exited through the flap as Nick turned to Carole who thrust Antonio's flashlight at him.

"Here —" she called, "You'll need this…"

Nick thanked her and began to open the flap. When she rose to follow, he stopped her.

"It's okay…" he assured her, "I think I know where he went. No point both of us getting soaked…" He was about to add that he'd be back shortly but could see in the spill of the flashlight's beam that she wasn't buying his reassurances either.

79.

The flashlight's beam cut through the sheets of rain like a searchlight at a Hollywood premiere. After less than a minute in the downpour, Nick looked as if he'd been dunked in the river, hair soaked tightly to his scalp, shirt clinging like plastic wrap to his torso. Water streamed down his face, collecting in rivulets and cascading from both sides of his jaw. Several times, he stopped to get his bearings.

As he neared the shaman's selap, he thought to announce himself, not wanting to startle the old man. He called out *'hello'* several times to no response. All that remained of last night's fire were thin wisps of bluish smoke barely visible in the shadows under the thatched overhang. At the entry flap to the hut's interior, Nick stopped and called his brother's name a couple times, then lowered the flashlight and pushed his head in through the opening.

"Hello...?? Anyone here...??"

His eyes gradually began to adjust and he could just make out a shape wedged into the selap's far corner. He slowly raised the flashlight and instantly recoiled, smacking his head on the bamboo framing. The old shaman was sitting upright in the corner, his face and body painted with white slashes and red flourishes like a skeleton from *'Dia del Muerte'*. He looked to be in a trance, chanting in a barely audible mumble while occasionally waving a small twig with dried leaves over the spent embers of a tiny cooking fire. His body was as gnarly and withered as the spindly branch he waved. As if this weren't creepy enough, there were about a dozen or so porcupine-like quills pierced into the sagging, shriveled flesh of the shaman's upper arms. Thin trickles of blood oozed down his painted skin while he stared into some far-off distance in his mind.

Leaning closer, Nick noticed something he'd missed last night: the opaque cloudiness in the old man's eyeballs from the cataracts that had claimed his sight. Nick only stopped gawping at the lurid spectacle when the shaman fell silent and broke the spell.

In the flashlight's spill, Nick noticed the old Penan's eyelids falling shut and, within seconds, his head gently drooped to his chest. Apparently, he had chanted himself into some sort of altered state, probably aided by ingesting one of his own concoctions and pain from the quills in his arms.

Obviously, Evan wasn't there, so Nick decided to inch back out. As he neared the flap, the shaman unexpectedly raised his head, cloudy eyes opened wide. Nick raised flashlight to notice the markings painted on the old man's face now lined up in the phantasmagoric outlines of a human skull. Suddenly, the shaman let loose with a shrieking howl as if trying to expel some demon. Terrified, Nick clumsily called out his brother's name.

"Evan!!" he blurted, "I'm Evan's *brother*!!"

This further agitated the old man — his upper body began to tremble as he raised his spindly arms and spewed gibberish like some possessed Pentecostal preacher lashing out in tongues.

"Evan!!" Nick repeated, louder now, *"I'm looking for Evan!!"*

Inexplicably, the shaman abruptly fell silent and lowered his arms. For half a minute or so, Nick didn't dare move. He gazed at the old Penan who slowly lifted an arm and pointed an accusatory finger at Nick. His mouth twisted in a snarl and a gurgling, growling sound boiled up in his throat.

"Hey…!" Nick shouted desperately, "It's *me!! Remember??* I was here *last night!!*"

The old man's pointed finger curled back and the arm slowly came down. For a moment, it looked as if the shaman did in fact, recall Nick's presence when, inexplicably, he fell over onto his side, knocking into a pan near the tiny smoldering fire.

"*Jesus!!!*" Nick yelled, frantically backing out the entry flap only to catch a foot and land face-first on the waterlogged ground with an audible '*oomph*'.

The impact momentarily knocked the wind out of him, and he lay there in the puddling water clutching his stomach and trying to catch his breath. The flashlight had flown from his grip, landing a couple meters away, its beam still shining. He rolled onto his hands and knees and crawled toward it.

Wiping mud and water from the flashlight with his filthy soaked shirt, Nick tried getting to his feet, but slipped on the greasy clay soil and landed on his butt. Leaning back on an arm, he tilted his head to the sky, letting the rain wash the mud and grime from his face. For half a minute or so, he sat like that, eyes shut, rain streaming over him, when he heard a kind of muted squawking sound somewhere in the din of the downpour. Something about it was vaguely familiar and he got to his feet, sweeping the flashlight's beam around the surrounding forest. Several more squawks followed in quick succession as he waved the beam around until it finally landed on a spot of reddish-orange in a tree… Cautiously, he stepped closer and couldn't believe his eyes: it was the beak of a large bird, with another semi-beak atop it that curved upward near its face with a flourish. Astonishingly, it looked to be the same sort of bird he'd encountered earlier…maybe even *that* very same bird. *Impossible*, he told himself, it couldn't be…

"*You* again…?" he called out in dismay, his flashlight fixed on the bird. If this were a kind of madness, he would no longer resist.

"Didn't you get the news…?" he asked, absurdly as the rain poured down. "It's not a fit night out for man or beast… Or *birds* for that matter…" Cautiously, he inched closer. "…Shouldn't you be hunkered down somewhere? Instead of out in this…?"

That he was speaking to what — an apparent hallucination? — in the middle of the night while standing in a tropical downpour somehow didn't feel as patently *crazy* as it should have.

"Sorry..." Nick continued, "...if I was rude when we met before... I must've dozed off..."

He began to move closer with a kind of strangely compliant ambivalence, like someone in a scopolamine haze.

"When I came to..." he went on, "You'd taken off... Anyway...turned out, I wasn't that far from where I'd been going in the first place..."

A couple meters from the tree, Nick stopped. The bird remained motionless in its perch, sheltered somehow from the heaviest rain. The beak was unquestionably stunning, its subtle gradations from yellow-orange to blood-orange looked almost air-brushed.

Going along with the delusion, Nick thought he'd ask about his brother when something spooked the creature and it alighted with a sonorous *whoosh*, disappearing into the night.

"Hey now...?" Nick called after it, "What's *this...?*" The words trailed off as he aimed the flashlight's beam in the direction the creature had flown. He then laughed, realizing his mental state had become as unsteady as his footing.

"*Hey!*" he called out again, "*Where you going...?? We just got started!...*"

Sweeping the flashlight around, Nick thought the rain's intensity had tapered a bit. Even so, visibility was still only four or five meters in any direction. Whatever had startled the bird, Nick could feel its presence nearby, watching him. *Stop this,* he told himself. *You need to find your brother.* He took a deep breath to steady the trembling in his stomach and turned to leave when another disturbance stirred the brush near him.

"*Who's there...??*" he called, anxiously sweeping the flashlight back and forth. "*Evan...? Is that you...??*"

On one of the passes, the beam caught a glint of movement and Nick tentatively moved toward it. Vines, leaves and wet bark glistened in the flashlight's beam as his entire body tensed.

"*I know someone's there...*"

Carefully inching closer, Nick thought he glimpsed a shape that didn't belong moving in the shadows in a tangle of brush.

"*Come out and show yourself...!*"

He gripped the flashlight tighter, ready to use it as a weapon if necessary, though it wouldn't be much of one… That he actually thought he might need to defend himself seemed a fitting burlesque of the entire situation.

When he reached a distance that felt close enough, Nick paused, leaving what he hoped was room to maneuver in the event of an attack. Swinging the flashlight from one spot to another over the brush, he felt like prey being stalked… Then, the brush rustled again. Instinctively, Nick stepped backward, heart pounding in his chest as he prepared to swing the flashlight like a hammer.

Slowly, a figure began to emerge from the shadows, wearing what appeared to be a military-grade rain suit. Water streamed down from the brim of a rain hat.

"Refreshing, isn't it…?" a voice said. Male, and vaguely familiar, Nick noted an accent.

"The rain…" the voice continued. "Breaks the humidity… You can actually *breathe* out here for a few hours…"

Nick noted that the rubberized rain suit was actually *two* parts — a poncho over rain pants, of the sort found in an army/navy surplus store.

"…Impossible to dry anything out, though…" the voice went on. "Clothes stay wet for days on end… Cotton's the worst… Always feels damp and clammy on the skin…"

The figure situated himself in the beam of the flashlight several meters from Nick. With a tilt of the head, water poured down from the brim of the rain hat. The head then tilted back with the brim hanging low over the eyes, and Nick slowly raised the flashlight onto the face — a face he immediately recognized: the confident visage of Wolcott's tag-along reporter, the Australian, *Ian.*

"…You know…the native people here, they didn't see the point of clothes," Ian explained, with a bland confidence. "The men, they just fashioned a kind of jungle codpiece to keep their nuts from flopping around. It's those damn Christian missionaries… They did it. Brought shame with Jesus…"

"*…You're fucking kidding…!?*" Nick uttered in astonishment. "*…What in the* hell *are* you *doing out here…?* Carole said you stayed back at Long Akah…? We thought you'd returned to Kuching…?"

"*Doing?*" Ian replied with a glib note in his tone. "What am I *doing*? Same as you," he answered, briefly removing his hat to run a hand through his hair. "…At the moment, I'm standing in a downpour…with a friend."

"Cut the bullshit…" Nick snapped, glaring at him, his eyes beginning to narrow. "How the hell did you find this place…? And what is all this, anyway?"

Ian remained silent. He again tilted his head slightly to let water pour from his hat.

"Listen…if you don't mind…" he said, "…It'd be easier to talk without that light in my eyes…"

Nick hesitantly lowered the beam enough to keep some spill on Ian's face.

"Thank you…" Ian kept his gaze on Nick, who saw that the flashlight's spill now produced a disturbing 'under-light' effect on the Australian's face reminiscent of a silent-era German horror film.

"…You know what works better than a flashlight out here…?" Ian then asked, while casually reaching a hand into an opening on his rain poncho. "…A set of *these*…" At this, he produced what looked to be a sophisticated pair of ski goggles. Undoing a catch on the elastic band that wrapped around the back of the head, he placed the goggles over his eyes and re-did the catch.

"…There…" he said, adjusting the fit. "They pick up *everything* in the infrared spectrum. Astonishing, really… So many things that only come out at night. Hiding during the day, sometimes right next to us. We never know they're there…"

With the night vision goggles and rain outfit, Ian resembled some futuristic dystopian fisherman.

"…Wait a minute…" Nick muttered, as several disparate threads began to coalesce.

"…*You*…? That *tracking* device…on Antonio's video deck… That was *you*…?"

He waited for a response but none came. Then, his carriage slackened and, for a brief moment, Nick felt like a man free-falling in an elevator after its cable snapped.

"…*Fucking hell*…" he murmured, "…It was *you*… You've been working for them all along…"

Ian removed the goggles and looked at Nick, a hint of something like pity in his demeanor.

"…*Jesus*…" Nick went on, shaking his head in disbelief. "…Unbelievable… You're not a goddamned reporter…"

The remark brought a wounded pout to Ian's face.

"Oh, but I *am*, mate…" he protested in mock defensiveness. "…It's where I started… Not much for job security… But you do meet people from *all* walks of life…"

"…*Wow*…" Nick uttered, with the bitter and astonished tone of someone realizing he's been taken by a grifter. "…Incredible… *Just fucking incredible*…" He shook his head. "And Wolcott has no idea…?"

Ian shrugged. "Why would he?"

Nick glared at the Australian with contempt.

"*Ian*…" he practically spat. "Probably not your real name either…" A quivering rage burned in him.

"Where's my brother?" he demanded, icily.

Ian silently studied Nick a moment then, produced a cigarette from inside his poncho. He lit it with a mighty drag, inhaled deeply and blew out a stream of bluish smoke that dissipated in curtains of rain.

"Tell me something, Nick…" Ian began at last, ignoring the question. "How much of his prognosis did your brother share with you…?"

The question further infuriated Nick; if its intention had been to remind him that Ian and his masters were in the business of knowing everything about everyone, including Evan, it wasn't necessary.

"No…?" Ian continued, taking silence as his answer. "He did *tell* you about it, though…? The cancer…?" Ian surmised from Nick's expression that he had.

"…Of course, he did… Well…maybe he left this out," he went on. "It's an aggressive form of cancer… I've seen the radiology report and prognosis. It metastasizes quickly. Migrates to other organs… Horrible… And I'm really sorry, Nick…" Ian then paused a beat. "I'm guessing you won't believe that, but I am…"

Nick was livid. "You *fucking bastard*…" he snarled. "You *miserable* fucking bastard…"

Ian reacted as if he half expected this.

"Yeah, sure, have at it…" he urged, strangely agreeable. "I'm a wretched human being, I know…" He looked down and took a drag from the cigarette. "But bear this in mind: if it wasn't me, it would've been somebody else. Your brother knew that… He understood how this has to work. It's a rough and tumble neighborhood where somebody's always trying to get over on somebody else. Individuals, businesses…nations. Everyone looking for an advantage while trying not to hand one to the other guy. Hardly news to you people in the academic world, I know. But it goes on every day, in every part of the world… You just hope there's some wisdom at the top."

The orange glow on the end of his cigarette brightened as he drew on it.

"Think of it as your tax dollars at work…" he added, exhaling another stream of bluish smoke.

"Thought you'd like to know," he then said, "Those men on the boat? Former military intelligence now in the employ of the political opposition, this informal *alliance* of Islamist and nativist interests unhappy with the current arrangement. They'd like the electorate to oust the party in charge, the heavily Chinese *BN* party that they say is hopelessly corrupt. Word is, they were looking to use you and/or your brother in some way that would embarrass the BN and sabotage its shaky coalition. Politics…"

Noticing his cigarette doused by the rain, Ian shrugged and threw it to the ground.

Nick stood there, numb, withered, furious and spent.

"Where is he…?" he asked once more, defiant. "Forget the bullshit and tell me where he is," he insisted. "I want to see him…"

"You *have* seen him, Nick," Ian answered, calmly. "…As he hoped you would…"

"How the hell would *you* know what he *hoped?*" Nick sneered.

Ian laughed. "*Really?* You're kidding, right? C'mon Nick, think about it. Your brother… clearly delighted to see you, sure. But did he seem genuinely *surprised…? Stunned* even, to think that, after all this time, you suddenly took an interest and decided to travel halfway around the world and find your way up here…?"

Nick struggled mightily to steady the trembling inside. He had, in fact, found his brother's initial reaction a bit confusing but, immersed in the moment, he filed it away.

"What are you driving at…?" he demanded, after a moment. "That he somehow *knew* I would show up here?"

A cryptic little smile briefly curled on Ian's lips.

"I don't know…" he remarked, "Maybe your brother felt the clock ticking and wanted to sort out some *old* business while he still had the chance… Not that long ago, a man in his position could easily find a way to put a bug in someone's ear. *Anywhere…*"

Ian let this sit for a few seconds.

"Your father," he then continued. "all these years later, out of the blue, hires an investigator to look for your brother? Just like that…?"

He fell silent and tilted his head in a way that further obscured his face under the hat. Nick's temples began to throb and a stabbing rage roiled in him. In that instant, he understood what Ian wanted him to: his brother would not be returning.

Nick thought he might scream, letting loose an anguished shrieking yowl from the pit of his soul. In truth though, he had nothing left. Like a dish rag corkscrewed ever tighter, he'd been wrung dry. The capacity for despair had been shorn bit by bit so that only blood, bone and numbness remained.

"He was dying of *cancer*, for Christ's sake…" Nick seethed, "…He wasn't a threat to anyone…"

Ian stared through the streaming rain. "That's not a call I get to make…" he answered.

'That's right,' thought Nick, feeling as though his legs just might buckle beneath him. *'Guys like you and me are way down the chain of command…'* At that moment, something else stirred in the brush behind Ian, and Nick instantly swept the flashlight around until the beam found two other figures in rainsuits recoiling in the shadows.

Several seconds passed in a strange sort of standoff until Ian calmly turned and spoke to them in their native tongue. He then turned back to Nick.

"My colleagues…" he said, flatly. "Reminding me it's time to go…"

Nick scowled helplessly at the Australian.

"What happens now…?" he asked, icily.

Ian shrugged. "Nothing happens now… We go home."

"…And what about me…?"

"What *about* you, Nick…?"

"I know the whole story. *All* of it. Including *you*…"

"Oh…I see…" Ian replied with mock enlightenment. His placid expression telegraphed the bland confidence of an unbeatable hand. To him, Nick must've seemed like a fly pestering an elephant.

"I can go to my congressman. Talk to the press," Nick protested.

"Yes…you *could*… But I think you know how that's going to work out. No politician is going to tread on national security interests. They couldn't even if they wanted to. And really, why would you expose yourself like that? Imagine how you'll come across. An almost forty-something, unmarried, part-time college instructor with a dysfunctional family background, teaching English as a second language at community colleges in California. A frustrated, delusional, middle-aged bachelor with a weakness for conspiracy theories. Not exactly the portrait of credibility, Nick…"

The rain had begun tapering to a lighter but still steady shower. Nick knew Ian was right: he'd get nowhere. With the infinite reach of the state, Ian's masters had an unbeatable hand. They could poison reputations and destroy lives using disinformation, character assassination, and frame-ups. Postal inspectors might show up at your workplace with questions about the child pornography in your mail; the FBI might detain you because your name turned up in documents seized during a sting on white supremacists. The imaginative ways to harass, intimidate and poison someone's character were limitless. And with such a bottomless well of both creative cunning and resources, violence was unnecessary.

"What did you do with him…?" Nick asked once more, his tone imbued with all the bitterness and resignation of the vanquished being dictated the terms of peace. "*Where* is he…?"

"…*Where*…?" Ian repeated, strangely serene. "…Why, he's all around you, Nick. Here…in the place he loved…"

Nick's lips quivered and he clenched his fists. The tears he could no longer choke back ran down his cheeks with the rain.

"Let it go, Nick…" Ian told him, softening now. "Get on with your life…"

At that, he turned and disappeared with his cohorts into the foresr.

The flashlight now hung limply at Nick's side, its beam pooling on the saturated ground. He could feel himself swaying ever so slightly, like a pole balanced on its end in the palm of someone's hand that, at any moment, would come crashing to earth.

80.

"The hours it must take to do this…" Antonio muttered, pressing a finger into the thatch roof of the shelter near the settlement's communal fire. He briefly glanced down at Carole, who tried to keep a brave face as she sat next to Phillip. Near them, Kelesau silently huddled with some other Penan unable to sleep. Weary and bereft, they stared empty-eyed into the fire waiting for word of Evan.

Phillip occasionally glanced up at Carole, his eyes anxious and fearful. She tried her best at a reassuring smile. To her surprise, the boy had stirred maternal instincts she assumed had long since atrophied. Like many women of her generation, family and parenthood had been deferred in order to pursue a career. And also like many of those women, she'd believed the timing would work itself out and, by then, she'd be better able to negotiate the balancing act of work and family. But somehow, the moment never announced itself, and now, in her early forties, childless with two failed marriages behind her, that door had effectively closed.

The boy's palpable distress rattled Antonio as well, who thought of his own son, also around Phillip's age, and the look on his face every time his father packed for another assignment.

"…It'll be okay…" he quietly murmured, poking at a spot of thatching near the boy. While he normally avoided this sort of empty prattle — the kind adults used when unable to parse life's harsher realities for children— here he was, doing just that.

Carole picked up on this and turned to the boy.

"Phillip…?" she said, as he glanced up from the fire.

"…You know…" she went on, gently, "…I was thinking, your mother could use some rest. Maybe you could take her back to your place… I promise I'll come get you as soon as your father and uncle return… That sound okay…?"

The boy's body language betrayed his reluctance, but he eventually nodded, then grudgingly stood and spoke to his mother in Penan. Kelesau looked over at Carole whose eyes conveyed an intuitive female understanding. A few seconds later, Kelesau rose to take the boy's hand and they started off. Carole then glanced down at her watch.

"How long has it been?" she asked, as Antonio moved closer.

"I don't know…" he answered, "…Twenty, thirty minutes…?"

She sucked in a breath and exhaled.

"I feel so helpless just sitting here waiting…" she complained.

"What else can we do…?" Antonio countered, "That was my only torch…"

She couldn't argue with this — they'd be lost in minutes out there in the dark.

"Let's give it another ten minutes," he suggested, "If they don't show by then…we wake the Penan."

He glanced over at the boatman sitting quietly by himself. "Seladang can do the talking," he added, as Carole nodded distractedly, and unconsciously bit her lower lip.

"I should've gone with him…" she insisted, a nauseating sense of déjà vu blackening her thoughts. Once again, her diminished judgment gnawed at her. "It was foolish to let him go by himself…"

"Oh sure, and then we'd be waiting here for *both* of you," Antonio commented. He watched her a moment then gazed out at the darkness.

"Don't go there," he counseled. "It hasn't been that long yet…"

"Sure," she said, "Only I keep thinking, Lt. what's-his-name' knows we have video of what happened. And he knows we're probably still out here…"

Antonio considered this. "True…" he replied, "But I can't see him ordering his military to sneak around out here at night. That's not how they do things. If they wanted, they'd just storm right in…"

"…Yeah, maybe…" she had to agree; the military they'd observed today was a blunt instrument, not a surgical one. Her mind then landed on something a colleague had once said to her, '*Find the interests and you've found your story.*' This colleague went on to remind her that the obvious interests were rarely the ones that counted.

"Why is it taking so long…?" she then asked, agitated. "What the hell is he doing??"

Antonio checked his watch. "Eight more minutes," he reminded her.

Several of those minutes had ticked away when Seladang got to his feet.

"There—" he said, pointing toward a speck of moving light in the distance, dipping in and out of view behind unseen trees, someone carrying a flashlight.

Carole and Antonio anxiously watched, certain it had to be Nick. Steadily moving their way, the person with the flashlight eventually emerged at the far edge of the Penan camp and began walking toward them — *Nick*. Their relief at seeing him was quickly tempered when they realized he was alone.

With the flashlight hanging limply at his side, he slowly approached as Carole glanced over at Antonio, the dread in his eyes mirroring hers.

A few meters shy of the shelter, Nick stopped. He stood there in the rain, drenched, numb and hollowed out. On the walk back through the forest, he'd let his conscious mind retreat to some inner space to collapse on itself. Now, they expected him to speak, to offer some explanation where none could ever suffice. Simple facts were all he had to offer, just paltry, unsatisfying facts.

Carole and the others stared in anxious silence. The rain had flattened Nick's hair to the contours of his skull, and the soaked tee-shirt clung to him like plastic wrap, revealing a torso in need of lunch. Water streamed down his chin and visibly sunken cheeks, and reddened, crestfallen eyes gave him the appearance of some rainforest revenant.

"...*Nick...?*" Carole softly intoned.

For what seemed like minutes, he stood there mute and unmoving, only to blink the rain from his eyes.

"...*You okay...?* " she then added, clearly seeing that he wasn't.

Nick's lips slowly began to form a word, then fell still, the thought slipping away. His mouth tightened and he gave a weak nod.

Unconsciously, Carole leaned back on her heels and her shoulders slackened. In that moment she knew Nick's brother would not be returning. There would be no story featuring the reunion of two estranged brothers set against a backdrop of turmoil around an indigenous land-rights conflict in far southeast Asia.

All that seemed far less important now, though perhaps, a different story might yet take shape, one with a glimmer of hope to offer a counterweight to all that had taken place here. She thought of Nick's nephew, who no longer had a father, and the boy's mother who now had no husband. And then there was Nick, who'd traveled far and endured much in search of a brother he scarcely knew. Few would've taken on such an endeavor and, whether part of some deeply personal desire to set the past right, or maybe just a futile stand against the ephemeral nature of life itself, it was remarkable that he had.

Over the steady drumming of rain splattering the ground, there came the sounds of people approaching. Penan unable to sleep had come out of their selaps and were heading toward the fire, Kelesau and Phillip among them.

Nick watched them draw near; he had been dreading this moment more than anything. Kelesau pulled up a few meters from him and stopped, gripping Phillip's hand ever tighter. She quickly registered the cast of Nick's eyes and her shoulders began to sag, the hope spilling from her spirit like air from a punctured balloon. For half a minute or so, she stood silently like that, pulling Phillip closer.

With no idea what to say or do, Nick simply gazed helplessly at them. At her side, Phillip searched his uncle's eyes for anything that might help explain what he now began to grasp.

What had happened? The unspoken question etched itself on the faces staring at him. They would want facts, of course; facts regarding the events and essential details of *what* had taken place out there. In this he had little to share. Ian and his associates had seen that those particulars would forever remain obscure. The bigger question of 'what happened' however, could never entirely be answered with facts because, facts alone were inadequate to explain how all this had come to pass, how a son of mid-twentieth century, small-town, rust-belt America had come to his end in a place so very far from where he started.

A minute or so passed as Nick met his nephew's gaze. He then approached Phillip and crouched down to the boy's level to look him in the eye. In all likelihood, his brother had been begun preparing his son for this very day, reminding him to stay strong and look after his mother, to use the English he had learned to be the voice of his people and speak for them as the outside world continued to press in.

Tomorrow... Nick thought. Tomorrow, he'd try to explain things in a way his nephew might understand, perhaps imparting some sense of his father's troubled soul and the hard-earned grace Evan had found in this rainforest. He would set aside his own misgivings about hitching the boy's future to a life freighted with constant struggle, strife, and hardship, an impossible burden for anyone to bear, let alone an eight-year-old boy. With time, Nick could only hope to find some measure of solace in the apt symmetry of a half-white, half-Penan boy helping to shepherd these nomads of the rainforest into a new century and a new millennium.

As he gazed into Phillip's glistening eyes, Nick clasped the boy's bony shoulders with both hands. He then pulled his nephew closer and embraced him as they both softly sobbed. *Tomorrow,* he would somehow find the words his nephew needed to hear. For now, it was enough to hold the boy and let the rain wash over them.

Epilogue

At only a few minutes past ten in the morning, the Kuching waterfront already felt steamy. The tropical sun glared through a thin haze in the pale blue sky. Scattered groups of workaday citizens — ethnic Chinese, ethnic Indians, peninsular Malays, Borneo Dayaks — all went about their business before the swelter of the afternoon. Out on the Sarawak River, wooden sampans shuttled people and goods between the banks, while on the streets and lanes, merchants raised the steel shutters and gates of shops, then began arranging produce, housewares, electronics, and other goods in eye-catching sidewalk displays.

At an open-air café near the main passenger wharf, Nick sipped a coffee and took it all in. He'd been in Kuching for a couple days now after the long journey back with Carole and Antonio (the boatman Seladang had parted from them further upriver). Clean-shaven and attired in new tropic weight pants and short sleeve oxford shirt, his sober mien suggested a man restored to solid ground after calamity. He looked thinner, somehow diminished, but returned to the world of the living. Without the facial stubble, his hollow cheeks presented a slightly cadaverous visage reminiscent of William Burroughs.

Pawed-over sections of newspapers sat in a pile to Nick's left, nearly covering the pack of cigarettes he now reached for. Lighting one with a deep drag, he gazed out toward the river and its morning traffic. It would be busy like this for several more hours before sensible people closed their shops and took 'siesta' time during the hottest part of the day, generally from 1:00 to 4:00 in the afternoon. With evening's relative cool, those same shops would open once more, plying their wares well into the balmy night.

Nick found this rhythm agreeable. Since returning to coastal Sarawak, the midday tropical sun felt more oppressive and harsh than it had in the Upper Baram, and he knew enough to sit out like this in the early morning or the twilight hours, when temperatures were almost pleasant and life's sharper edges seemed blunted.

For several days now, his thoughts had been circling around all that had taken place. He remained untroubled by his choice of fabrication over truth to explain what had taken place with his brother. No one questioned his story of finding smeared footprints on a patch of riverbank where Evan had, apparently, accidentally slid into the dark roiling current of the Baram. Though he suspected many had their doubts, especially Carole and Antonio, they graciously kept their skepticism to themselves out of respect for Nick and his brother's family.

Before leaving the Upper Baram, Nick had written out his contact information for Phillip and Kelesau. In an unspoken compact with his brother, Nick resolved to see to it that Phillip entered the new century and new millennium armored with knowledge to help him and the Penan navigate whatever lay ahead. He promised to return the following year, reminding them that they were *family*, and that he and Phillip would correspond by mail until then. He had assured his nephew that, once back in Los Angeles, he'd send regular shipments of pens, paper, and postage, along with money and books to help with the boy's ongoing education. Seladang had been enlisted to help ensure the packages arrived at their destination.

As he stared absently out at the Sarawak river, Nick replayed the last morning with his nephew, not really sure he'd done right by the boy. No one slept much that final night and, as daylight returned, a devastated Phillip had asked him point blank, if his father had really fallen into the Baram River. Nick faltered, surprised by the boy's perceptiveness, then answered that yes, as far as he could tell, he had.

Nick understood that his nephew deserved to know the truth, but that would have to wait. The truth required a more complete understanding of his brother's history, and what of that convoluted and nuanced story could his nephew grasp at that age? One day, *yes*... when the boy was older, he would explain *everything* as he understood it for the boy. On that final morning however, a meager shard of truth had to suffice. He told Phillip that his father had an illness that impaired his faculties and that he tried to keep that from everyone. The boy looked skeptical, but eventually seemed to accept this explanation for his father accidentally falling in the river. In his nephew's demeanor, Nick thought he recognized something of his brother at that age: an ability perhaps, to apprehend that the world beyond our little corner of it was far larger and more confusing than we could possibly imagine.

When the time came for final goodbyes, Nick had hugged his nephew and Kelesau one last time before joining Carole and Antonio who were already disappearing into the forest behind Seladang. As he started off, he turned for a final wave. Fighting back a tear, he was reminded of the fundamental uncertainty of what we take to be life's seemingly fixed bearings. Maybe Phillip would one day come to understand, as Nick had, that most of us simply puzzled our way through the circumstances of our existence. And, like those ancient mariners who navigated uncharted waters, we were likely to wash up in unforeseen places.

Kelesau and the Penan had made no fuss about Evan's corporeal remains. Their take on death aligned with Nick's belief that, who and what we had been in this life, had little to do with the empty vessel left behind. Still, on a personal level, he found solace in the fact that somewhere out there in the dark heart of Borneo, the molecules of his brother's body would become part of the soil in this place where he found whatever had so eluded him in life.

Just then, a taxi pulled up in front of the café and honked. Nick watched as the curbside rear door swung open and Carole emerged. A second later, the taxi's other rear door opened and Antonio stepped out, sharply dressed in a crisp pair of chinos and polo shirt, a wrist brace on his injured arm. This brief rendezvous had been arranged the night before when Carole said she and Antonio would pass by the next day on their way to the airport.

Nick got up and met her half-way, where she extended both arms to embrace him. With her fashionable, business-savvy tropic-weight outfit, she projected an air of professionalism befitting a globe-trotting journalist. Behind her, Antonio extended his uninjured left arm in greeting.

"Nick…" he murmured, with genuine affinity as Nick grasped the proffered hand.

"Didn't I read that you're never supposed to shake with your left hand in Asia…?" Nick remarked with a winking smirk.

"One-armed people exempted," Antonio replied, grinning appreciatively.

"Any word on your replacement passport?" Carole asked Nick.

"Tomorrow…" he answered, "So they say…"

Reaching into her satchel, she removed an envelope and handed it to him.

"I know you've had some cash wired from the US…" she began, adding, "…But Derek wanted you to have this as well. Just in case. Along with your return ticket to KL."

"Thank him for me," he remarked, clearly humbled by the gesture. "That wasn't necessary…"

Carole waved this off. "Forget it…" she replied, "Think of it as a *fixer's* fee…"

Nick held the envelope and tapped it a couple of times on his other palm.

"Okay," he said, "Though that's the first time I've ever been accused of fixing *anything*..."

She smiled, encouraged by the sliver of levity.

"By the way, Antonio got some terrific footage," she continued, treading carefully. "I spoke to my executive producer in London and he thinks we should keep at it. Wants us to get some comment from the government in Kuala Lumpur about what happened up there." At this, she paused, an earnestness in her eyes. "We're going to get this out, Nick. That boy's death... it won't be in vain."

Nick was pleased but dubious. Since returning to Kuching, he continued to wrangle with the idea of sharing the thornier aspects of his brother's story with Carole so she might better understand the full measure of what they were scratching around in. Perhaps she'd see the folly of chasing phantoms that could never be found, let alone held accountable.

In the end, he decided against it. Ian had likely already vanished into the ether where he would eventually pop-up elsewhere with a new identity and a new assignment. And Nick saw no good reason to put the Peace Corps' otherwise stellar record in jeopardy with this can of worms. They had been an unwitting party in the whole mess and, he felt, should remain unscathed.

By now, he suspected the entire debacle with his brother must have laid bare the major flaws in the *'experimental'* program and rightly sealed its fate. Even if Carole kept digging, as was her nature, she'd inevitably end up in a cul-de-sac of mirrors. In time, the entire episode would dissolve away and the official line on his brother would remain unchanged. The world would go on about its business, oblivious to the infernal machinations that kept it all running.

"We'll let you know when it airs," Carole added.

"I'll look forward to it," he assured her just as the taxi driver honked.

"He thinks we're cutting it close," Antonio said, checking his watch. "Better get going,"

He said a final goodbye to Nick and started for the taxi while Carole and Nick faced each other for several awkward seconds, neither quite sure what to say.

"You'll be back in LA soon..." Carole finally said, "Any thoughts about a service or memorial for your brother?"

"Uh…not really…" Nick answered, with a note of ambivalence. "I have no idea what he would've wanted…" He paused, considering. "Besides…" he continued, "Evan's life was *here... This* was his home… Whatever I might try to do, it should be *here* where people knew him…" He hesitated before finishing. "Maybe next year when I return. Now that I've got family to visit…"

The taxi honked, longer this time, the driver pointing to his watch.

"Better get moving…" Nick told her. "…Only two flights out each day…"

"True…" Carole agreed, glancing around at the morning's flurry of activity. "But seeing all this, I suspect it won't be that way forever." She then extended a hand. "Goodbye, Nick…"

As they shook, Nick searched her eyes, for what, he didn't really know.

"Take care of yourself, Carole," he said, holding his grip just slightly longer than necessary.

She held his gaze a moment before turning to depart. Once inside the cab, she rolled the window down.

"Hey…" she called out, "On occasion, I *do* get to Los Angeles," she said, adding, "Are you easy enough to find?"

Nick smiled warmly. "*Very...*" he answered.

With that, she raised the window and the taxi pulled away, disappearing in the rush of late morning traffic.

Returning to his table, Nick finished his coffee standing, then placed some money under the empty cup and wandered toward the river esplanade. Along the way, he passed workers unloading crates of produce and other goods from boats, merchants setting up kiosks, and citizens engaged in the hurly-burly of another day's business. The faces were a mosaic of ethnicities, a living tapestry reflecting the history of human migration in this part of the world: Chinese, Malays, south Asians, Arabs and Dayaks. His nephew now conferred a sliver of American-Irish DNA to the mix. Future generations would dilute it even further and, with time, that sliver would become little more than a vestigial trace, as remote and insignificant as the smidgen of Neanderthal DNA buried deep in the Eurasian genome.

Gazing up into the hazy late-morning sky, Nick reflected on how we are all, in some way or another, shackled by the dictates of heredity and the particulars of our upbringing. In this sense, the essential trajectory and parameters of our lives had been laid down at birth, casting doubt on the notion that any of us truly had free will.

As he leaned on the riverwalk's rail with the sun in his face, Nick closed his eyes and took a deep breath. He began to imagine himself floating upward, body lighter than air. Like a raptor riding the thermals, he gazed down upon the city's boisterous commerce. Out on the Sarawak River, sampans spewed puffs of bluish exhaust from poorly tuned two-stroke motors, whisking people and goods back and forth, while in the crush of morning traffic, pedal-powered rickshaws, scooters, motorcycles, taxis and bicycles all vied for position.

Rising ever higher, Kuching began to stretch out wider before him, its boundaries pushing further into scatter-shot settlements and industrial operations at its outer fringes. Beyond the city, the manicured green expanses of sprawling palm oil plantations stretched from the coastal plains and lowlands of Sarawak up toward the verdant central highlands. Floating now through vaporous, wispy clouds, Nick passed over the rugged upper reaches of Mt. Kinabalu, the highest point in Borneo, its rocky summit visible through thin patches of mist clinging to its flanks.

Soon, the entire island stretched out below him, the ragged brown scars of recently cut forest bumping into the re-greening monocultures of palm oil plantations. Here and there, scattered plumes of smoke wafted skyward from burning piles of logging debris, while offshore, the Java Sea and South China Sea shimmered in the tropical sun. Further west, numerous tiny smears and blotches marked the passage of container ships and oil tankers through the Straits of Malacca. For two thousand-plus miles, you could draw a line south from Ho Chi Minh City in Vietnam, all the way to Darwin, in northern Australia, and right in the middle would be Borneo, at one time, the very definition of *remote*, a place about as far off as you could get, in an age when distance still had power to stir the imagination.

Acknowledgments

A huge note of gratitude goes out to all those who've been patient and
helpful, in both this endeavor and in friendship, namely, Jeff Schiro, Veron-
ica Sive, Katherine Sheneman, John Vitollo, Michael Pond and William
McKnight. And I can't forget the untold number of coffee shops and hotel
rooms around the world where much of this novel got worked out in fits
and starts. Finally, I'd like to acknowledge the inspiration and friendship
of those who've departed too soon and who brought much light to this life:
Fellow writers Robert Haber and Brian Kellow, photographer Lynn Webb,
and old friend from the wayback time, Richard 'Dick' Dassance.

About the Author

Robert Demyan has been roaming the globe as
a freelance travel writer and photographer since
1990. A graduate of New York University, his
work has appeared in numerous travel industry
and lifestyle magazines and his photography
has been represented by various stock photo
agencies, including the Leo de Wys Agency in
New York City, and Alamy in the United Kingdom.
This is his first novel.

www.ingramcontent.com/pod-product-compliance
Lightning Source LLC
Chambersburg PA
CBHW021041310726
48969CB00006B/1762